Buffy the Vampire Slayer™

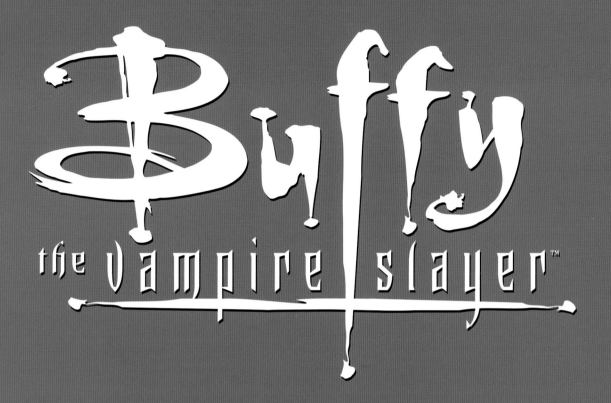

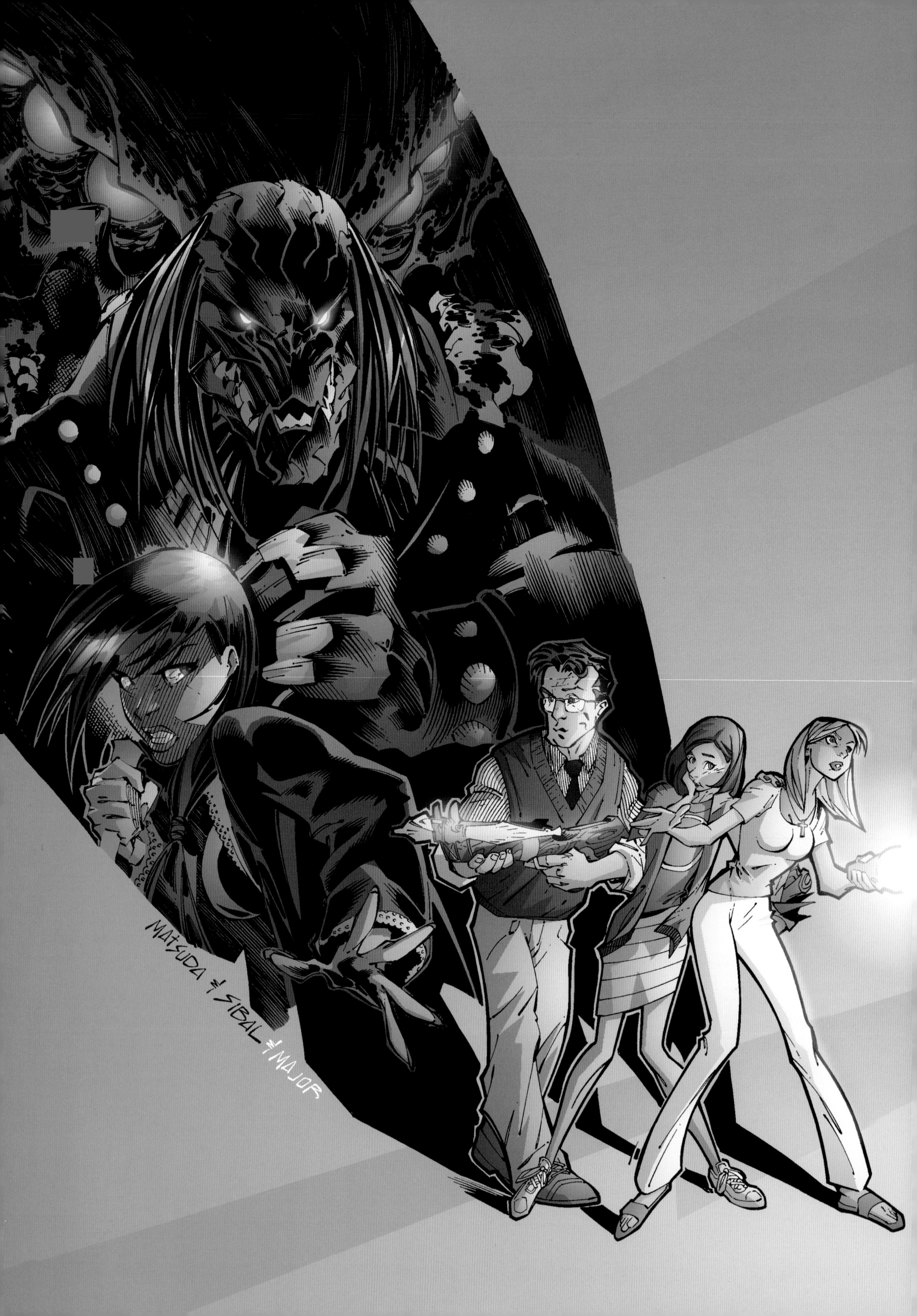
MATSUDA
SIBAL
MAJOR

Buffy the Vampire Slayer™

PANEL TO PANEL

THE ART OF THE COMICS
THE FIRST SEVEN SEASONS

Featuring

BRIAN HORTON

PAUL LEE

JEFF MATSUDA

CLIFF RICHARDS

CHRIS BACHALO

JOE BENNETT

J. SCOTT CAMPBELL

RANDY GREEN

GUY MAJOR

ERIC POWELL

TIM SALE

RYAN SOOK

DAVE STEWART

JOHN TOTLEBEN

CHRISTIAN ZANIER

and more

Text by
SCOTT ALLIE

Based on the television series created by
JOSS WHEDON

DARK HORSE BOOKS®

Pencils by Jeff Matsuda, inks by Jon Sibal, colors by Guy Major. Cover, *Buffy the Vampire Slayer* #22, June 2000.

Publisher
Mike Richardson

Editors
Scott Allie & Katie Moody

Assistant Editor
Sierra Hahn

Collection Designer
Heidi Whitcomb

Art Director
Lia Ribacchi

Cover Illustration
Pencils by Chris Bachalo, inks by Tim Townsend, colors by Liquid! Cover, *Buffy the Vampire Slayer (BTVS)* #2, October 1998.

Back Cover Illustration
Pencils by Jeff Matsuda, inks by Andy Owens, colors by Guy Major. Cover, *BTVS* #25, August 2000.

Special thanks to Michael Boretz, Debbie Olshan at Twentieth Century Fox, David Campiti at Glass House Graphics, Diego Gutierrez, Caroline Kallas, George Snyder, and Brett Matthews.

Published by
Dark Horse Books
A division of
Dark Horse Comics, Inc.
10956 SE Main Street
Milwaukie, OR 97222

darkhorse.com

To find a comics shop in your area, call the Comic Shop Locator Service toll-free at (888) 266-4226.

First edition: November 2007
ISBN: 978-1-59307-836-2

10 9 8 7 6 5 4 3 2 1
Printed in China

From 1998 to 2003, I worked on a series of comics based on Joss Whedon's television show, *Buffy the Vampire Slayer*. When I asked for the assignment, I'd never seen an episode. By the time we'd canceled the comic-book series, I'd edited books written by a handful of the show's writers, and had worked with Joss himself on his first comics. Over those six years, the book went through tremendous changes. *Panel to Panel* is an intense trip down Memory Lane for me, reliving the evolution of the book through the work of the artists, some of whom I discovered, some of whom were already big names, and big fans of Joss.

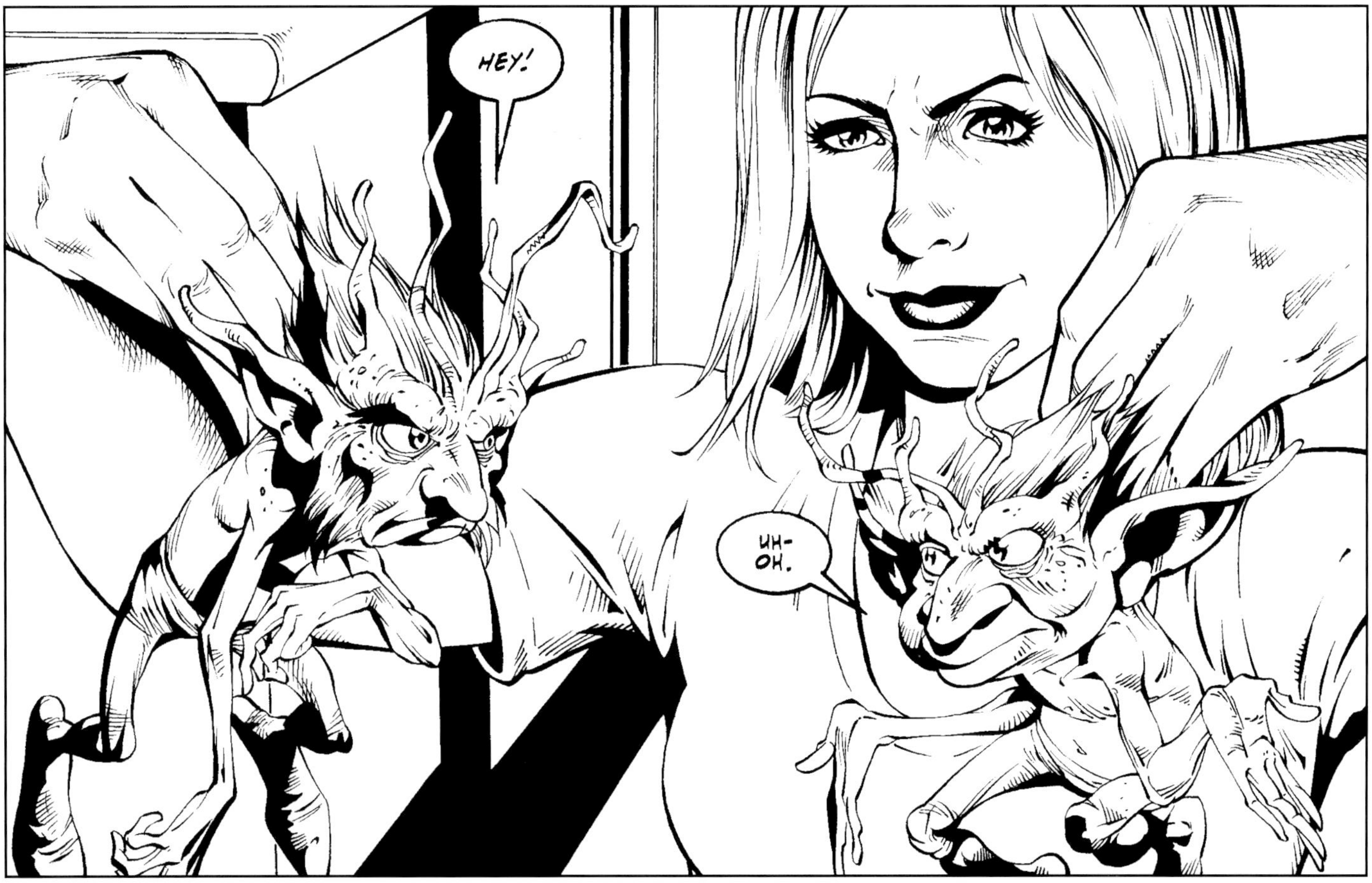
HEY!
UH-OH.

This panel is from the first Buffy comics story ever published, "The MacGuffins." "MacGuffins" was supposed to be drawn by Randy Green, who decided at the last minute to take another assignment. He was replaced by Luke Ross, who's since developed a radically different style. We did this story while simultaneously working on the graphic novel *The Dust Waltz* and the first issue of the monthly series.

Script by Jen Van Meter, pencils by Luke Ross, inks by Rick Ketcham, letters by Steve Dutro. Interiors, *Dark Horse Presents Annual*, August 1998.

WE WERE STRONGLY ADVISED that photo covers on the series would increase sales dramatically, so every issue had two covers. No matter how good the art covers were, by superstars like Art Adams, who lived in Portland at the time—or, frankly, how boring the photo covers—the photo covers always sold better. I enlisted Dave Stewart, then on staff at Dark Horse, to augment the photos, so they wouldn't simply be the same publicity shots fans had seen before. Stewart has always been among my favorite people to work with, as Eisner Award–winning colorist on *Hellboy*, *Fray*, and *Buffy the Vampire Slayer* Season Eight.

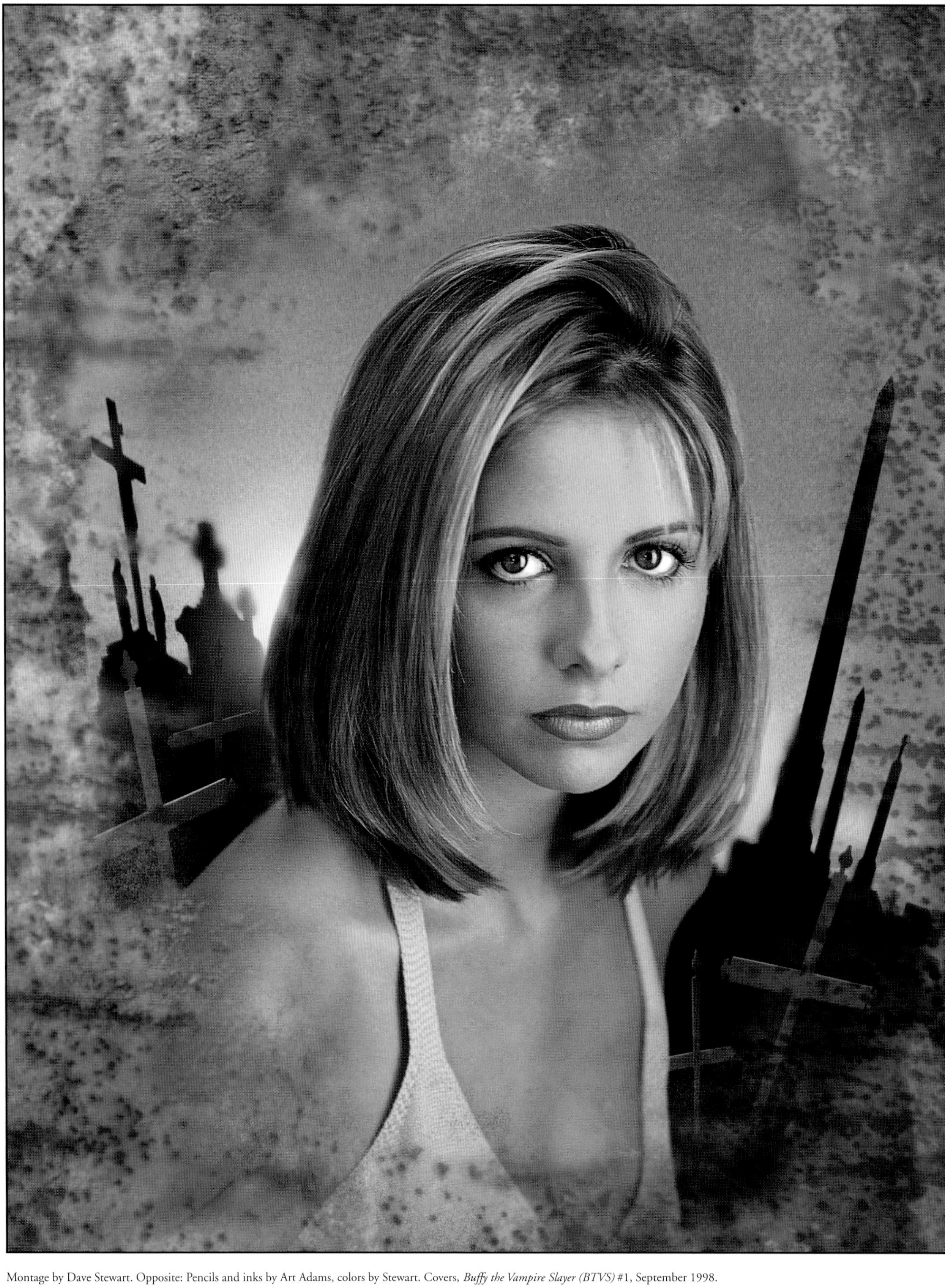

 Montage by Dave Stewart. Opposite: Pencils and inks by Art Adams, colors by Stewart. Covers, *Buffy the Vampire Slayer (BTVS)* #1, September 1998.

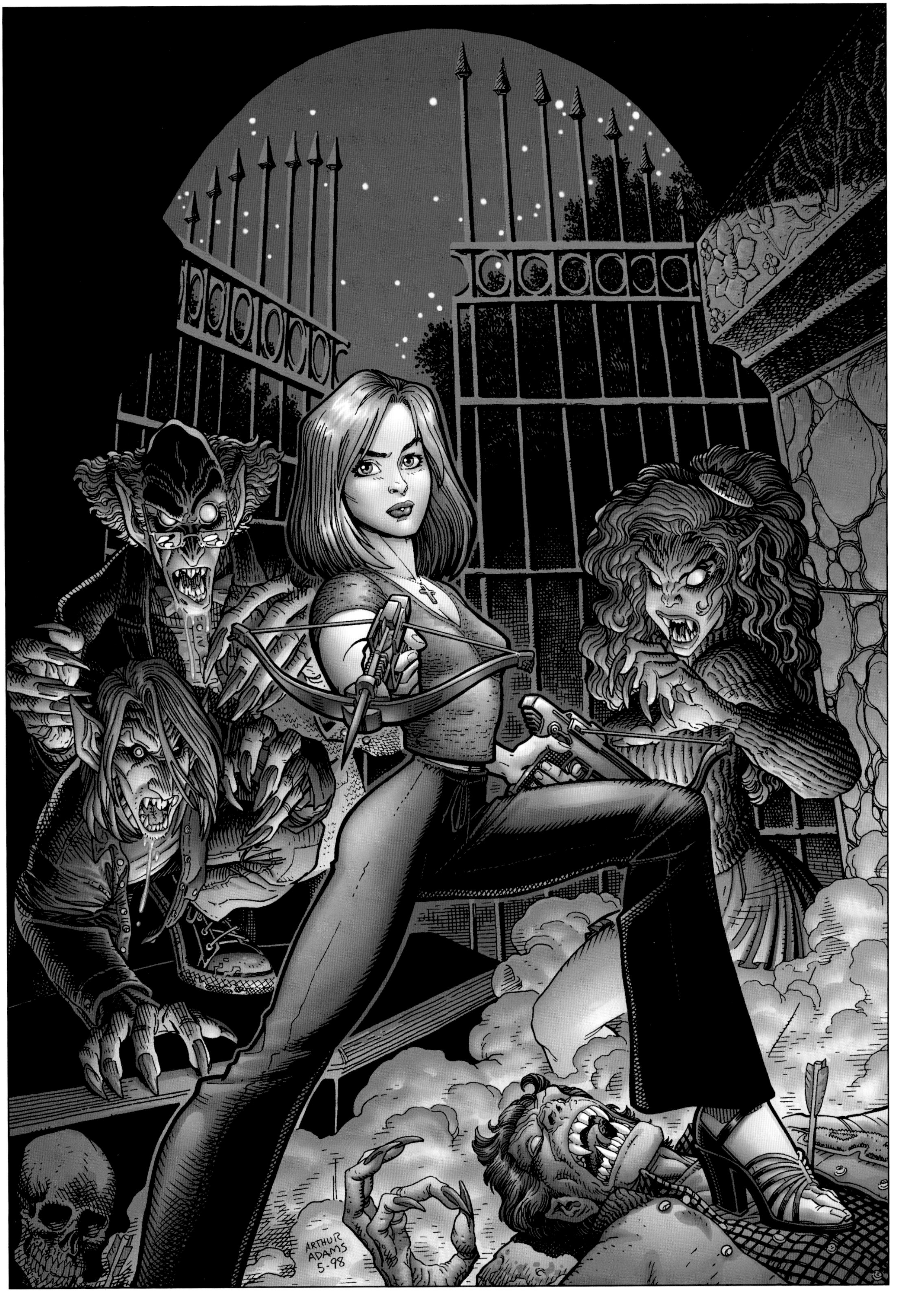
ARTHUR
ADAMS
5-98

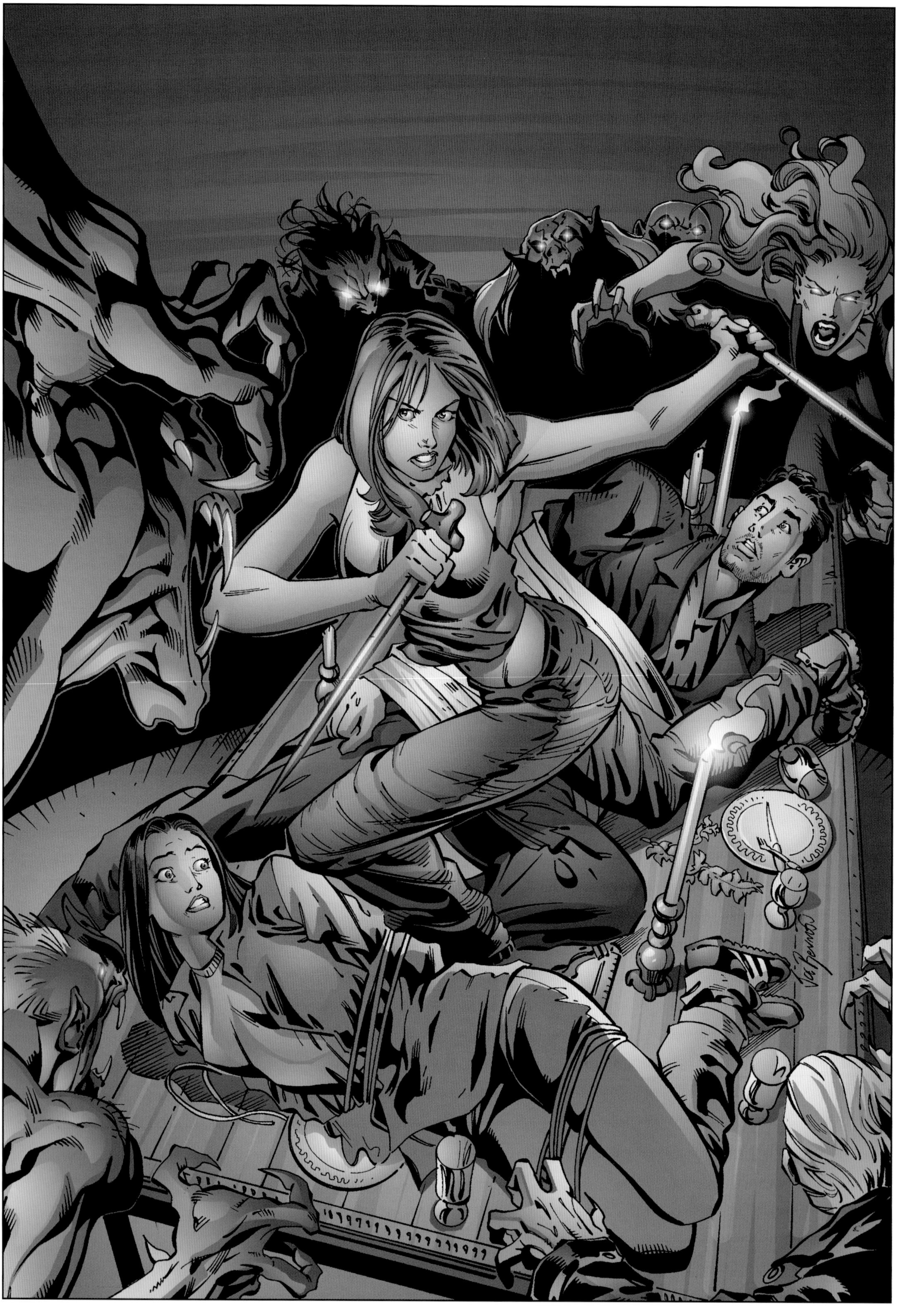

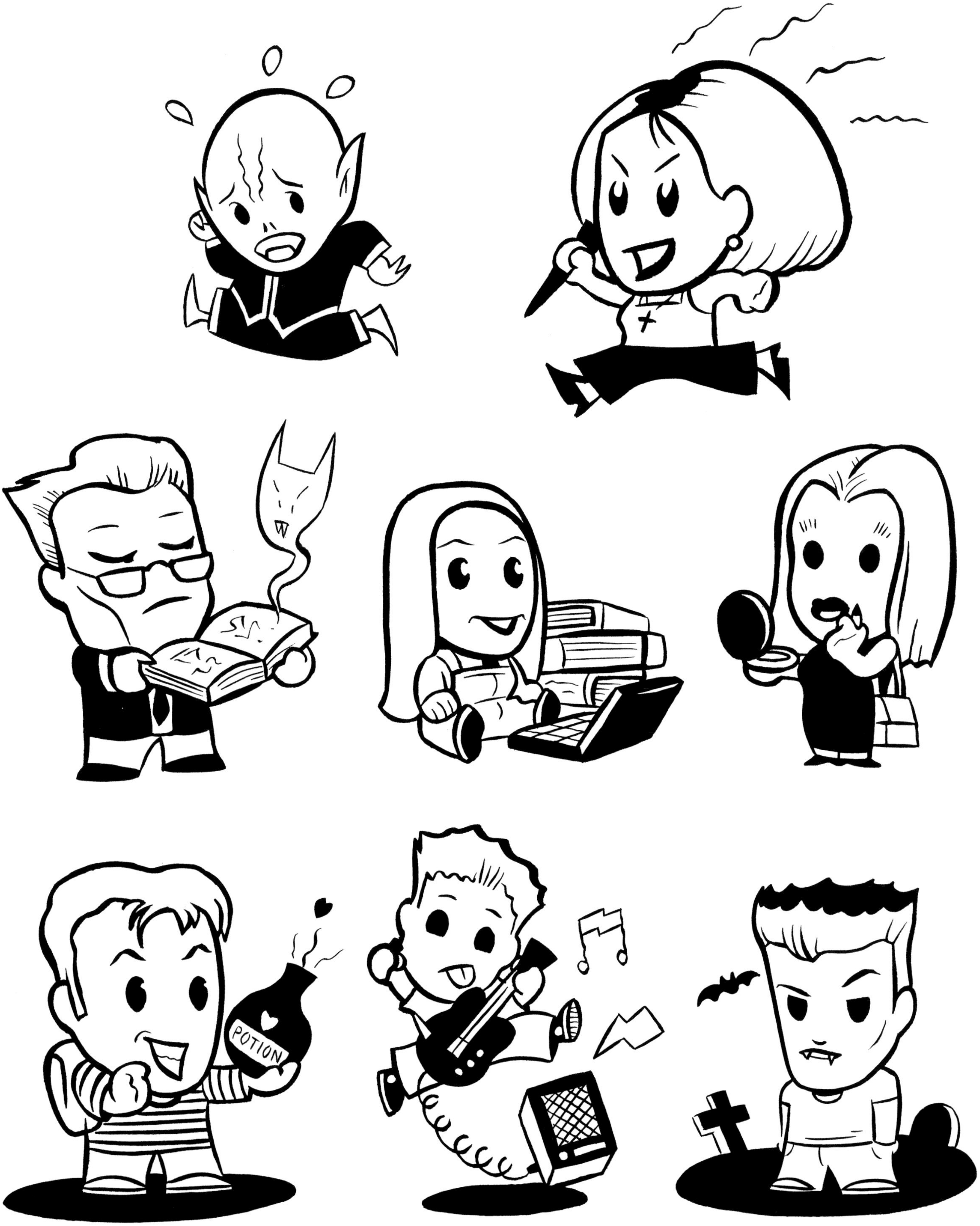
POTION

AFTER RANDY GREEN passed on *Buffy*, I replaced him with Joe Bennett in time for the first issue. Bennett did a few covers during his fairly brief stint. Andi Watson, who'd become popular writing and drawing *Skeleton Key* at Slave Labor, wrote the monthly series until *Buffy* #19.

Opposite: Pencils by Bennett, inks by Rick Ketcham, colors by Guy Major. Cover, *BTVS* #3, November 1998. Above: Pencils and inks by Watson. Letter-column art, *BTVS* #4, December1998.

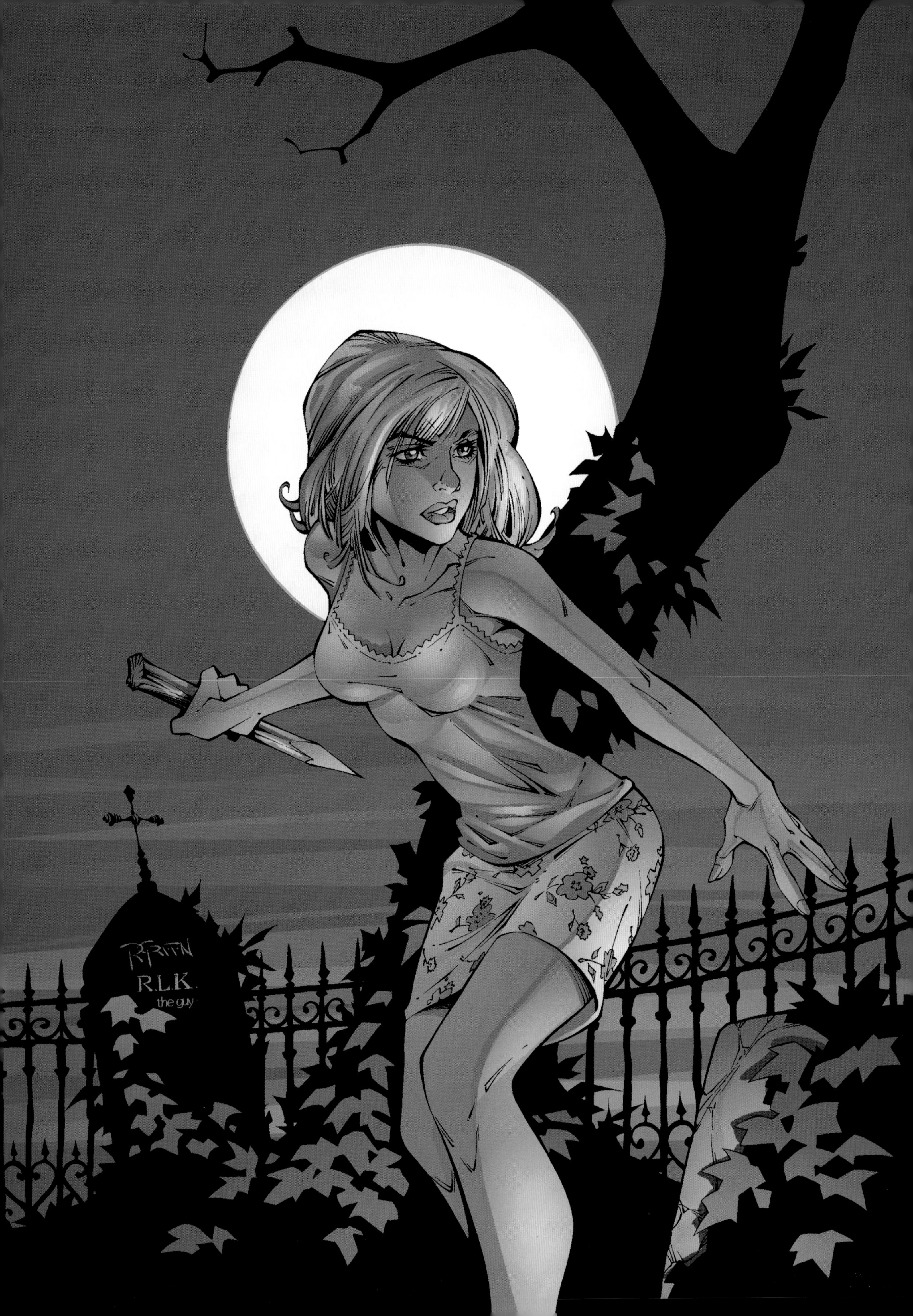
R.L.K.
the guy

I EVENTUALLY GOT RANDY GREEN to draw the girl for me. Meanwhile, we were already launching a spinoff series. Established Buffy novelist Christopher Golden, with whom I'd worked on some Hellboy novels, pitched an adaptation of Joss's original screenplay, minus the camp of the film, and done in the style of the TV show, called *The Origin*. On this *Origin* cover, Joe Bennett didn't want his name on a tombstone for fear it would bring bad luck.

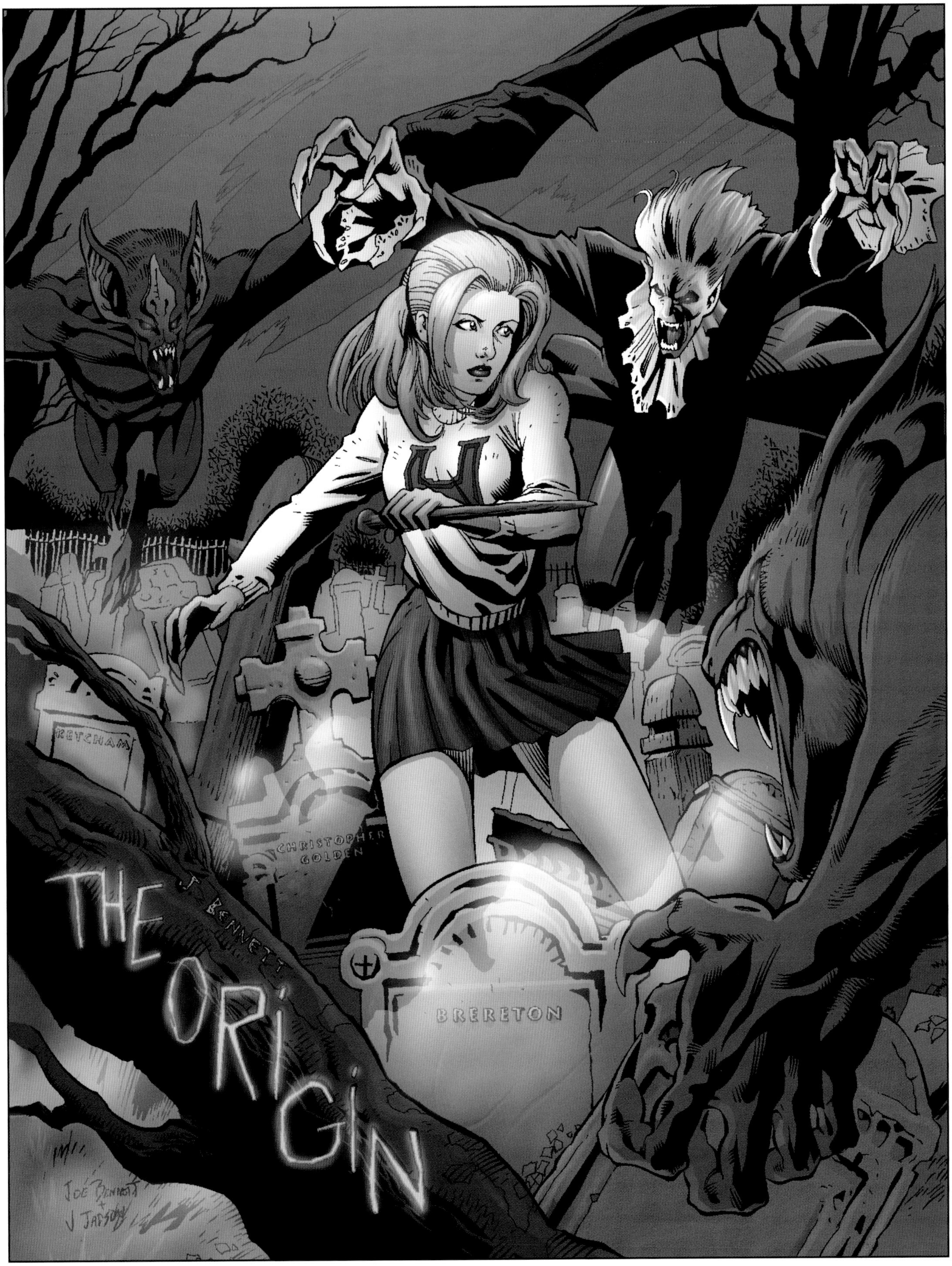

THE ORIGIN
KETCHAM
CHRISTOPHER GOLDEN
J. BENNETT
BRERETON

Opposite: Pencils by Green, inks by Rick Ketcham, colors by Guy Major. Cover, *BTVS* #5, November 1999. Above: Pencils by Bennett, inks by J. Jadsen and René Micheletti, colors by Jeromy Cox and Major. Cover, *BTVS: The Origin* #2, February 1999.

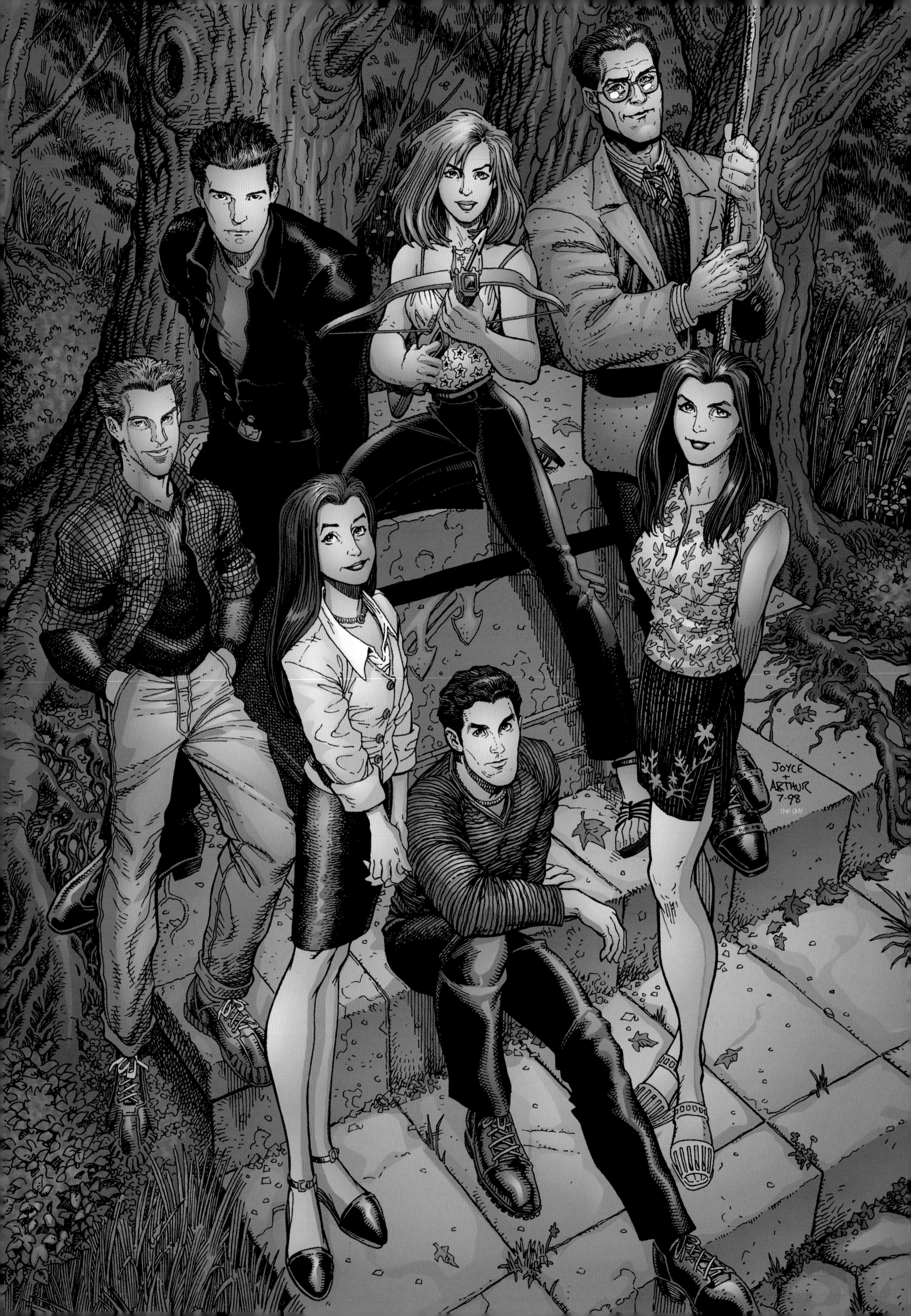
JOYCE
+
ARTHUR
7-98

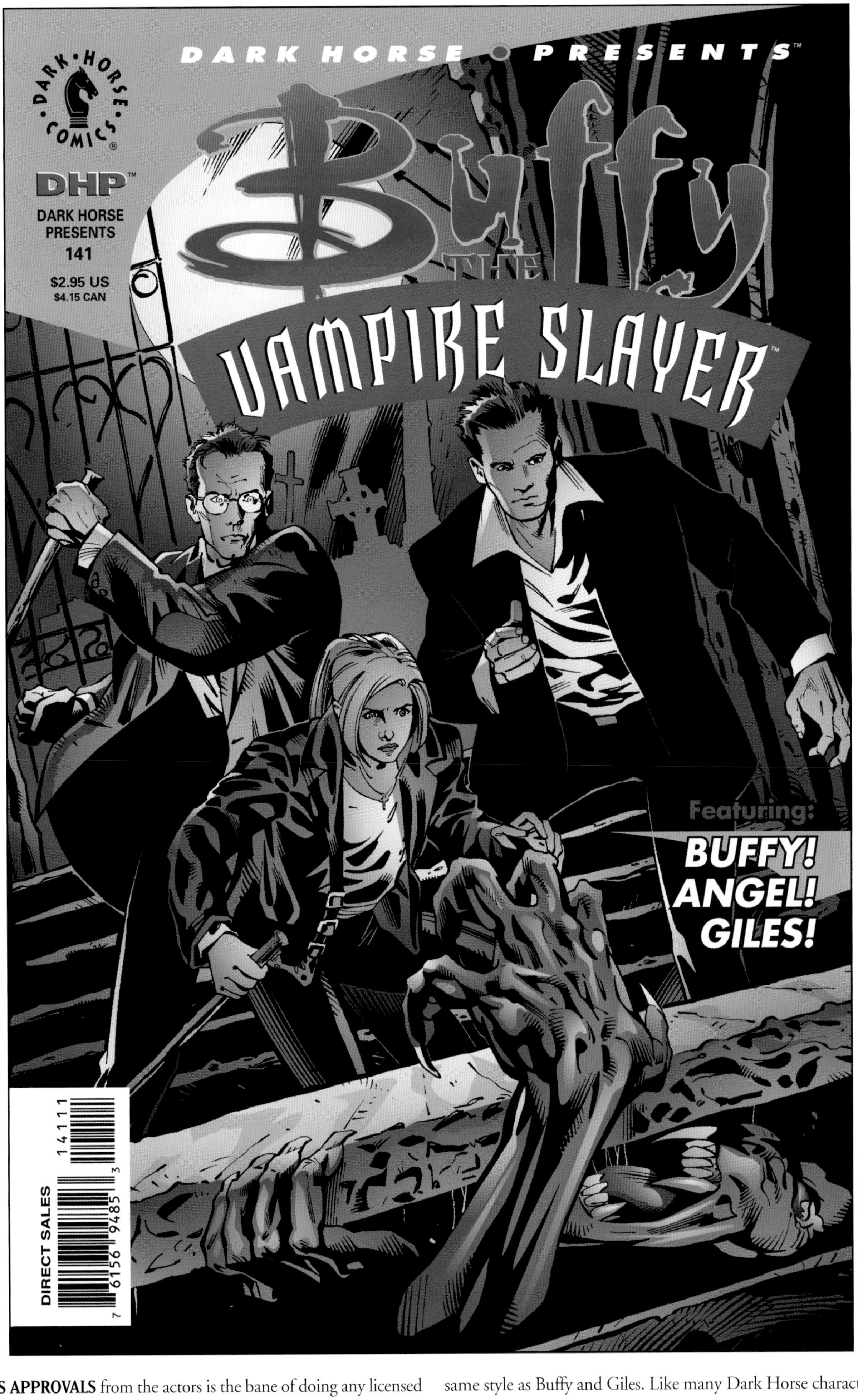
DARK HORSE PRESENTS™
DARK HORSE COMICS®
DHP™
DARK HORSE PRESENTS
141
$2.95 US
$4.15 CAN
Buffy
THE
VAMPIRE SLAYER™
Featuring:
BUFFY!
ANGEL!
GILES!
DIRECT SALES

LIKENESS APPROVALS from the actors is the bane of doing any licensed comic. Art Adams met with approval trouble with Angel's likeness, resulting in an Angel who doesn't quite look like he was drawn in the same style as Buffy and Giles. Like many Dark Horse characters, Buffy had made her debut in *Dark Horse Presents*—less than a year later, we dedicated an entire issue to her, with *DHP* editor Randy Stradley.

Opposite: Pencils and inks by Adams and Joyce Chin, colors by Guy Major. Cover, *BTVS* #6, March 1999. Above: Art by Joe Bennett, colors by Major. Cover, *Dark Horse Presents* #141, March 1999.

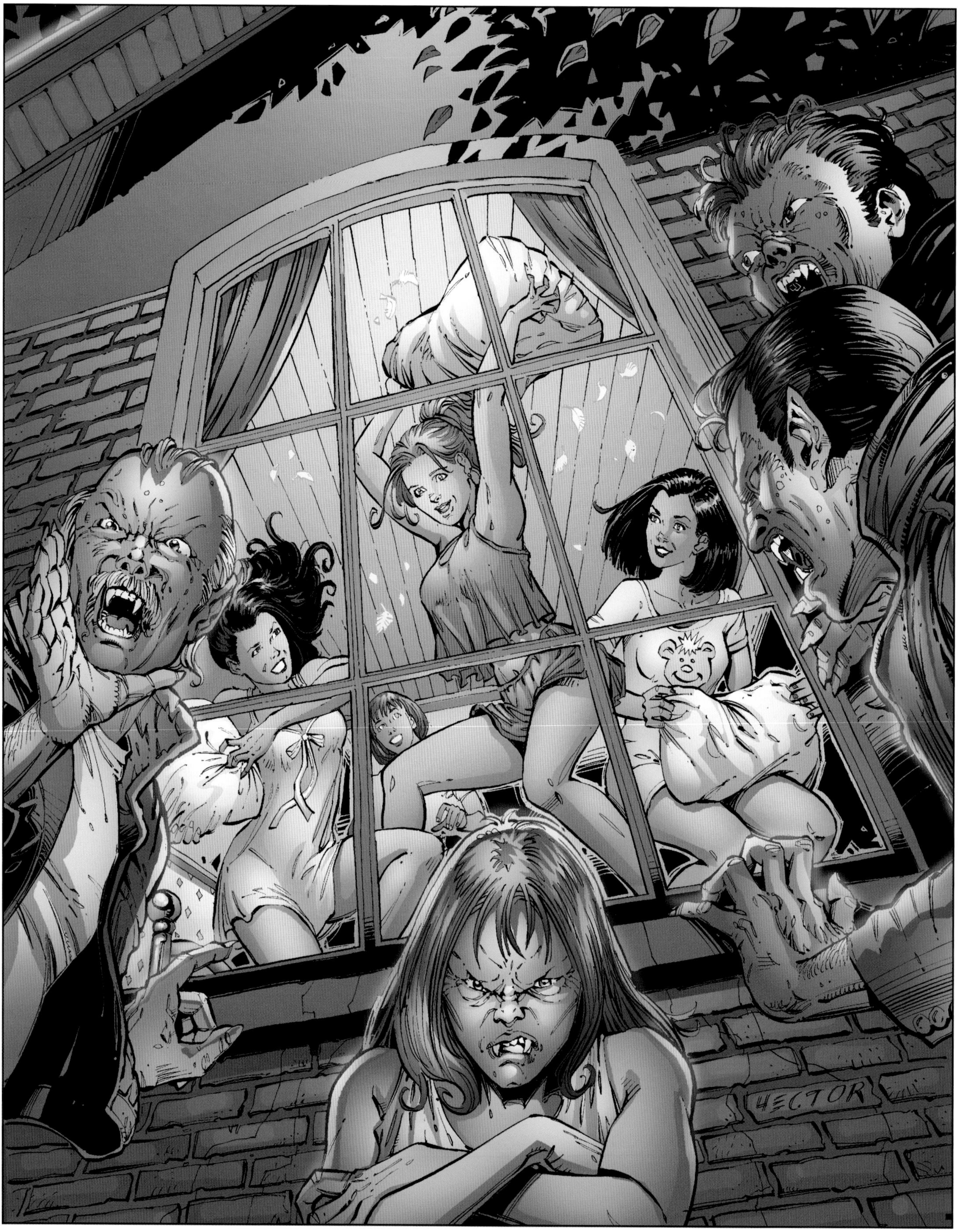
HECTOR

WHILE JOE BENNETT was drawing the spinoff *Buffy: The Origin*, he was replaced on the monthly by Hector Gomez, who'd drawn the graphic novel *The Dust Waltz*. Gomez was the favorite artist of Caroline Kallas, my approvals contact at Joss's office. Up until this point, I'd had no contact with Joss. Christopher Golden, who was writing *The Watcher's Guide* for Pocket Books, met James ("Spike") Marsters on the set of the show. The two proposed writing a comic together, focusing on Spike and Dru. I saw the opportunity to use a different kind of artist than I'd been using on *Buffy*. Mike Mignola and I had had our eyes on Ryan Sook for a while, and I thought a story about a couple of vampires on the road would be perfect for him. When the book came out, word got back to me that Joss loved Sook's work.

Above: Art by Gomez, colors by Guy Major. Cover, *BTVS* #7, March 1999. Opposite: Script by Marsters and Golden, pencils and inks by Sook, colors by Major, letters by Pat Brosseau. Interiors, *BTVS: Spike and Dru*, December 2000.

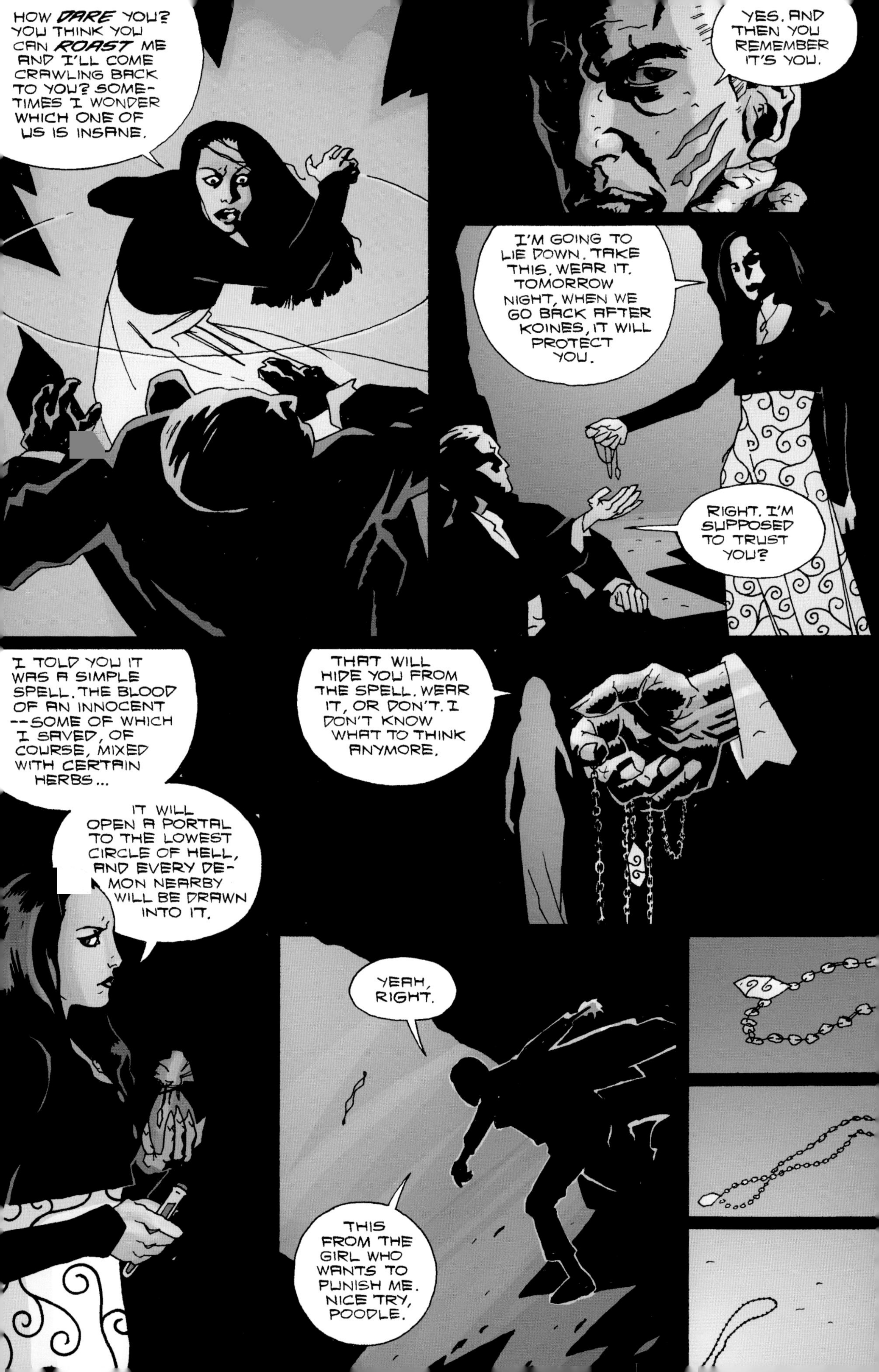
HOW DARE YOU? YOU THINK YOU CAN ROAST ME AND I'LL COME CRAWLING BACK TO YOU? SOMETIMES I WONDER WHICH ONE OF US IS INSANE.
YES. AND THEN YOU REMEMBER IT'S YOU.
I'M GOING TO LIE DOWN. TAKE THIS. WEAR IT. TOMORROW NIGHT, WHEN WE GO BACK AFTER KOINES, IT WILL PROTECT YOU.
RIGHT. I'M SUPPOSED TO TRUST YOU?
I TOLD YOU IT WAS A SIMPLE SPELL. THE BLOOD OF AN INNOCENT --SOME OF WHICH I SAVED, OF COURSE, MIXED WITH CERTAIN HERBS...
IT WILL OPEN A PORTAL TO THE LOWEST CIRCLE OF HELL, AND EVERY DEMON NEARBY WILL BE DRAWN INTO IT.
THAT WILL HIDE YOU FROM THE SPELL. WEAR IT, OR DON'T. I DON'T KNOW WHAT TO THINK ANYMORE.
YEAH, RIGHT.
THIS FROM THE GIRL WHO WANTS TO PUNISH ME. NICE TRY, POODLE.

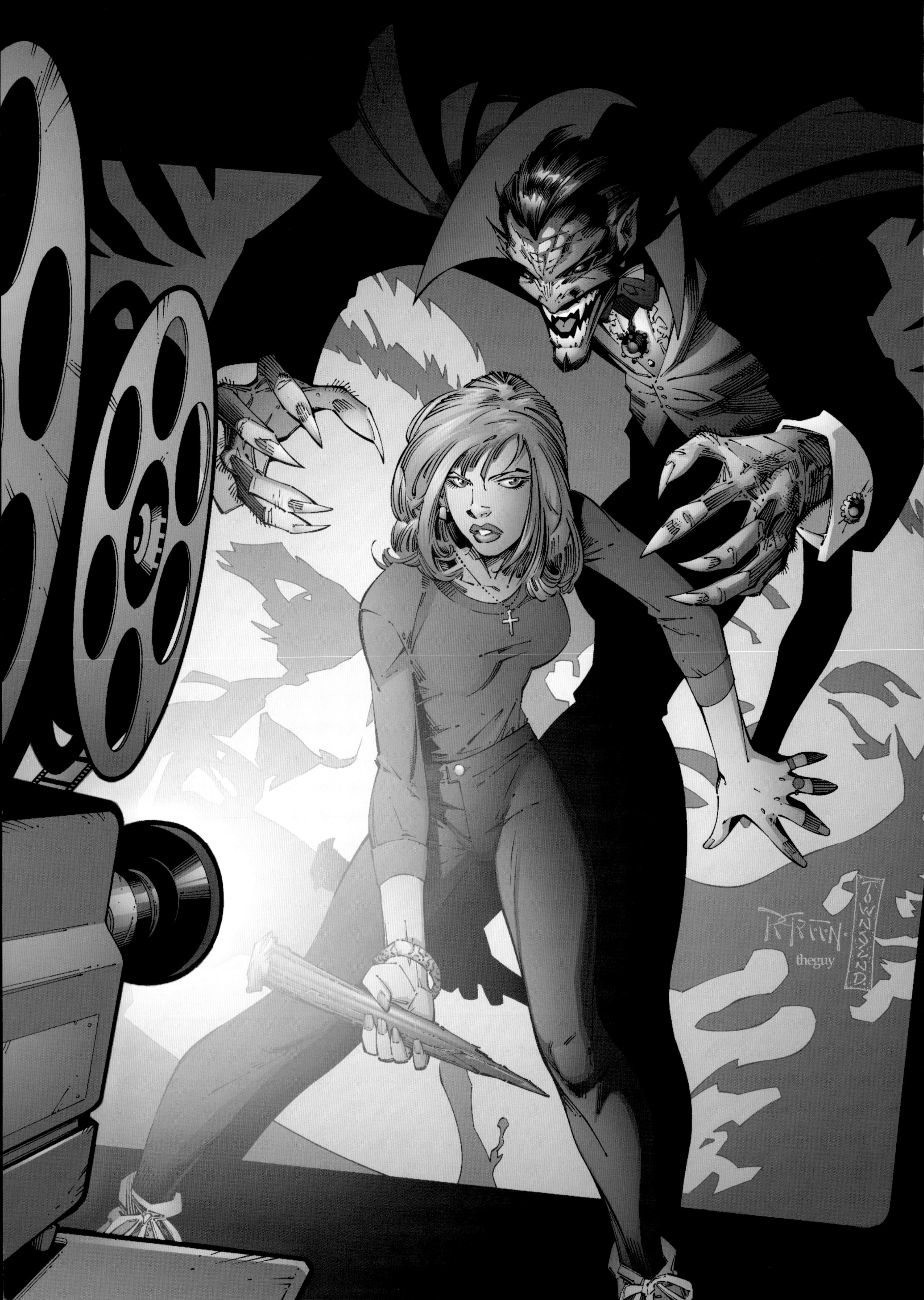
theguy
TOWNSEND

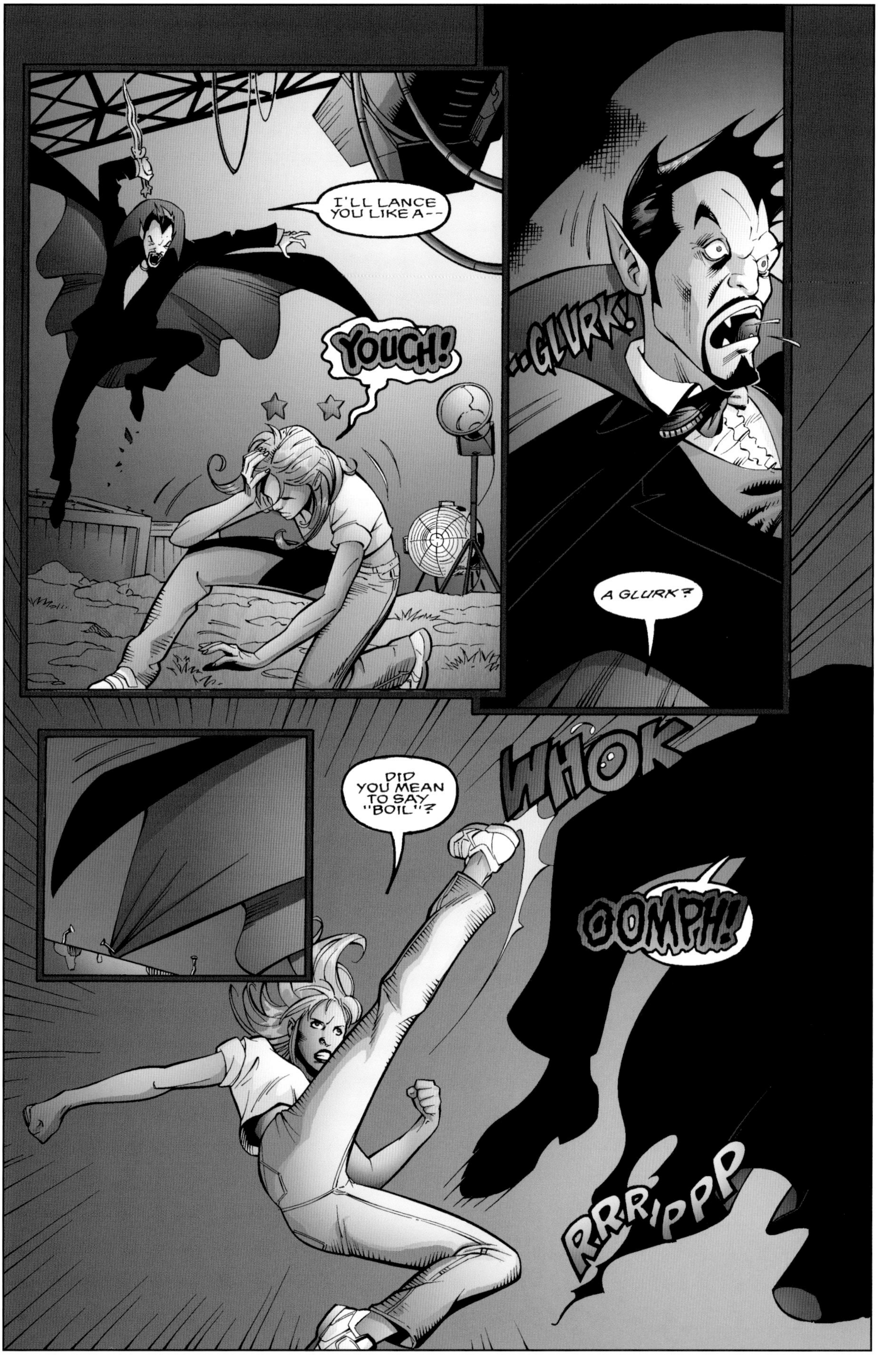
I'LL LANCE YOU LIKE A--
YOUCH!
--GLURK!
A GLURK?
DID YOU MEAN TO SAY "BOIL"?
WHOK
OOMPH!
RRRIPPP

I DIDN'T KNOW at the time that the fill-in artist I hired for *Buffy* #8, Cliff Richards, would go on to dominate the series, drawing more than fifty stories for me. As I write this, Joss just decided to hire Cliff to draw an issue of Season Eight. I'd grow to love not only Cliff's ability to draw great likenesses, while never looking like he was tracing photos, but more importantly his acting and his storytelling. At first I was unsure of his storytelling, and asked my friend, *Body Bags* artist Jason Pearson (one of the best comic-book artists around), to lay out *Buffy* #8, with Richards drawing over those layouts.

Opposite: Pencils by Randy Green, inks by Tim Townsend, colors by Guy Major. Above: Script by Andi Watson, layouts by Pearson, pencils by Richards, inks by Joe Pimentel, colors by Major, letters by Janice Chiang. Cover and interiors, *BTVS* #8, April 1999.

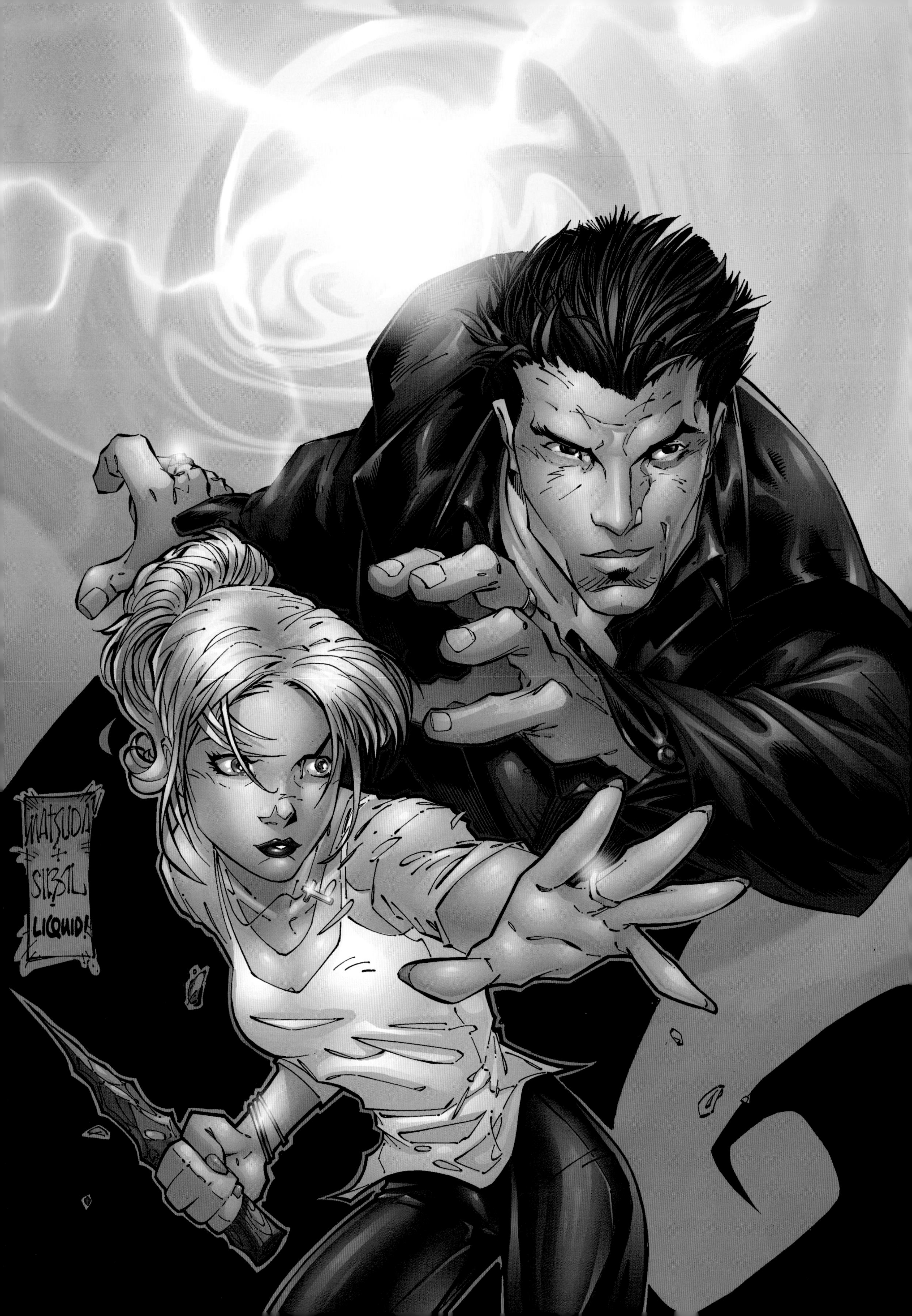

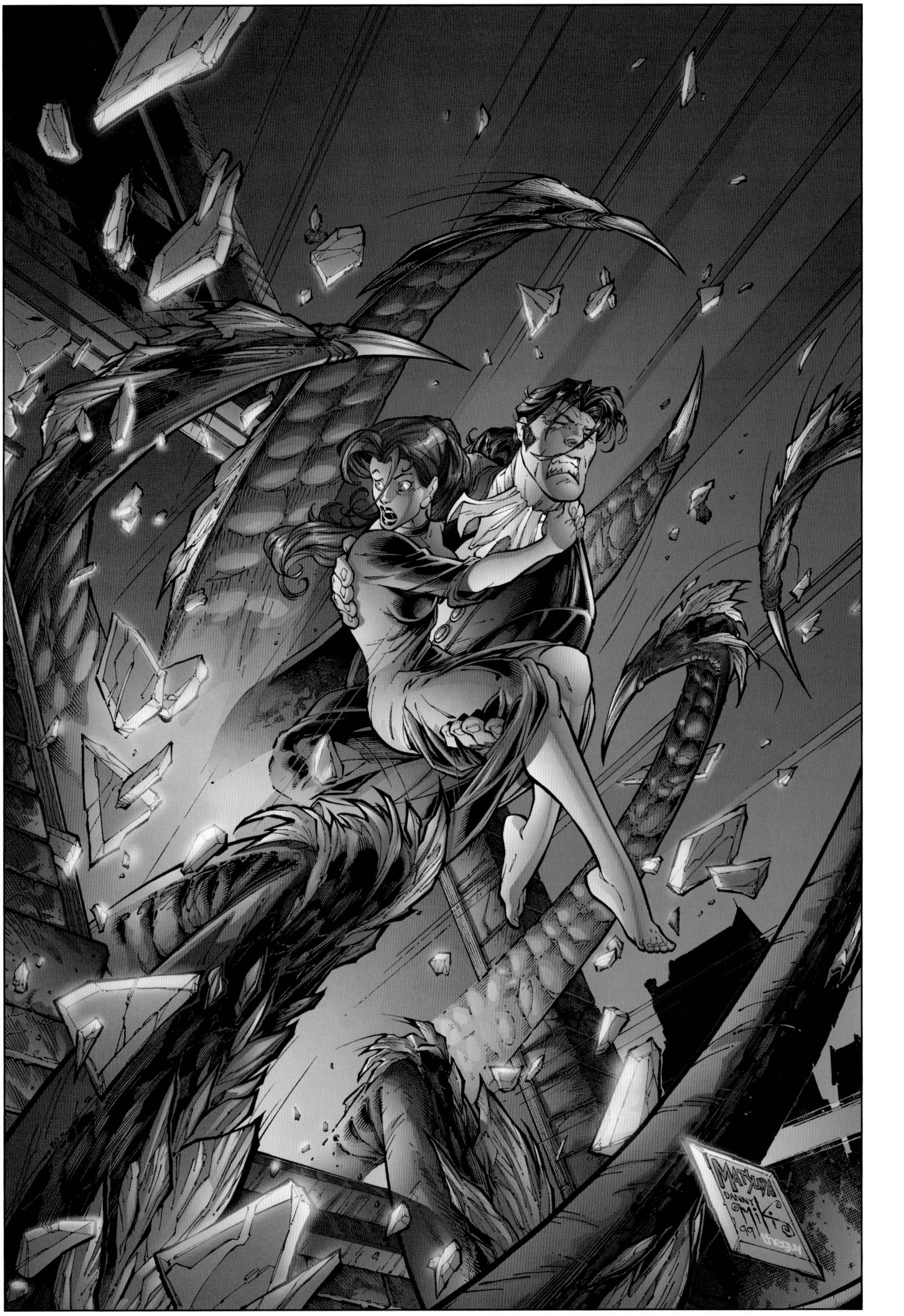

JEFF MATSUDA called me saying he was a huge fan of the television show, and wanted to get involved in the *Buffy* comics. Jeff was an incredibly popular comics artist before mostly abandoning the medium for animation, working on *Jackie Chan Adventures* before becoming the art director for *The Batman* cartoon. He had no time to do interior work, but he quickly fell into heavy rotation as a cover artist on the monthly book and miniseries. We framed his very first *Angel* cover, alongside a high-quality print of the colored version, and gave it to Joss to decorate his office at the old Mutant Enemy location in Santa Monica. I should ask him where that thing is now.

Opposite: Pencils by Matsuda, inks by Jon Sibal, colors by Liquid! Above: Pencils by Matsuda, inks by Danny Miki, colors by Guy Major. Covers, *BTVS: Angel* #1 and #2, May and June 1999.

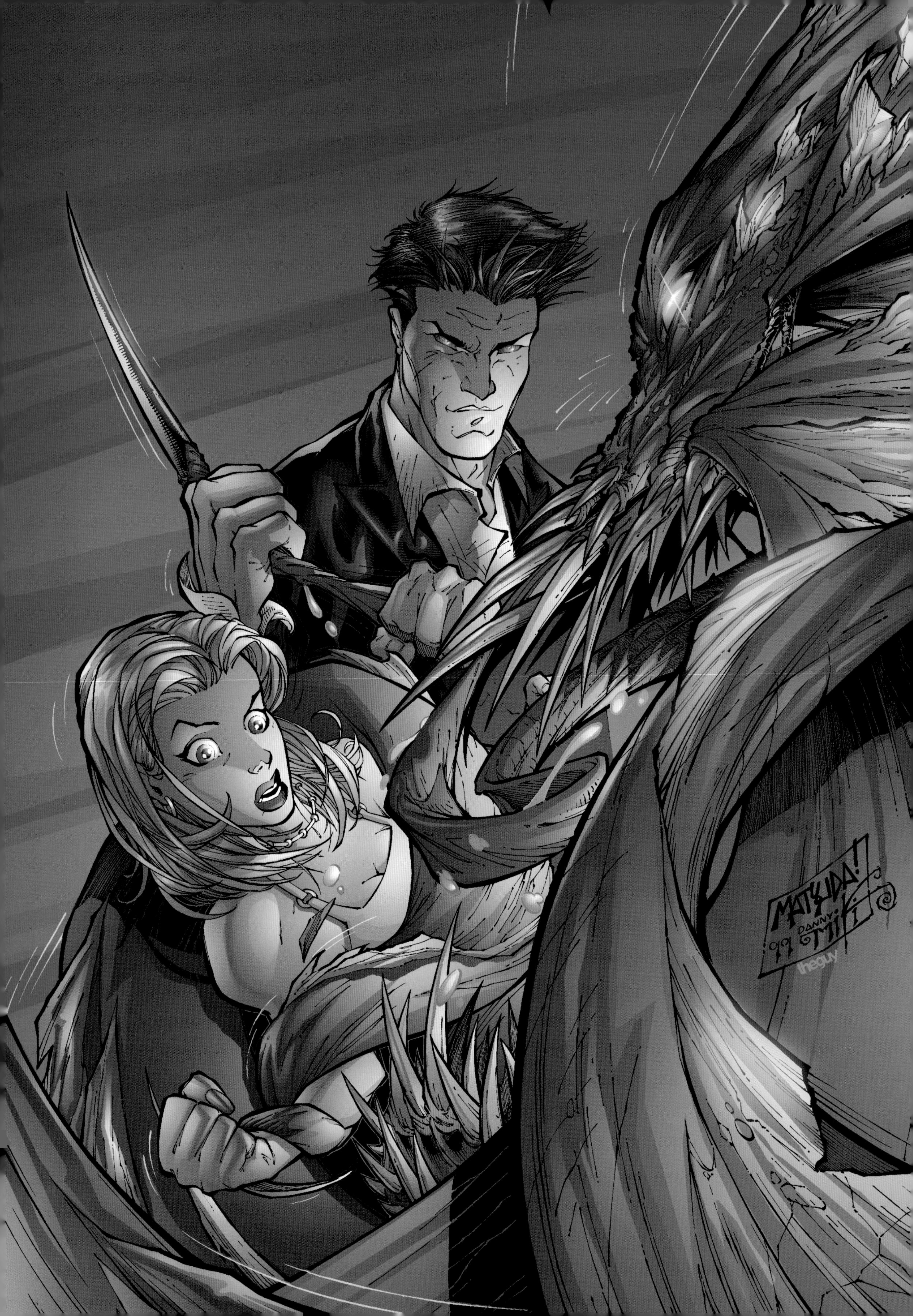
MATSUDA!
theguy

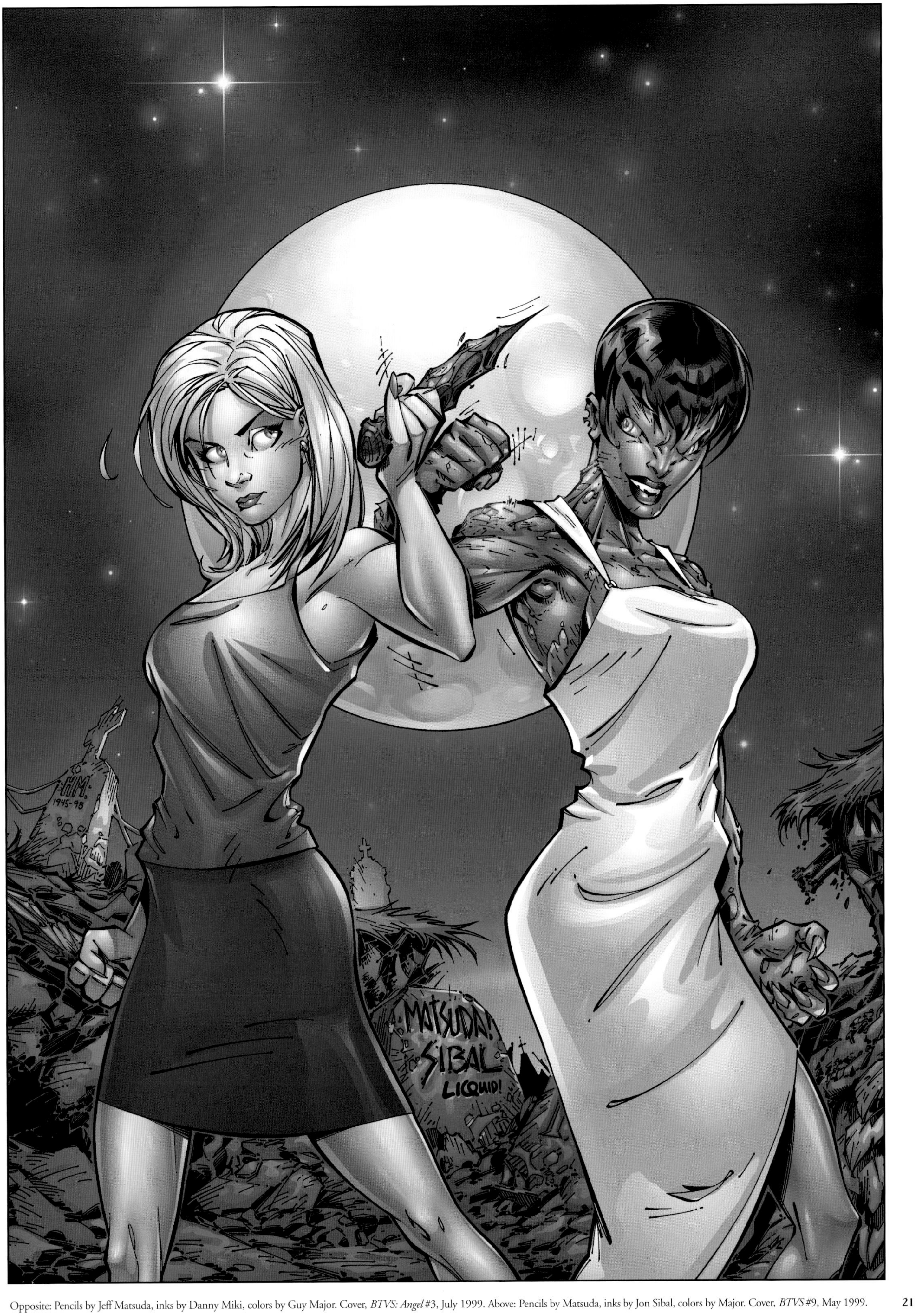
H.M.
1945-98
MATSUDA!
SIBAL
LICQUID!

Opposite: Pencils by Jeff Matsuda, inks by Danny Miki, colors by Guy Major. Cover, *BTVS: Angel* #3, July 1999. Above: Pencils by Matsuda, inks by Jon Sibal, colors by Major. Cover, *BTVS* #9, May 1999.

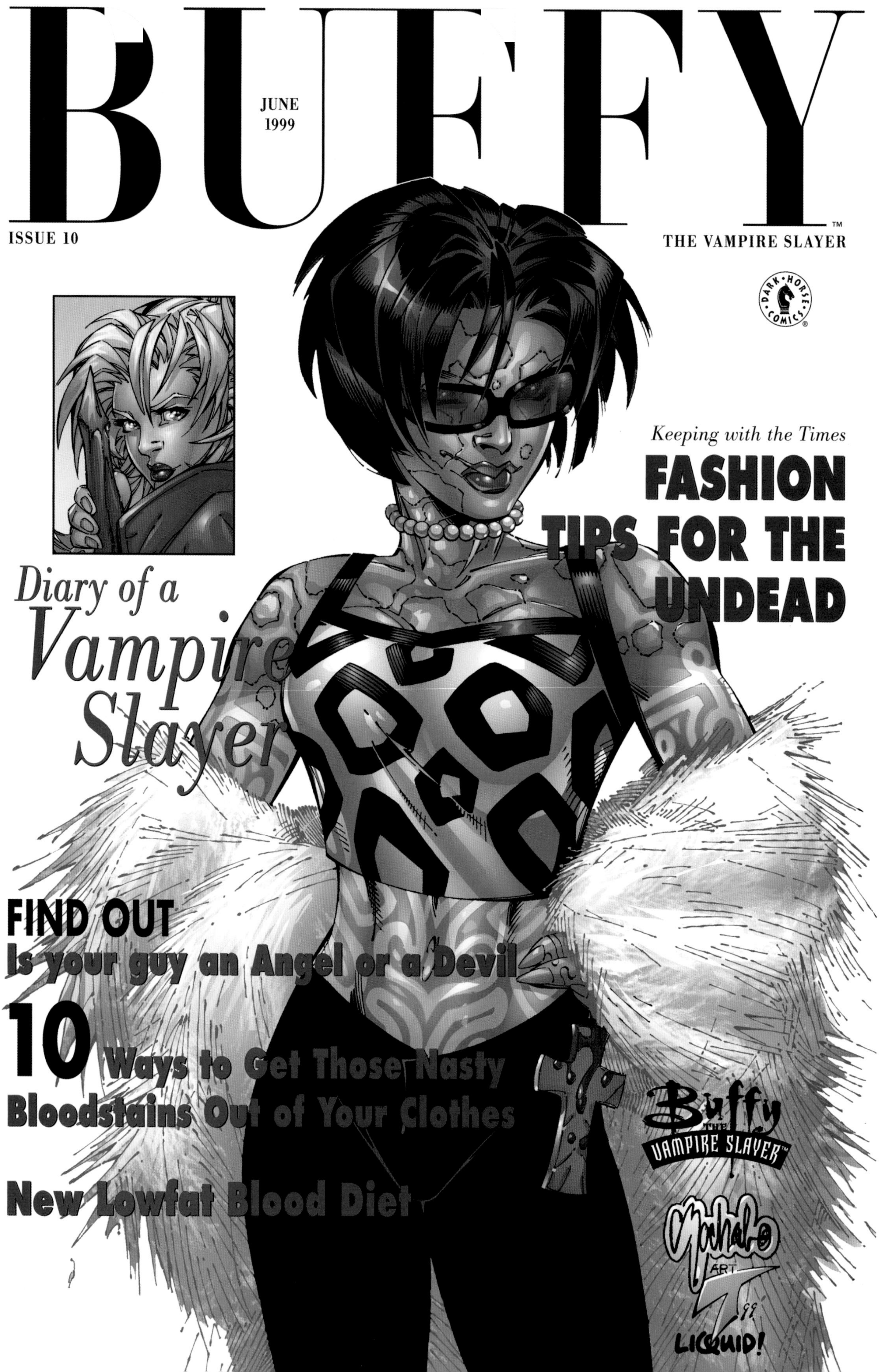
BUFFY
JUNE
1999
ISSUE 10
THE VAMPIRE SLAYER
DARK HORSE COMICS
Keeping with the Times
FASHION TIPS FOR THE UNDEAD
Diary of a Vampire Slayer
FIND OUT
Is your guy an Angel or a Devil
10 Ways to Get Those Nasty Bloodstains Out of Your Clothes
New Lowfat Blood Diet
Buffy THE VAMPIRE SLAYER
LIQUID!

A STORY ABOUT a group of vampiric models (which began in *Buffy* #9) led to the high-concept cover on the facing page. The marketing gang thought it was funny, but insisted we include Buffy. I'm not sure the little cameo satisfied them. There are not a whole lot of covers without our main girl.

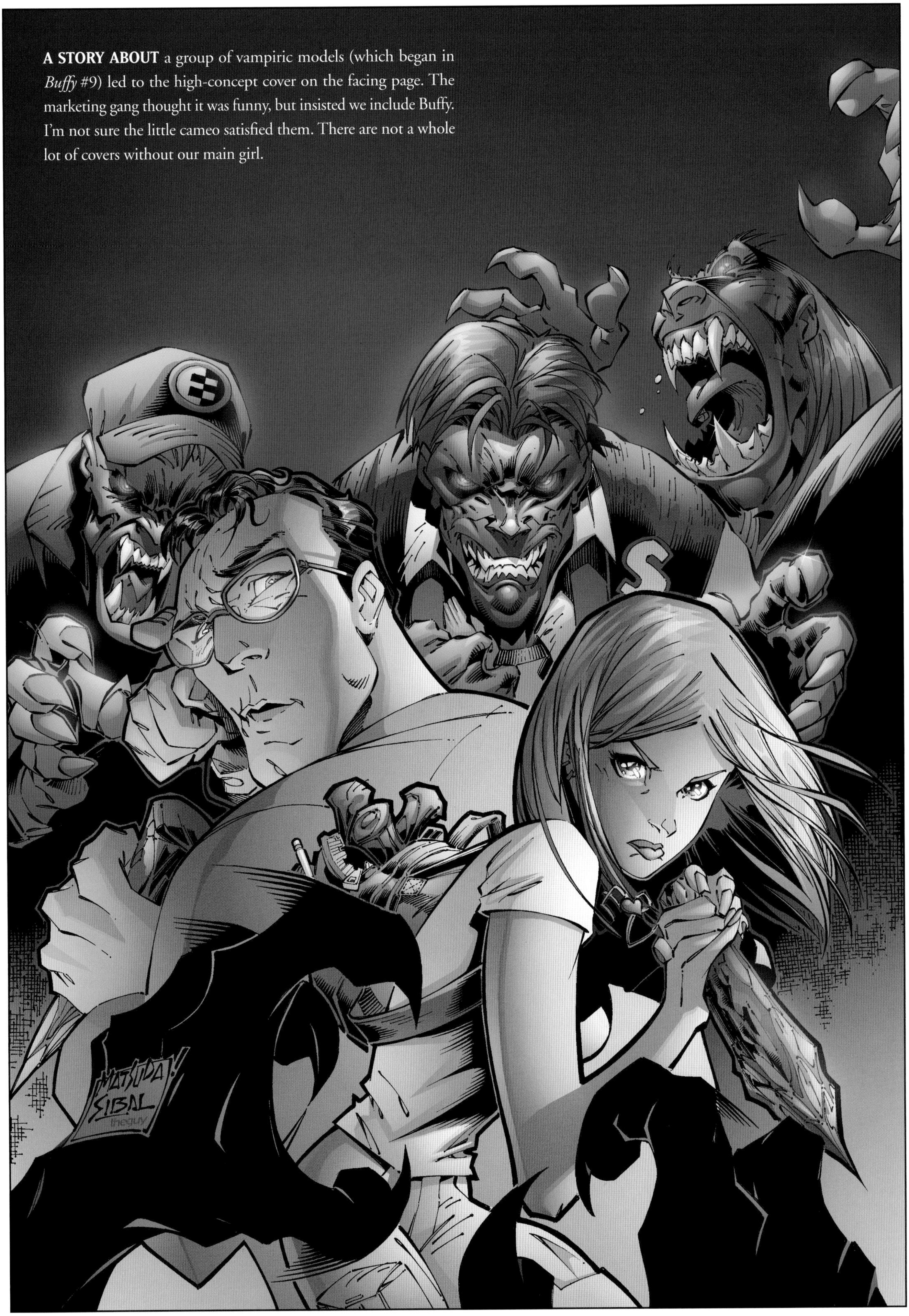
MATSUDA!
SIBAL
theguy

Opposite: Pencils by Chris Bachalo, inks by Art Thibert, colors by Liquid!, design by Kristen Burda. Above: Pencils by Jeff Matsuda, inks by Jon Sibal, colors by Guy Major. Covers, *BTVS* #10 and #11, June and July 1999.

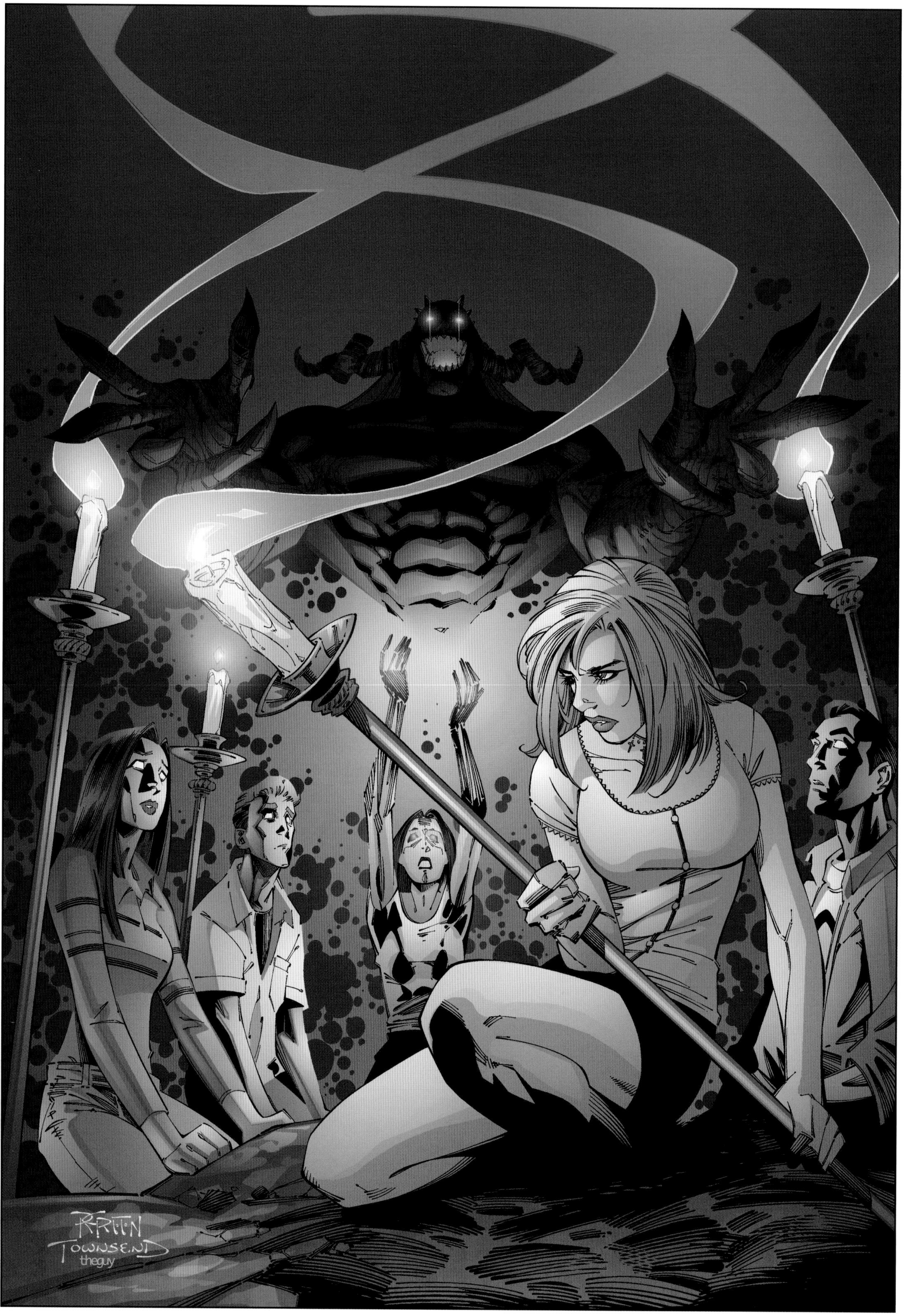
TOWNSEND
theguy

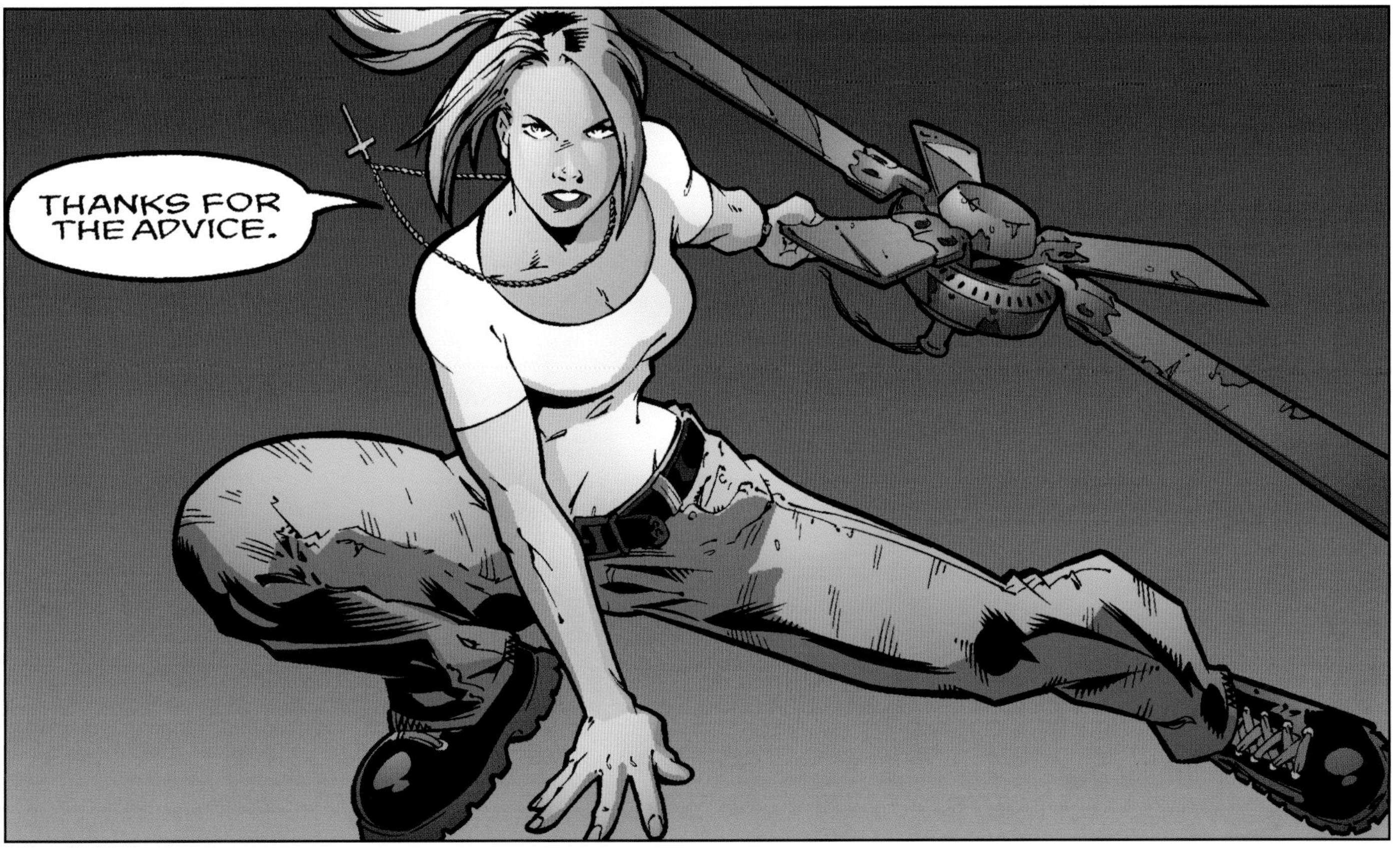
THANKS FOR
THE ADVICE.

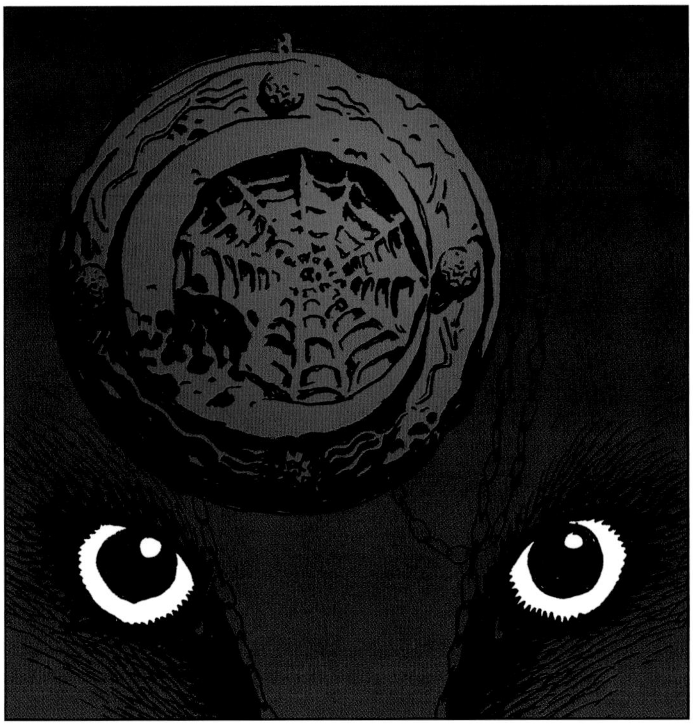

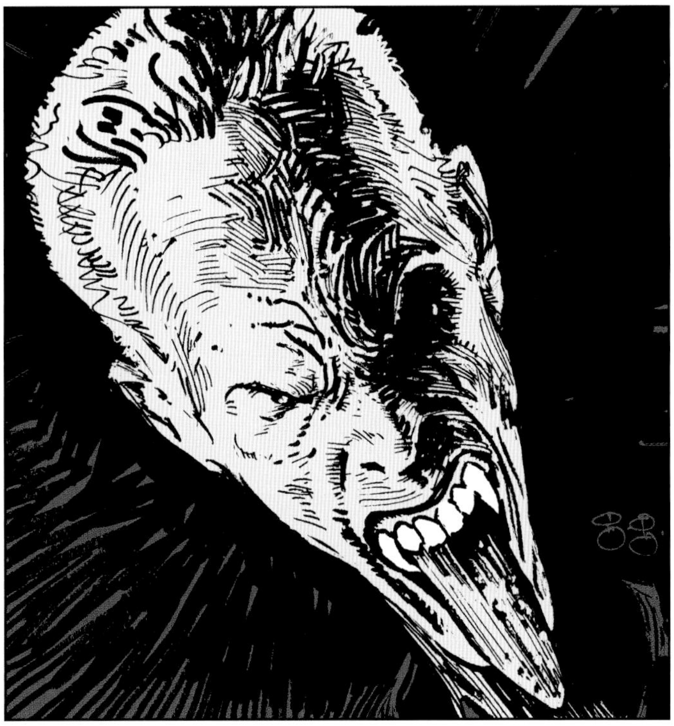

BUFFY #12 was the first issue of the monthly not written by Andi Watson. Christopher Golden joined Christian Zanier—who would go on to be the regular artist on our monthly *Angel* series, launching a few months later. This issue also marked the first time I worked with inker Andy Owens, whom I met through Jeff Matsuda. Owens would go on to work with Joss on *Fray* and *Buffy the Vampire Slayer* Season Eight.

At the same time, we were putting together the first and only *Buffy Annual*, which contained various features, broken up by the above spot illustrations by Ryan Sook and Gary Gianni. Sook and Cliff Richards drew the stories in the book, which also featured a pinup gallery. Sook's story was written by Doug Petrie, who'd seen his work in *Spike and Dru.* Petrie became the first writer from the *Buffy* show to cross over into comics. Around this time, I had my first meeting with Joss. He told me that he wanted Sook to be the regular artist on our upcoming *Angel* series, but the schedule made it impossible. Fans had a very mixed reaction to Sook, and I wonder what they'd have done if he'd been hired for that job. At that meeting, we also talked about the possibility of Joss writing a Faith miniseries. That idea ultimately transformed into the comics series *Fray.*

Opposite: Pencils by Randy Green, inks by Tim Townsend, colors by Guy Major. Cover, *BTVS* #12, August 1999. Top: Script by Golden, pencils by Zanier, inks by Owens, colors by Major. Interiors, *BTVS* #12, August 1999. Above left: Pencils and inks by Sook. Above right: Pencils and inks by Gianni. Chapter breaks, *BTVS Annual*, August 1999.

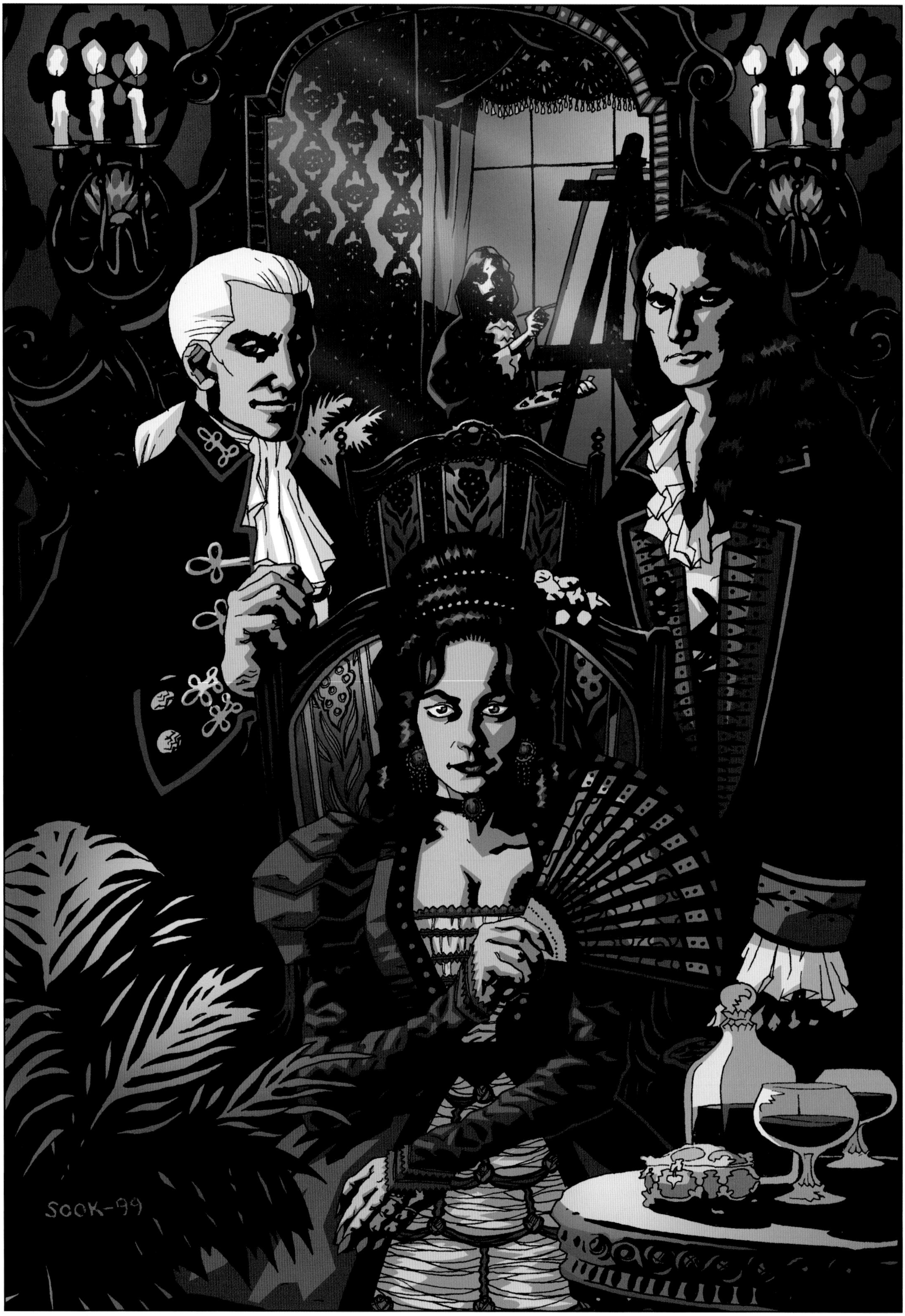
SOOK-99

 Pencils and inks by Ryan Sook, colors by Guy Major. Opposite: Pencils by Jeff Matsuda, inks by Andy Owens, colors by Major. Pinups, *BTVS Annual*, August 1999.

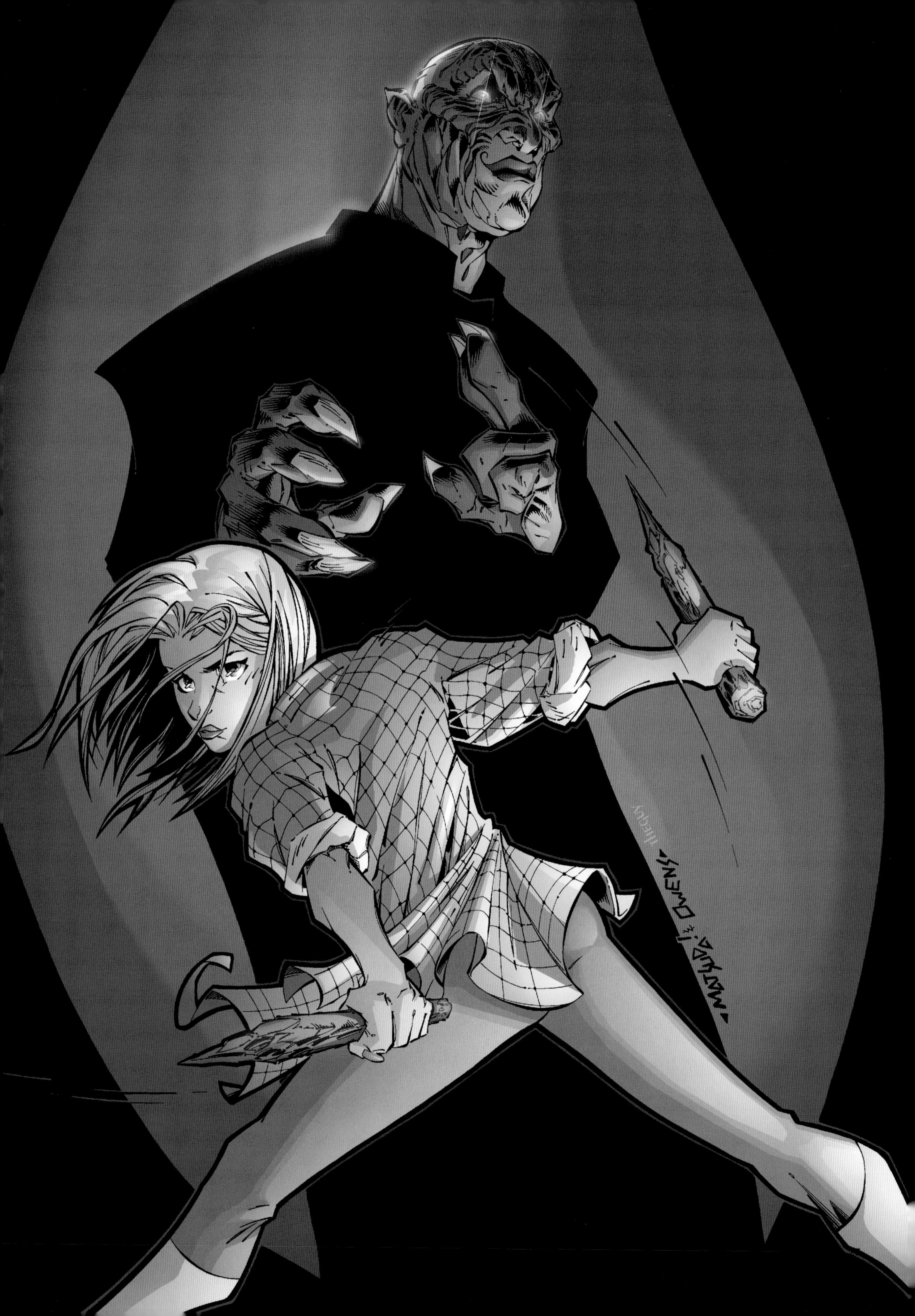

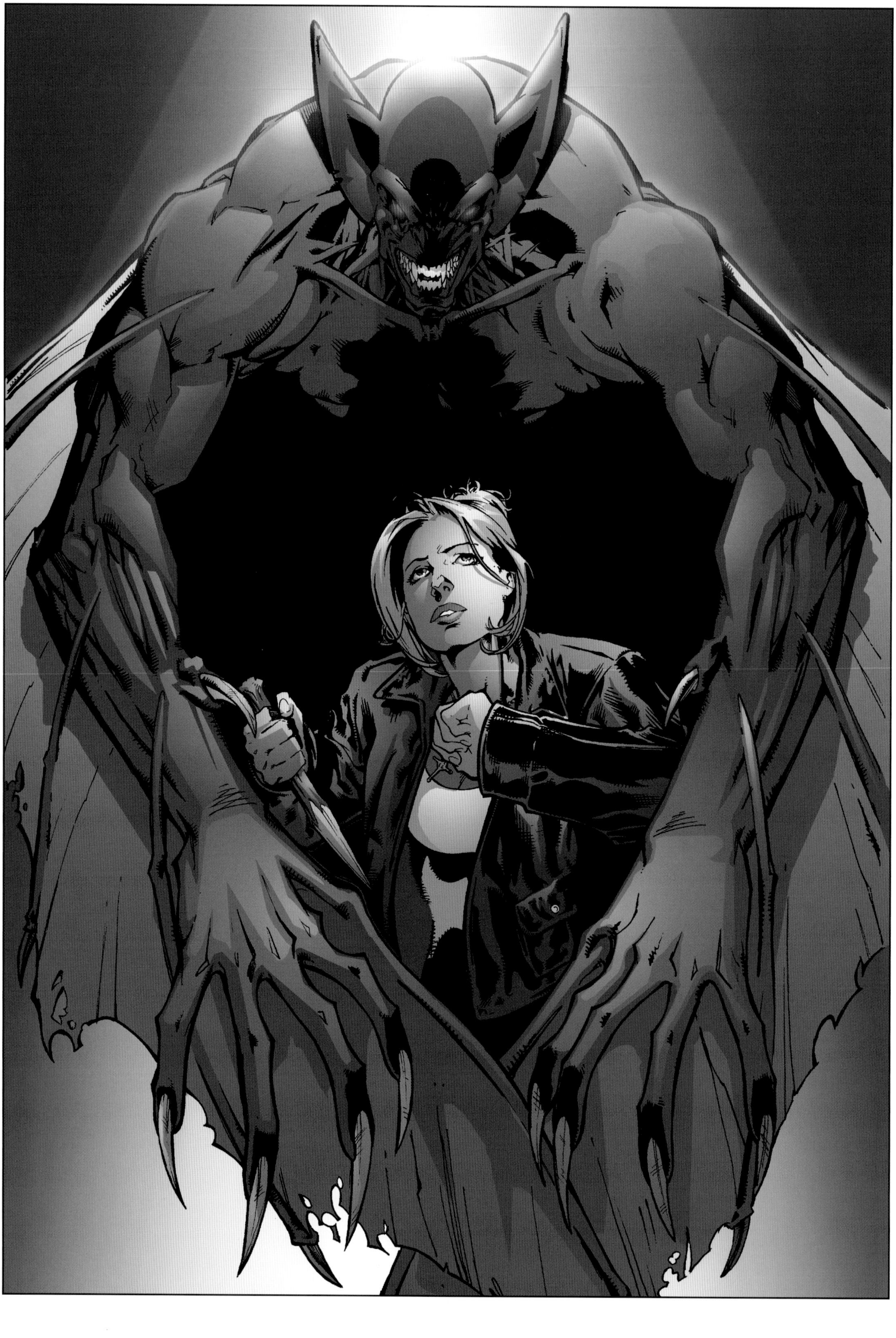

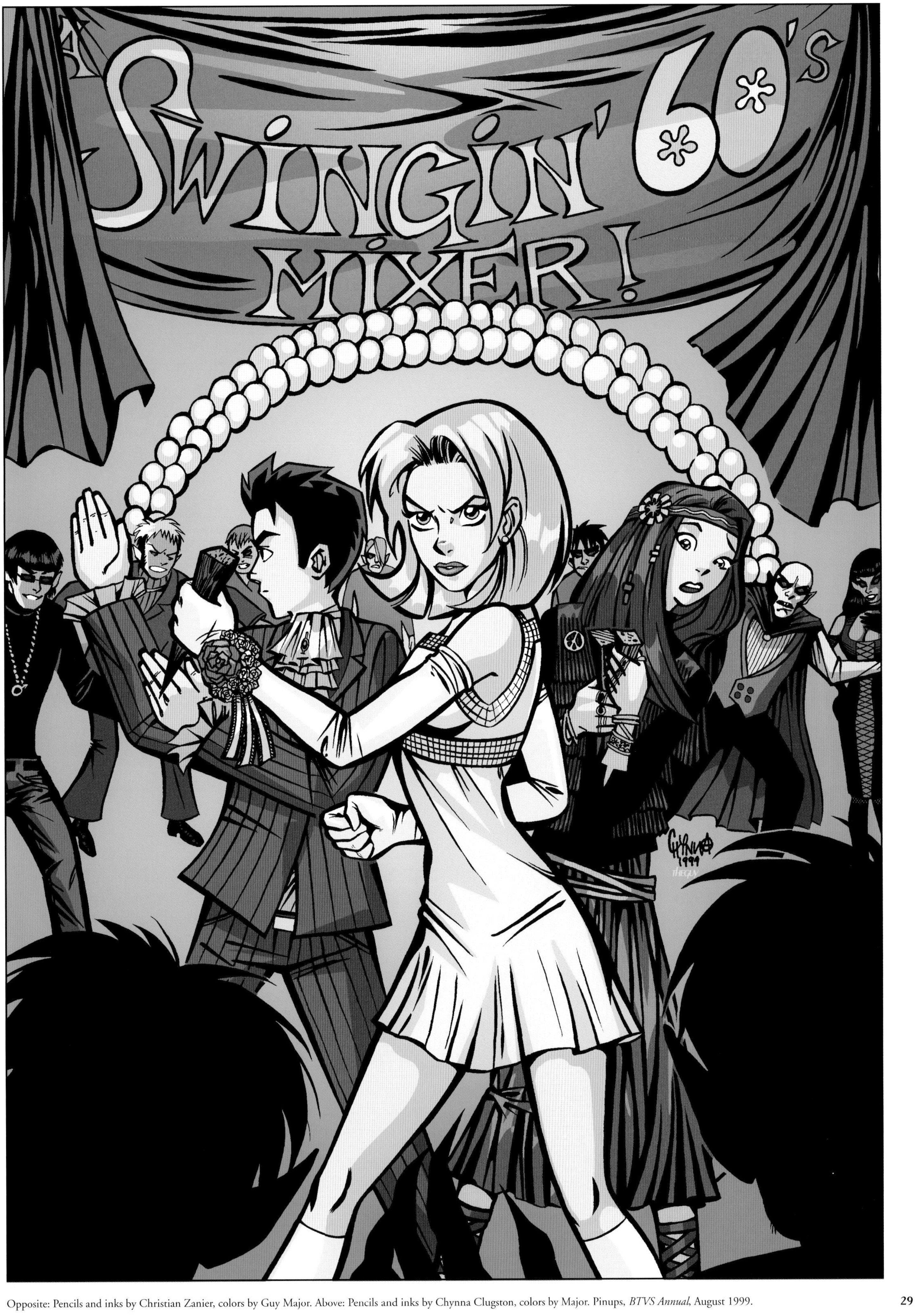
A SWINGIN' 60's MIXER!

Opposite: Pencils and inks by Christian Zanier, colors by Guy Major. Above: Pencils and inks by Chynna Clugston, colors by Major. Pinups, *BTVS Annual*, August 1999.

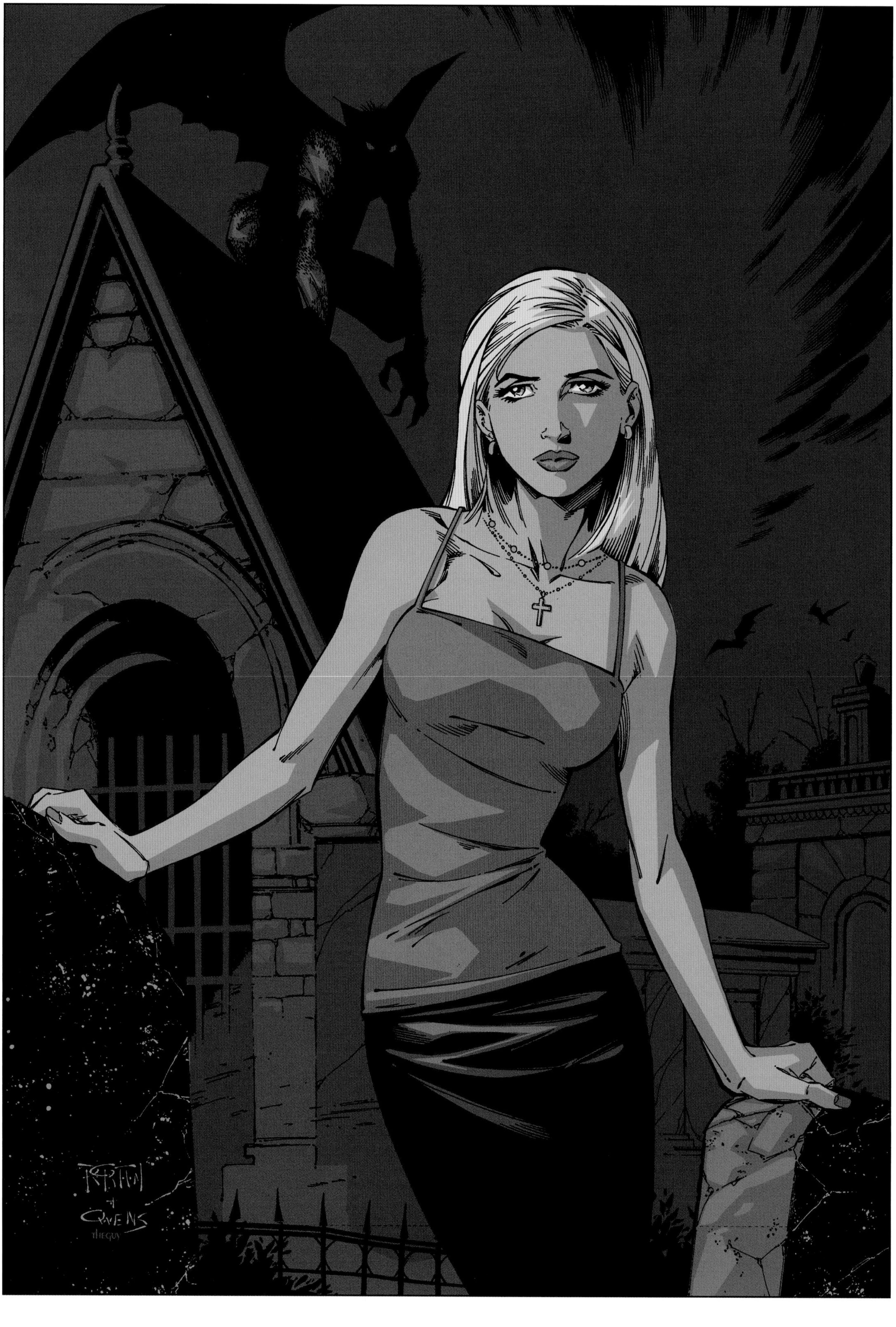

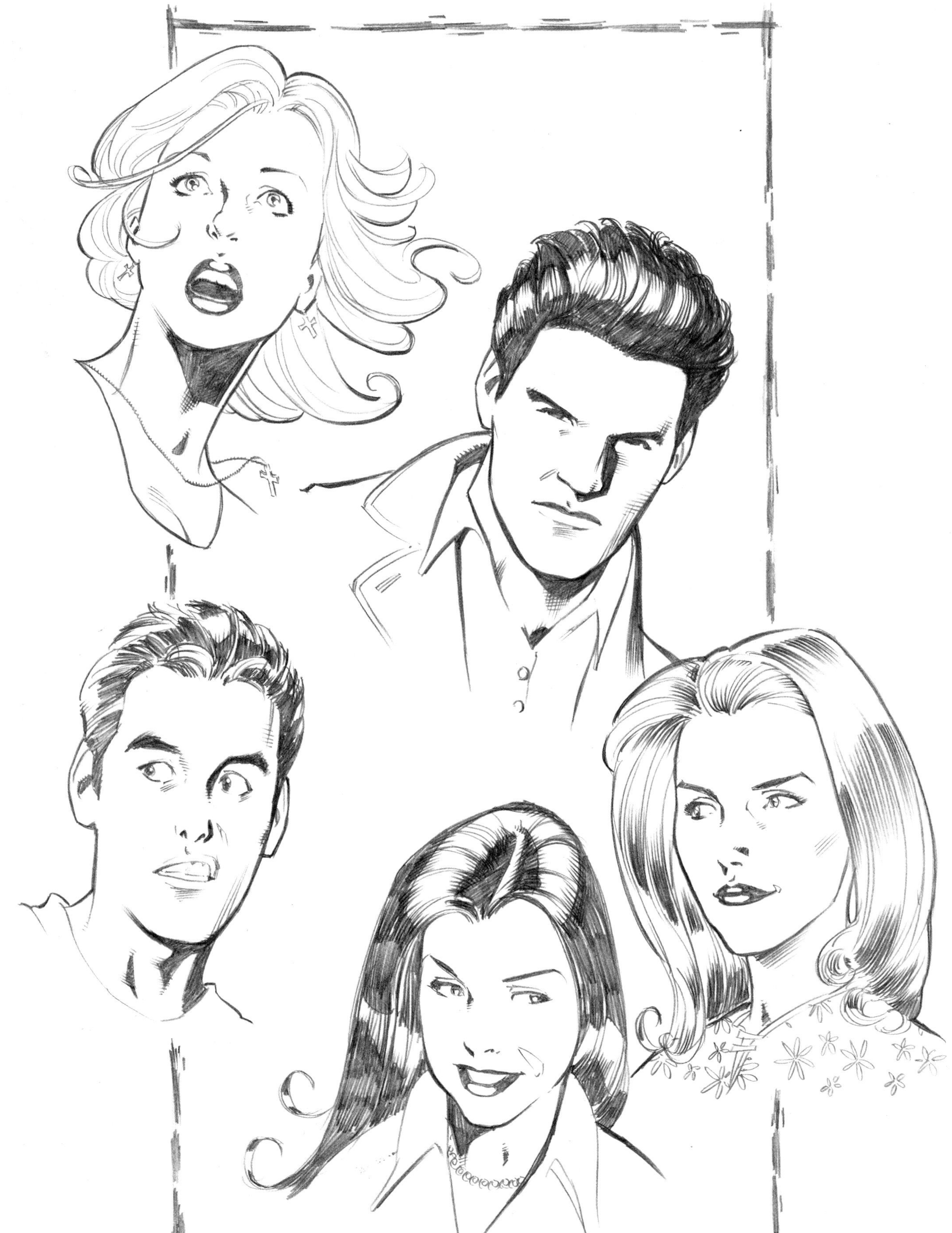

WHEN THE ANNUAL was done, Cliff Richards jumped in as the regular artist on the series. Starting with *Buffy* #13, he only missed a handful of the next fifty issues, and he only missed those because I wanted to play it safe while he was drawing side projects for me such as *Haunted* and *Chaos Bleeds*. These are some of the sketches that had gotten Cliff the job on *Buffy* #8.

Opposite: Pencils by Randy Green, inks by Andy Owens, colors by Guy Major. Pinup, *BTVS Annual*, August 1999. Above: Sketches by Richards, mid-1999.

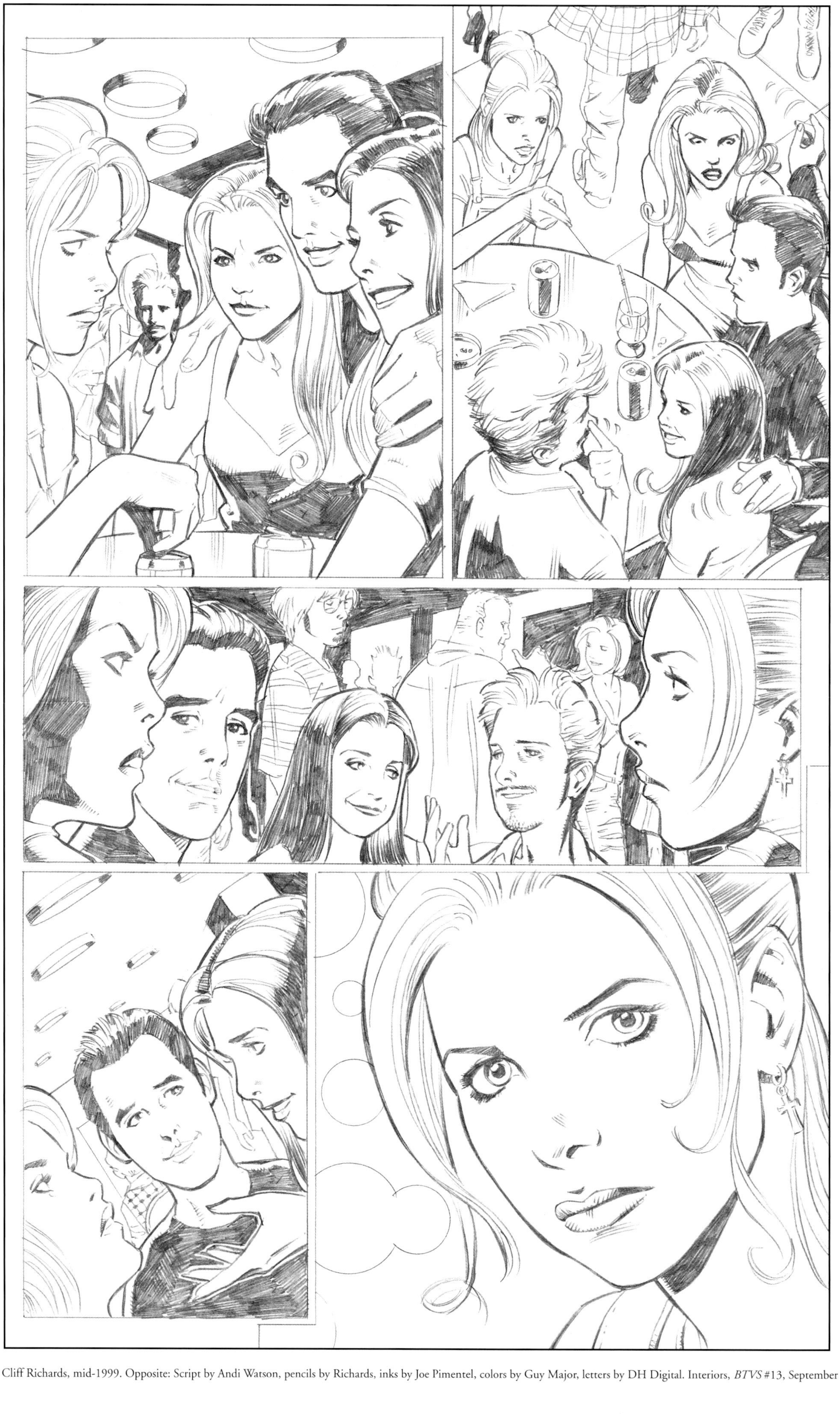

 Pencils by Cliff Richards, mid-1999. Opposite: Script by Andi Watson, pencils by Richards, inks by Joe Pimentel, colors by Guy Major, letters by DH Digital. Interiors, *BTVS* #13, September 1999.

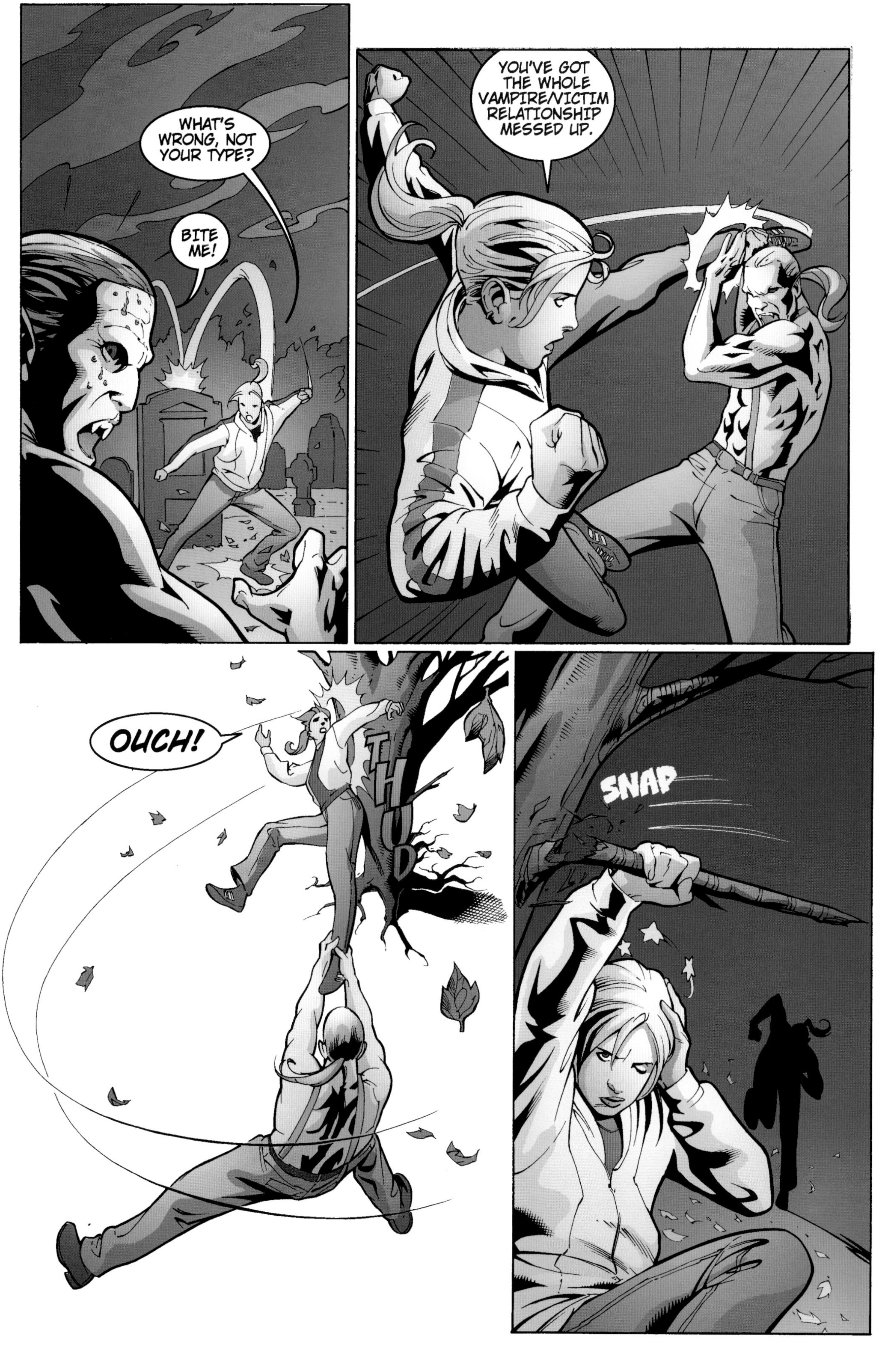
WHAT'S WRONG, NOT YOUR TYPE?
BITE ME!
YOU'VE GOT THE WHOLE VAMPIRE/VICTIM RELATIONSHIP MESSED UP.
OUCH!
THUD
SNAP

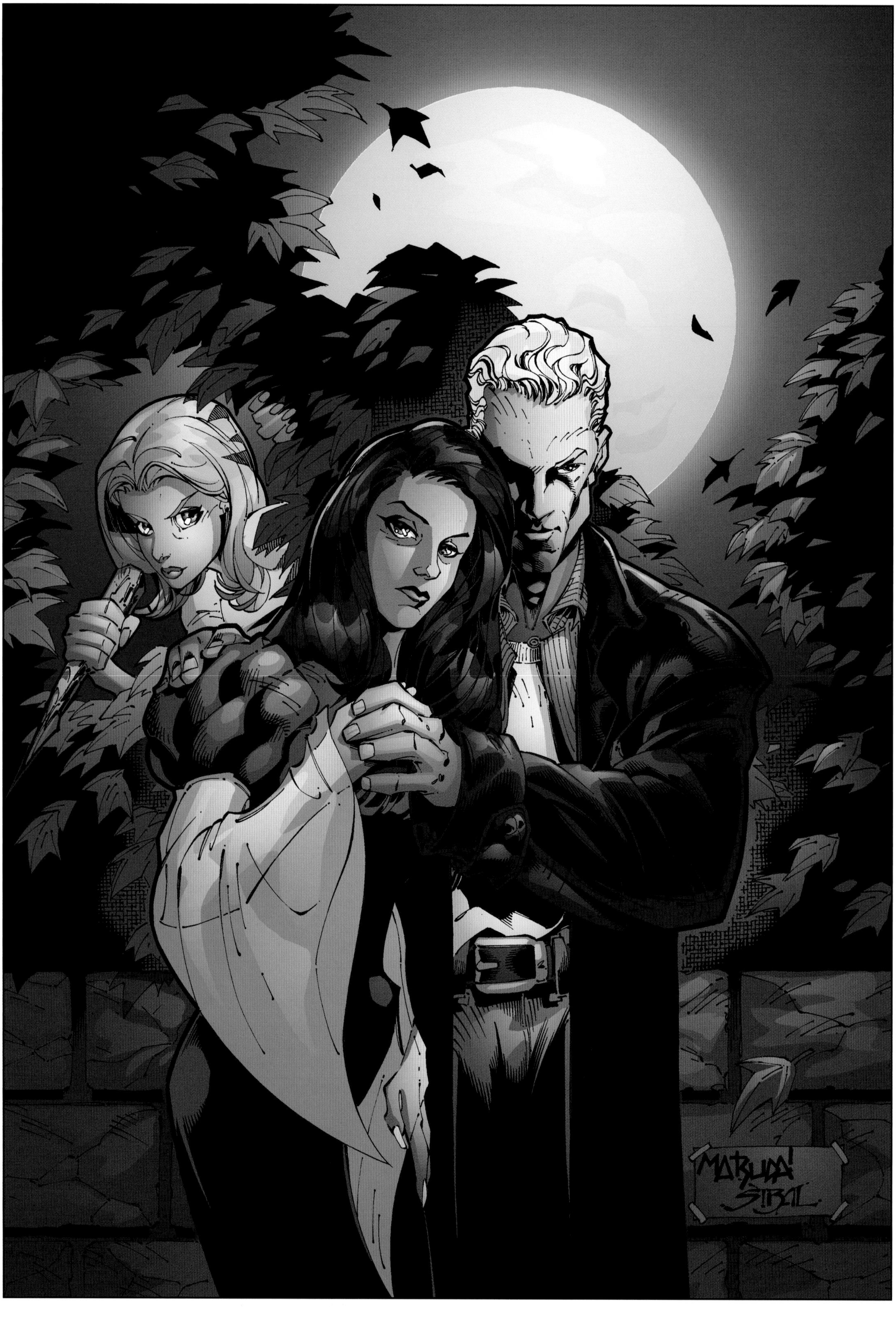

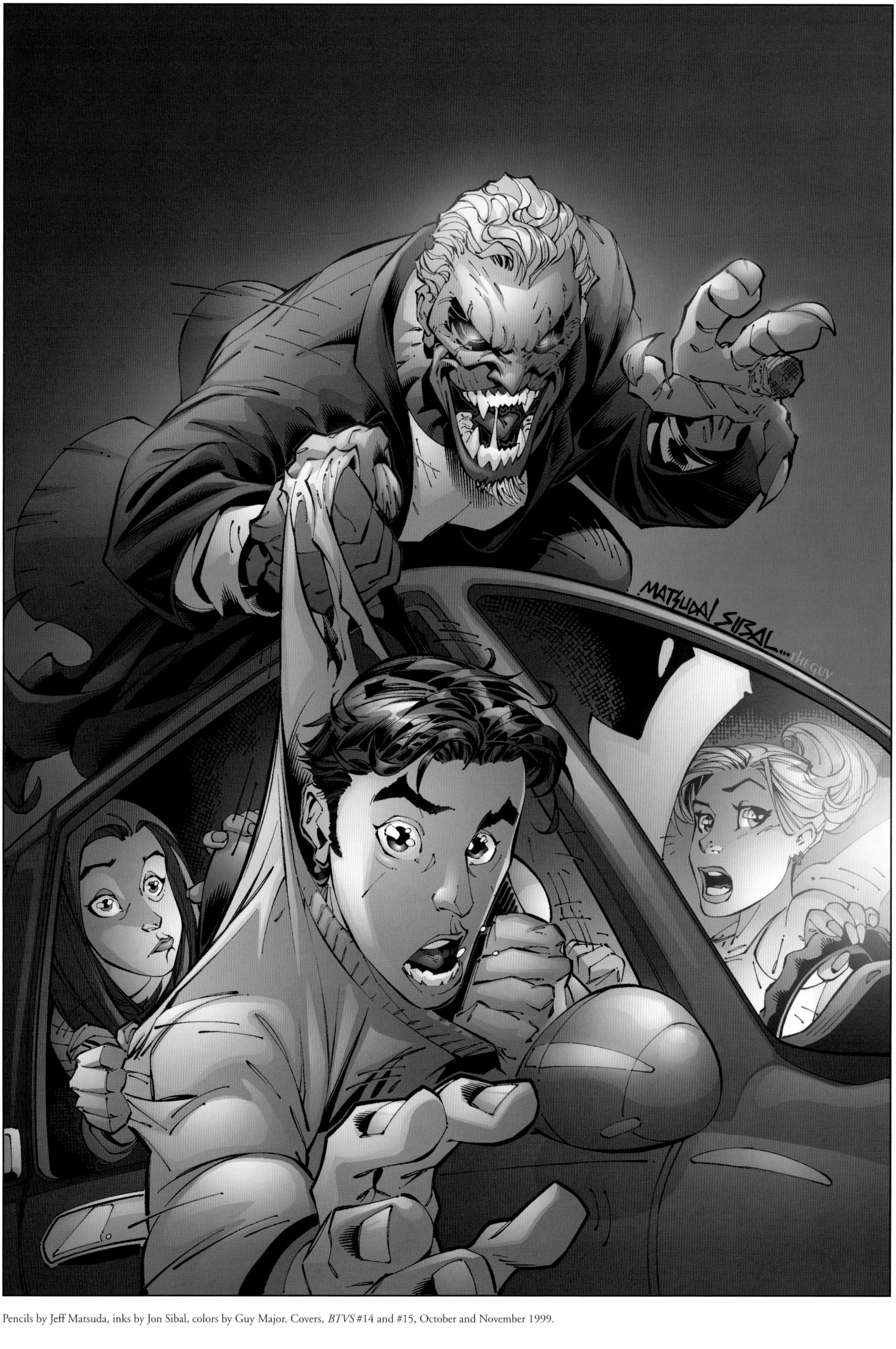
MATSUDA/SIBAL...THEGUY

Pencils by Jeff Matsuda, inks by Jon Sibal, colors by Guy Major. Covers, *BTVS* #14 and #15, October and November 1999.

JEFF MATSUDA SPOOFED his own *Buffy* #9 cover (see page 21) as a doppleganger Buffy grown in a lab appears in Sunnydale. In subsequent issues, an unsuccessful attempt from the same lab showed up as a sympathetic, Quasimodo-type character. *Buffy* #9 had been the start of the three-part *Bad Blood* arc (#9-11). We continued that story in the *Crash Test Demons* arc (#13-15), and wrapped it up in *Pale Reflections* (#17-19). This trilogy was our first attempt at imitating a "season" in comics form, and it wound up being Andi Watson's swan song.

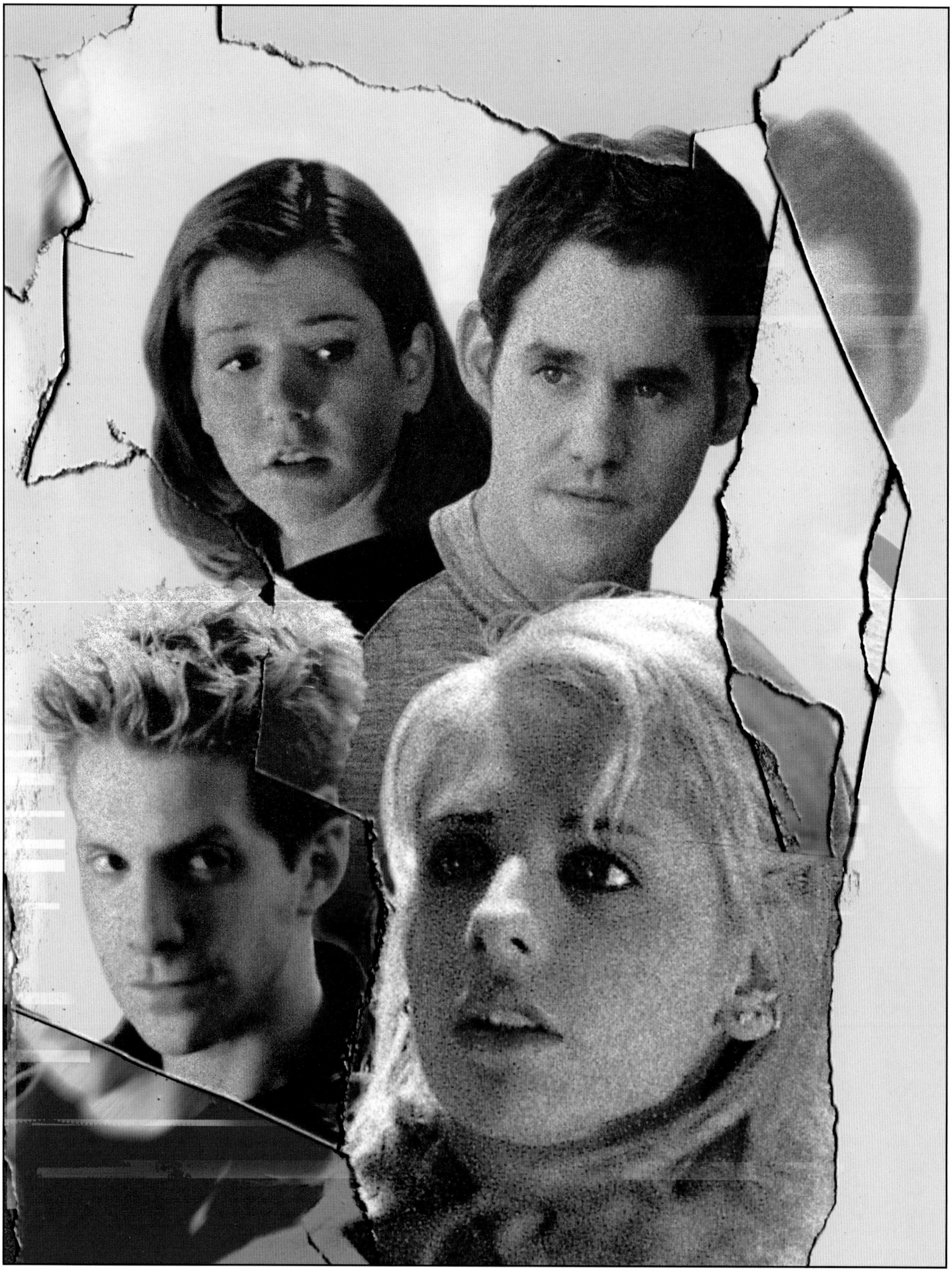

 Montage by Dave Stewart. Cover, *BTVS* #15, November 1999. Opposite: Pencils by Matsuda, inks by Jon Sibal, colors by Guy Major. Cover, *BTVS* #17, January 2000.

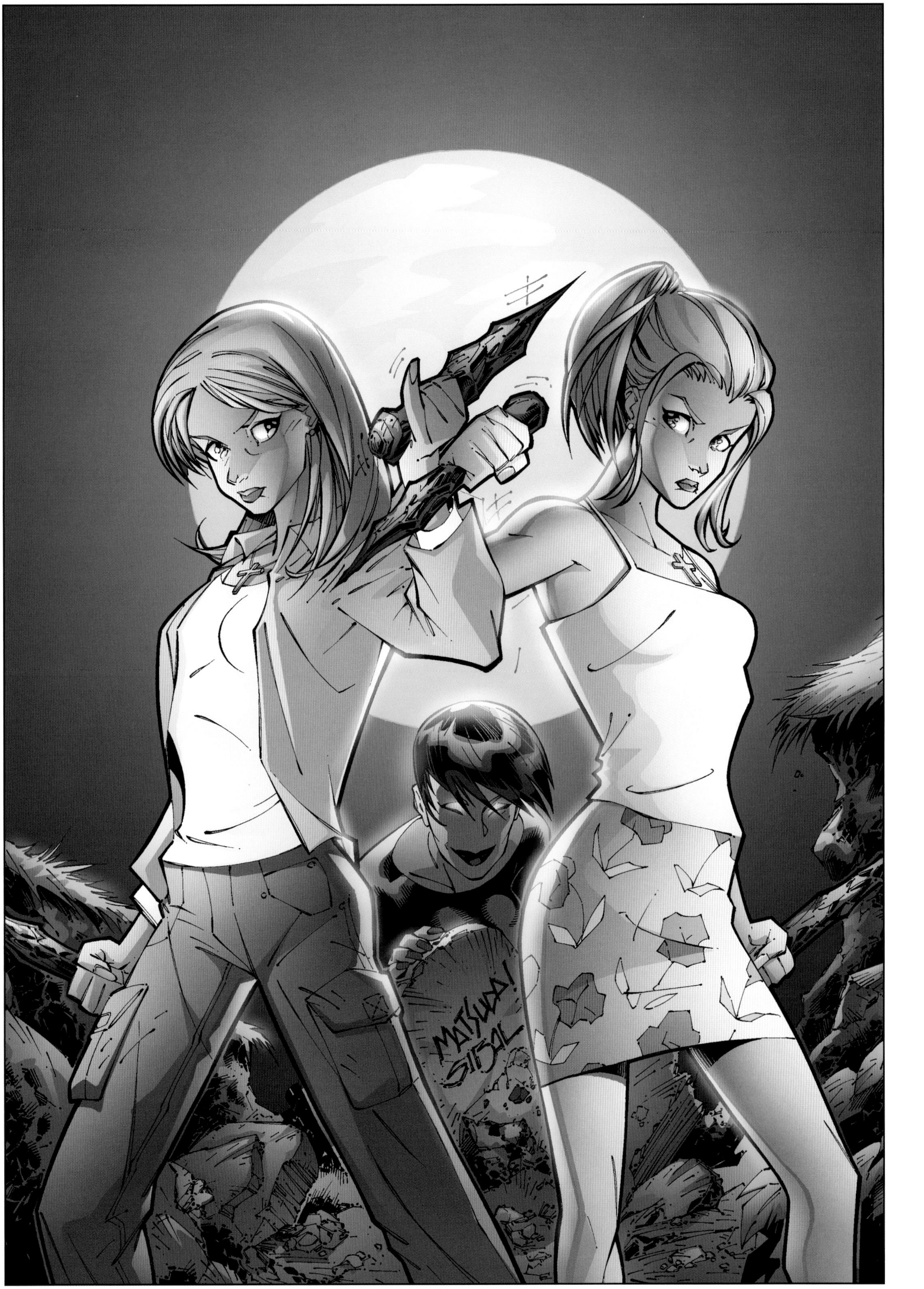
MATSUDA!
SIBAL

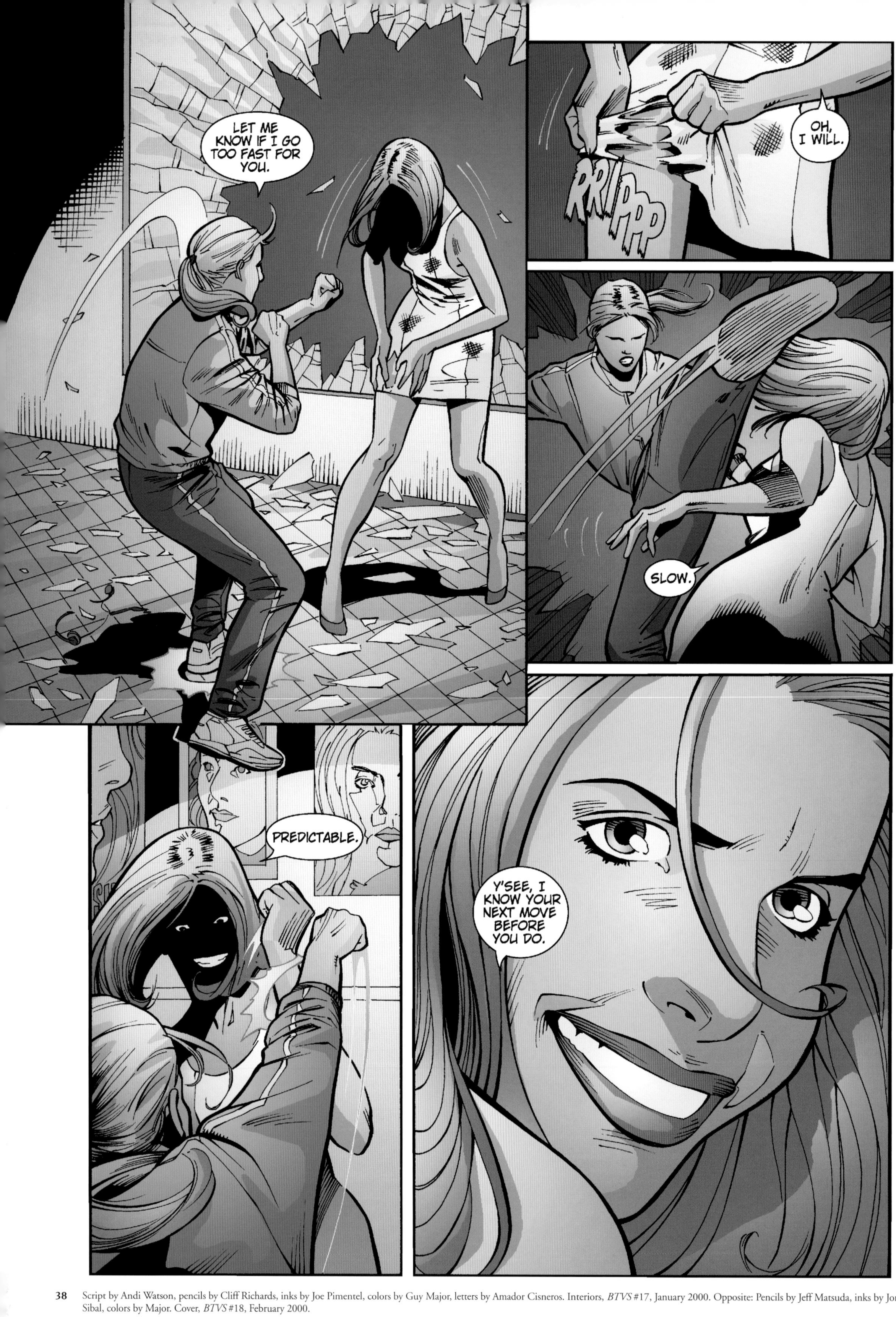
LET ME KNOW IF I GO TOO FAST FOR YOU.
RRIPPP
OH, I WILL.
SLOW.
PREDICTABLE.
Y'SEE, I KNOW YOUR NEXT MOVE BEFORE YOU DO.

 Script by Andi Watson, pencils by Cliff Richards, inks by Joe Pimentel, colors by Guy Major, letters by Amador Cisneros. Interiors, *BTVS* #17, January 2000. Opposite: Pencils by Jeff Matsuda, inks by Jon Sibal, colors by Major. Cover, *BTVS* #18, February 2000.

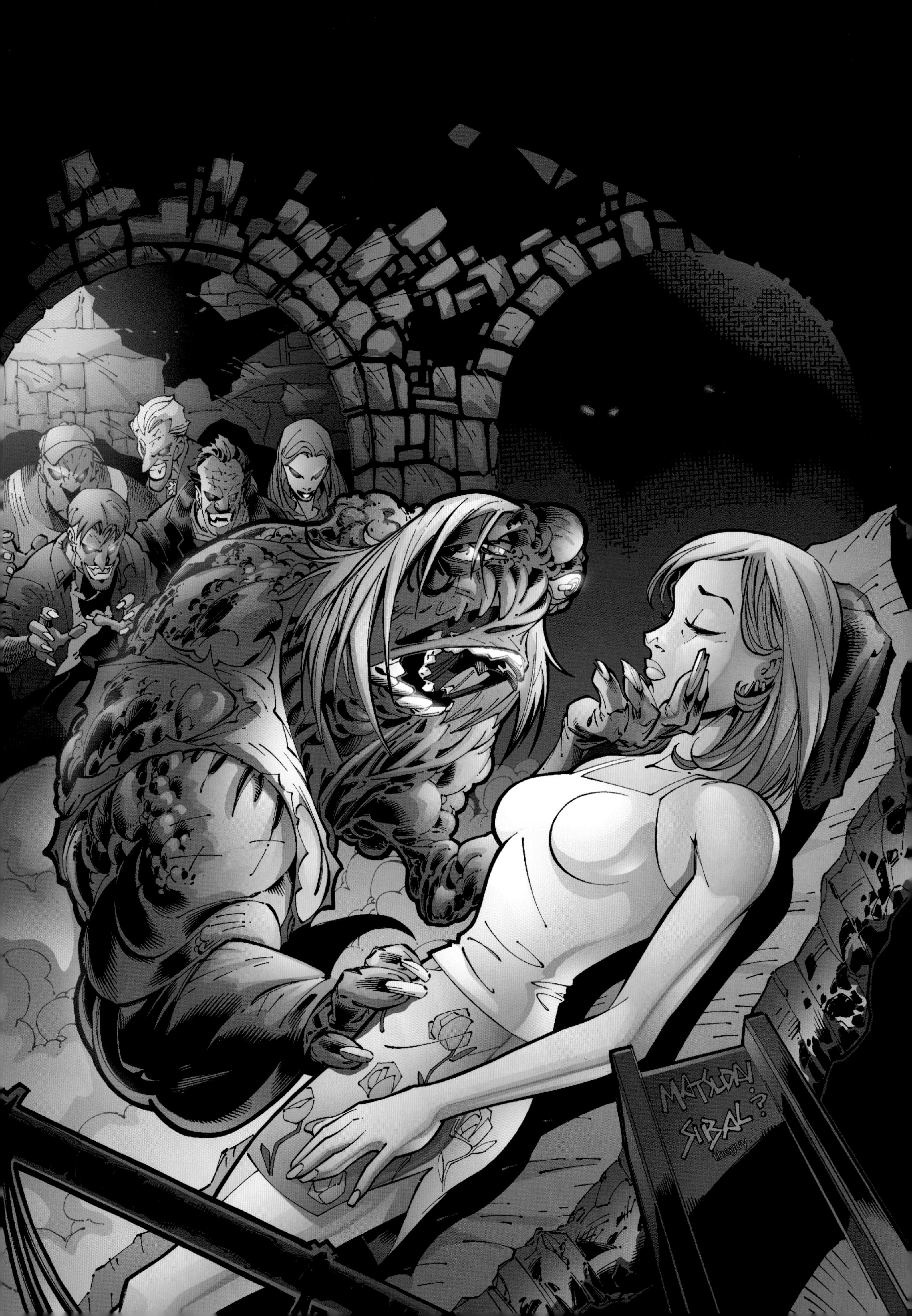
theguy.

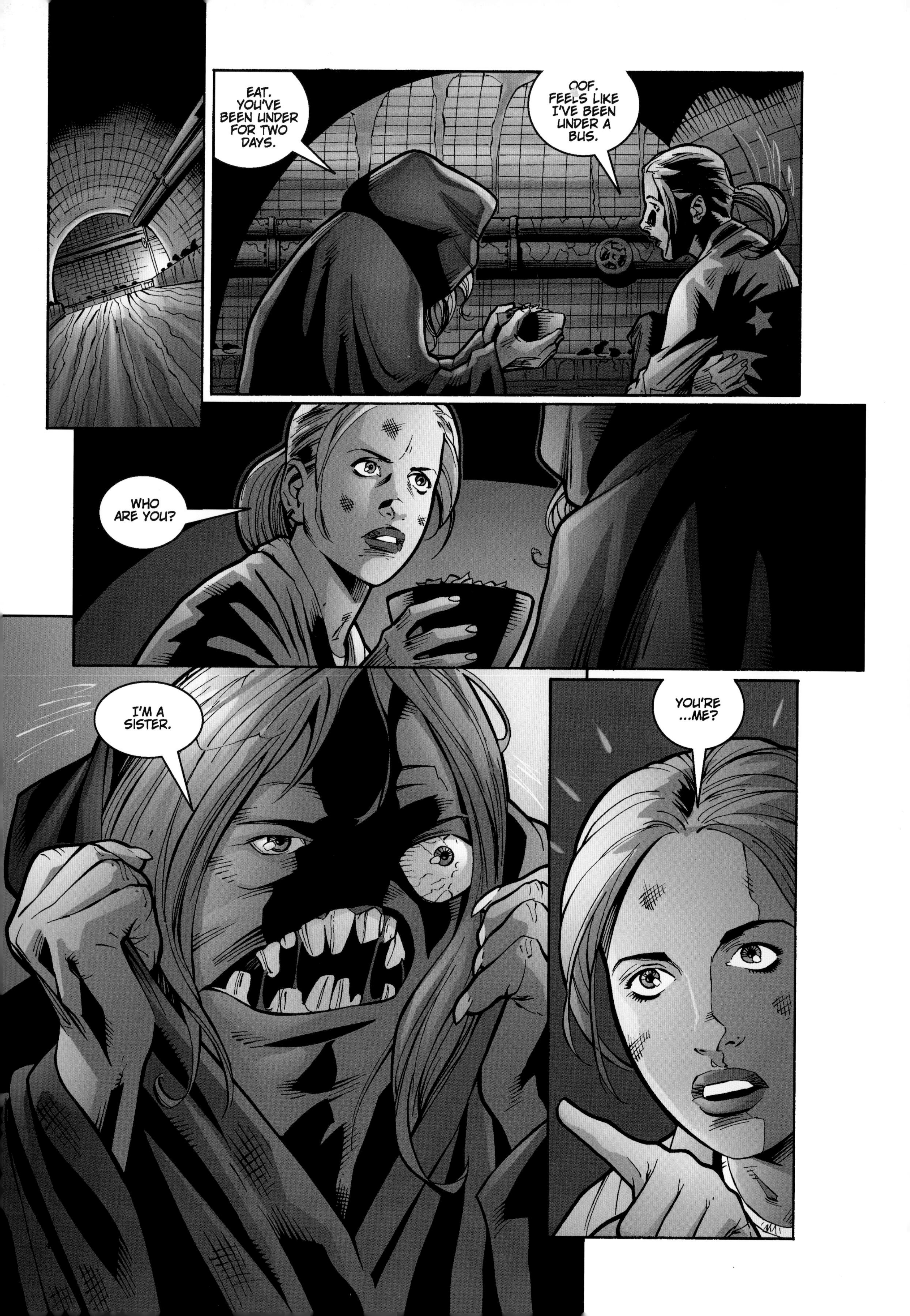
EAT. YOU'VE BEEN UNDER FOR TWO DAYS.
OOF. FEELS LIKE I'VE BEEN UNDER A BUS.
WHO ARE YOU?
I'M A SISTER.
YOU'RE ...ME?

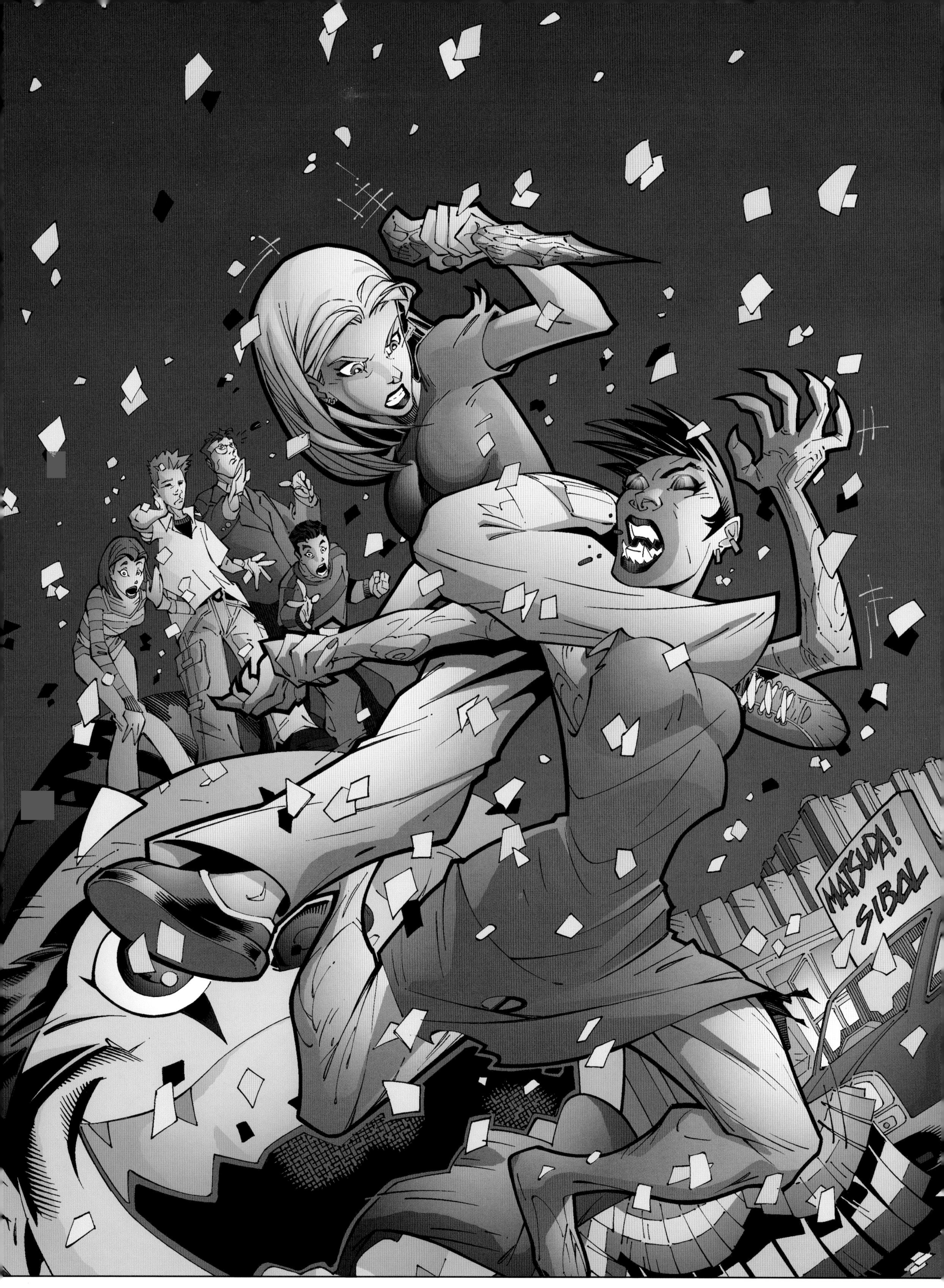
MATSUDA!
SIBAL

Opposite: Script by Andi Watson, pencils by Cliff Richards, inks by Joe Pimentel, colors by Guy Major, letters by Amador Cisneros. Interiors, *BTVS* #18, February 2000. Above: Pencils by Jeff Matsuda, inks by Jon Sibal, colors by Major. Cover, *BTVS* #19, March 2000.

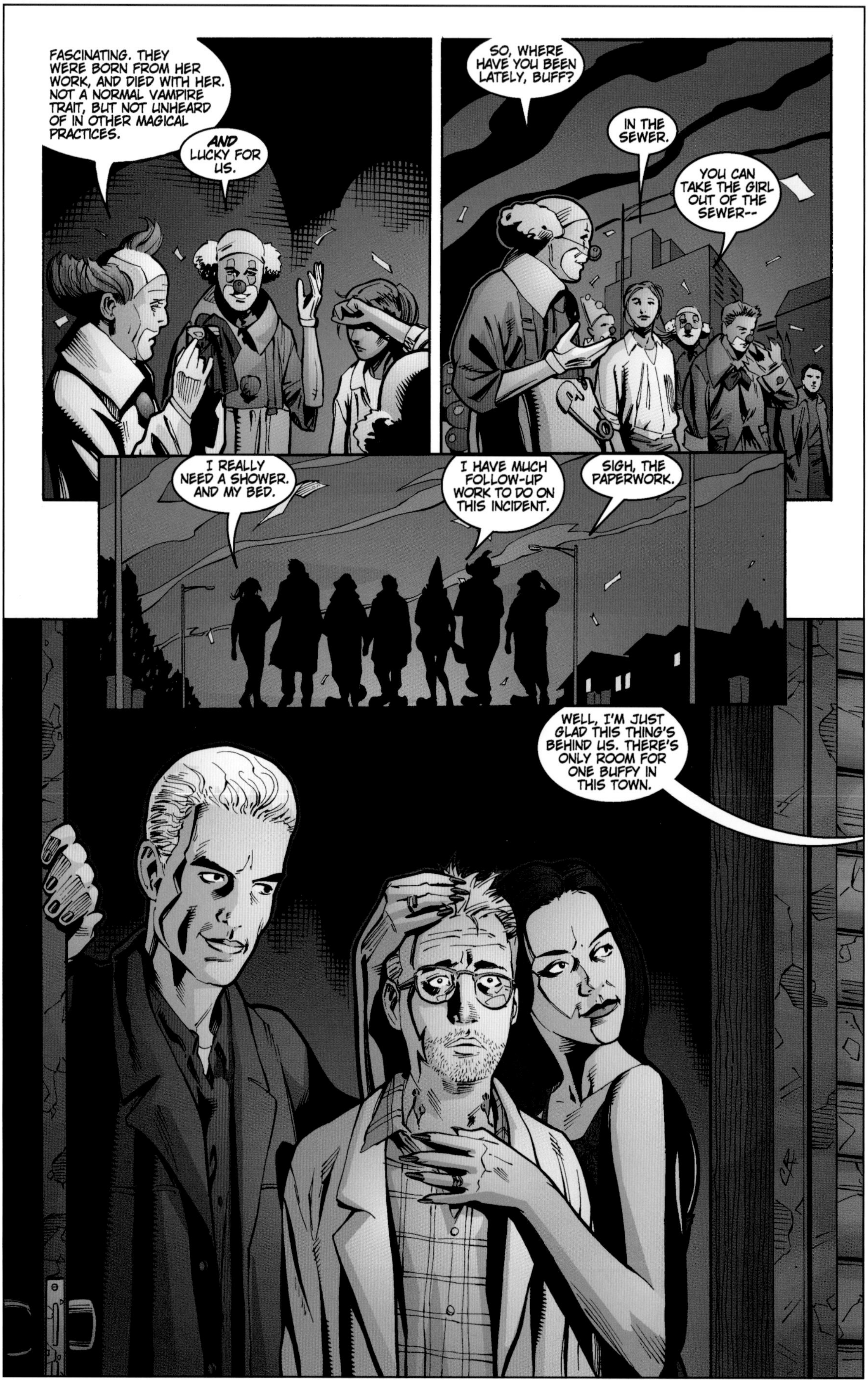
FASCINATING. THEY WERE BORN FROM HER WORK, AND DIED WITH HER. NOT A NORMAL VAMPIRE TRAIT, BUT NOT UNHEARD OF IN OTHER MAGICAL PRACTICES.
AND LUCKY FOR US.
SO, WHERE HAVE YOU BEEN LATELY, BUFF?
IN THE SEWER.
YOU CAN TAKE THE GIRL OUT OF THE SEWER--
I REALLY NEED A SHOWER. AND MY BED.
I HAVE MUCH FOLLOW-UP WORK TO DO ON THIS INCIDENT.
SIGH, THE PAPERWORK.
WELL, I'M JUST GLAD THIS THING'S BEHIND US. THERE'S ONLY ROOM FOR ONE BUFFY IN THIS TOWN.

WITH ANDI WATSON'S story over, we were ready to start fresh. When we first began *Buffy*, the cover artist we wanted was J. Scott Campbell—one of the most popular artists of modern times, and a master at drawing cute girls. However, he didn't initially meet with actor approval. A huge fan of the show, he was willing to really work for the job, and was able to do this cover for us, nearly two years later. This cover was done with no specific story in mind. *Buffy* #20 was a standalone story by Doug Petrie, who was hard at work on the graphic novel *Ring of Fire* with Ryan Sook.

 Above: Script by Watson, pencils by Cliff Richards, inks by Joe Pimentel, colors by Guy Major, letters by Amador Cisneros. Interiors, *BTVS* #19, March 2000. Opposite: Pencils by J. Scott Campbell, inks by Alex Garner, colors by Major. Cover, *BTVS* #20, April 2000.

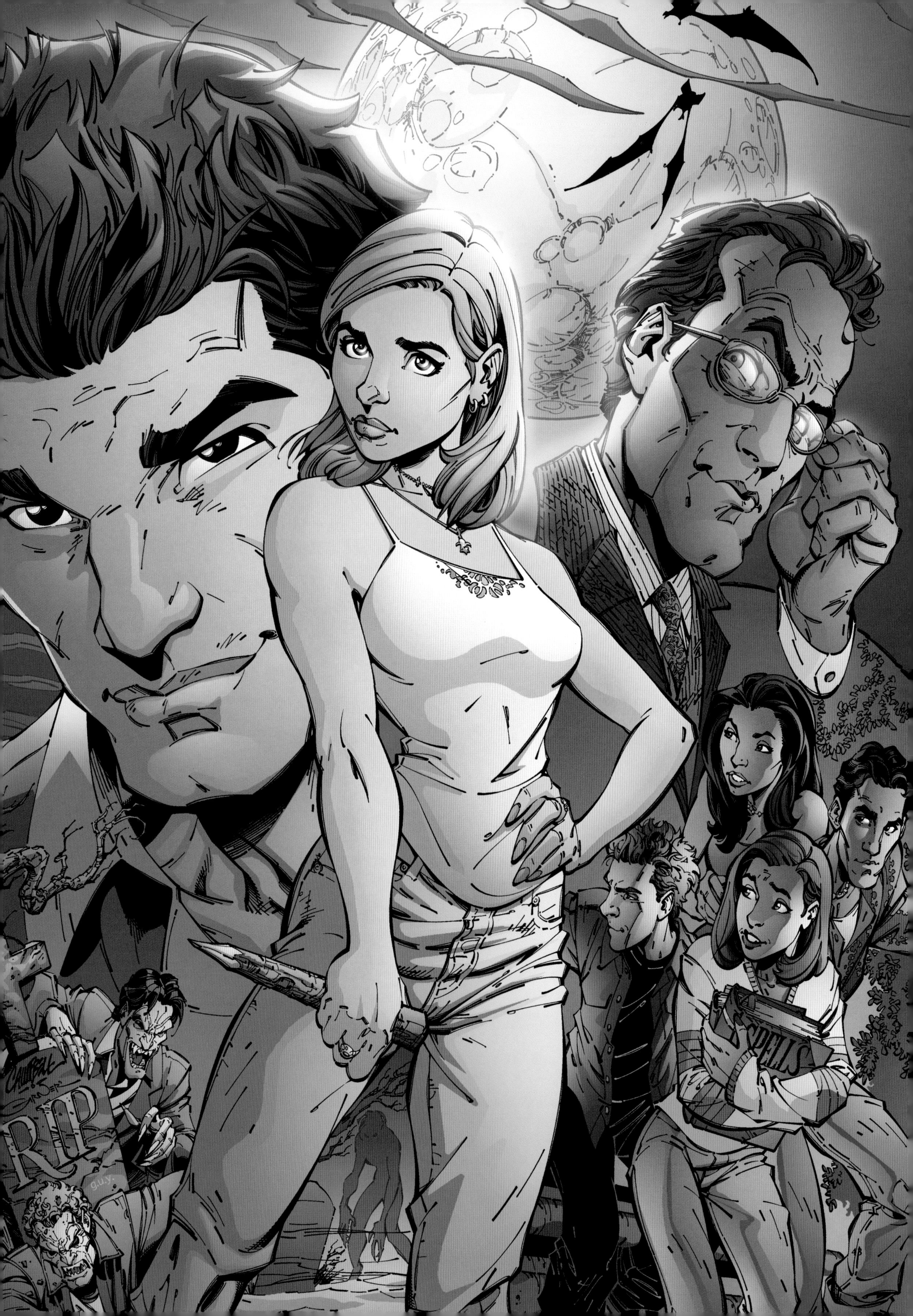
RIP
SPELLS

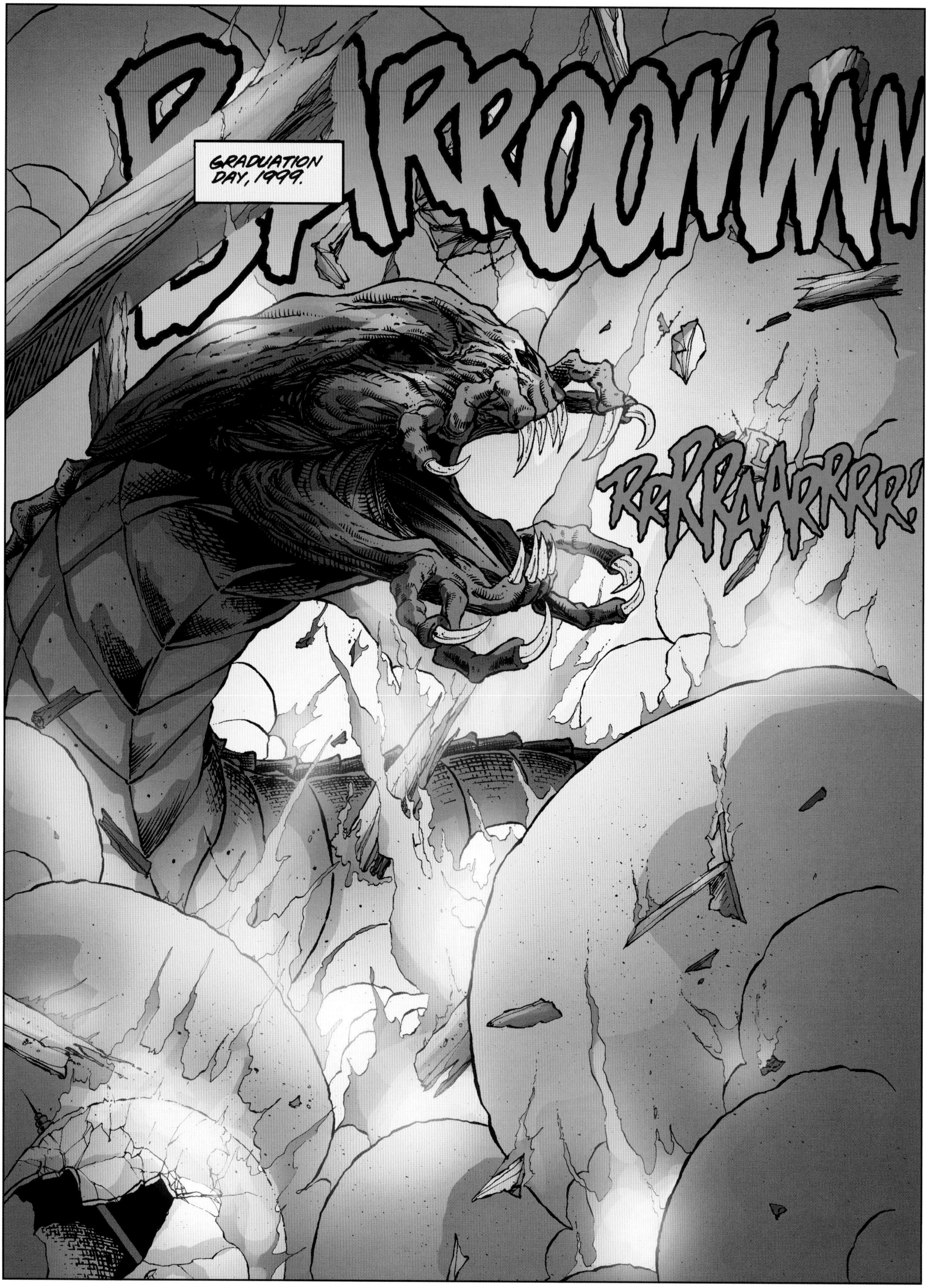
BARROOMMM
GRADUATION DAY, 1999.
RRRRAARRRR!

AFTER DOUG PETRIE'S post-graduation story, Chris Golden took up the reins of the monthly for a few issues. Jeff Matsuda drew the covers for Golden's *Blood of Carthage* arc, influencing the interiors of the books by designing some of the monsters.

 Script by Petrie, pencils by Jason Minor, inks by Curtis Arnold, colors by Guy Major, letters by John Costanza. Interiors, *BTVS* #20, April 2000. Opposite: Pencils by Matsuda, inks by Jon Sibal, colors by Major. Cover, *BTVS* #21, May 2000. Inset: Sketch by Matsuda.

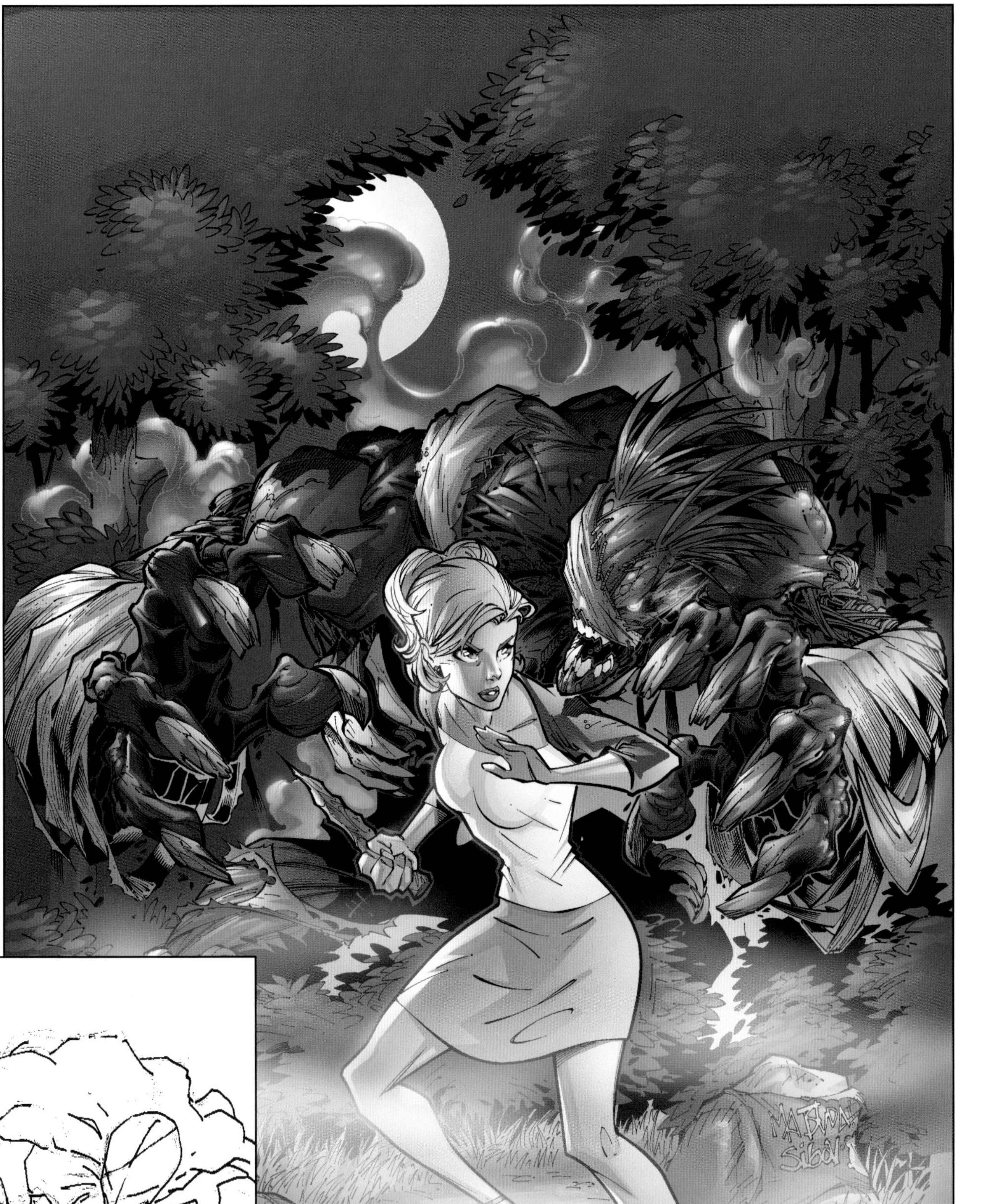

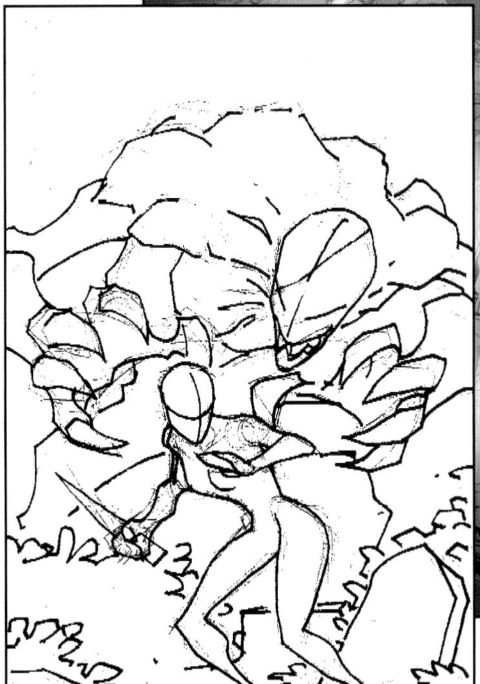

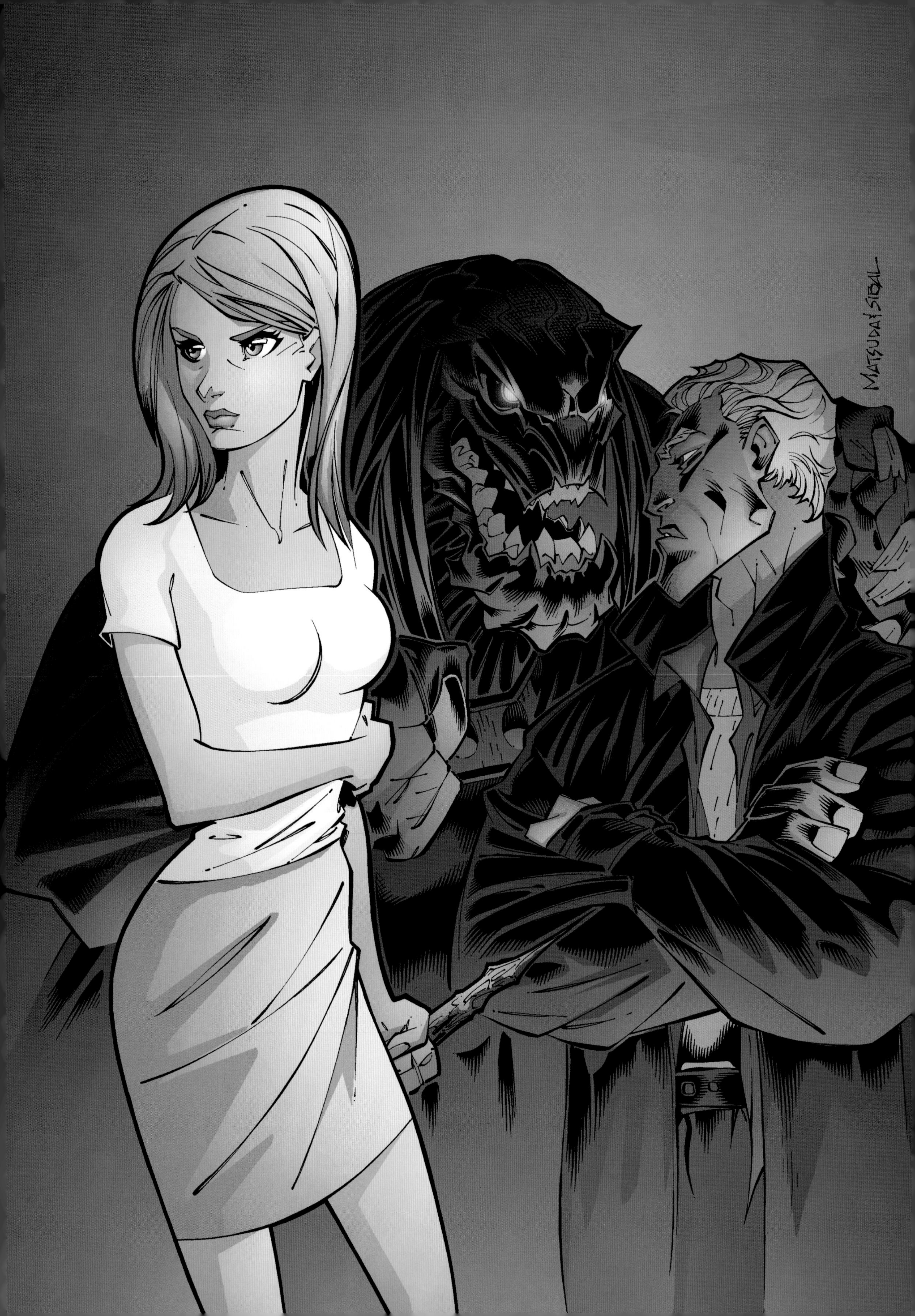
MATSUDA&SIBAL

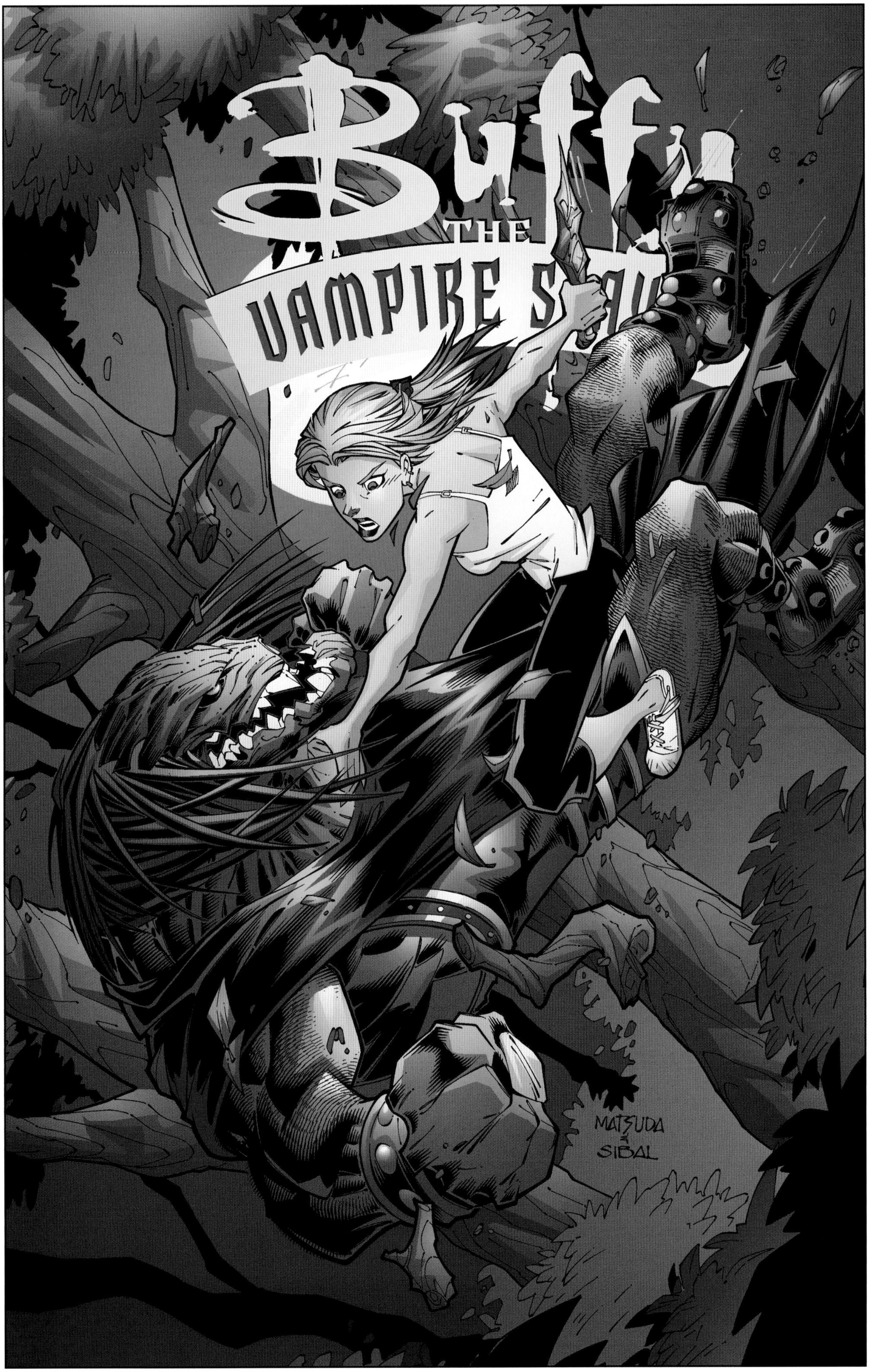
Buffy
THE
VAMPIRE S
MATSUDA
&
SIBAL

Opposite and above: Pencils by Jeff Matsuda, inks by Jon Sibal, colors by Guy Major. Covers, *BTVS* #23 and #24, June and July 2000. Following two pages: Pencils by Matsuda, inks by Andy Owens, colors by Major. Cover, *BTVS* #25, August 2000.

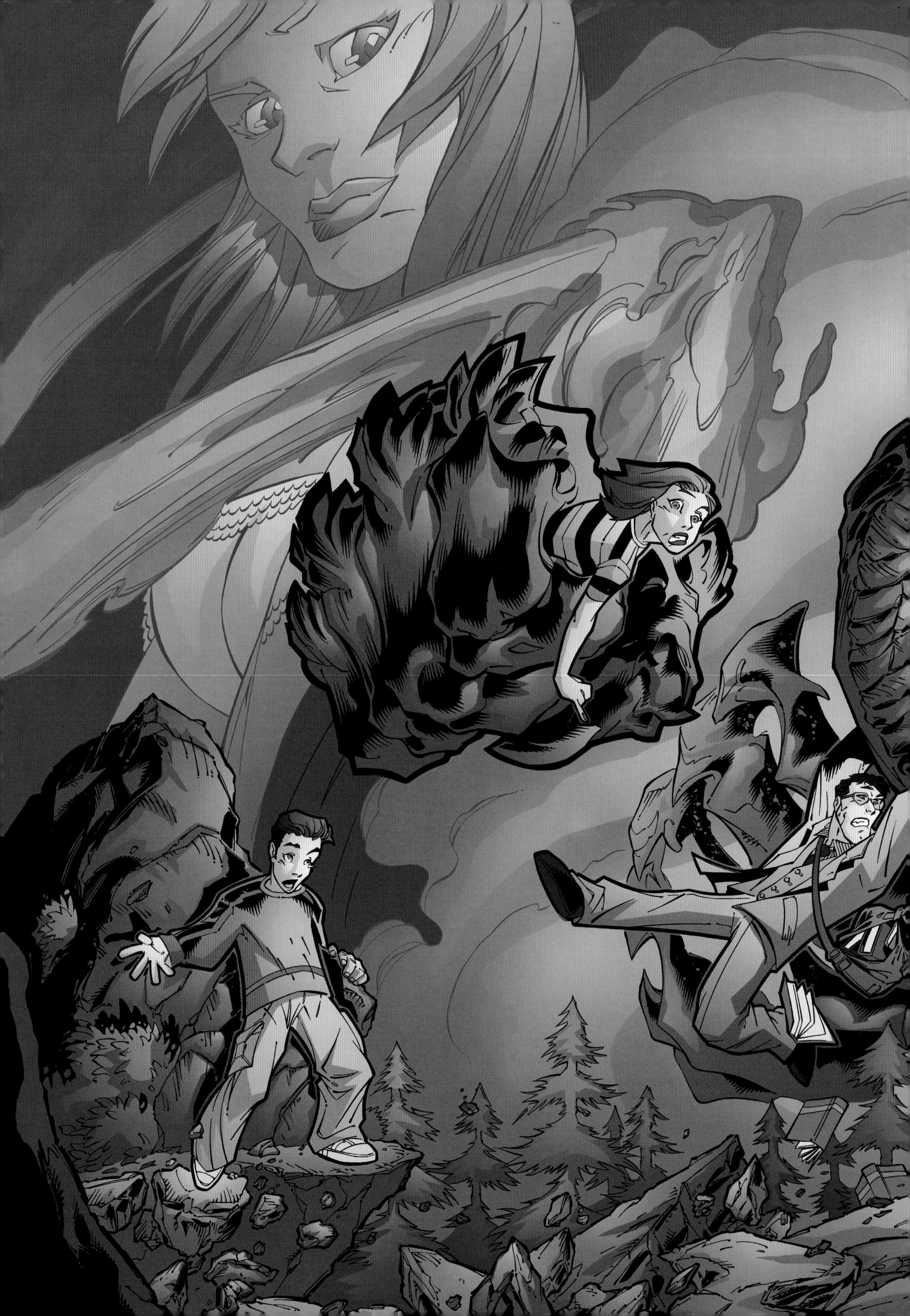

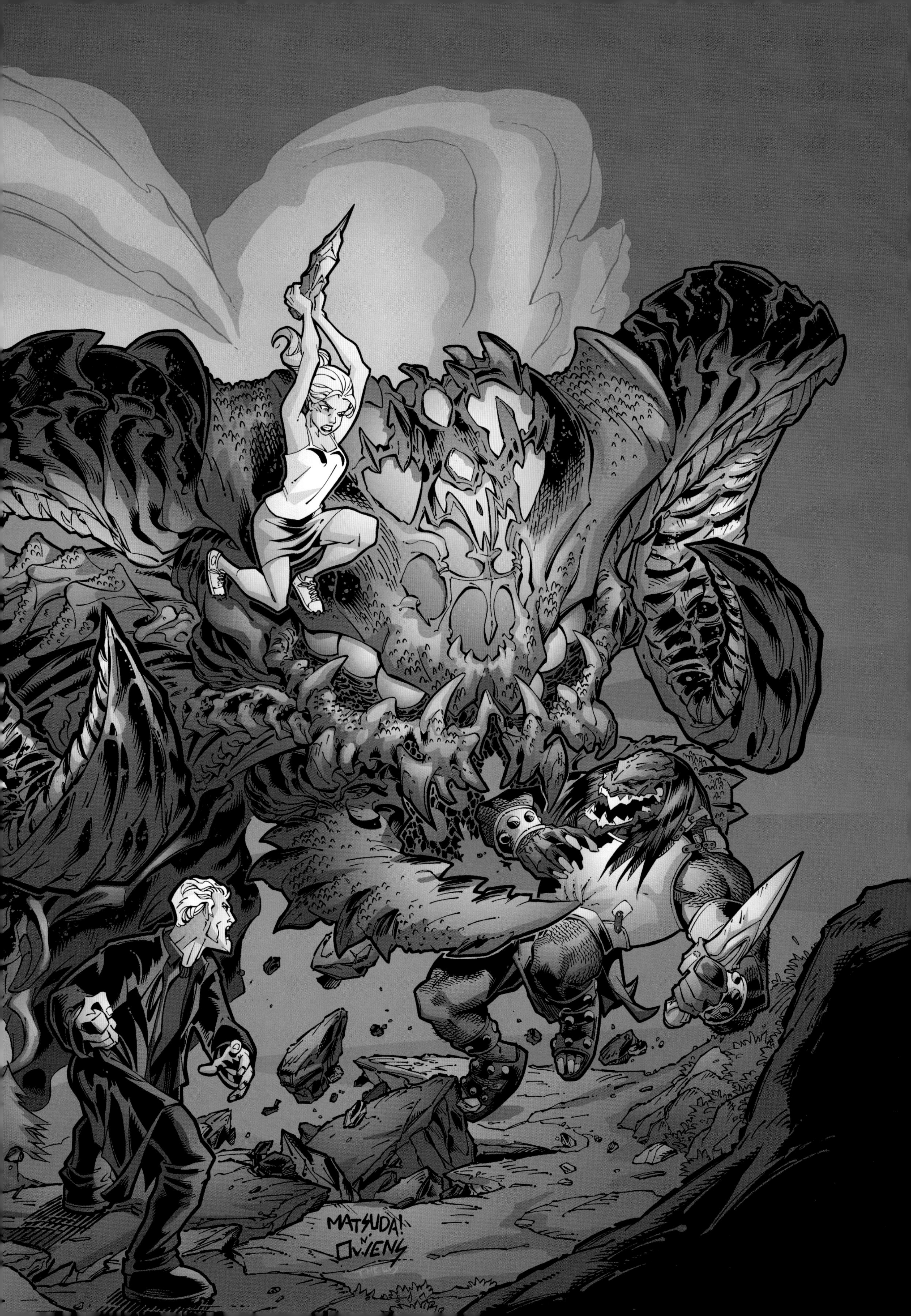
MATSUDA!
OWENS

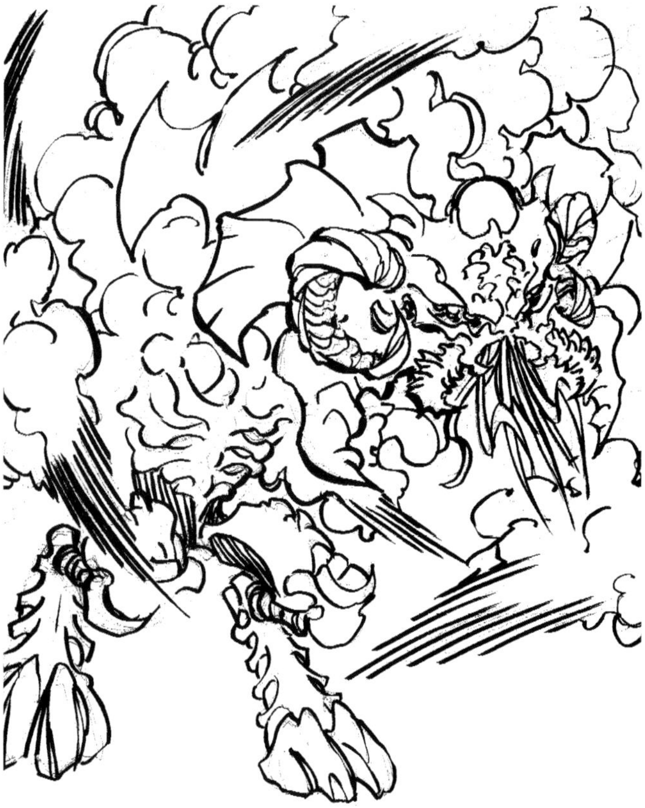

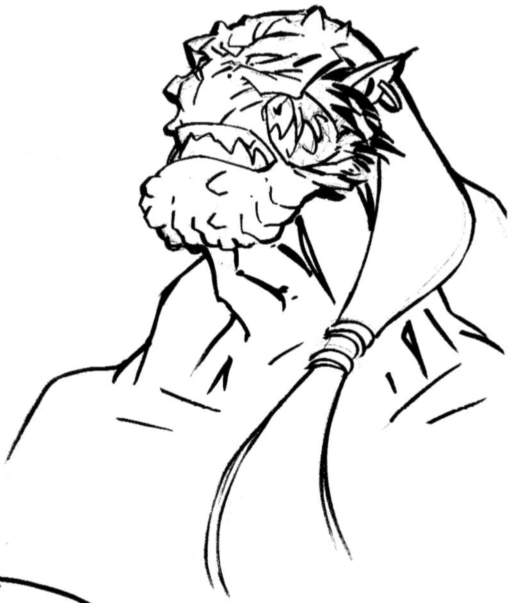

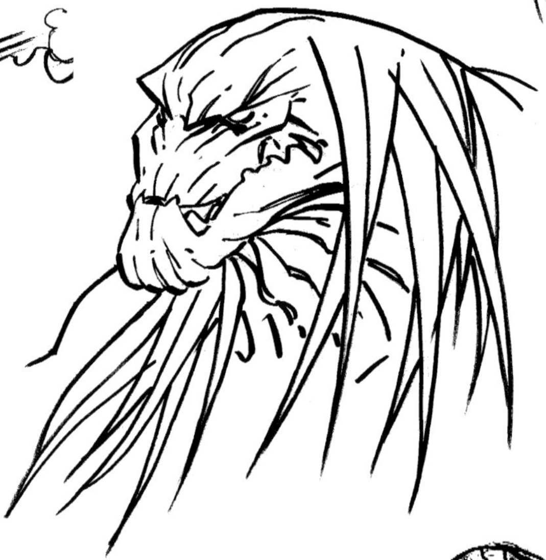

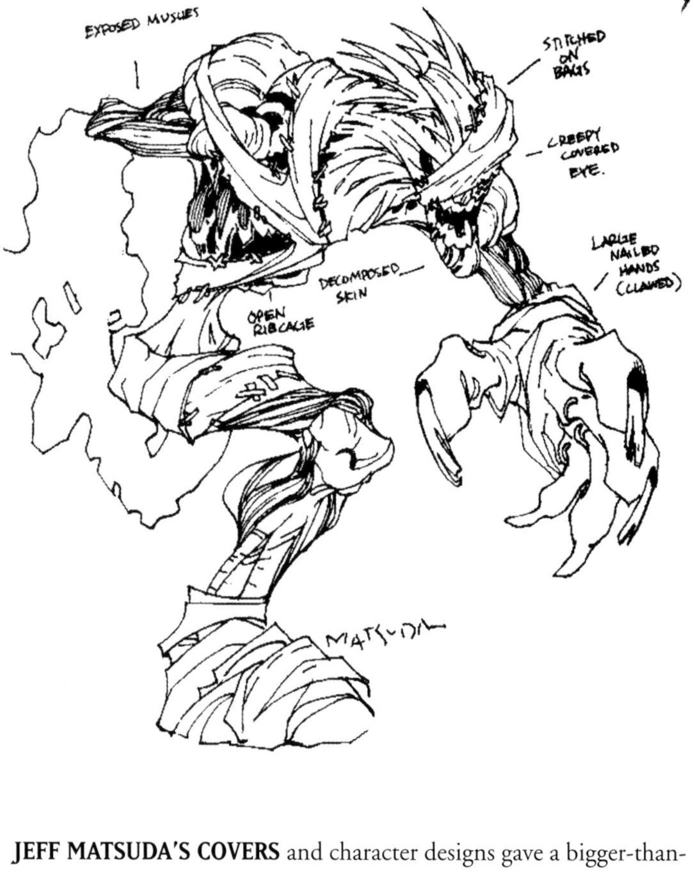
EXPOSED MUSLES
STITCHED ON BAGS
CREEPY COVERED EYE.
LARGE NAILED HANDS (CLAWED)
DECOMPOSED SKIN
OPEN RIBCAGE
MATSUDA

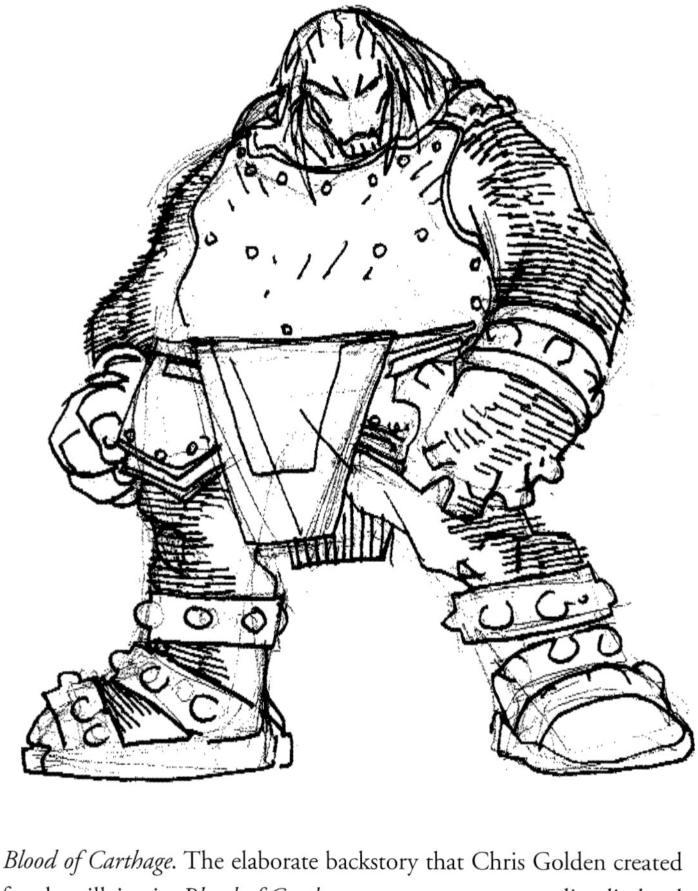

JEFF MATSUDA'S COVERS and character designs gave a bigger-than-life, superhero edge to Cliff Richards's realism. *Buffy* is as much a horror story as an action-adventure story, particularly in the case of *Blood of Carthage.* The elaborate backstory that Chris Golden created for the villains in *Blood of Carthage* gave an excuse to enlist die-hard *Buffy* fans Paul Lee and Brian Horton to draw flashbacks.

 Sketches by Matsuda. Early 2000. Opposite: Script by Golden, layouts by Lee, finishes by Horton, colors by Guy Major, letters by Michelle Madsen. Interiors, *BTVS* #24, July 2000.

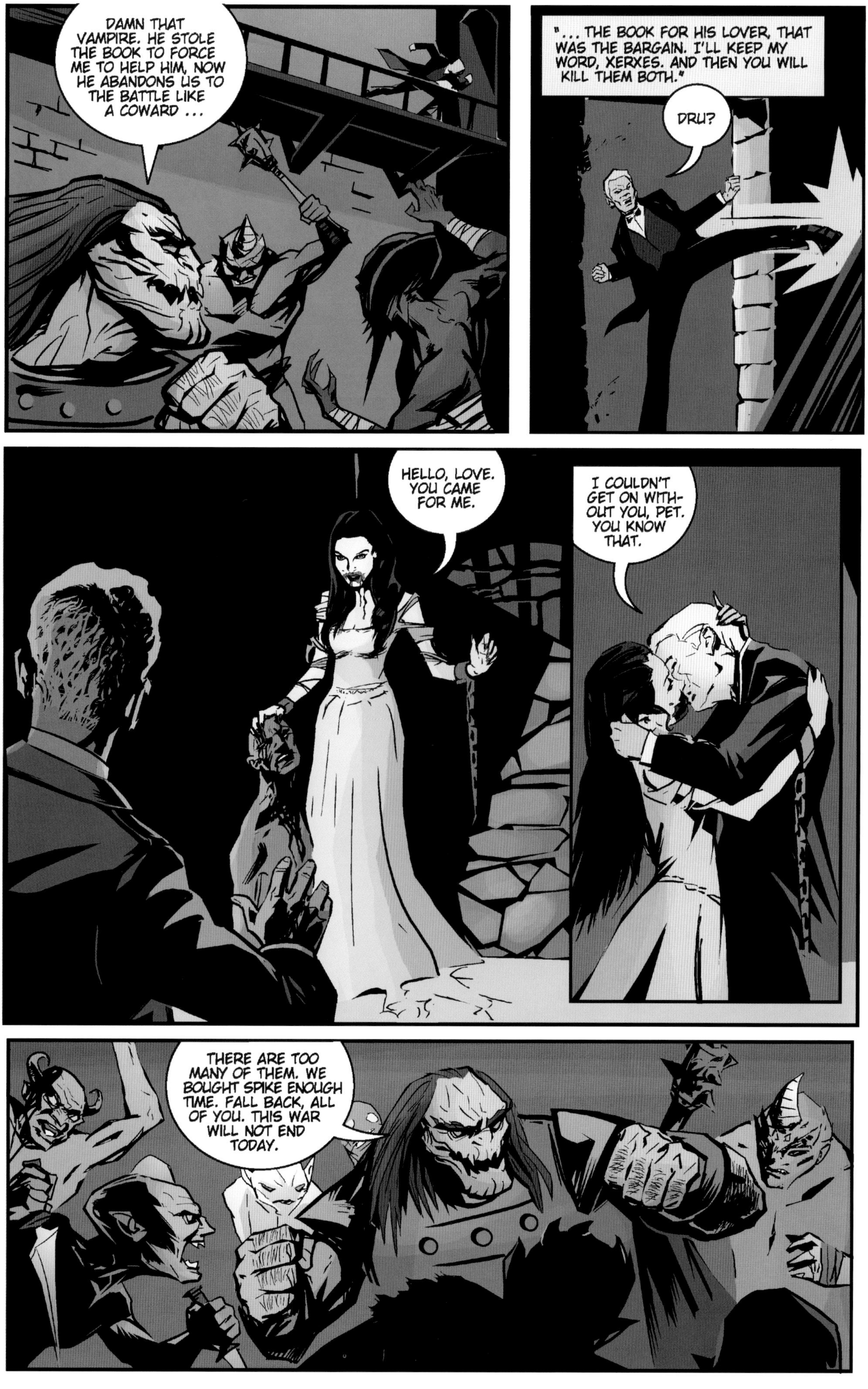
DAMN THAT VAMPIRE. HE STOLE THE BOOK TO FORCE ME TO HELP HIM, NOW HE ABANDONS US TO THE BATTLE LIKE A COWARD ...
"... THE BOOK FOR HIS LOVER, THAT WAS THE BARGAIN. I'LL KEEP MY WORD, XERXES. AND THEN YOU WILL KILL THEM BOTH."
DRU?
HELLO, LOVE. YOU CAME FOR ME.
I COULDN'T GET ON WITH-OUT YOU, PET. YOU KNOW THAT.
THERE ARE TOO MANY OF THEM. WE BOUGHT SPIKE ENOUGH TIME. FALL BACK, ALL OF YOU. THIS WAR WILL NOT END TODAY.

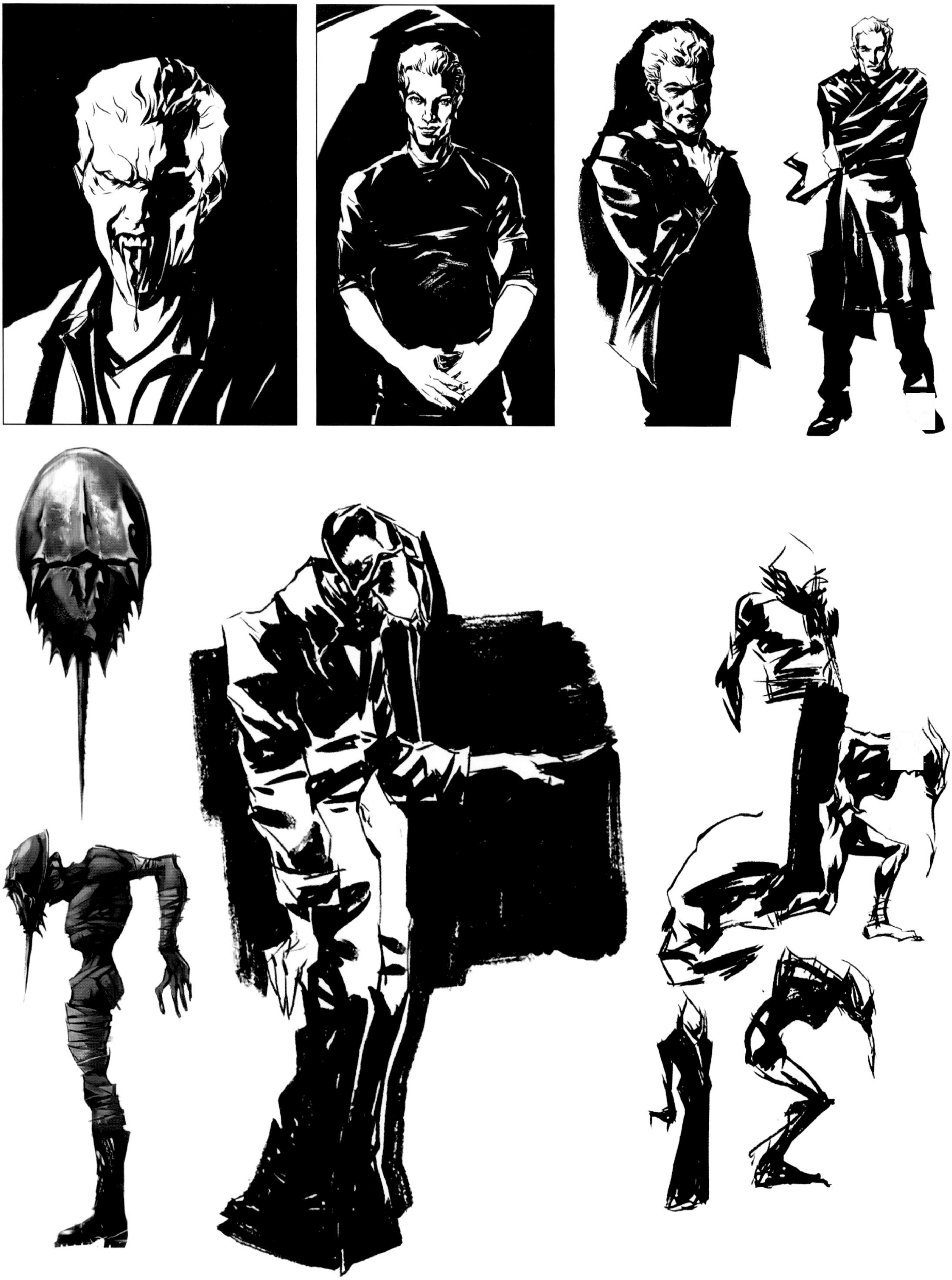

BRIAN HORTON also designed some of the characters for *Blood of Carthage.* In a world full of monsters, it makes sense to me that they wouldn't all follow a single design sense. Because the flashbacks were set many years in the past, the only character that Paul Lee and Horton had to audition for was Spike—although eventually they'd wind up drawing and painting almost every character in the series.

 Character sketches by Horton, early 2000. Opposite: Layouts by Lee, finishes by Horton, colors by Guy Major. Interiors, *BTVS* #25, August 2000.

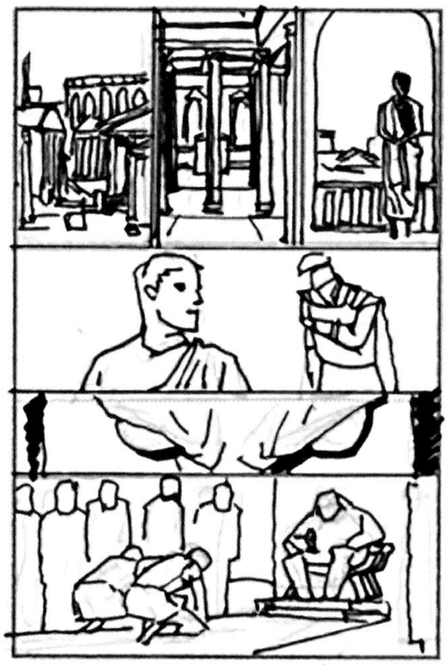

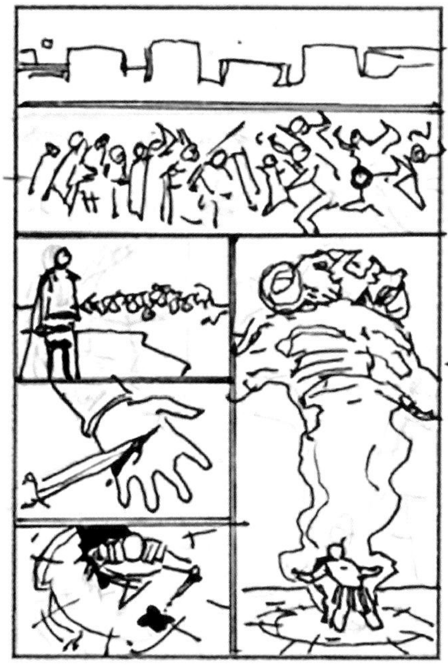

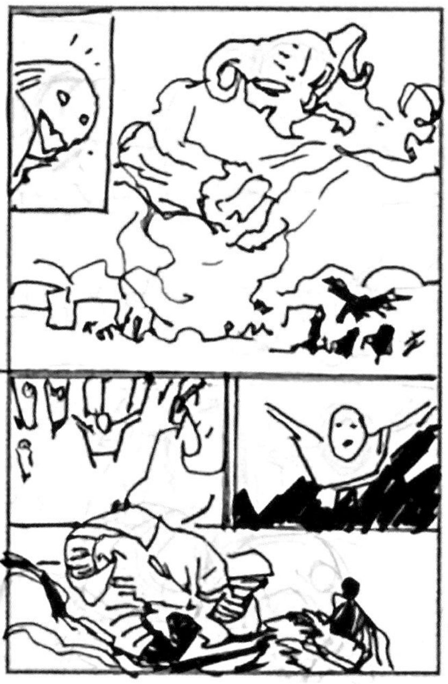

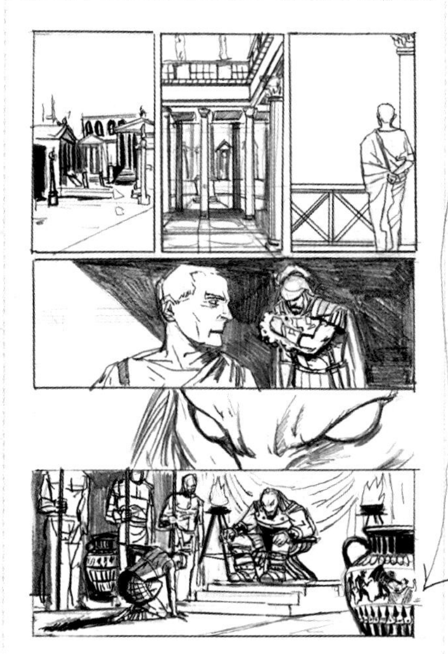

2

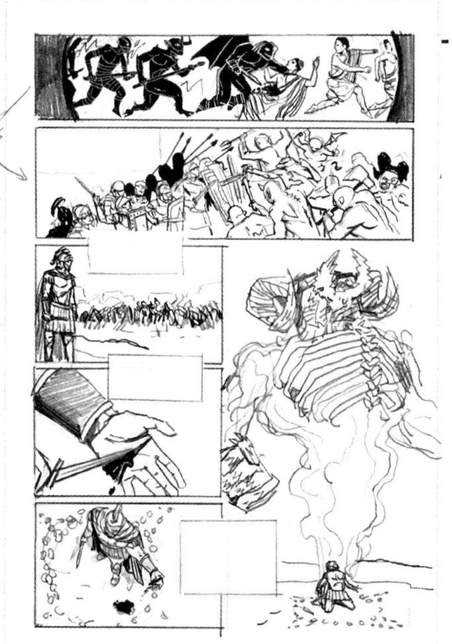

3

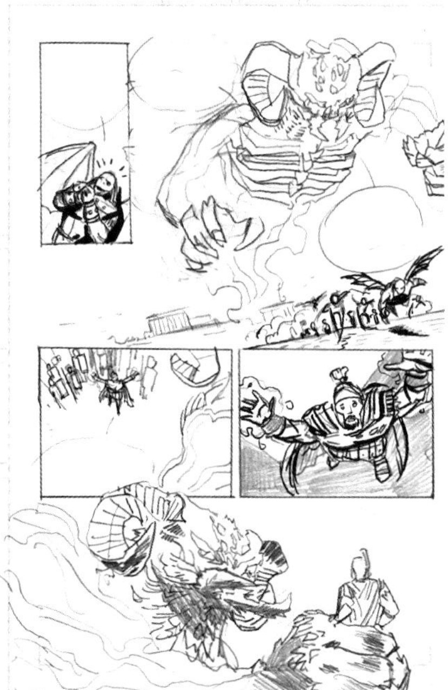

4

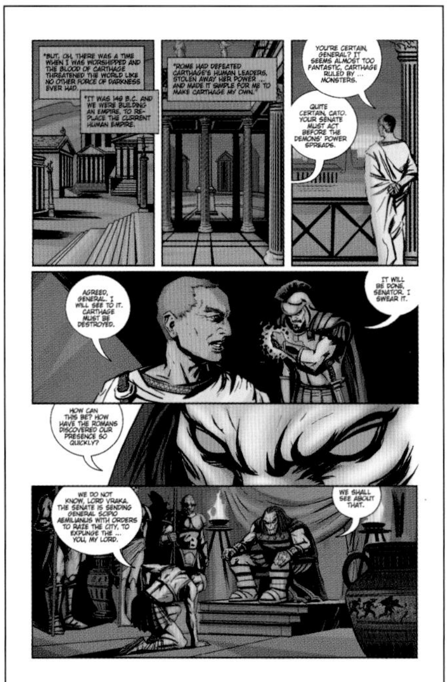
"BUT, OH, THERE WAS A TIME WHEN I WAS WORSHIPPED AND THE BLOOD OF CARTHAGE THREATENED THE WORLD LIKE NO OTHER FORCE OF DARKNESS EVER HAD.
"IT WAS 146 B.C. AND WE WERE BUILDING AN EMPIRE, TO REPLACE THE CURRENT HUMAN EMPIRE.
"ROME HAD DEFEATED CARTHAGE'S HUMAN LEADERS, STOLEN AWAY HER POWER ... AND MADE IT SIMPLE FOR ME TO MAKE CARTHAGE MY OWN."
YOU'RE CERTAIN, GENERAL? IT SEEMS ALMOST TOO FANTASTIC, CARTHAGE RULED BY ... MONSTERS.
QUITE CERTAIN, CATO. YOUR SENATE MUST ACT BEFORE THE DEMONS' POWER SPREADS.
AGREED, GENERAL. I WILL SEE TO IT. CARTHAGE MUST BE DESTROYED.
IT WILL BE DONE, SENATOR. I SWEAR IT.
HOW CAN THIS BE? HOW HAVE THE ROMANS DISCOVERED OUR PRESENCE SO QUICKLY?
WE DO NOT KNOW, LORD VRAKA. THE SENATE IS SENDING GENERAL SCIPIO AEMILIANUS WITH ORDERS TO RAZE THE CITY, TO EXPUNGE THE ... YOU, MY LORD.
WE SHALL SEE ABOUT THAT.

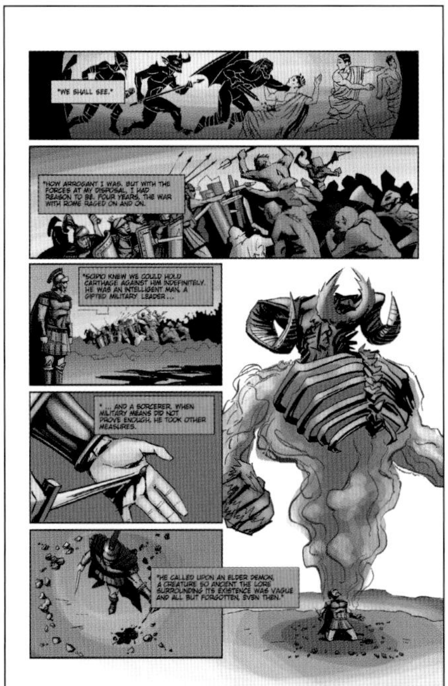
"WE SHALL SEE."
"HOW ARROGANT I WAS. BUT WITH THE FORCES AT MY DISPOSAL, I HAD REASON TO BE. FOUR YEARS, THE WAR WITH ROME RAGED ON AND ON.
"SCIPIO KNEW WE COULD HOLD CARTHAGE AGAINST HIM INDEFINITELY. HE WAS AN INTELLIGENT MAN, A GIFTED MILITARY LEADER ...
" ... AND A SORCERER. WHEN MILITARY MEANS DID NOT PROVE ENOUGH, HE TOOK OTHER MEASURES.
"HE CALLED UPON AN ELDER DEMON, A CREATURE SO ANCIENT THE LORE SURROUNDING ITS EXISTENCE WAS VAGUE AND ALL BUT FORGOTTEN, EVEN THEN."

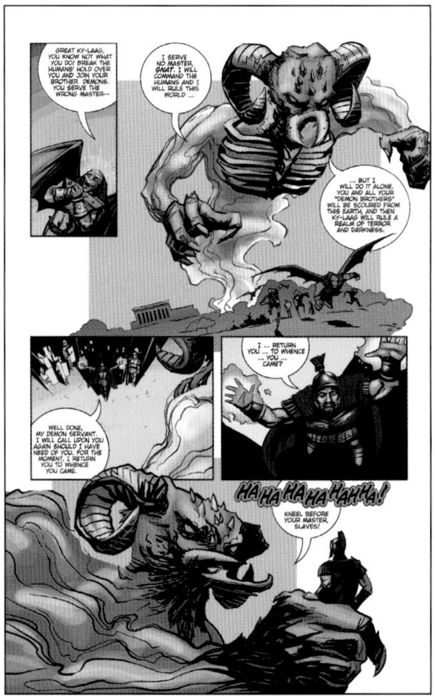
GREAT KY-LAAG, YOU KNOW NOT WHAT YOU DO! BREAK THE HUMANS' HOLD OVER YOU AND JOIN YOUR BROTHER DEMONS. YOU SERVE THE WRONG MASTER--
I SERVE NO MASTER, GNAT. I WILL COMMAND THE HUMANS AND I WILL RULE THIS WORLD ...
... BUT I WILL DO IT ALONE. YOU AND ALL YOUR "DEMON BROTHERS" WILL BE SCOURED FROM THIS EARTH, AND THEN KY-LAAG WILL RULE A REALM OF TERROR AND DARKNESS.
I ... RETURN YOU ... TO WHENCE ... YOU ... CAME?
WELL DONE, MY DEMON SERVANT. I WILL CALL UPON YOU AGAIN SHOULD I HAVE NEED OF YOU. FOR THE MOMENT, I RETURN YOU TO WHENCE YOU CAME.
HA HA HA HA HAHHA!
KNEEL BEFORE YOUR MASTER, SLAVES!

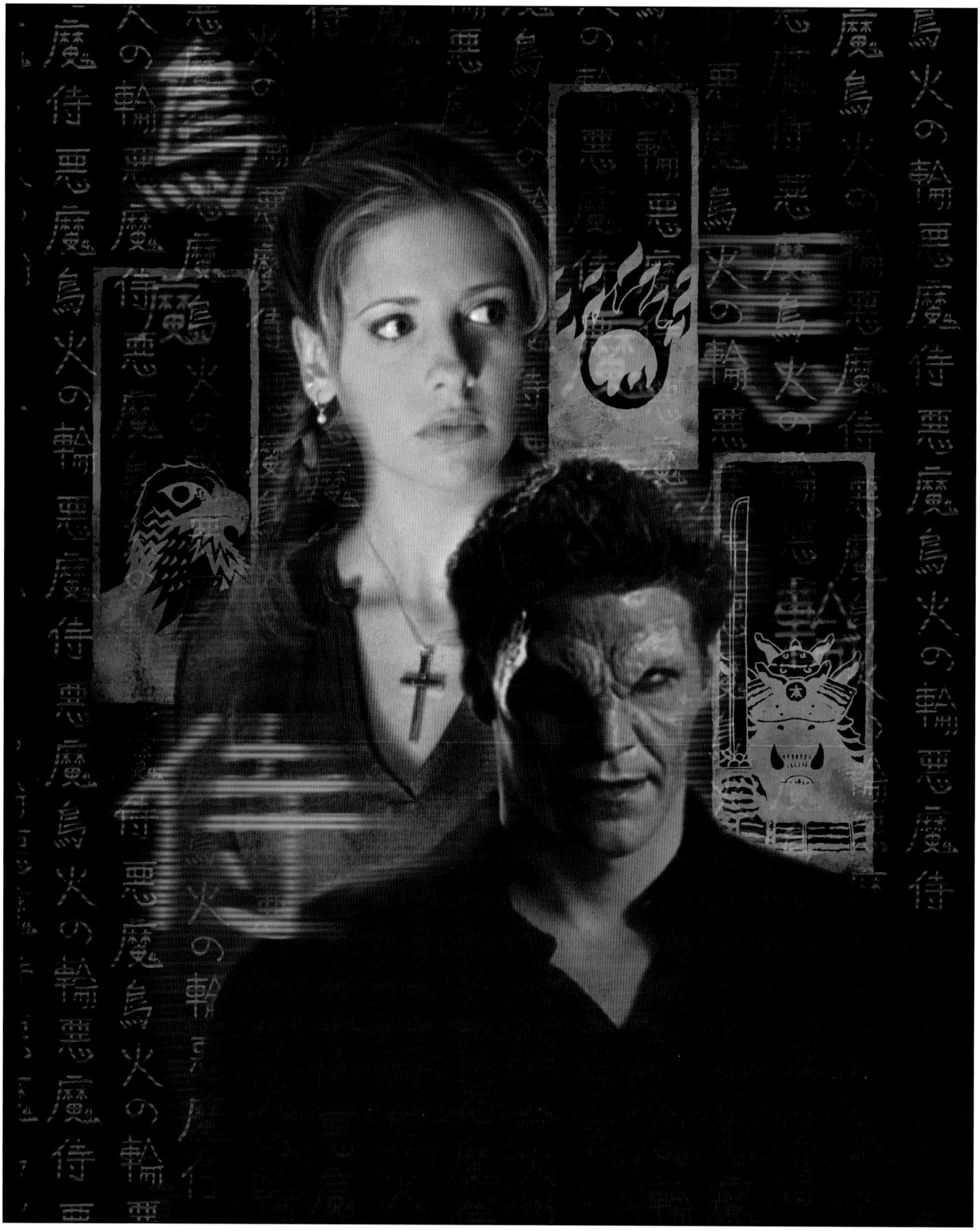

IT TOOK NEARLY a year to make *Ring of Fire*, but in late 2000 Dark Horse released the first major comics work by a *Buffy* television writer. Doug Petrie, who'd warmed up on a short story in the *Buffy Annual* and on *Buffy* #20, teamed with Ryan Sook for a massive story set during Season Two of the television series, shortly after Angelus had killed Jenny Calendar. While we loved Sook's artwork, our marketing department felt it imperative that we do photo covers on trade paperbacks, with which we hoped to reach mainstream fans through bookstores. Dave Stewart incorporated art that Ryan had created for chapter breaks in the graphic novel, so that there was at least a little of Ryan's style on the cover. This remains one of my favorite Buffy projects. The combination of Doug's positive experience on the book, and Ryan's great work, was an important factor in connecting Joss with me and Dark Horse, ultimately leading to the debut of *Fray* the next year.

Montage by Stewart, pencils and inks by Sook. Opposite: Script by Petrie, pencils by Sook, inking assist by Tim Goodyear, colors by Stewart, letters by Clem Robins. Cover and interiors, *BTVS: Ring of Fire*, August 2000.

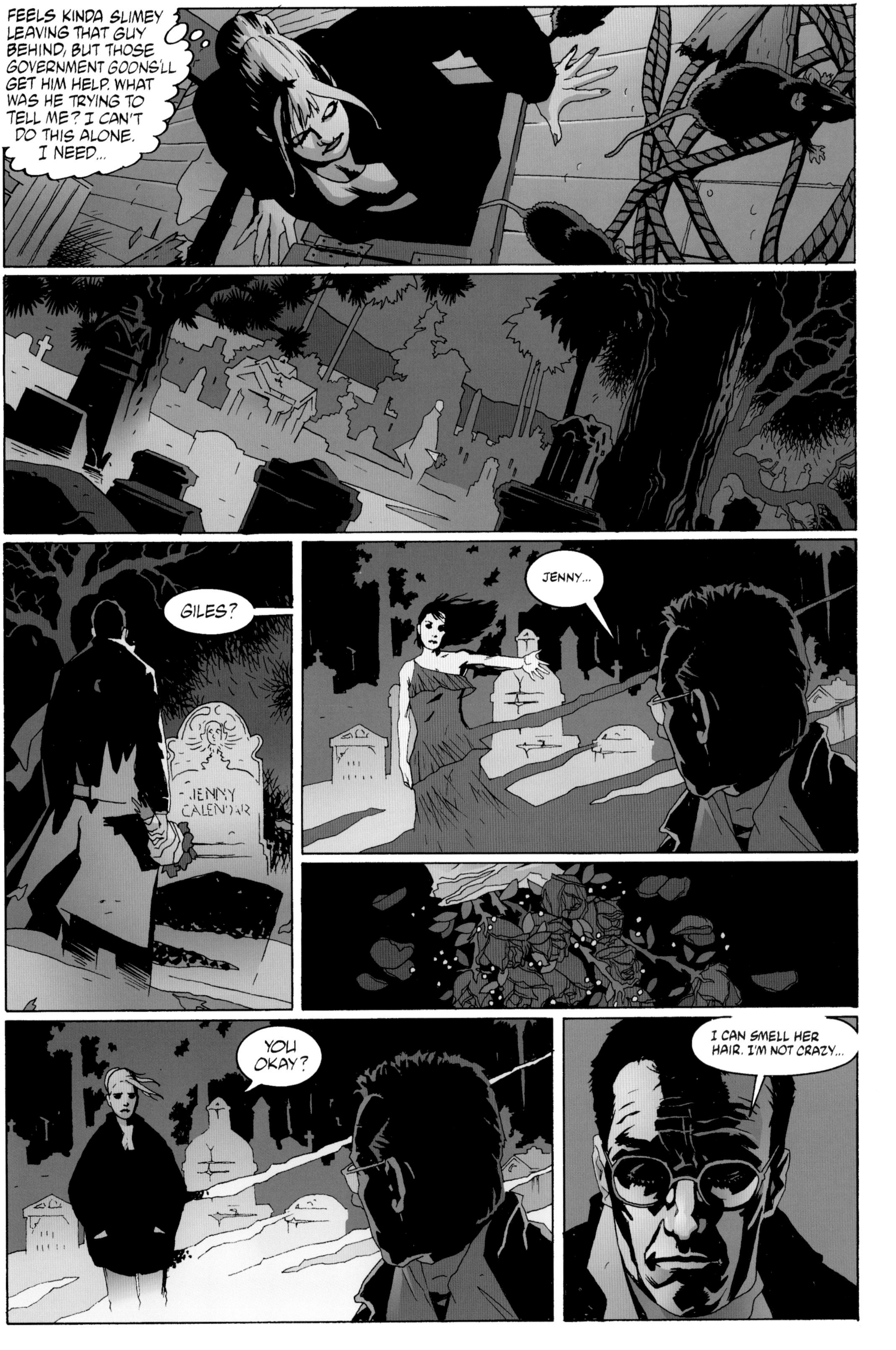
FEELS KINDA SLIMEY LEAVING THAT GUY BEHIND, BUT THOSE GOVERNMENT GOONS'LL GET HIM HELP. WHAT WAS HE TRYING TO TELL ME? I CAN'T DO THIS ALONE. I NEED...
GILES?
JENNY CALENDAR
JENNY...
YOU OKAY?
I CAN SMELL HER HAIR. I'M NOT CRAZY...

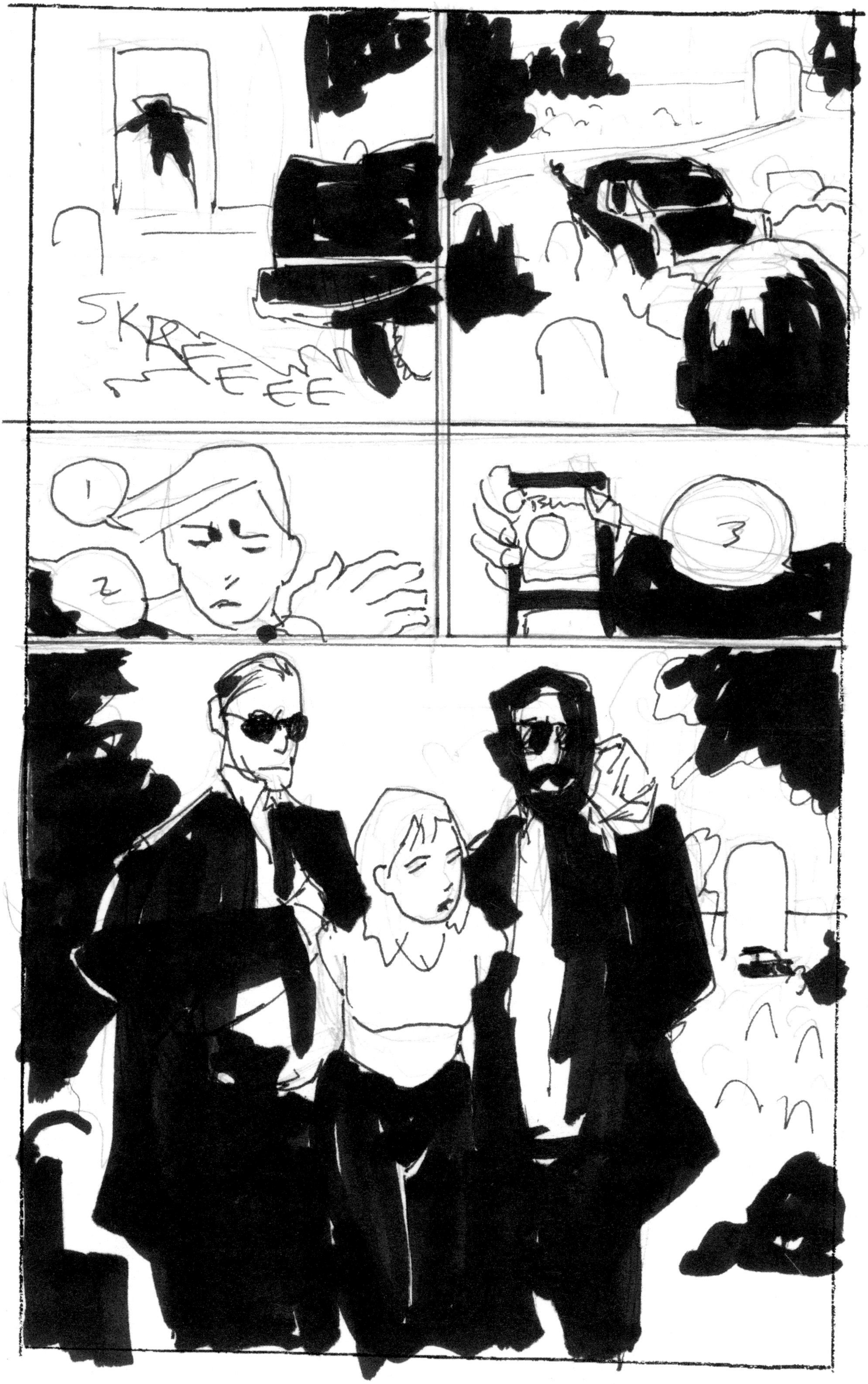
SKREEEEEE
1
2
3

 Layouts, pencils, and inks by Ryan Sook. Late 1999.

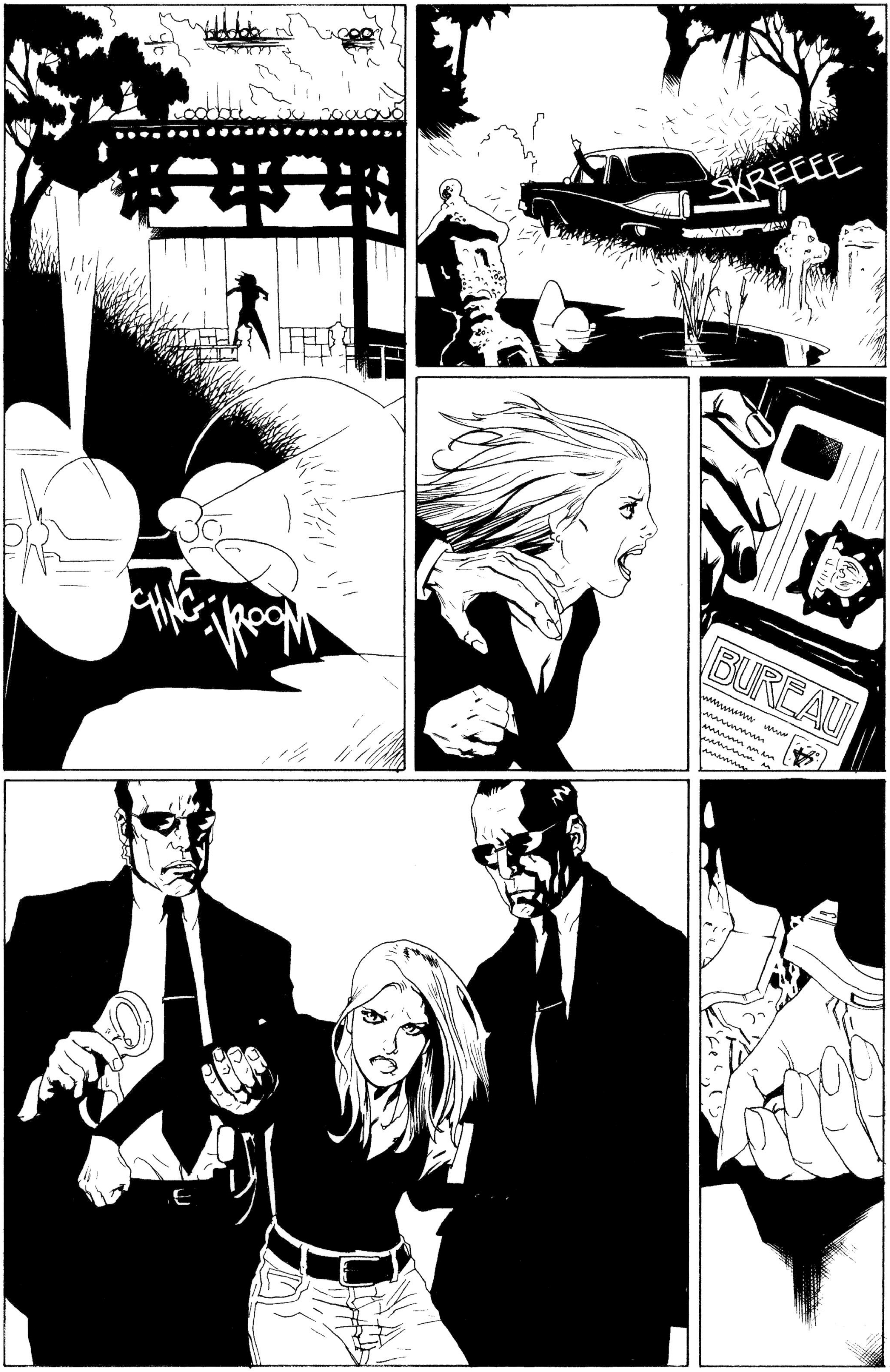
CHNG-VROOM
SKREEEE
BUREAU

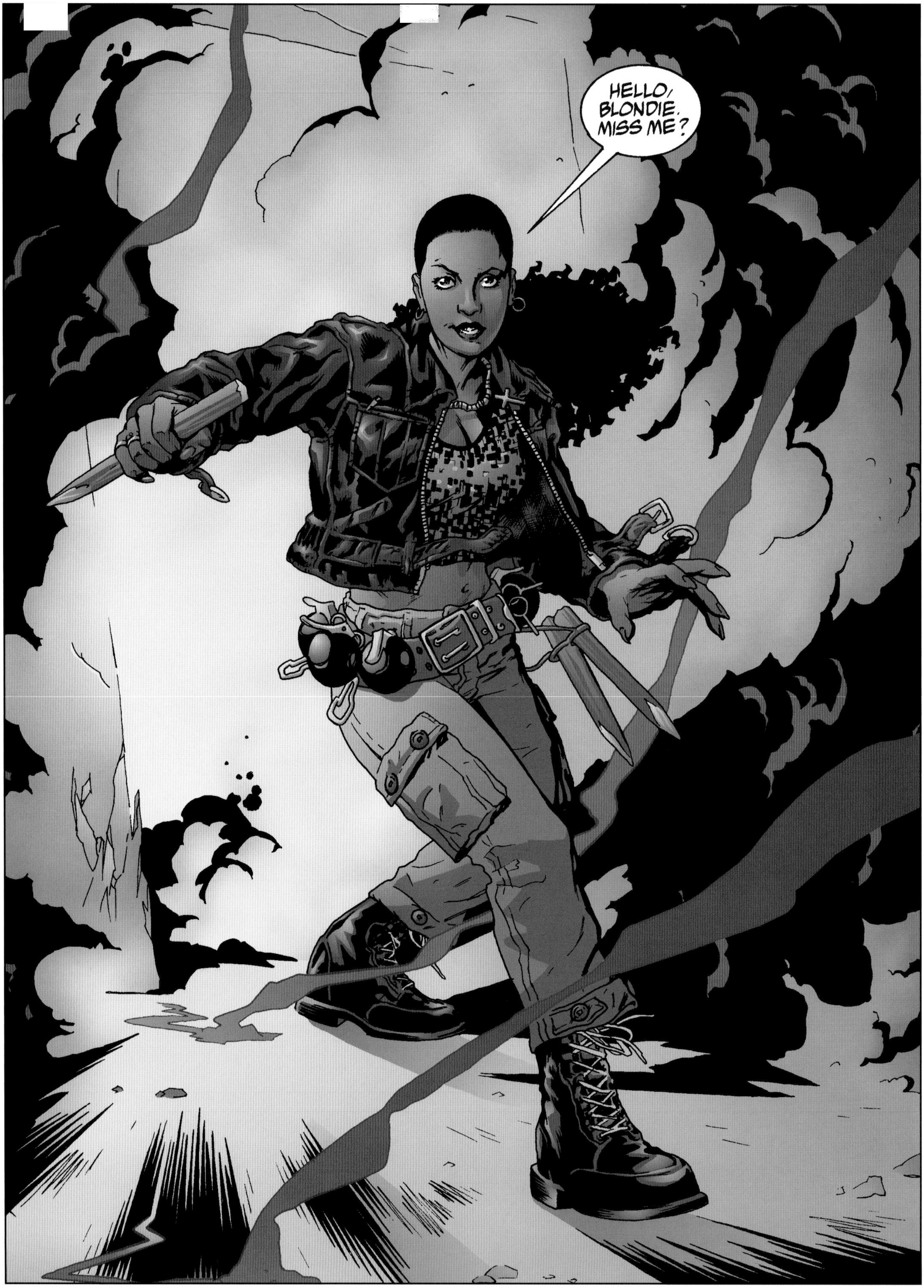
HELLO, BLONDIE. MISS ME?

DOUG PETRIE AND RYAN SOOK offer the only appearance of Kendra in the comics. And while Sarah Michelle Gellar did not always do her own stunts, Ryan drew his own sound effects.

 Script by Petrie, pencils and inks by Sook, inking assist by Tim Goodyear, colors by Dave Stewart, letters by Clem Robins. Interiors, *BTVS: Ring of Fire*, August 2000.

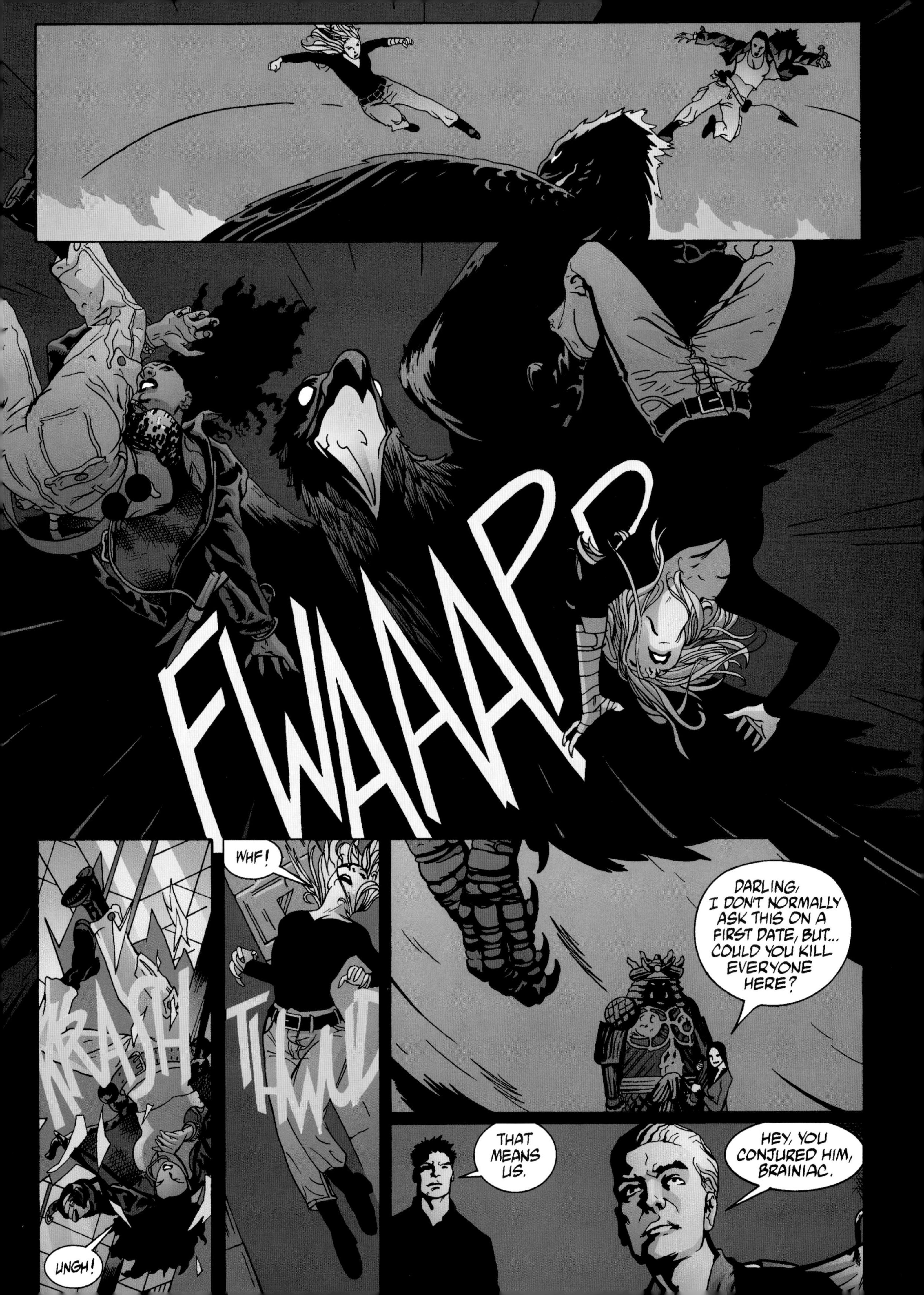
FWAAAP
KRASH
UNGH!
WHF!
THUD
DARLING, I DON'T NORMALLY ASK THIS ON A FIRST DATE, BUT... COULD YOU KILL EVERYONE HERE?
THAT MEANS US.
HEY, YOU CONJURED HIM, BRAINIAC.

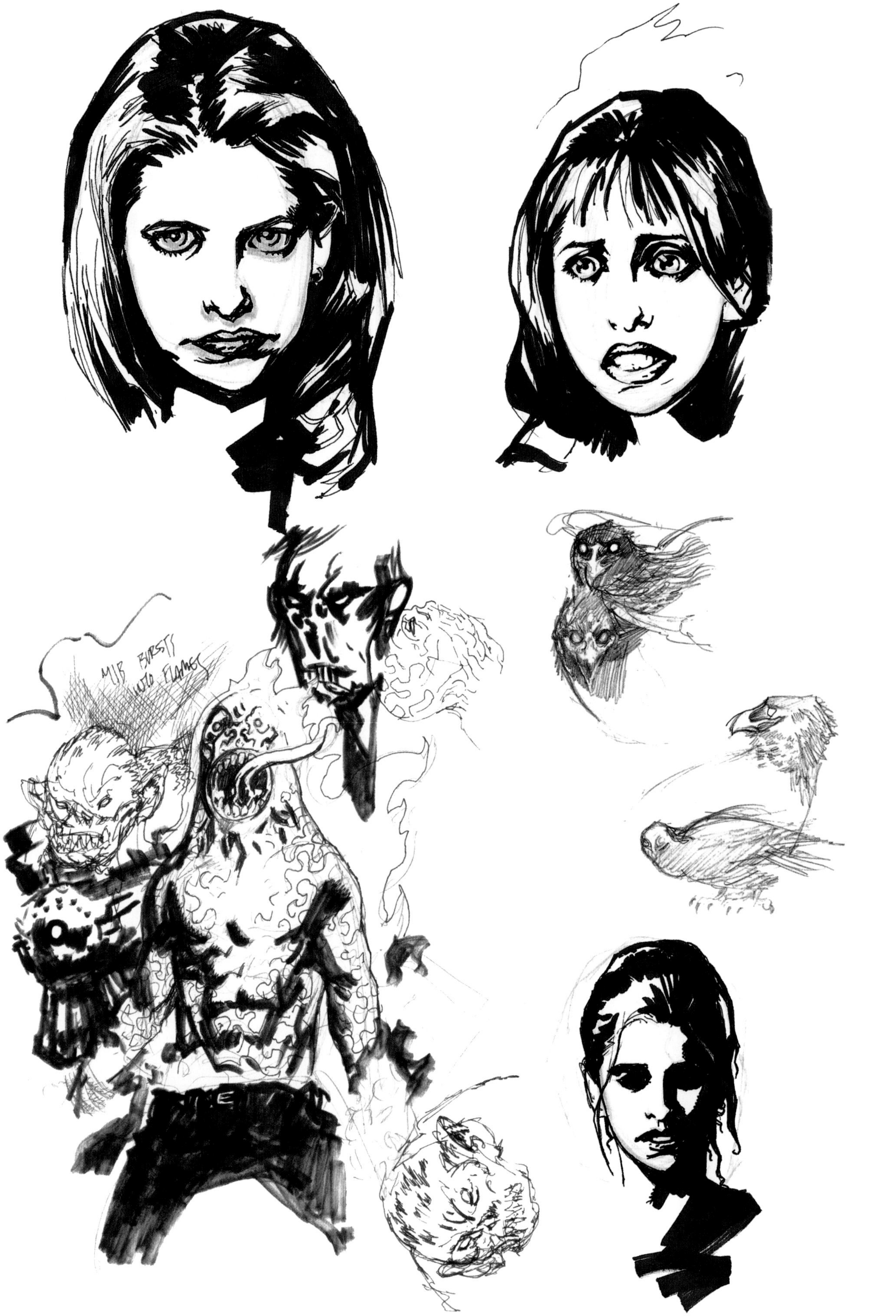
MIB BURSTS INTO FLAMES

RING OF FIRE included a sketchbook, featuring Ryan Sook's character designs for some of the monsters, as well as his original audition pieces for Buffy herself. Whereas most artists audition with a few headshots, Sook's initial tryouts included the page on the right.

 Sketches by Sook. 1999.

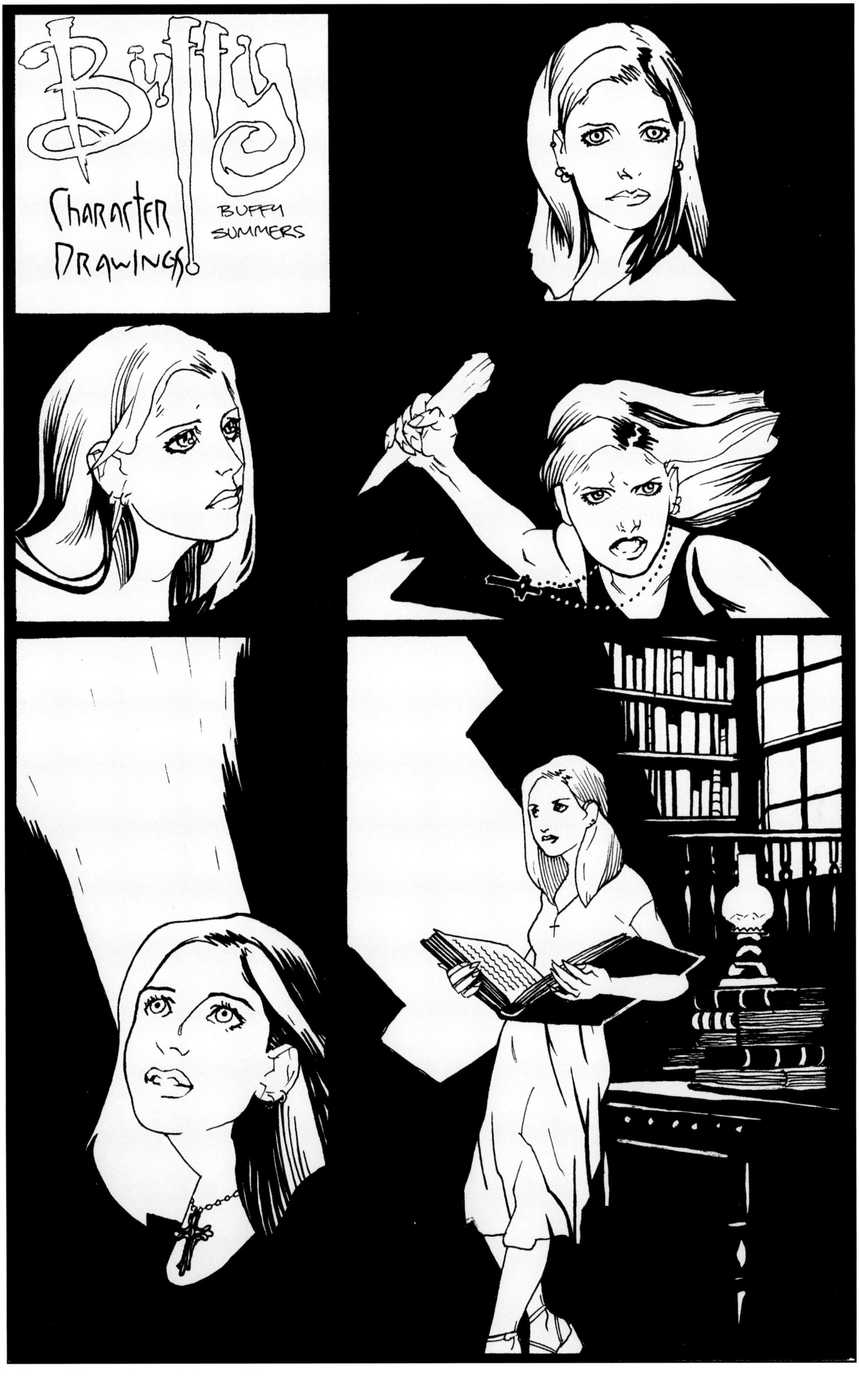
Buffy
Character Drawings
Buffy Summers

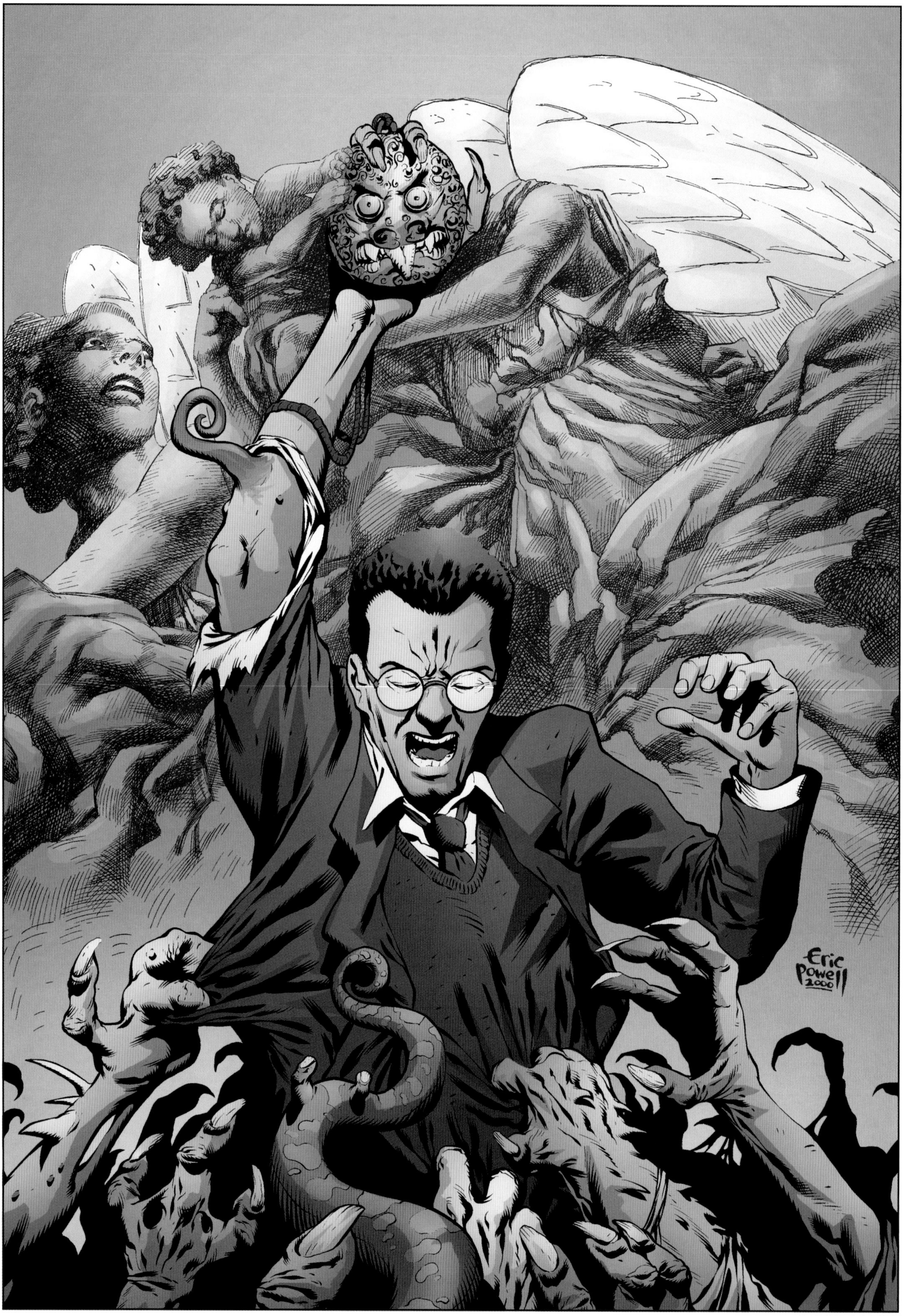

Eric Powell 2000

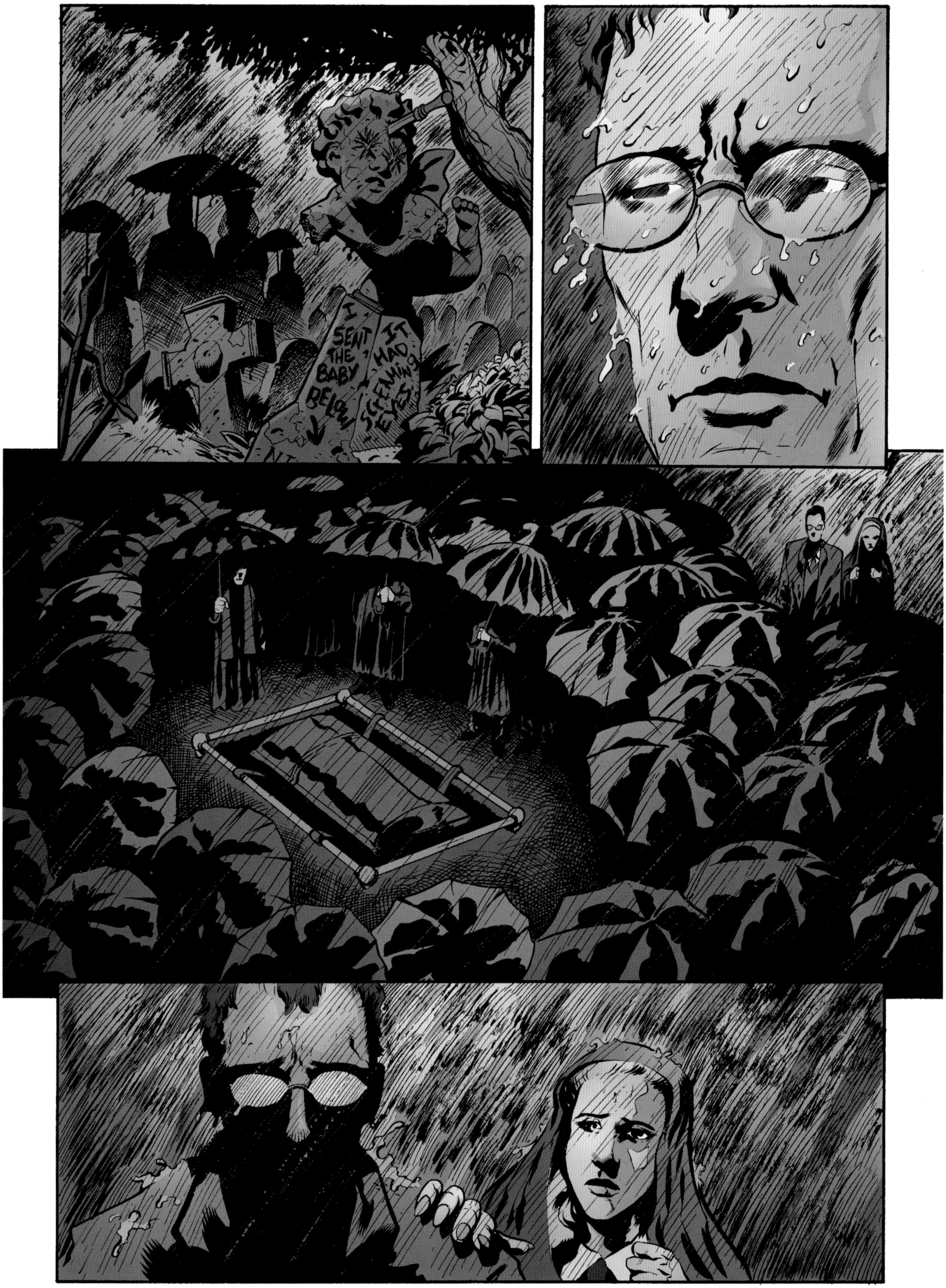
I SENT THE BABY BELOW
IT HAD SCREAMING EYES

I REGRET THAT in those first six years of doing *Buffy* comics, we only did one *Giles* comic. Christopher Golden brought in artist Eric Powell, who'd already done some work on our *Angel* series. Eric continued to do great work on *Buffy* and *Angel* comics until I could finally set up his own creator-owned book at Dark Horse, *The Goon*, the same year that Dark Horse stopped publishing the *Buffy* comics.

Script by Golden and Tom Sniegoski, pencils and inks by Powell, colors by Guy Major. Cover and interiors, *BTVS: Giles*, October 2000.

IN OCTOBER 2000, I launched a three-month promotion called *Autumnals*, turning *Buffy* into more of a horror comic, which we reflected in the covers. This was my first chance to work with one of my heroes, John Totleben.

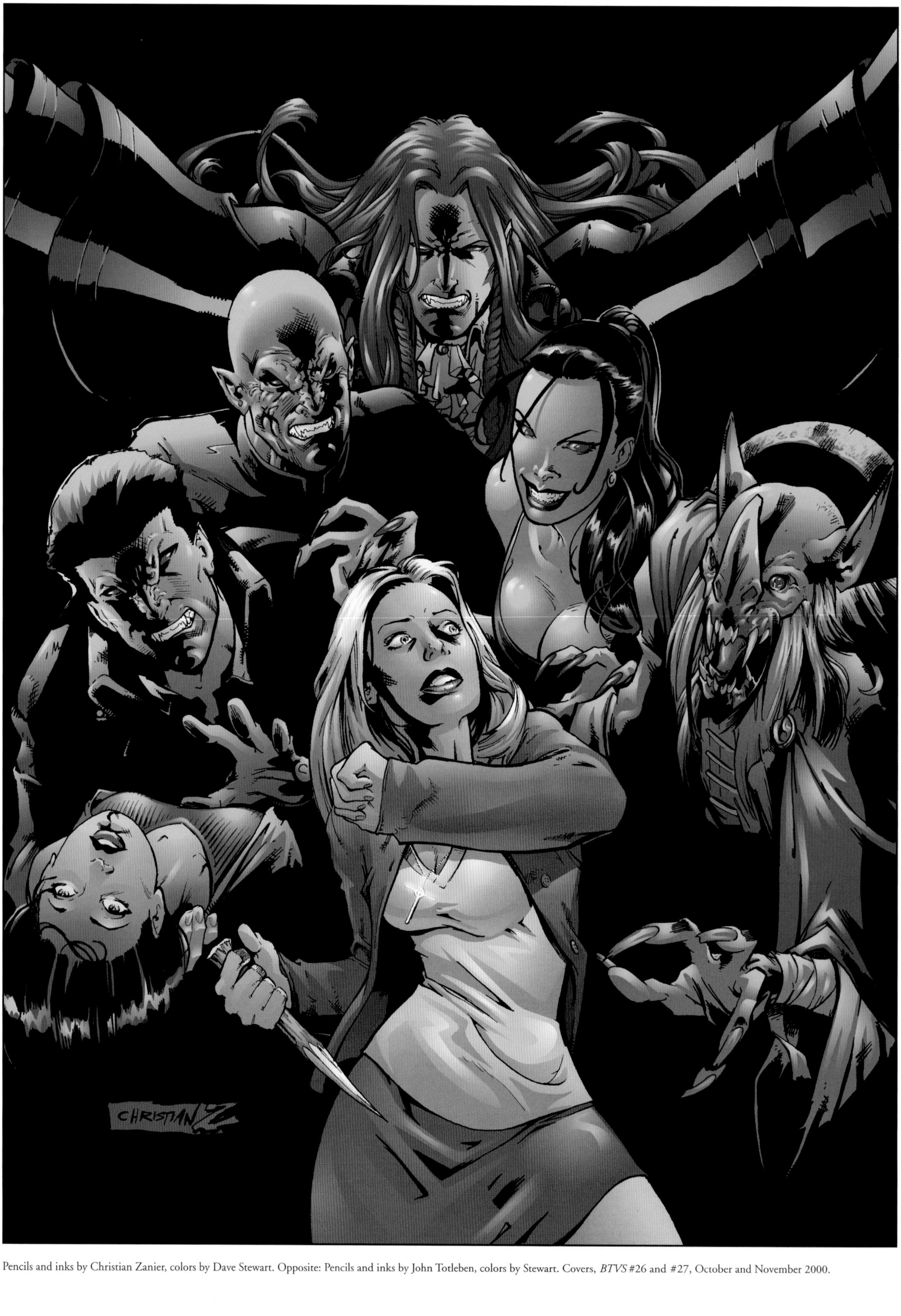
CHRISTIAN Z

 Pencils and inks by Christian Zanier, colors by Dave Stewart. Opposite: Pencils and inks by John Totleben, colors by Stewart. Covers, *BTVS* #26 and #27, October and November 2000.

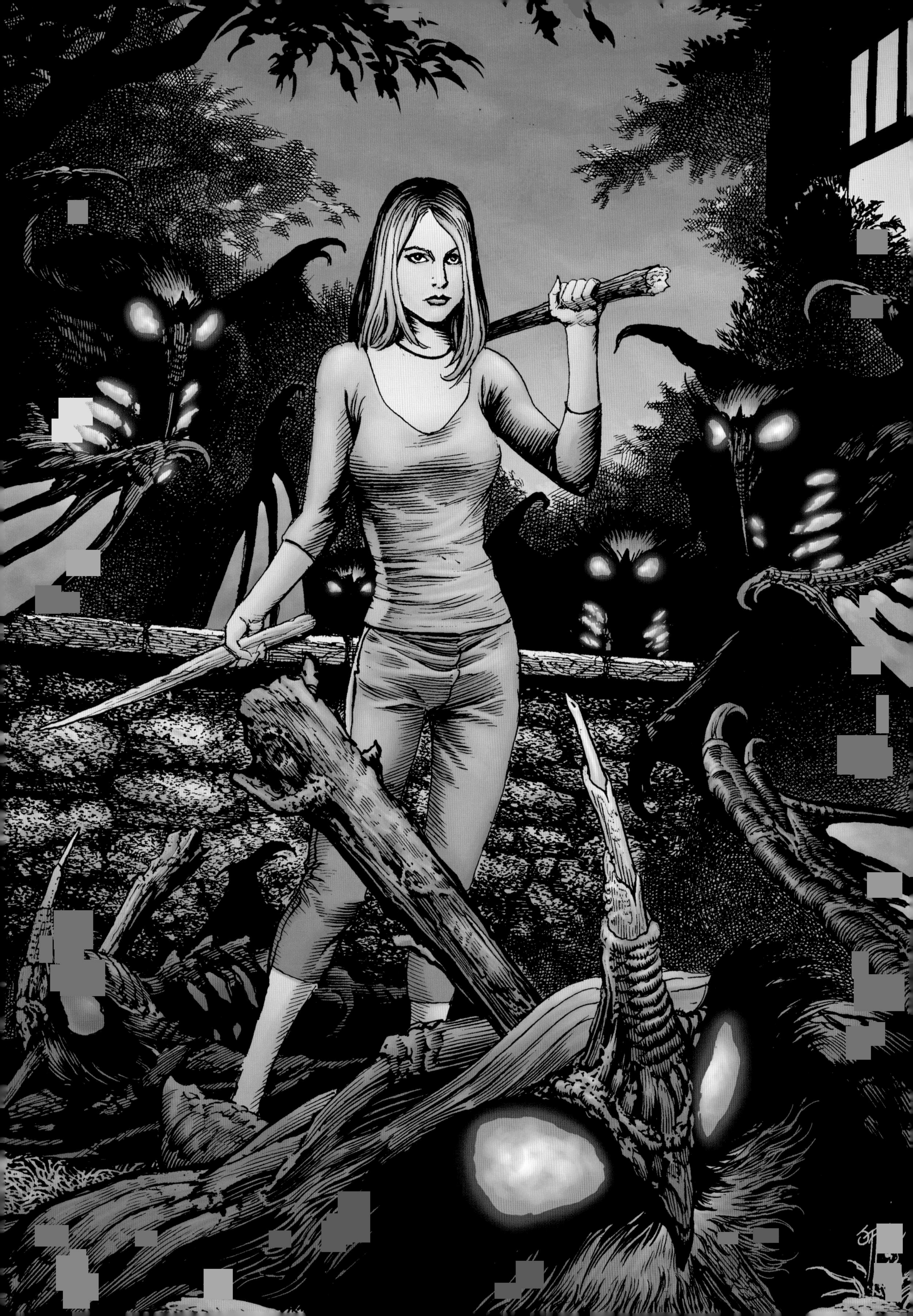

I'D BEEN GOING back and forth between writers ever since Andi Watson left. I asked Tom Fassbender and Jim Pascoe, a writing team whom I'd known for a while, to write *Buffy* #28. That same month, we released a third *Spike and Dru* comic. Ryan Sook provided the cover, but had to back out of the interiors at the last minute. Eric Powell joined Golden again, but the book was rushed under a terrible deadline, and not Powell's finest work.

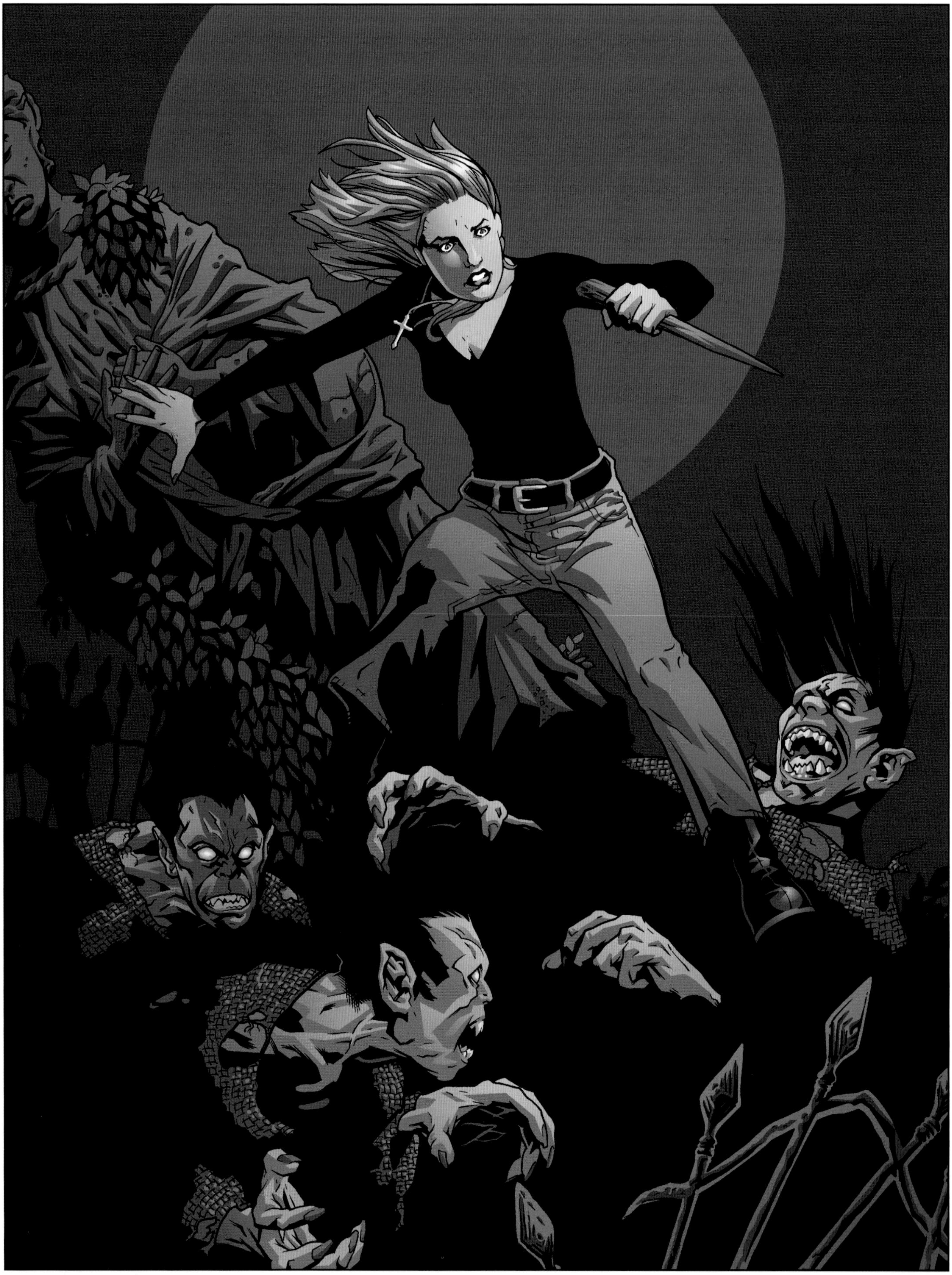

 Pencils by Sook, inks by Galen Showman, colors by Dave Stewart. Cover, *BTVS* #28, December 2000. Opposite: Pencils and inks by Sook, colors by Guy Major. Cover, *BTVS: Spike and Dru* #3, December 2000.

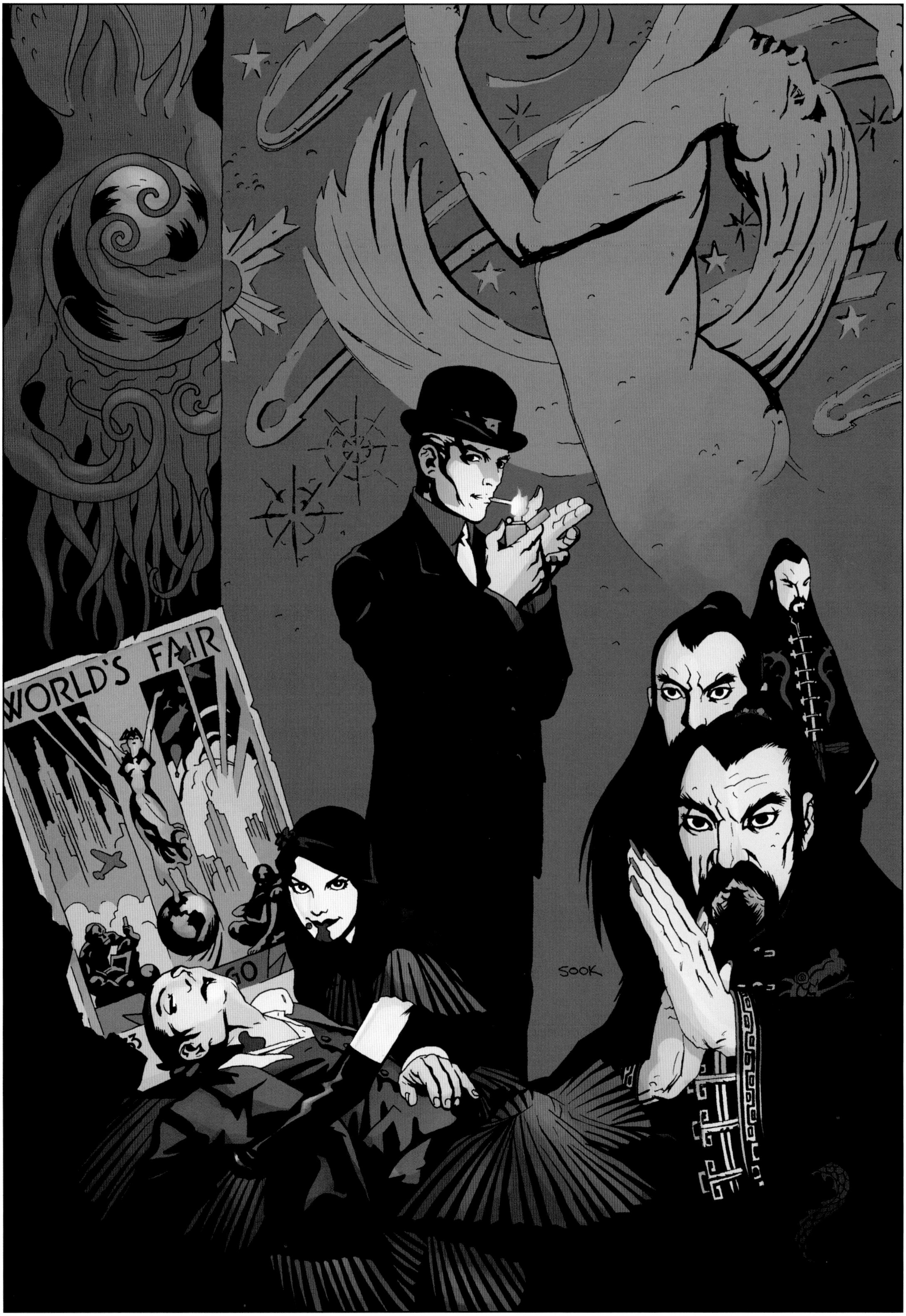
WORLD'S FAIR
SOOK

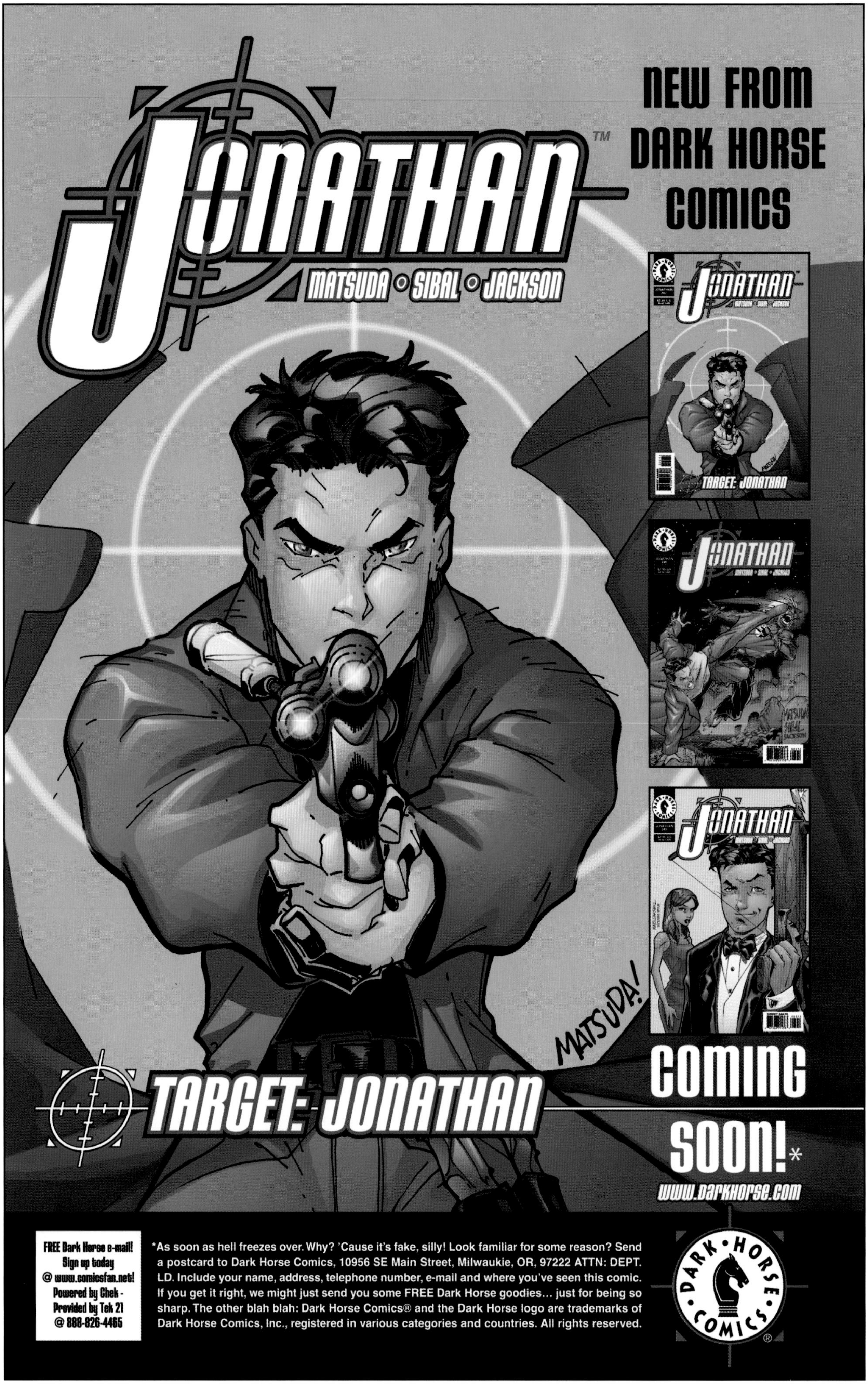
JONATHAN™
MATSUDA • SIBAL • JACKSON
NEW FROM DARK HORSE COMICS
MATSUDA!
TARGET: JONATHAN
COMING SOON!*
www.darkhorse.com
FREE Dark Horse e-mail! Sign up today @ www.comicsfan.net! Powered by Chek - Provided by Tek 21 @ 888-826-4465
*As soon as hell freezes over. Why? 'Cause it's fake, silly! Look familiar for some reason? Send a postcard to Dark Horse Comics, 10956 SE Main Street, Milwaukie, OR, 97222 ATTN: DEPT. LD. Include your name, address, telephone number, e-mail and where you've seen this comic. If you get it right, we might just send you some FREE Dark Horse goodies… just for being so sharp. The other blah blah: Dark Horse Comics® and the Dark Horse logo are trademarks of Dark Horse Comics, Inc., registered in various categories and countries. All rights reserved.
DARK HORSE COMICS®

THE *BUFFY* SEASON FOUR episode "Superstar," written by Jane Espenson, turned the nerdy Jonathan Levinson into a cross between James Bond and Michael Jordan. The episode also featured some props that we created for the show—a group of comic books about Jonathan's exploits. When the producers—not Joss himself—contacted me to create the covers, I knew I had to give Jeff Matsuda his chance to "appear" in his favorite show. Dark Horse also made up an ad for the book, which of course didn't exist. We ran the ad in our *Buffy* book the month the show aired.

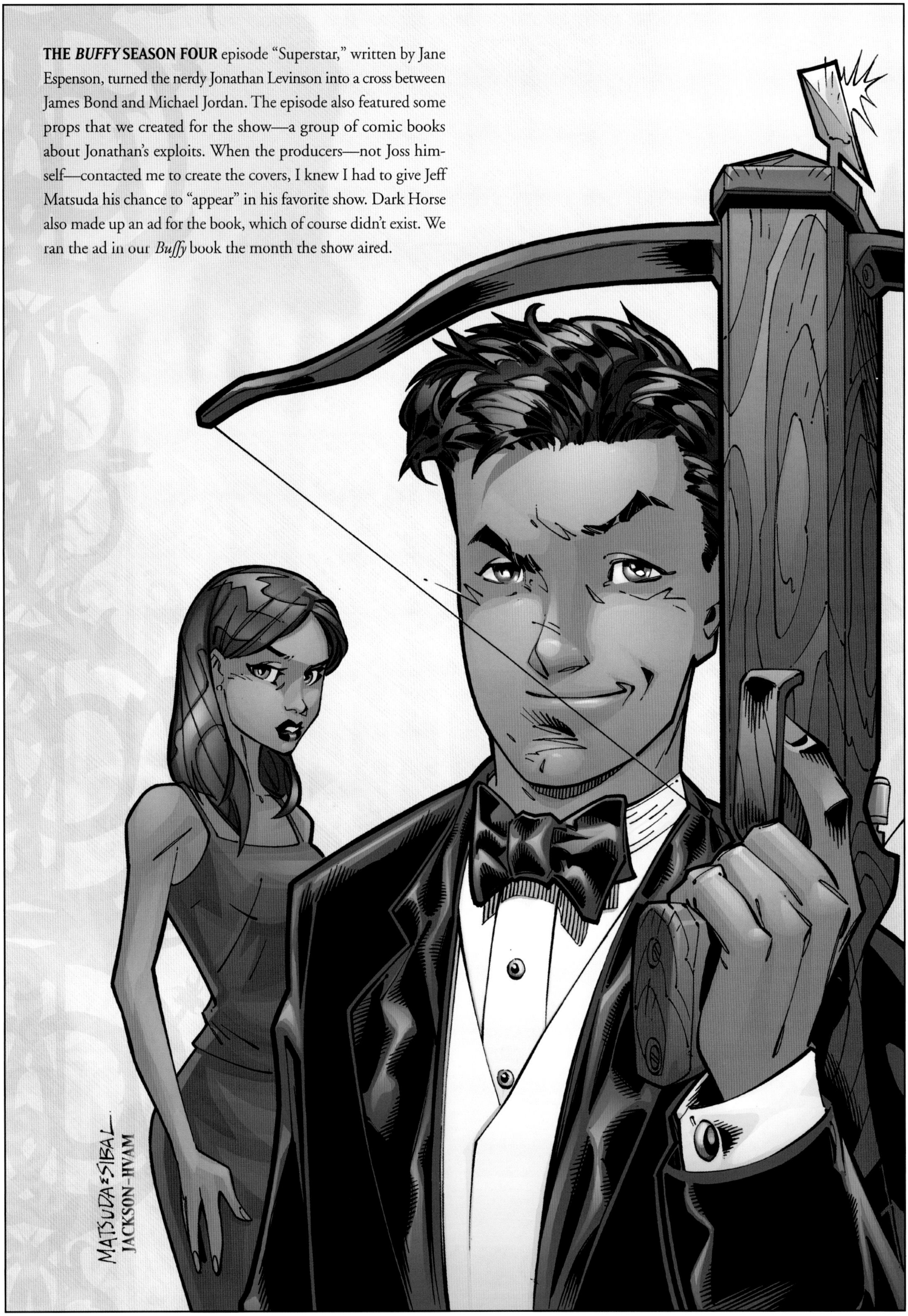
MATSUDA & SIBAL
JACKSON-HVAM

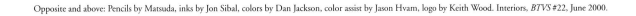

Opposite and above: Pencils by Matsuda, inks by Jon Sibal, colors by Dan Jackson, color assist by Jason Hvam, logo by Keith Wood. Interiors, *BTVS* #22, June 2000.

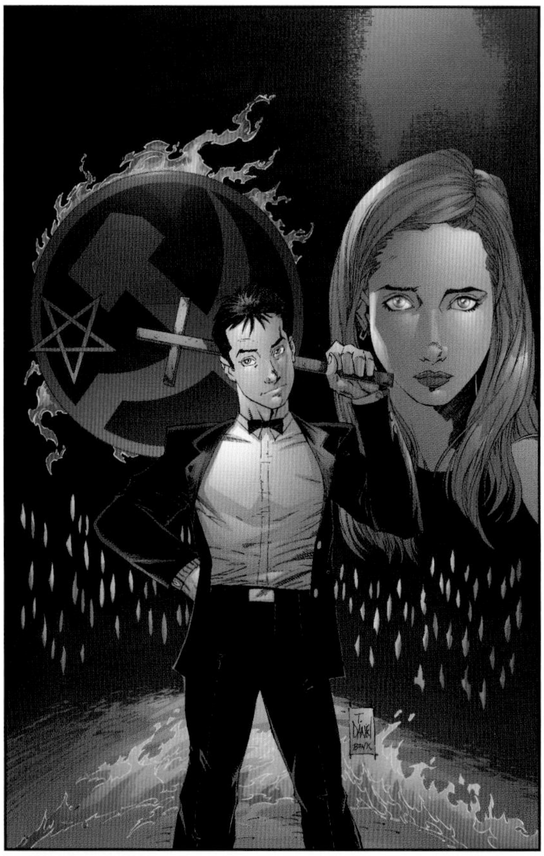

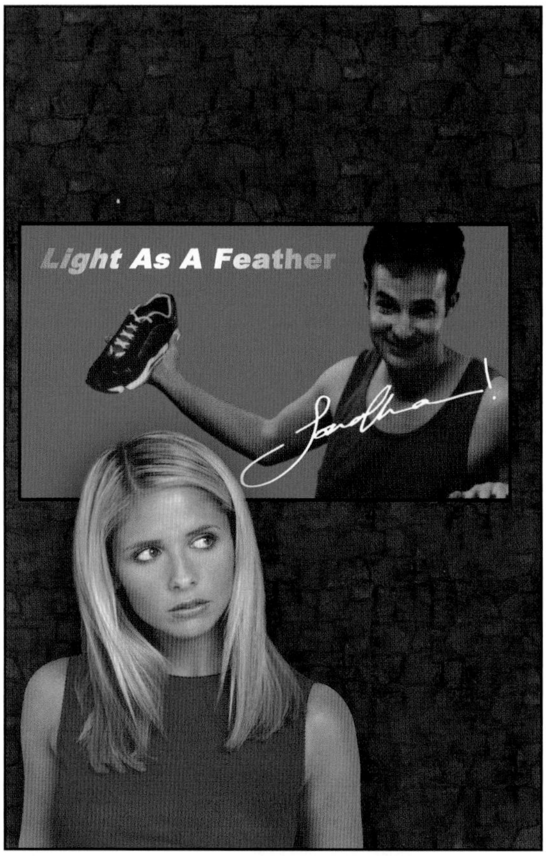
Light As A Feather

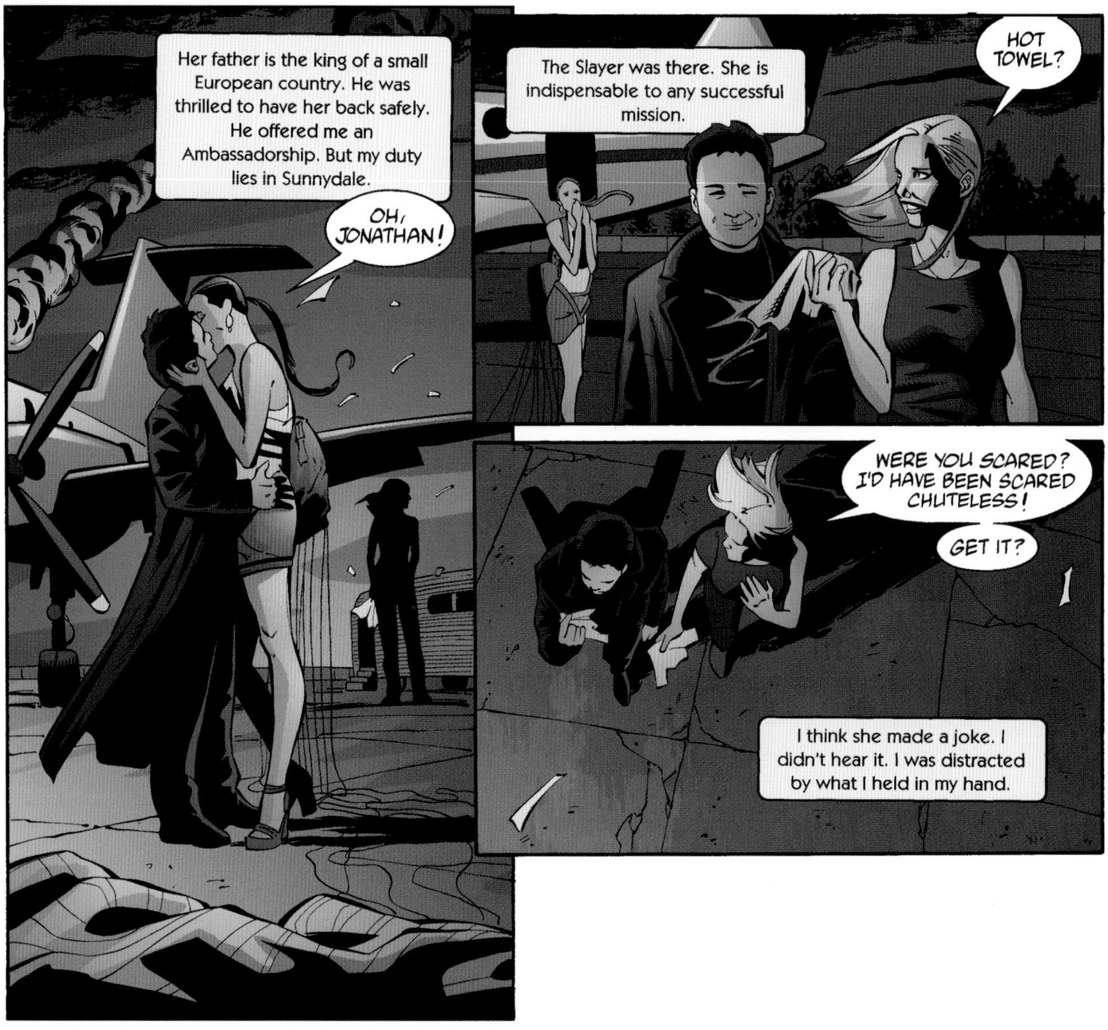
Her father is the king of a small European country. He was thrilled to have her back safely. He offered me an Ambassadorship. But my duty lies in Sunnydale.
OH, JONATHAN!
The Slayer was there. She is indispensable to any successful mission.
HOT TOWEL?
WERE YOU SCARED? I'D HAVE BEEN SCARED CHUTELESS!
GET IT?
I think she made a joke. I didn't hear it. I was distracted by what I held in my hand.

JANE ESPENSON LOVED the Jonathan character, and offered to write a comic about him, a prequel to "Superstar," making her the second writer from the show whom I got to work with. The month the book was due to come out, Dark Horse was heavily promoting a new book by Tony Daniel. Part of the promotion was to have him do covers for a variety of Dark Horse books, including *Jonathan.*

 Top left: Pencils by Daniel, inks by Bonk, colors uncredited. Top right: Montage by Keith Wood. Bottom and opposite: Script by Espenson, pencils by Cliff Richards, inks by Andy Owens, colors by Guy Major, letters by Clem Robins. Covers and interiors, *BTVS: Jonathan*, January 2001.

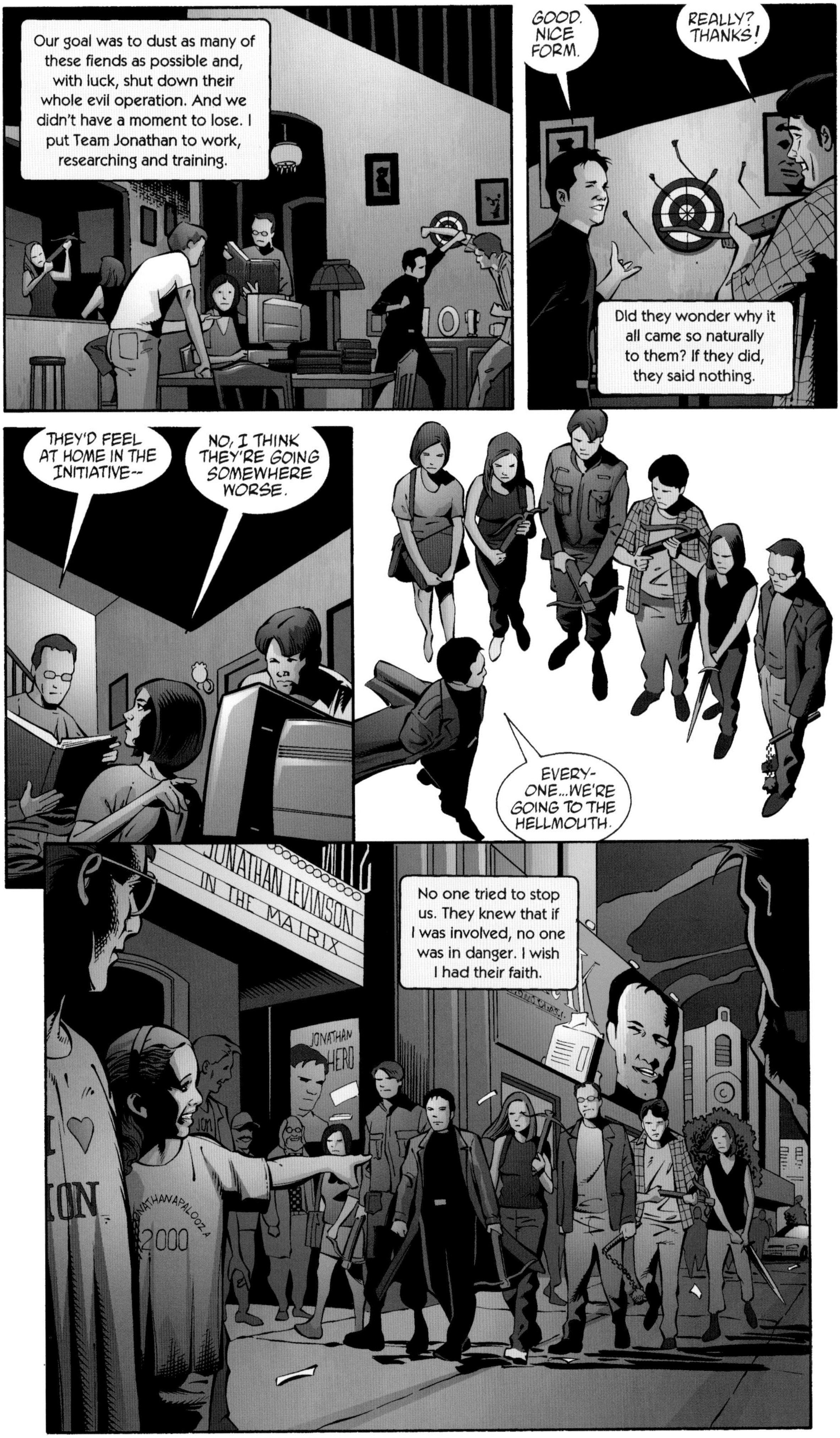

Our goal was to dust as many of these fiends as possible and, with luck, shut down their whole evil operation. And we didn't have a moment to lose. I put Team Jonathan to work, researching and training.
GOOD. NICE FORM.
REALLY? THANKS!
Did they wonder why it all came so naturally to them? If they did, they said nothing.
THEY'D FEEL AT HOME IN THE INITIATIVE--
NO, I THINK THEY'RE GOING SOMEWHERE WORSE.
EVERY-ONE...WE'RE GOING TO THE HELLMOUTH.
JONATHAN LEVINSON IN THE MATRIX
No one tried to stop us. They knew that if I was involved, no one was in danger. I wish I had their faith.
JONATHAN HERO
JONATHANAPALOOZA 2000

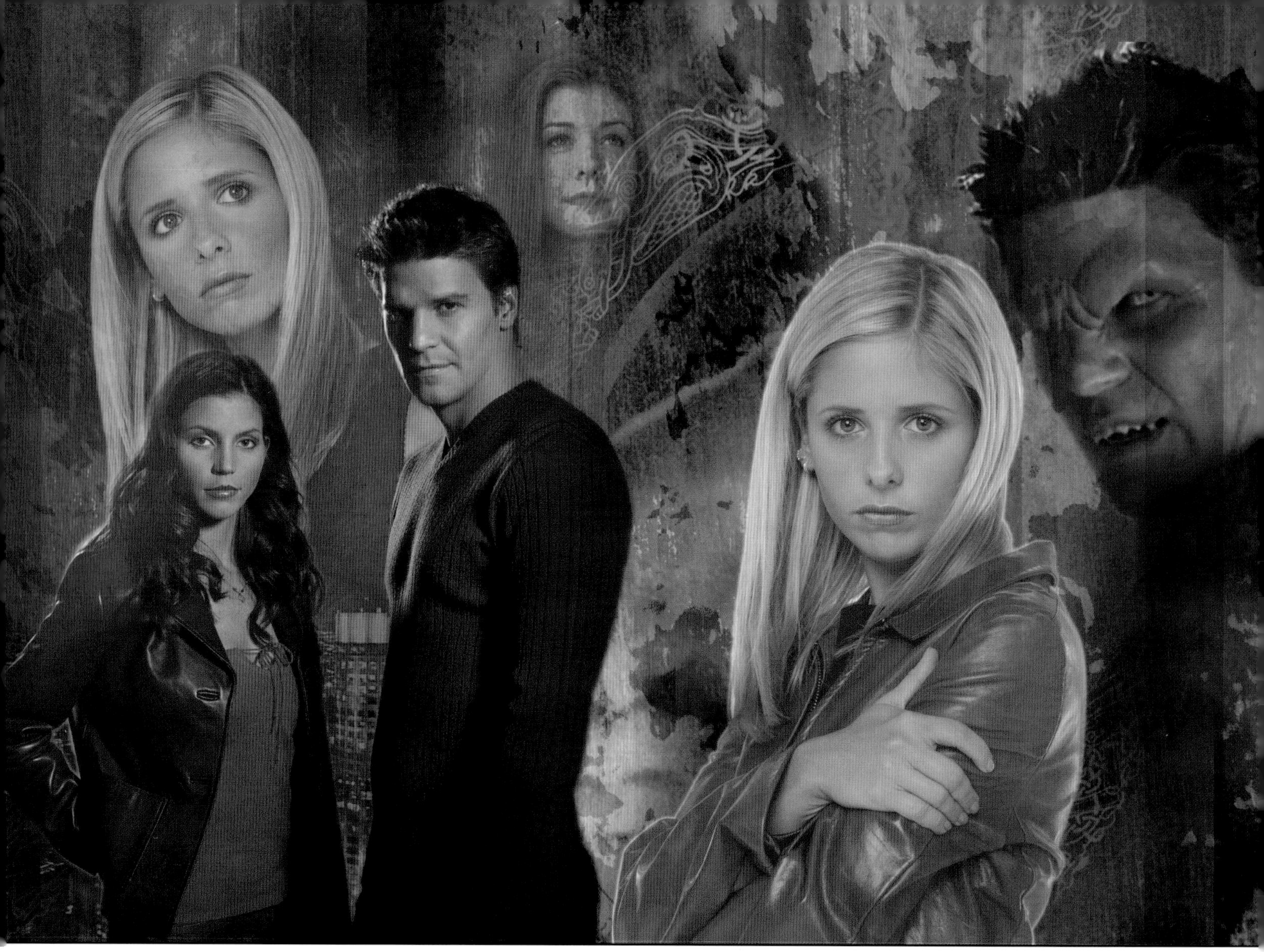

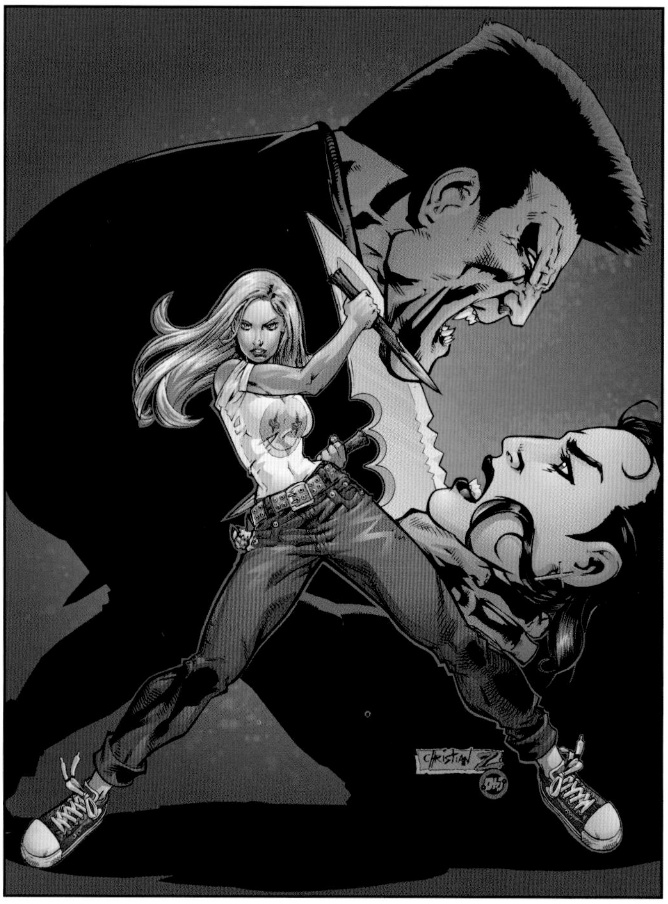

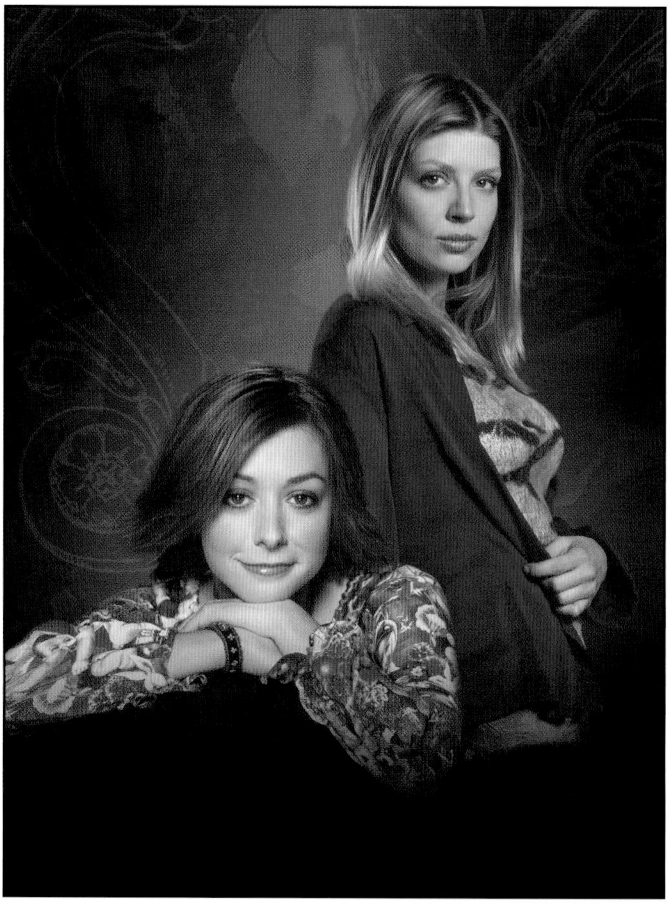

 Top: Montage by Keith Wood. Covers, *Angel* #15 and #16, *BTVS* #29 and #30, January and February 2001. Bottom left: Pencils by Christian Zanier, inks by Andrew Pepoy, colors by Stewart. Cover, *BTVS* #30, February 2001.

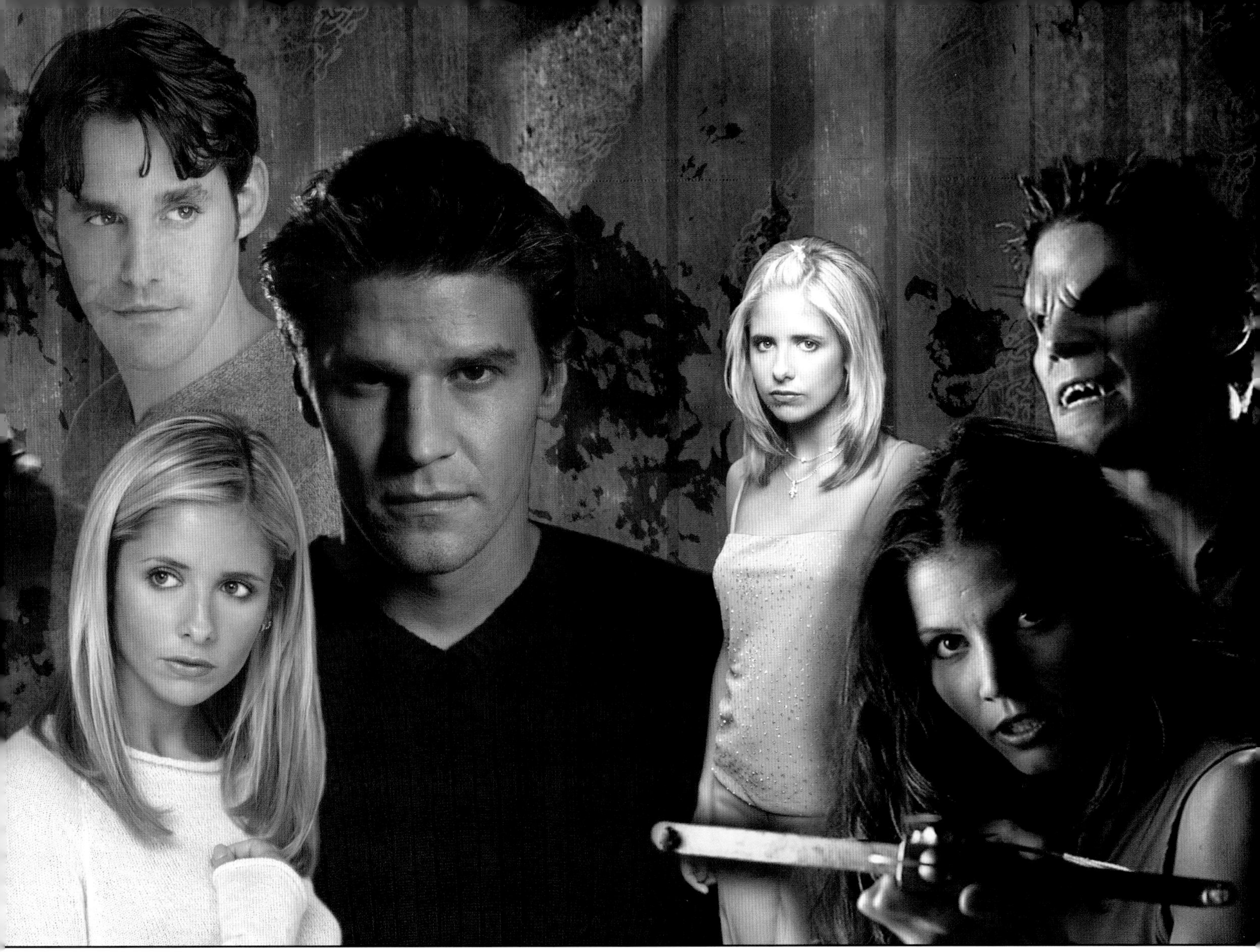

WE PUBLISHED A CROSSOVER between our *Buffy* and *Angel* series for two months, effectively making it a biweekly story—all tied up with one sprawling photocover. Chris Golden wrote the crossover with his frequent co-writer Tom Sniegoski. A month later, Golden brought another actor from *Buffy* into the comics fold, writing a Willow and Tara story with Amber ("Tara") Benson. The story was drawn by independent-comics superstar Terry Moore, who'd been winning awards and fans for his series *Strangers in Paradise*, in which he wrote and drew female characters more honestly and compellingly than most artists in the history of comics. When he fell behind schedule, Eric Powell pitched in on backgrounds. The photocover looks like a simple publicity still with texture in the background, but there were no stills of the women together, so we combined two shots of them to get this.

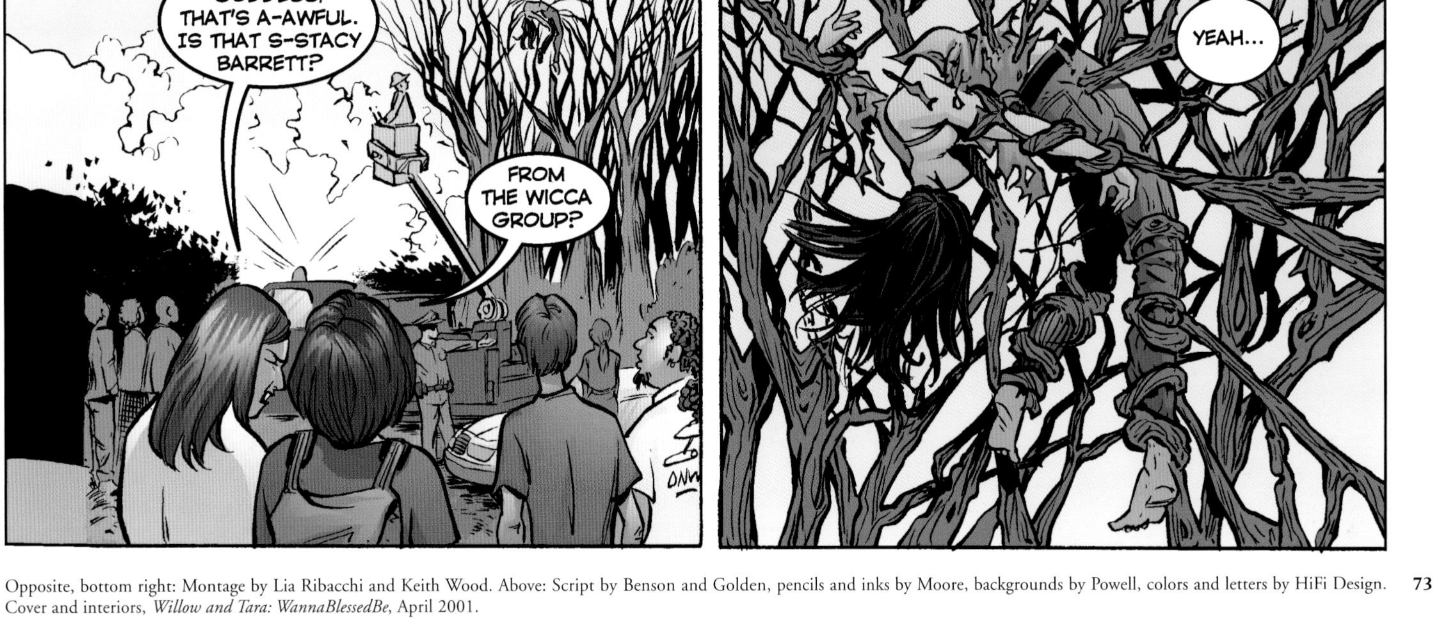
GODDESS, THAT'S A-AWFUL. IS THAT S-STACY BARRETT?
FROM THE WICCA GROUP?
YEAH...

Opposite, bottom right: Montage by Lia Ribacchi and Keith Wood. Above: Script by Benson and Golden, pencils and inks by Moore, backgrounds by Powell, colors and letters by HiFi Design. Cover and interiors, *Willow and Tara: WannaBlessedBe*, April 2001.

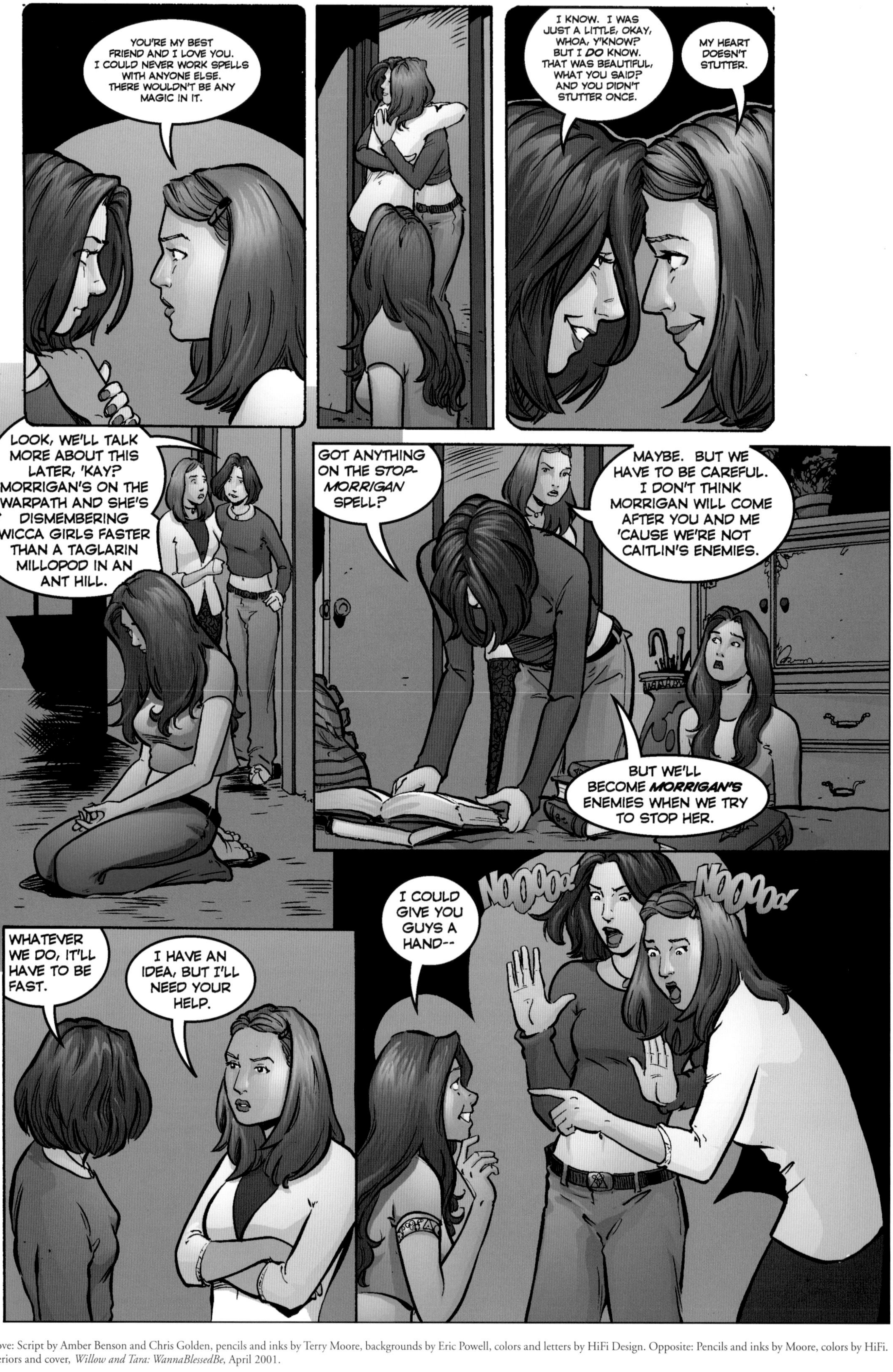
YOU'RE MY BEST FRIEND AND I LOVE YOU. I COULD NEVER WORK SPELLS WITH ANYONE ELSE. THERE WOULDN'T BE ANY MAGIC IN IT.
I KNOW. I WAS JUST A LITTLE, OKAY, WHOA, Y'KNOW? BUT I DO KNOW. THAT WAS BEAUTIFUL, WHAT YOU SAID? AND YOU DIDN'T STUTTER ONCE.
MY HEART DOESN'T STUTTER.
LOOK, WE'LL TALK MORE ABOUT THIS LATER, 'KAY? MORRIGAN'S ON THE WARPATH AND SHE'S DISMEMBERING WICCA GIRLS FASTER THAN A TAGLARIN MILLOPOD IN AN ANT HILL.
GOT ANYTHING ON THE STOP-MORRIGAN SPELL?
MAYBE. BUT WE HAVE TO BE CAREFUL. I DON'T THINK MORRIGAN WILL COME AFTER YOU AND ME 'CAUSE WE'RE NOT CAITLIN'S ENEMIES.
BUT WE'LL BECOME MORRIGAN'S ENEMIES WHEN WE TRY TO STOP HER.
WHATEVER WE DO, IT'LL HAVE TO BE FAST.
I HAVE AN IDEA, BUT I'LL NEED YOUR HELP.
I COULD GIVE YOU GUYS A HAND--
NOOOOO!
NOOOOO!

Above: Script by Amber Benson and Chris Golden, pencils and inks by Terry Moore, backgrounds by Eric Powell, colors and letters by HiFi Design. Opposite: Pencils and inks by Moore, colors by HiFi. Interiors and cover, *Willow and Tara: WannaBlessedBe*, April 2001.

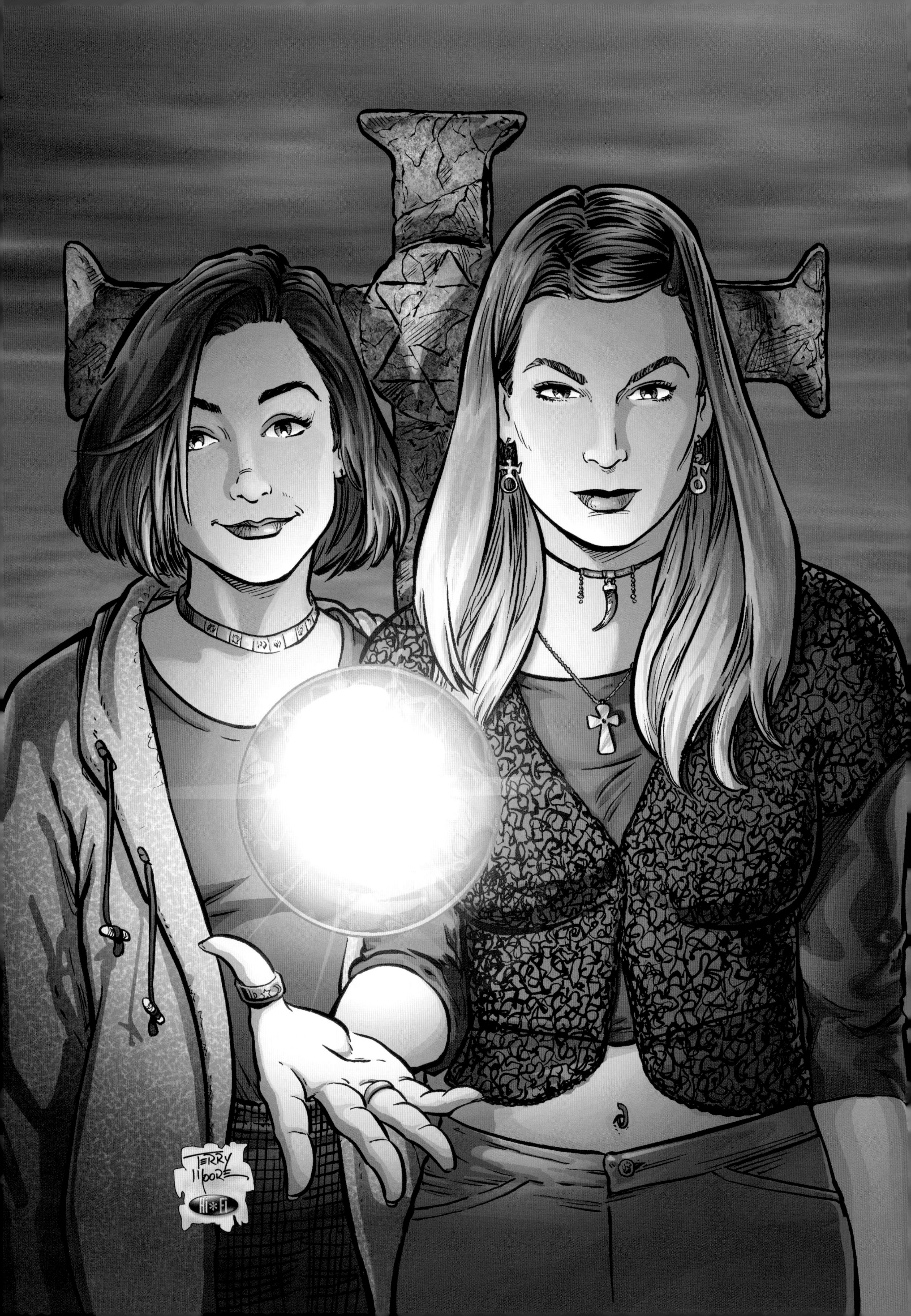
TERRY MOORE
HI*FI

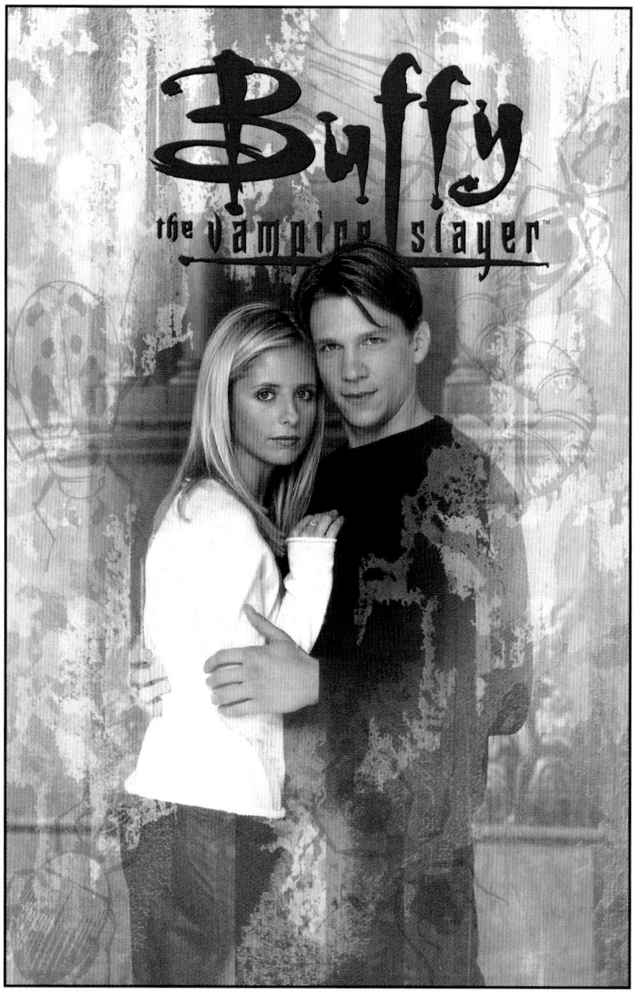
Buffy
the vampire slayer
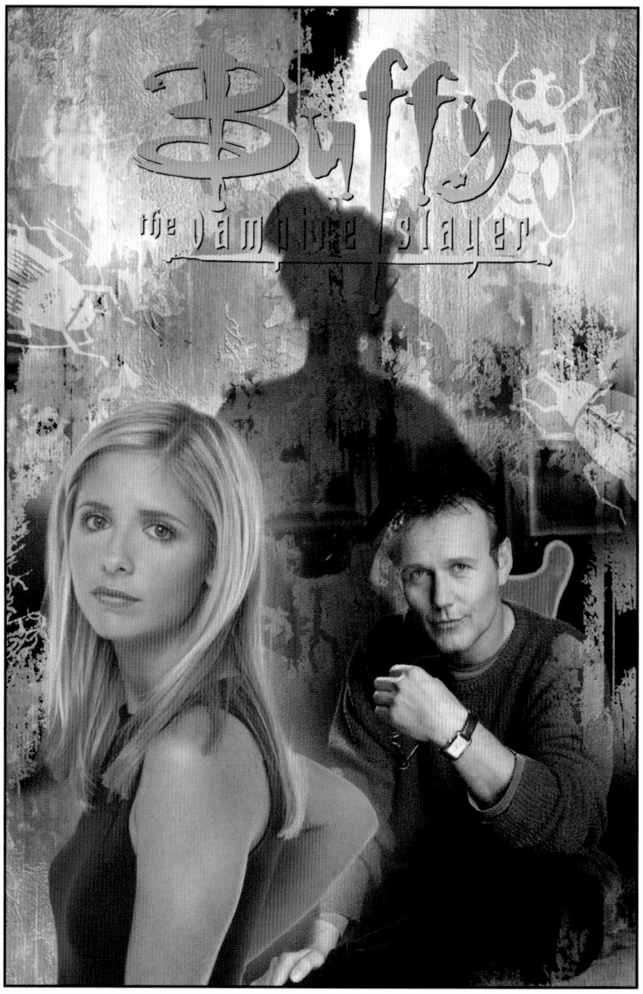
Buffy
the vampire slayer
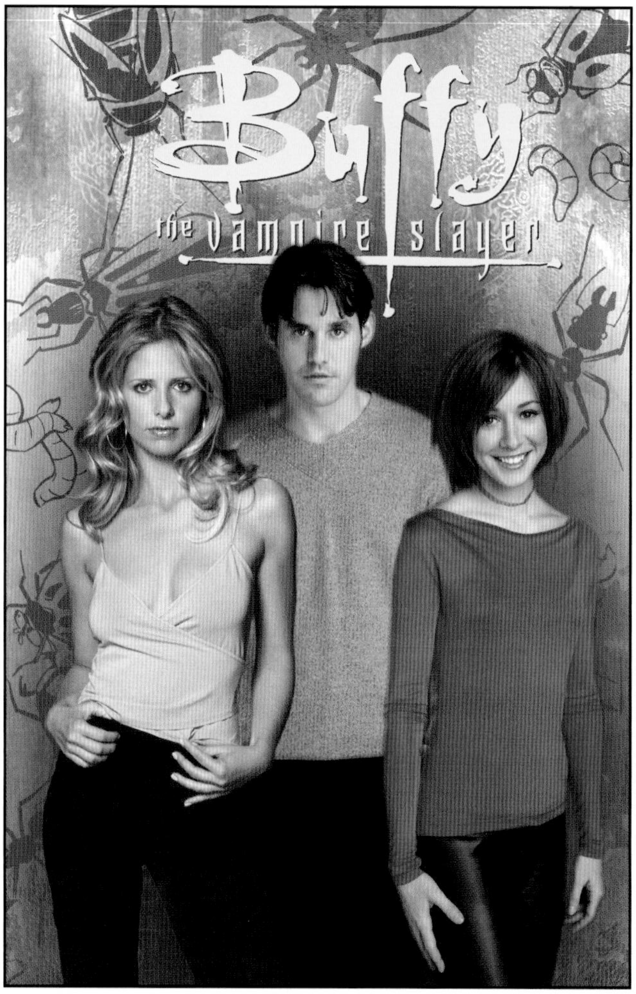
Buffy
the vampire slayer
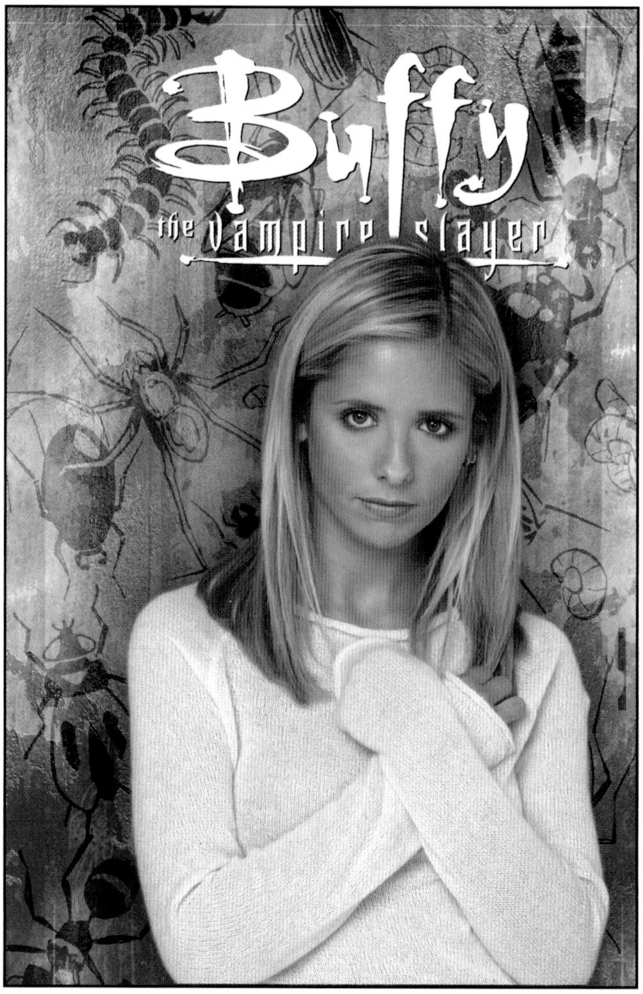
Buffy
the vampire slayer

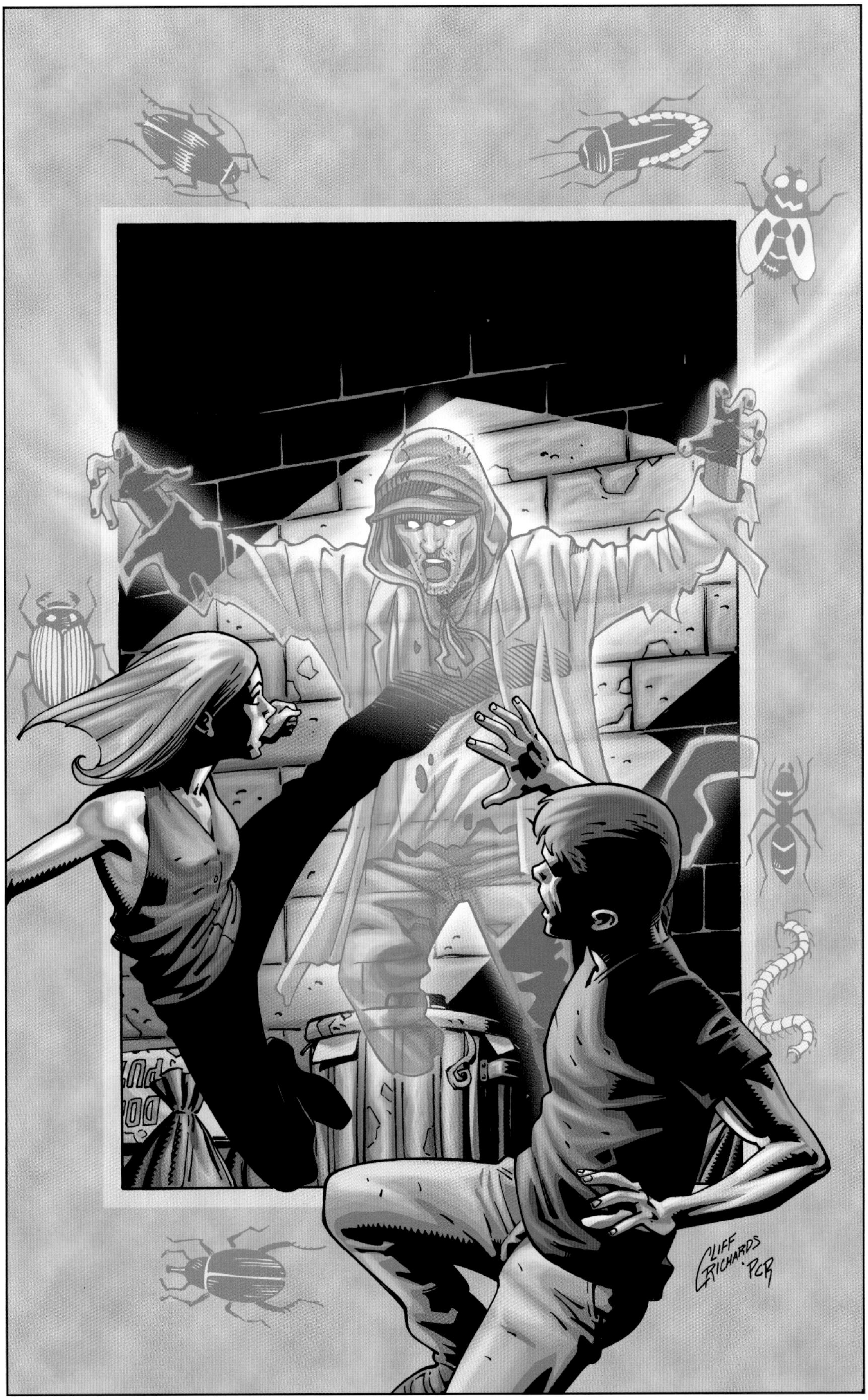
CLIFF RICHARDS
PCR

AS DAVE STEWART'S coloring career picked up, he grew bored with the photo covers, and I recruited Dark Horse staff designer Keith Wood. For the story *Out of the Woodwork* in the monthly title, Wood incorporated insects from Cliff Richards's pencilled covers. This was the beginning of a brief stint of thematically connected sets of photo covers. For the art covers, I let our then–Art Director Mark Cox take the reins. In magazine publishing the Art Director dictates the covers, but this is unusual in comics. Mark provided Cliff with sketches for each cover, and worked closely with him and the colorist for the final piece. One of my favorite artists, P. Craig Russell, signed up to ink Richards's covers.

Opposite: Montages by Wood. Covers, *BTVS* #31–34, March–June 2001. Above and following two pages: Pencils by Richards, inks by Russell, colors by Dave McCaig. Covers, *BTVS* #31–33, March–May 2001.

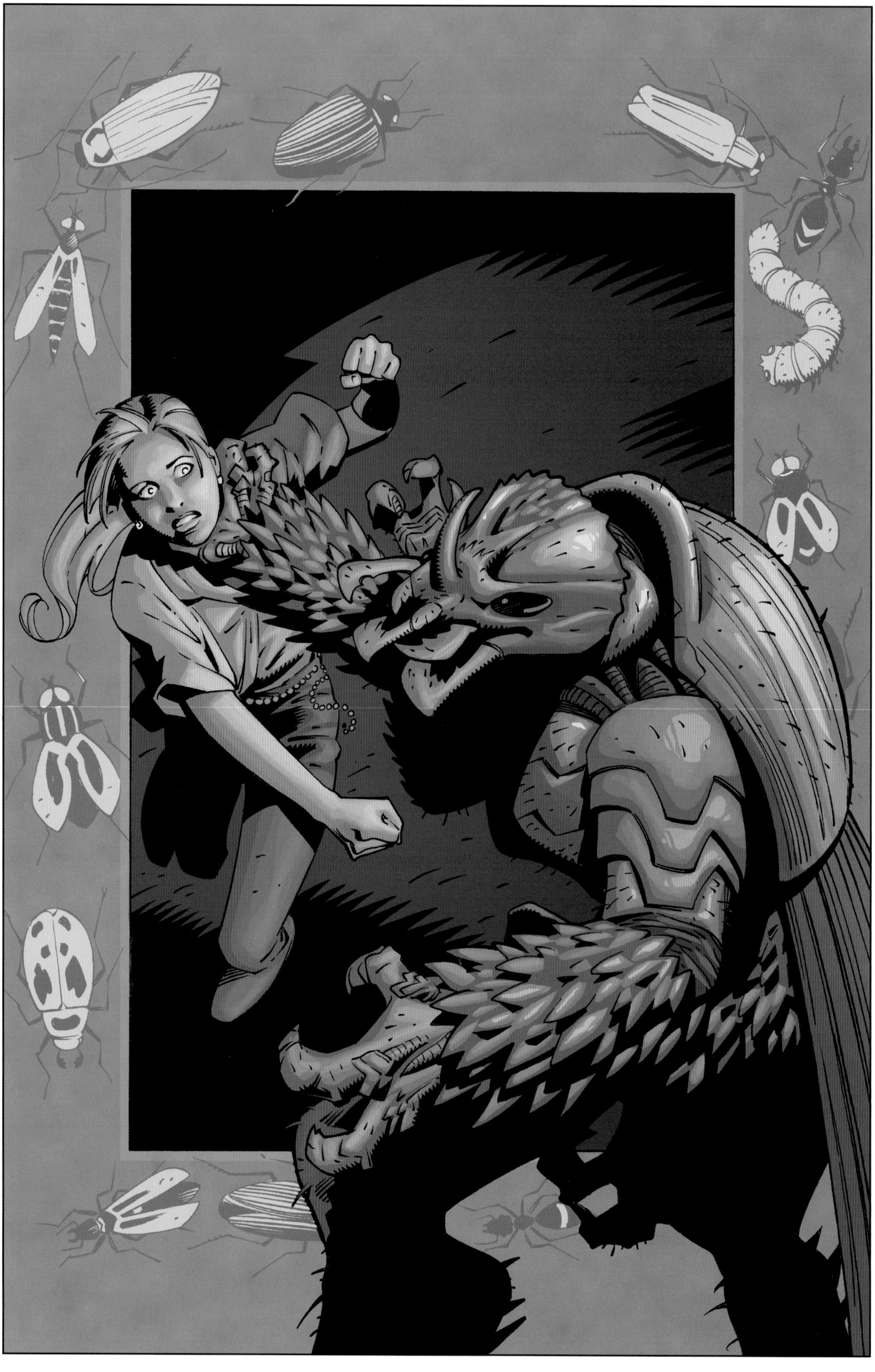

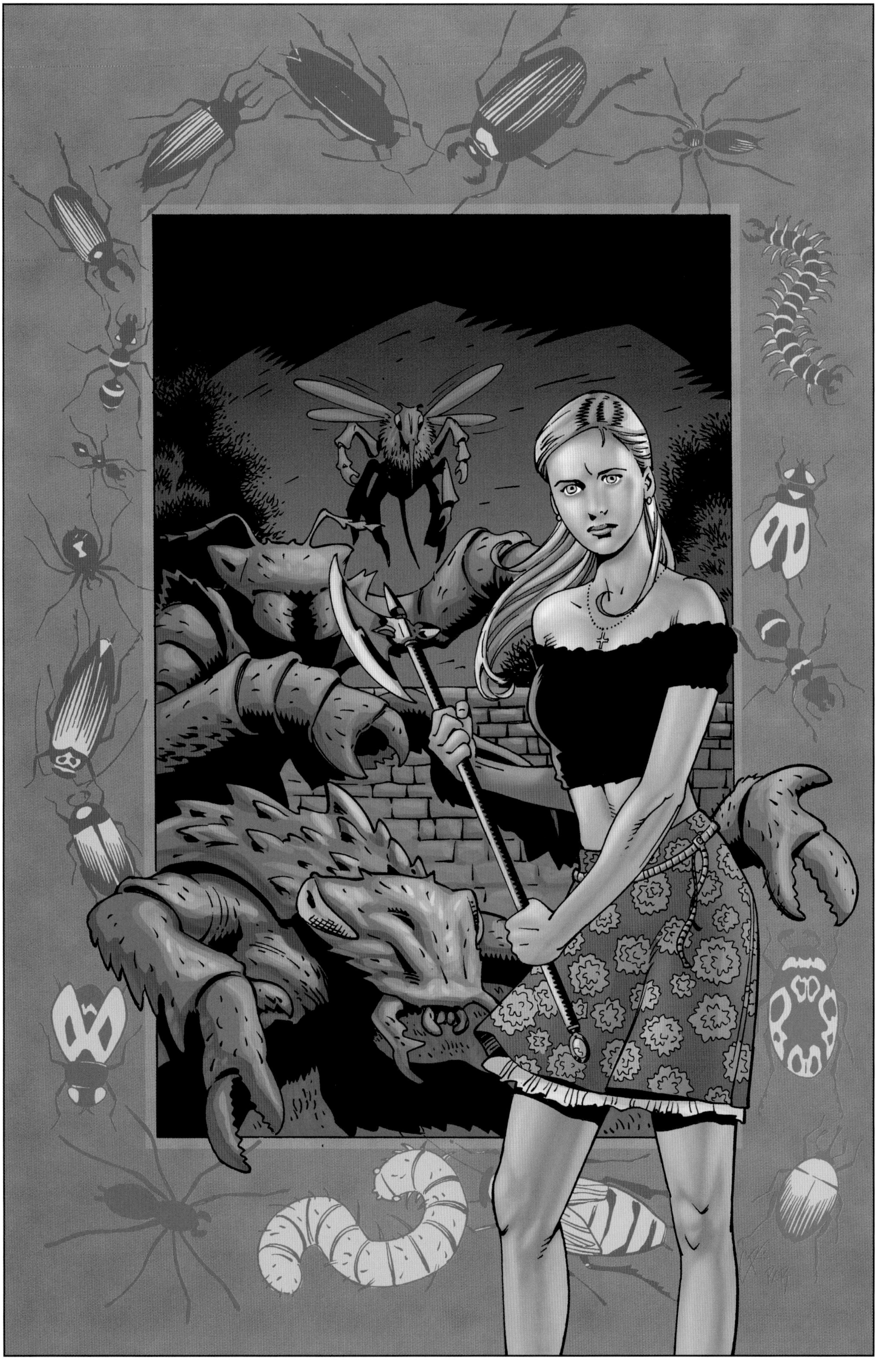

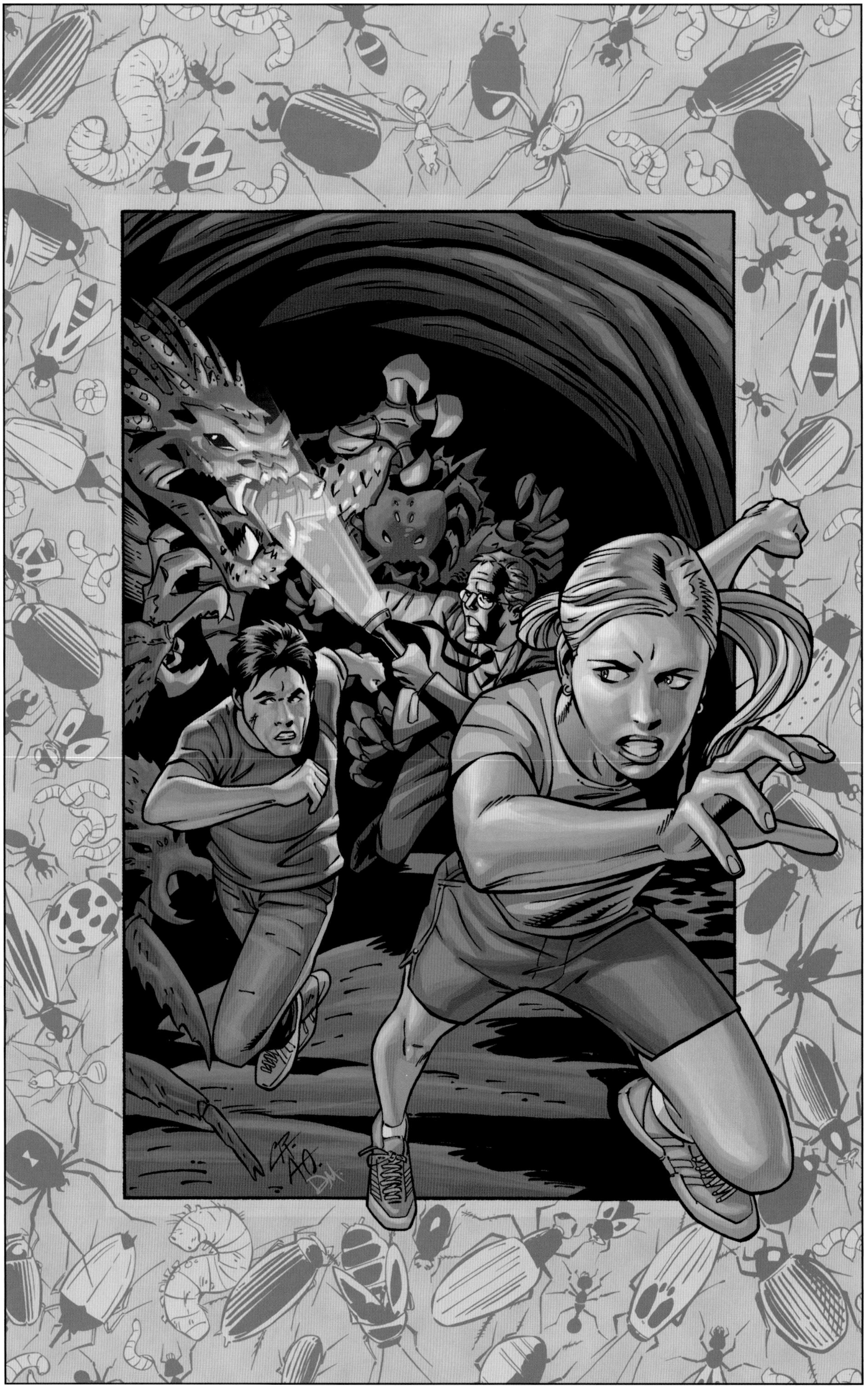

WHEN THE MONTHLY covers fell behind schedule, Andy Owens saved the day, inking the final cover to *Buffy* #34. By then, Andy was working on Joss's *Fray*. John Totleben returned to bring a scary edge to our *Oz* miniseries.

 Above: Pencils by Cliff Richards, inks by Owens, colors by Dave McCaig. Cover, *BTVS* #34, June 2001. Opposite and following two pages: Pencils and inks by Totleben, colors by Dave Stewart. Covers, *BTVS: Oz* #1–3, July–September 2001.

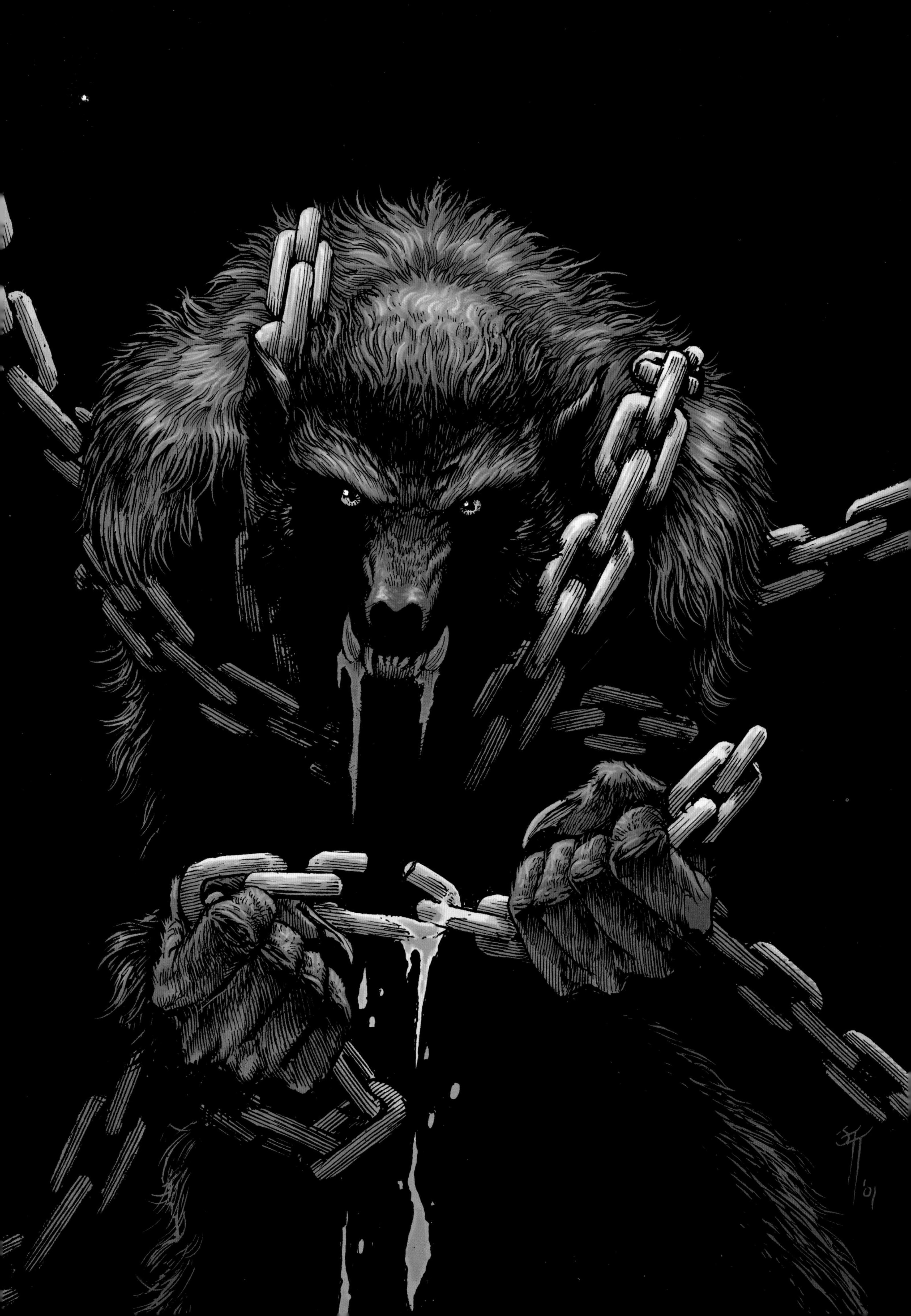

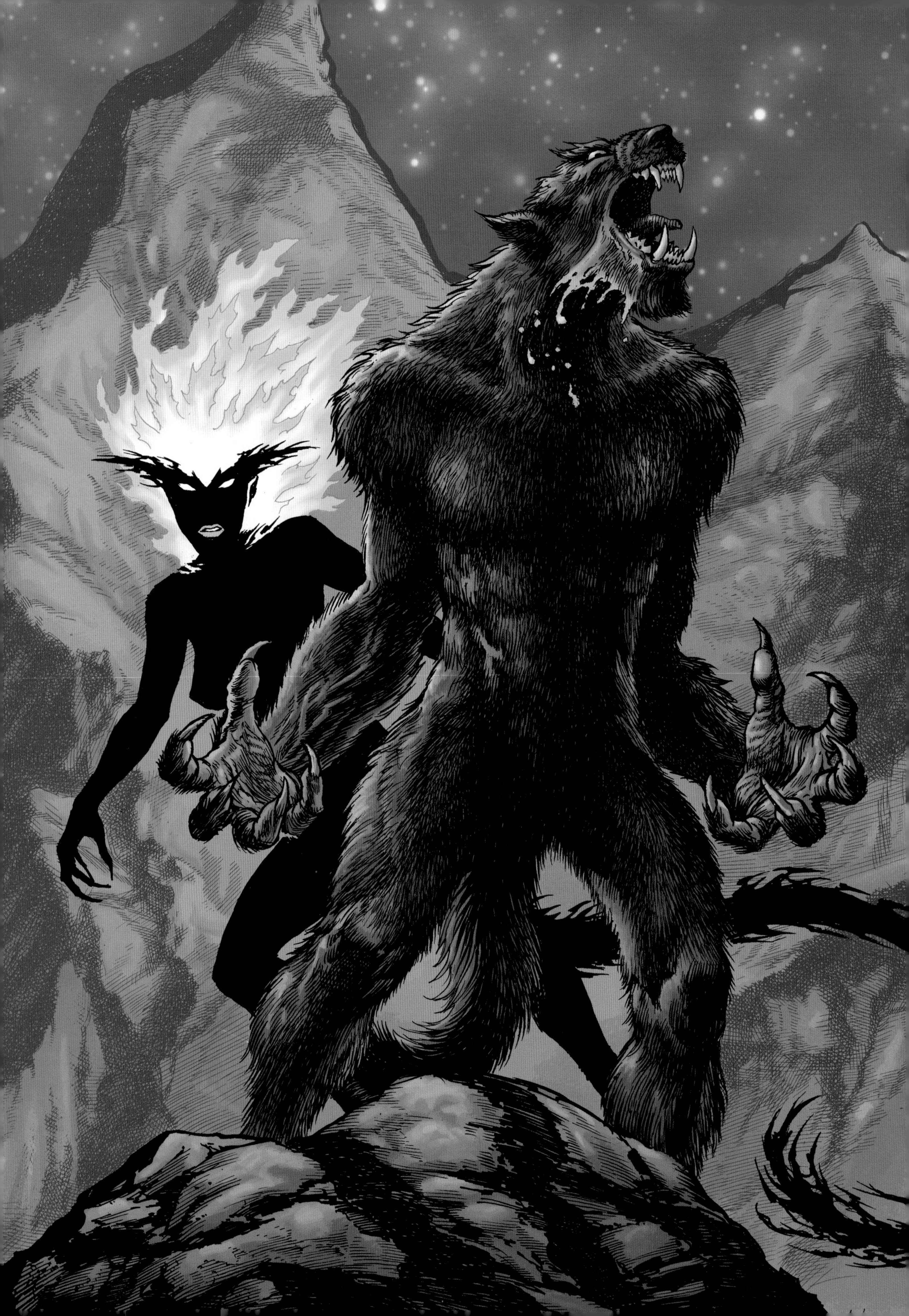

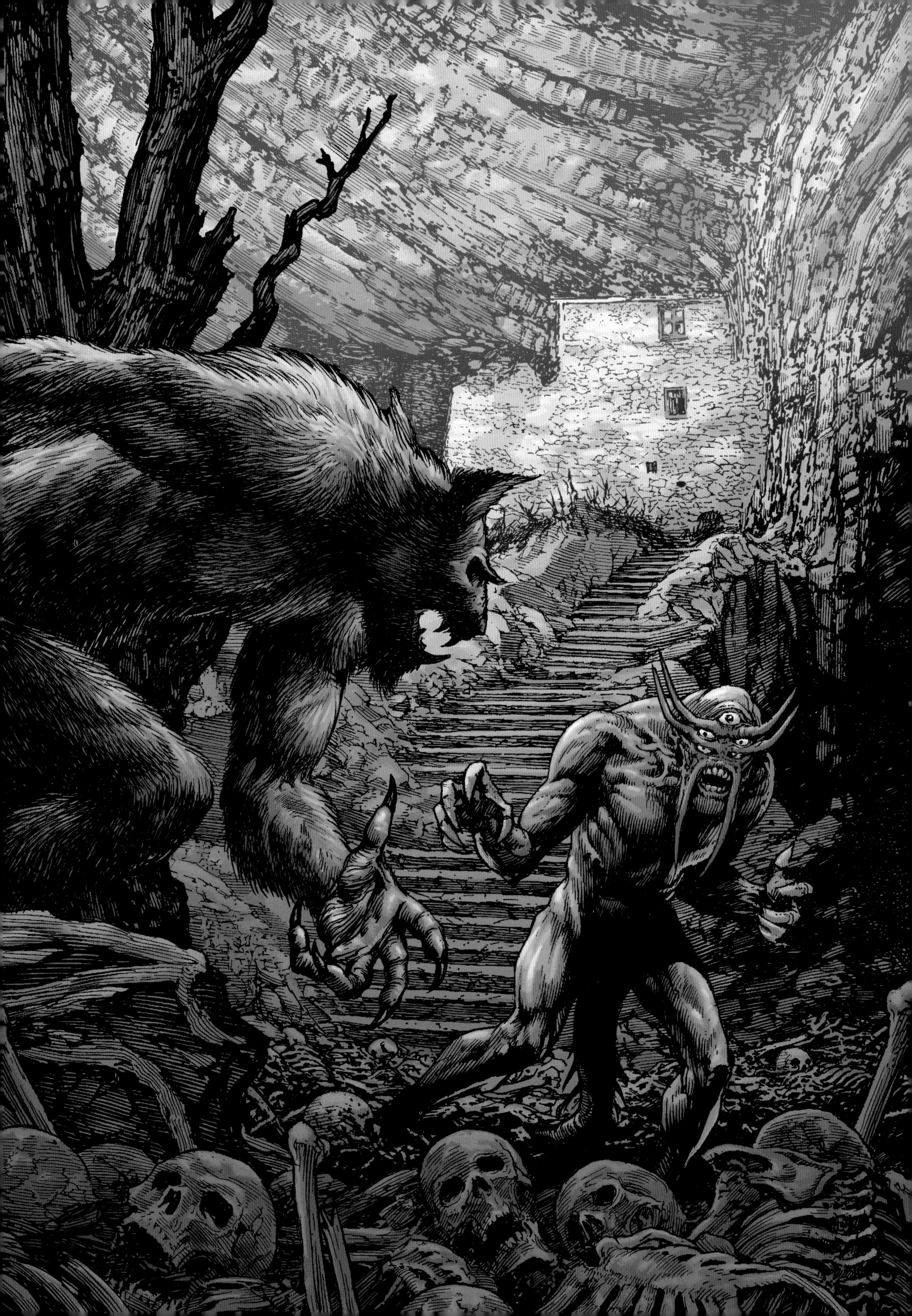

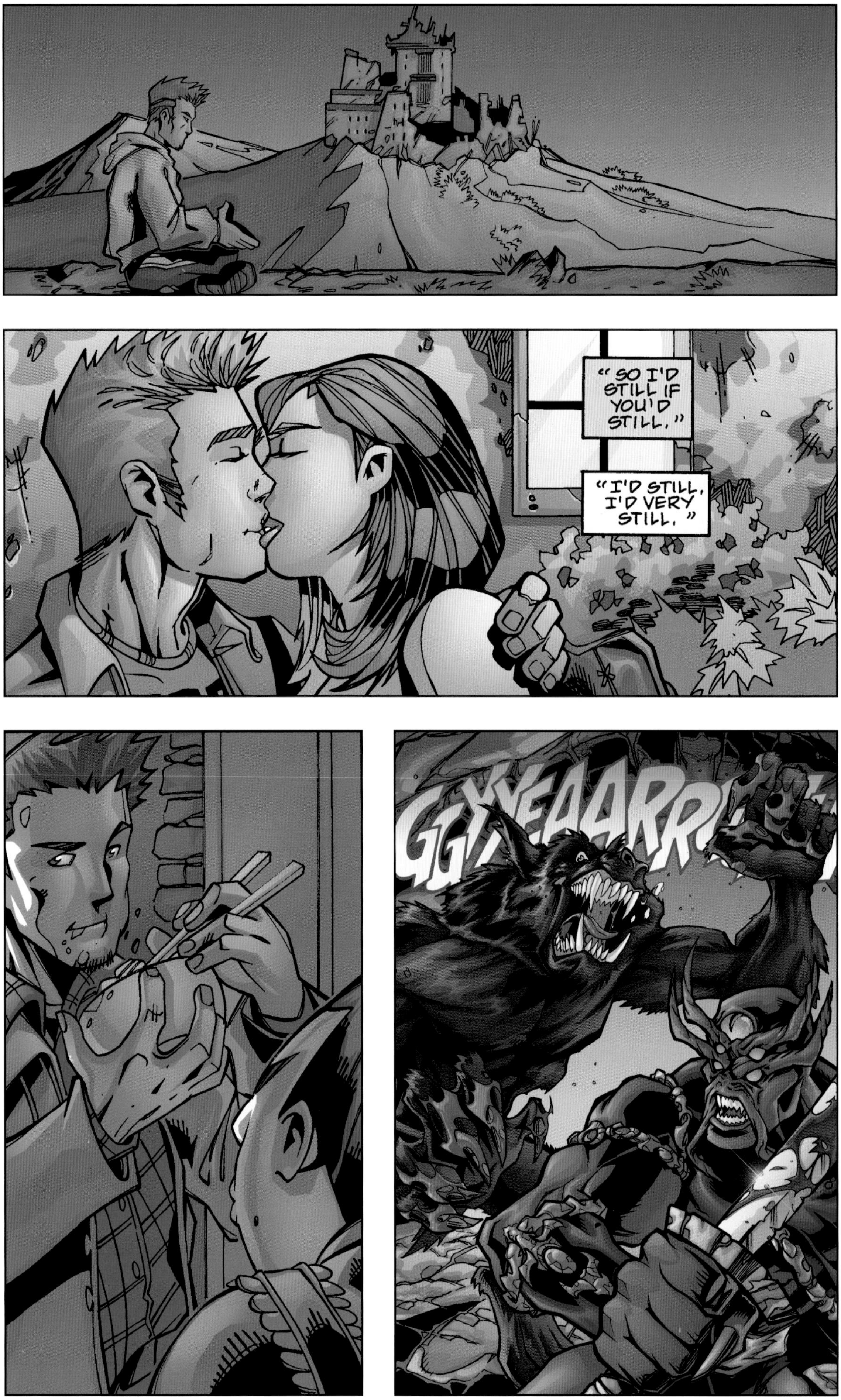
"SO I'D STILL IF YOU'D STILL."
"I'D STILL, I'D VERY STILL."

LOGAN LUBERA CAME ON to draw interiors for *Oz*, which was an odd match to John Totleben's creepy covers. Lubera fell behind schedule, and Herb Apon stepped in to draw the last half of *Oz* #3. The two styles sync up a lot better than Lubera's and Totleben's, at least. Time was so pressing that Apon's pages were colored over the pencils. The name listed as colorist, Helen Bach, was a pseudonym used by Dark Horse staffers on rush jobs.

 Script by Chris Golden, pencils by Lubera and Valentine de Landro, inks by Craig Yeung, color by Halo and Percy Melbye, letters by Vickie Williams. Bottom right: Pencils by Apon, colors by Helen Bach. Interiors, *BTVS: Oz* #1–3, July–September 2001.

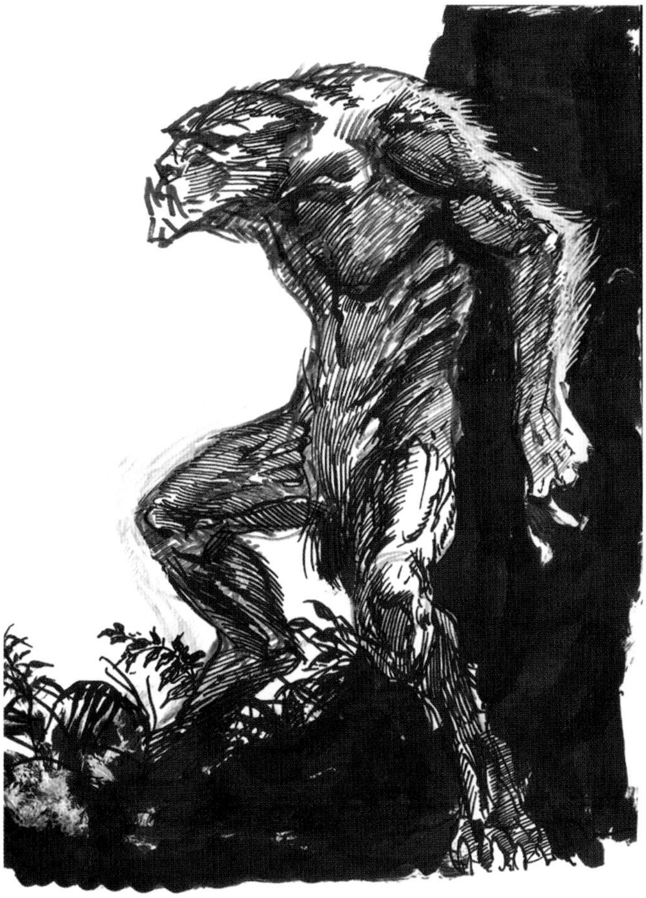

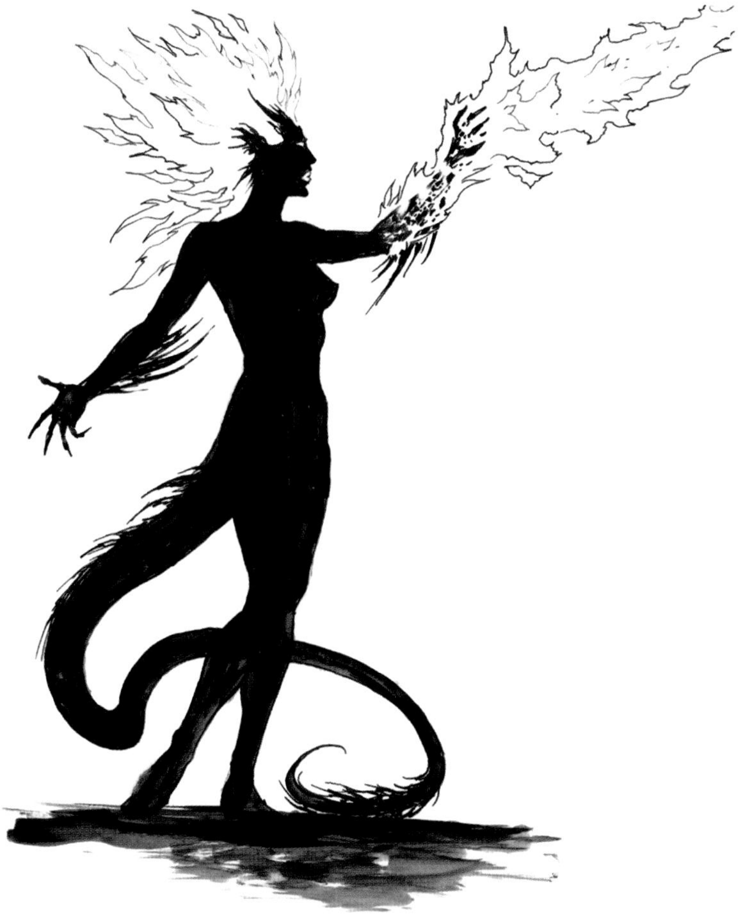

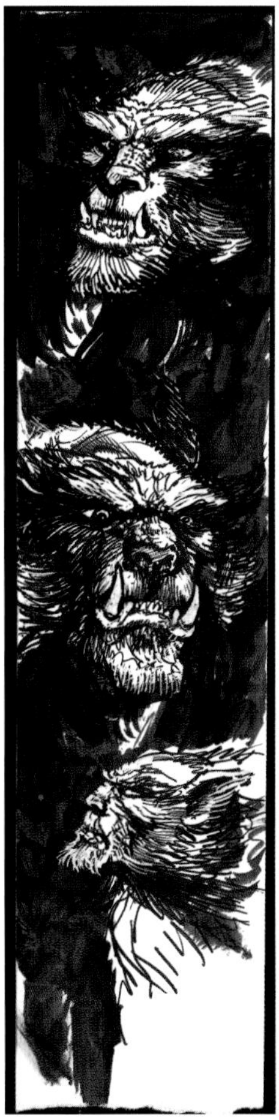

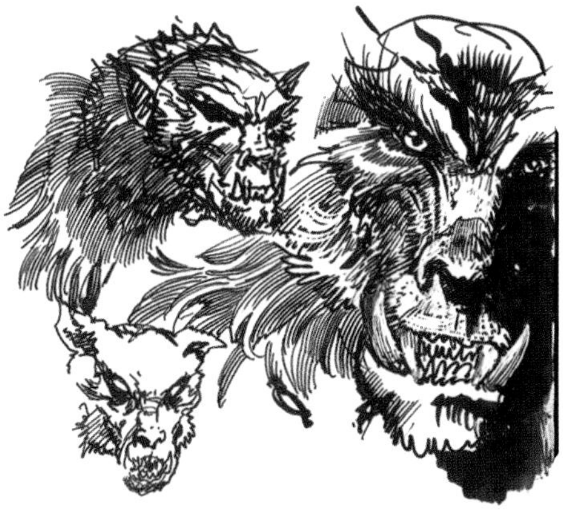

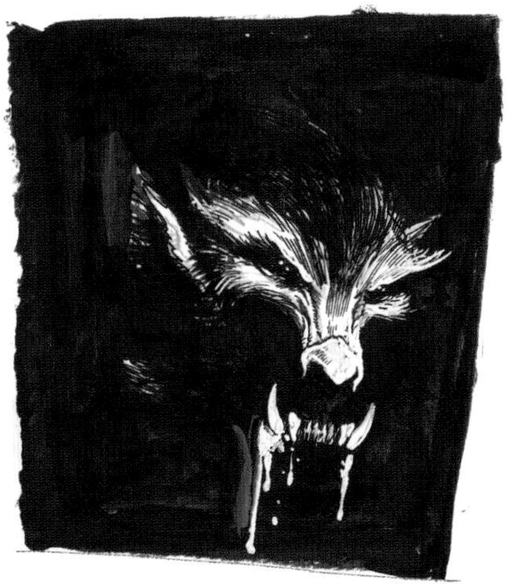

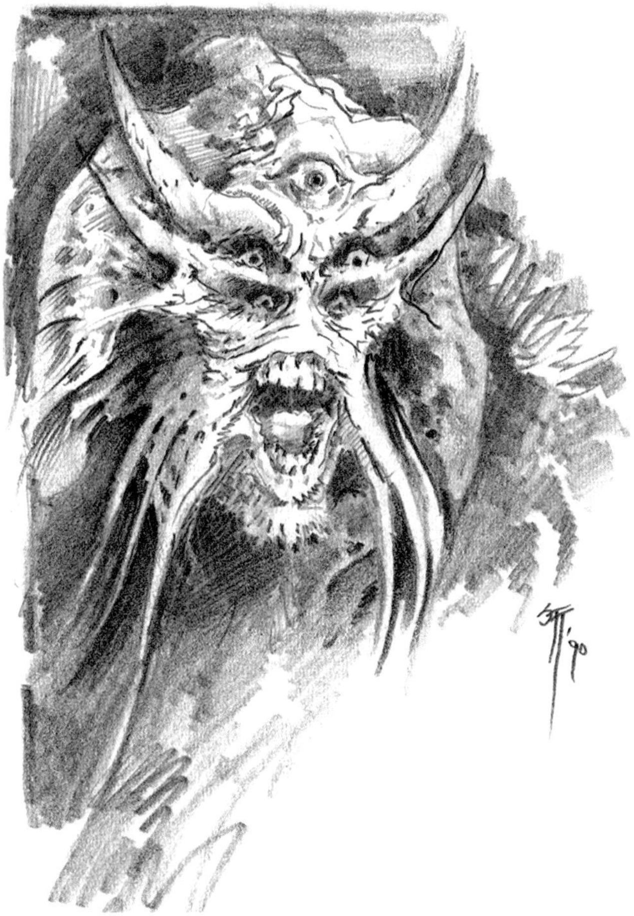

KNOWING THAT BUDGET had limited Oz's werewolf look on the show, I had John Totleben create a look specifically for Dark Horse's version of the character. He also provided other designs, including the design of the villain—which you'll notice was dated 1990. It was something Totleben had lying around that suited our needs. I was happy to get any monsters from his wild imagination.

Sketches and character designs by Totleben, 1990 and 2001.

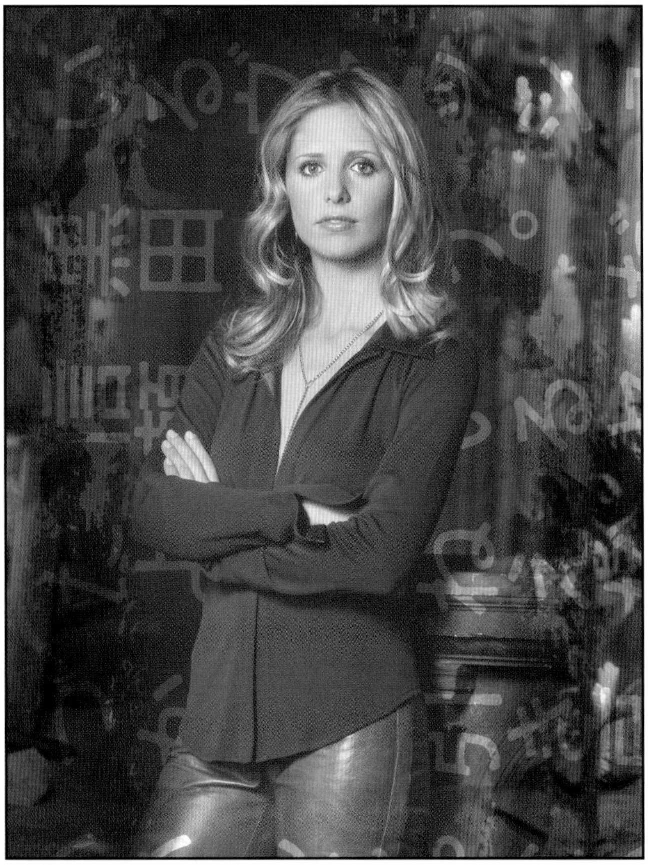

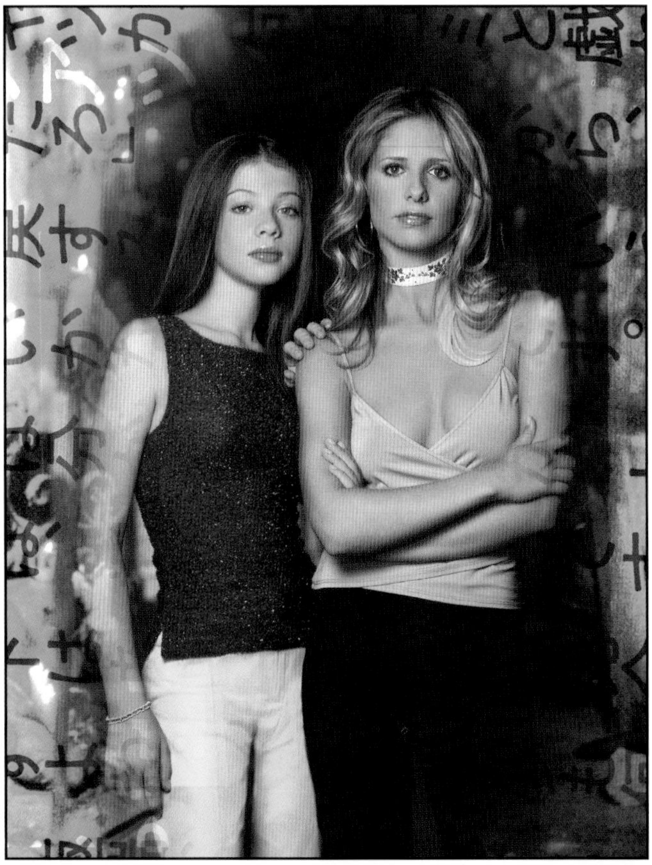

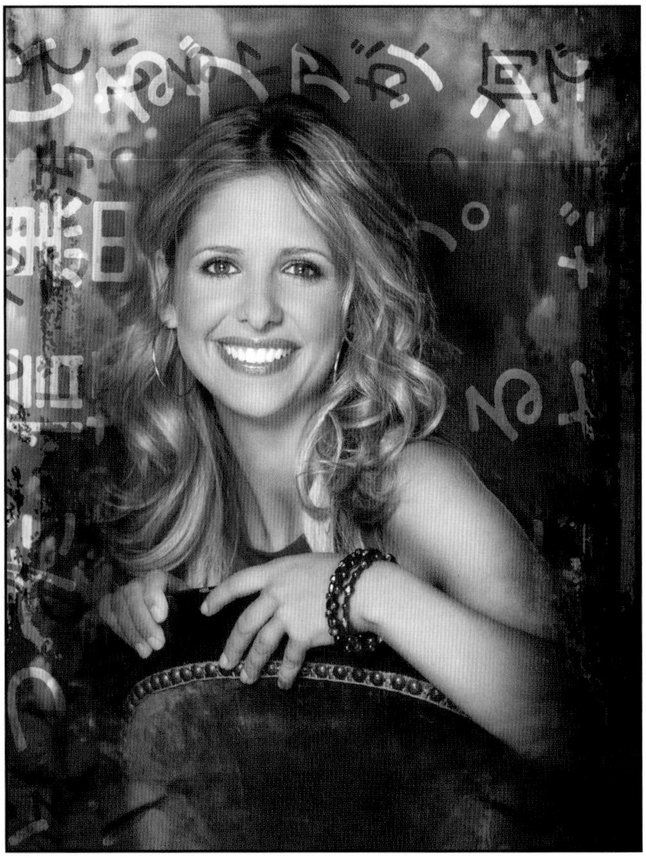

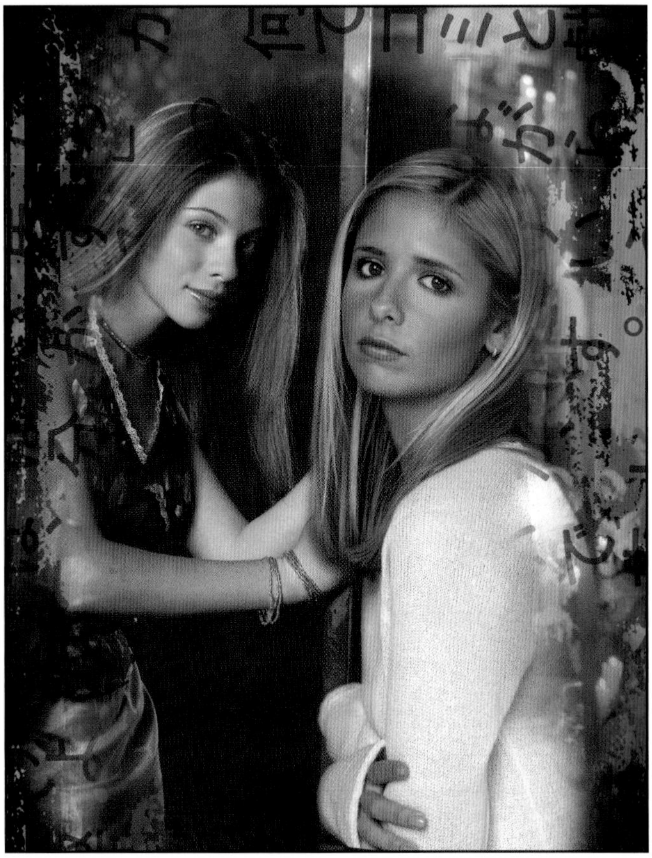

WITH *FALSE MEMORIES*, we stepped into Season Five of the television series, which meant introducing Dawn to comics. To do so, we did a story that delved into the idea of the characters' memories of Dawn having been there during past adventures. I hear that this was fertile territory for fan fiction. The Chinese characters on the cover reflect a powerful Chinese vampire, who'd been a Slayer. Buffy and friends recalled such key events as Dawn pulling Buffy out of the water after the Master had left her for dead clear back in Season One. Dave McCaig developed a computer-rendered style, fairly cutting edge at the time, to approximate watercolors for the backgrounds of the covers, which he also used for the "false memory" sections of the interior pages. During *False Memories*, Cliff Richards's longtime inker Joe Pimentel moved on, and Will Conrad took over. Conrad would later pencil the hugely successful *Serenity* comics series, written by Joss Whedon and Brett Matthews.

Montages by Keith Wood. Covers, *BTVS* #35–38, July, August, September, and November 2001. Following three pages: Pencils by Richards, inks by Joe Pimentel, colors by McCaig. Covers, *BTVS* #35–37, July–September 2001. Fourth page following: Pencils by Richards, inks by Owens, colors by McCaig. Cover, *BTVS* #38, November 2001.

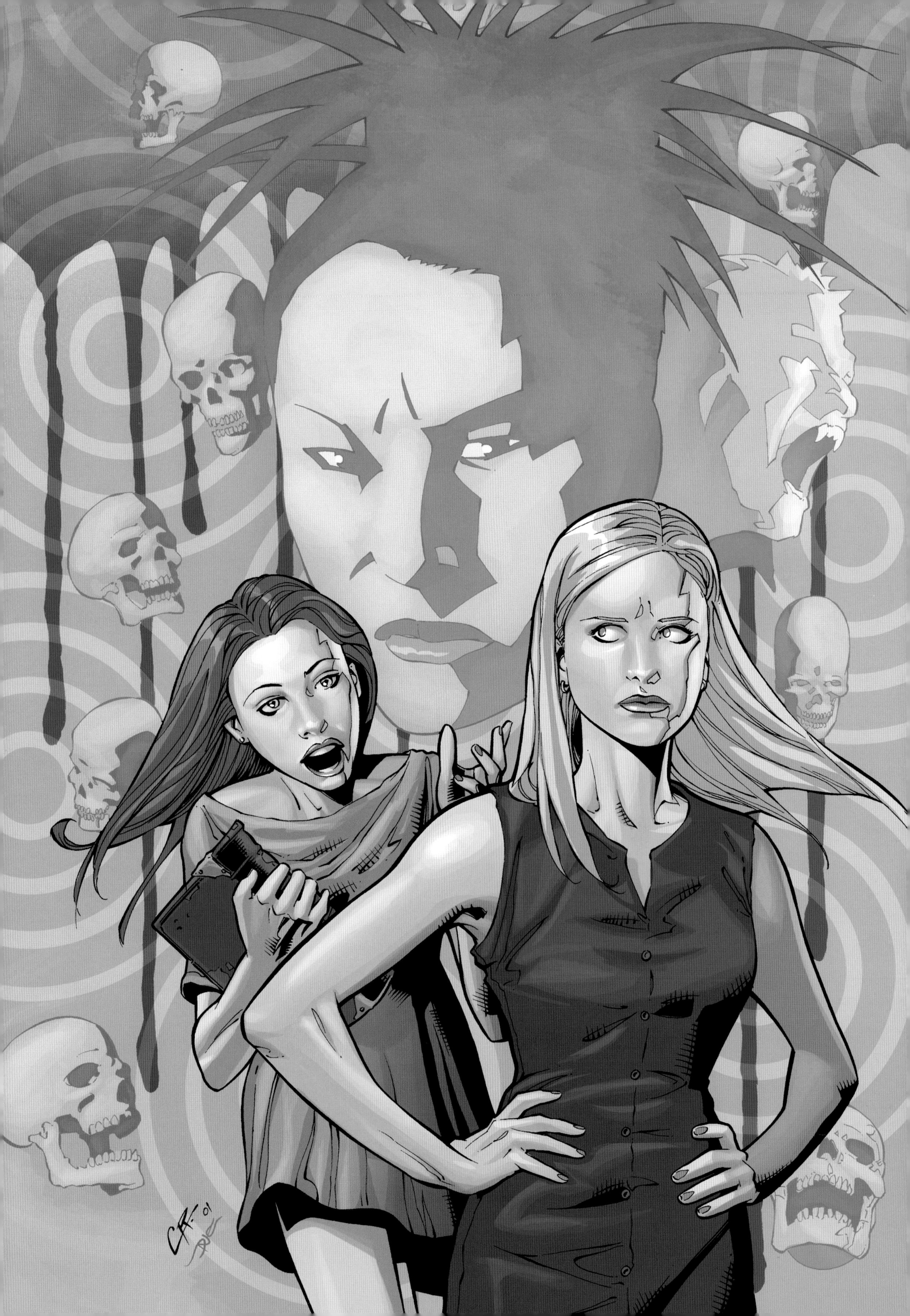

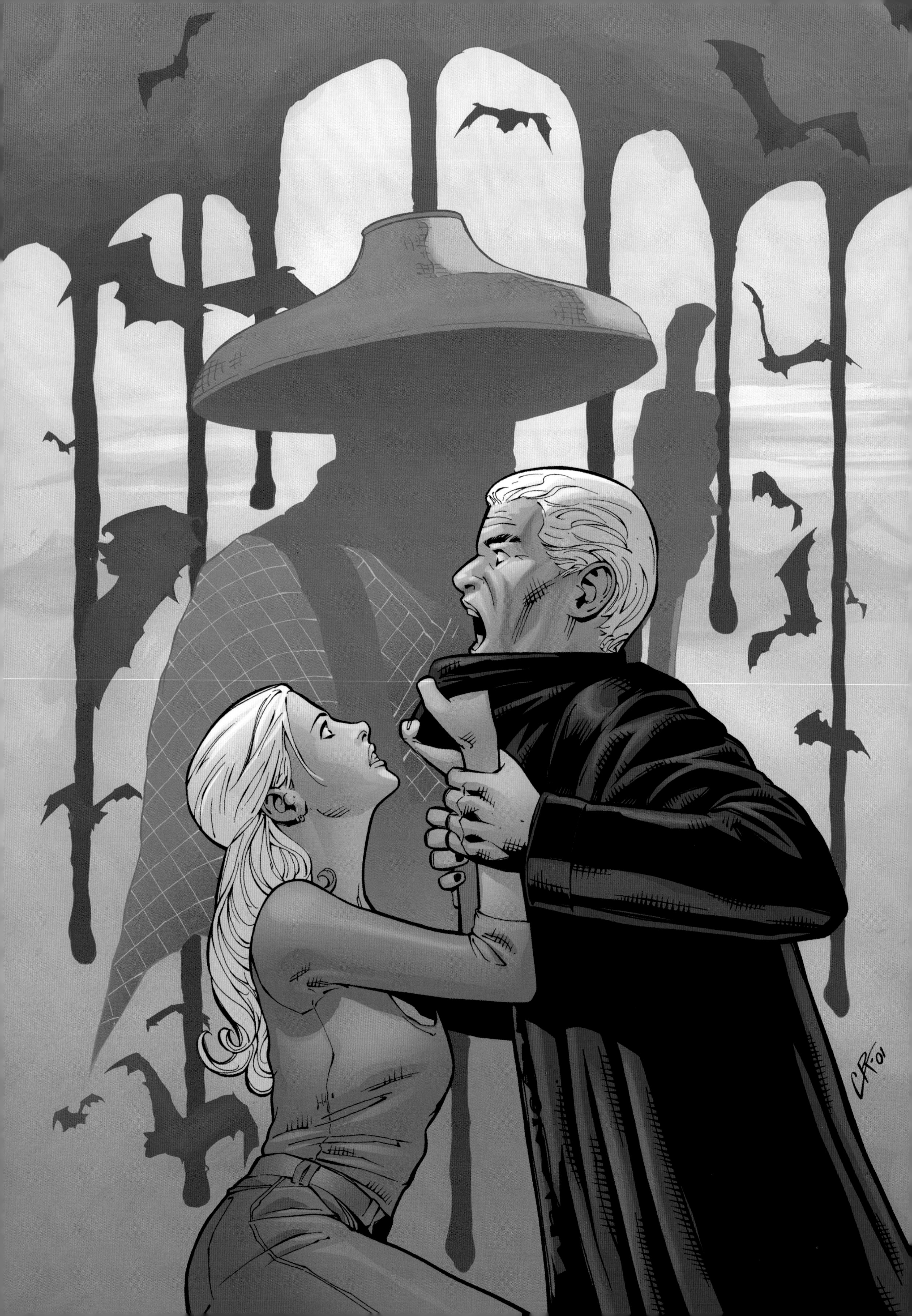
CR'01

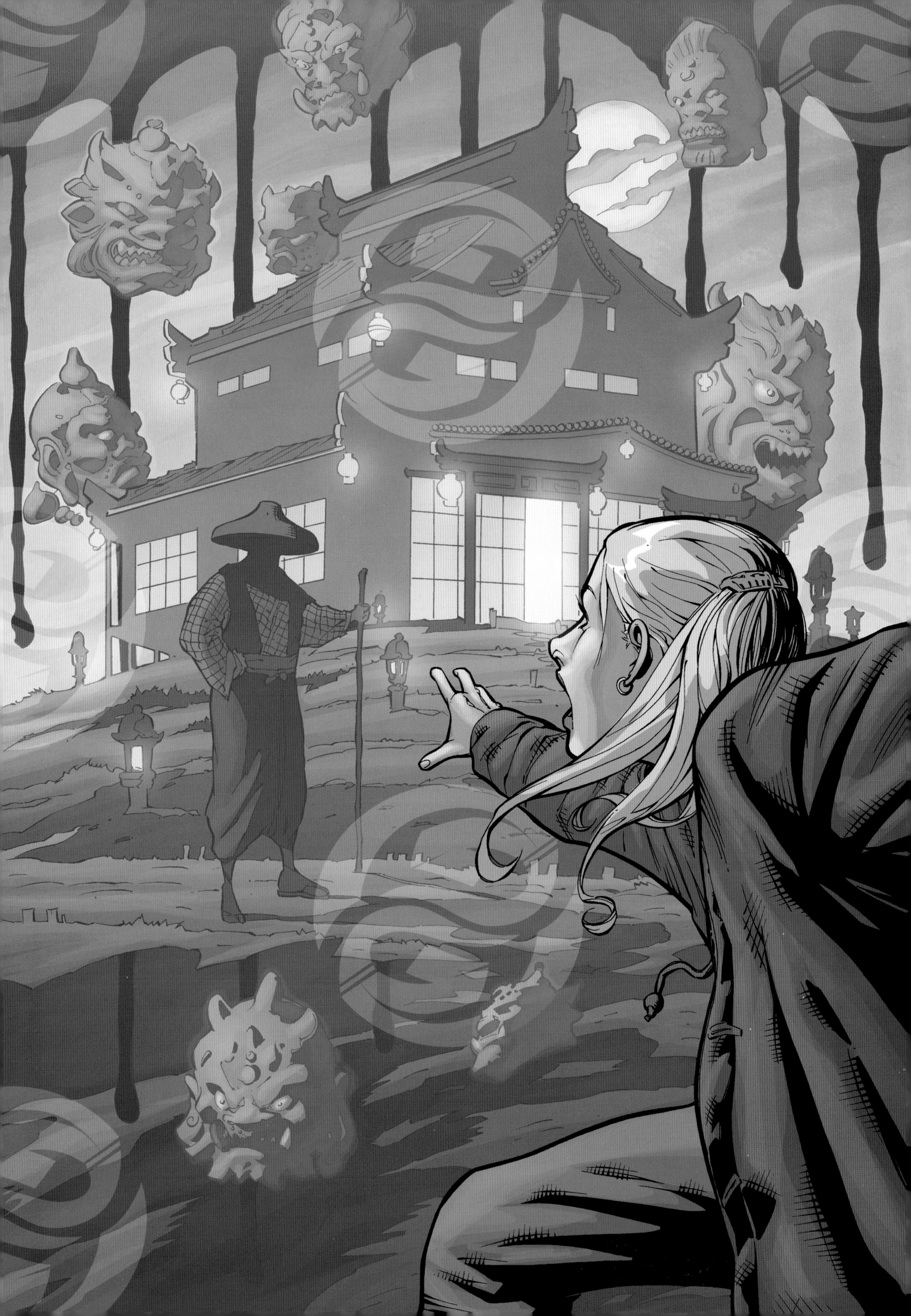

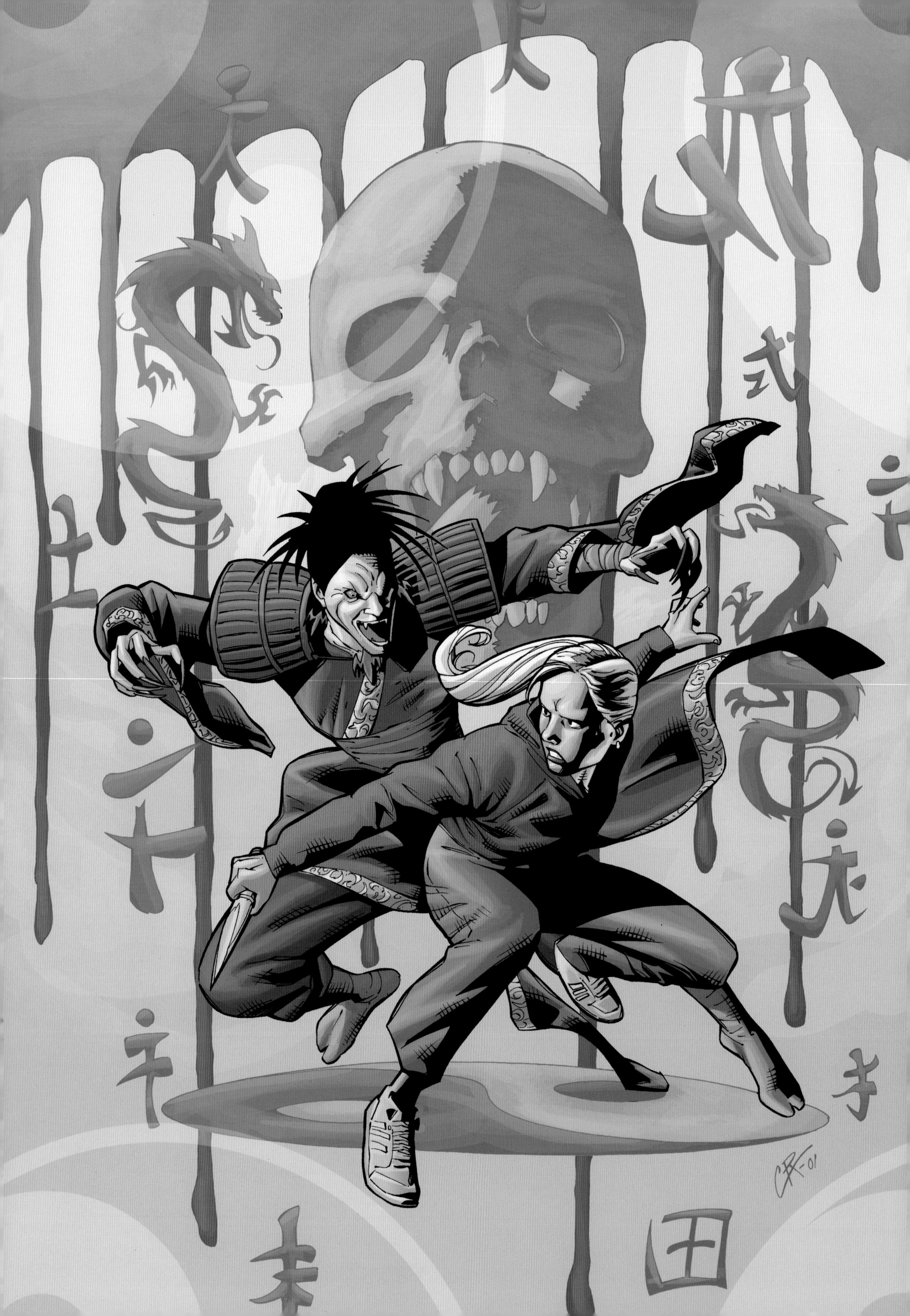

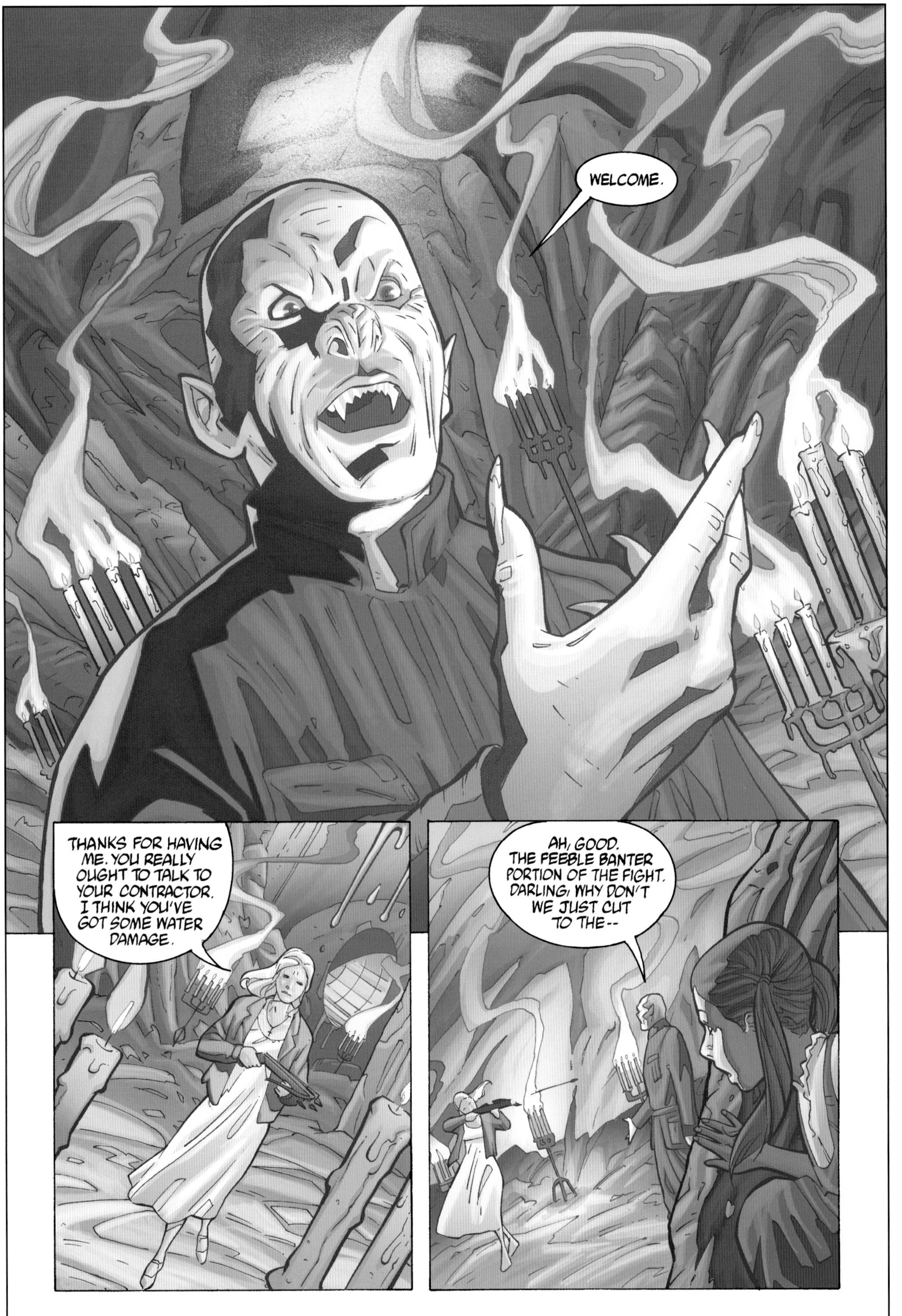
WELCOME.
THANKS FOR HAVING ME. YOU REALLY OUGHT TO TALK TO YOUR CONTRACTOR. I THINK YOU'VE GOT SOME WATER DAMAGE.
AH, GOOD. THE FEEBLE BANTER PORTION OF THE FIGHT. DARLING, WHY DON'T WE JUST CUT TO THE--

Above and following two pages: Script by Tom Fassbender and Jim Pascoe, pencils by Cliff Richards, inks by Joe Pimentel and Will Conrad, colors by Dave McCaig, letters by Clem Robins. Interiors, *BTVS* #35, July 2001.

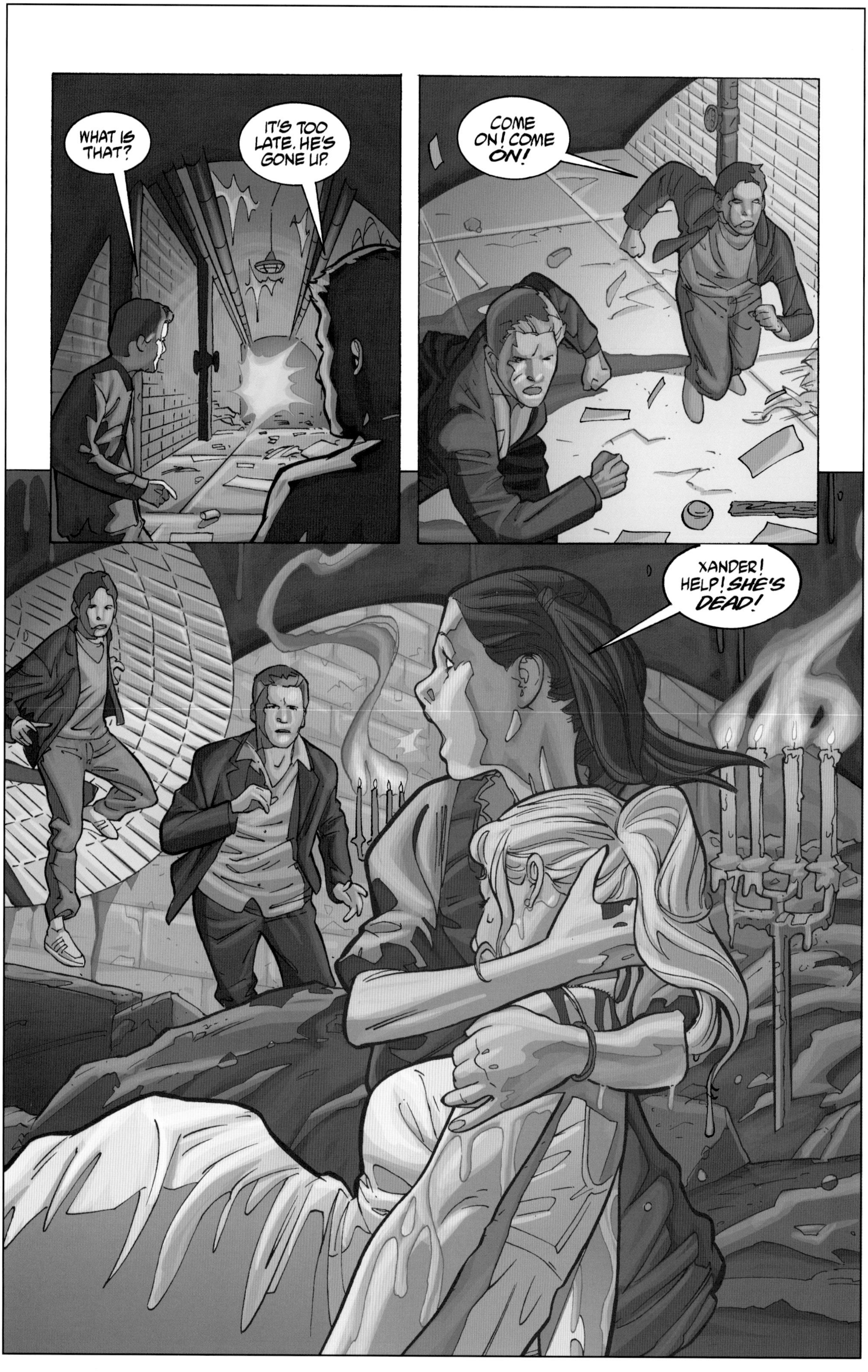
WHAT IS THAT?
IT'S TOO LATE. HE'S GONE UP.
COME ON! COME ON!
XANDER! HELP! SHE'S DEAD!

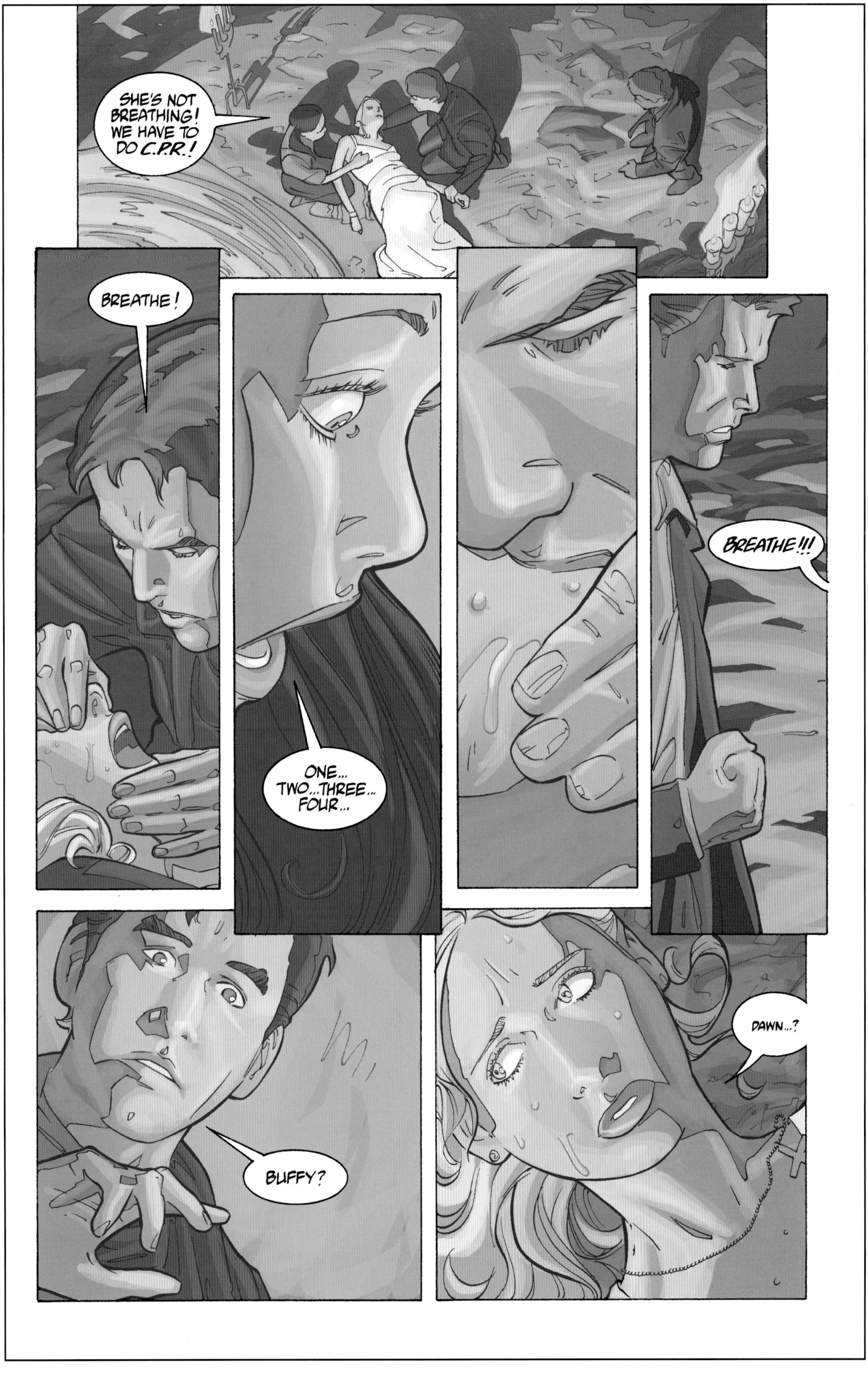
SHE'S NOT BREATHING! WE HAVE TO DO C.P.R.!
BREATHE!
ONE... TWO...THREE... FOUR...
BREATHE!!!
BUFFY?
DAWN...?

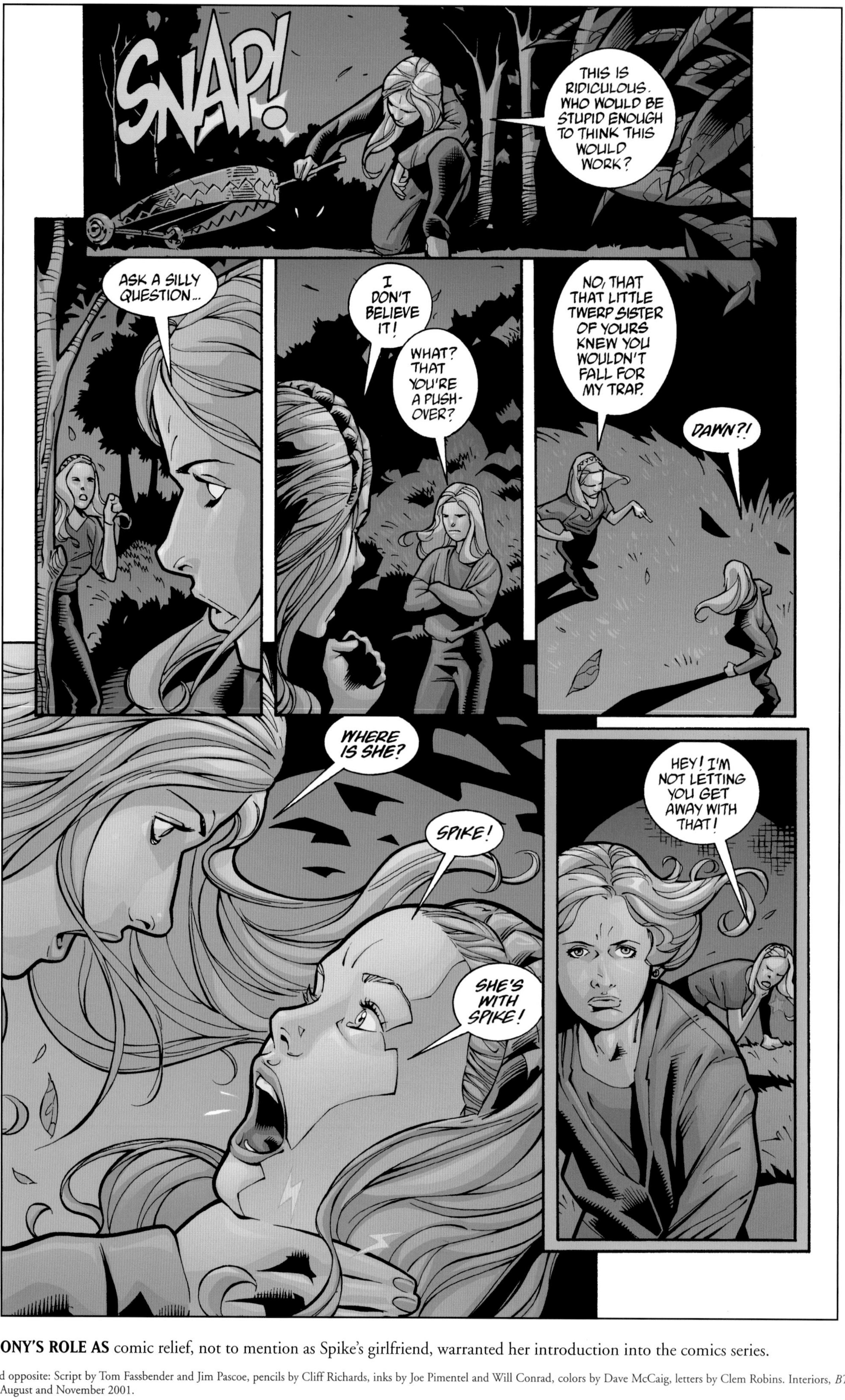
SNAP!
THIS IS RIDICULOUS. WHO WOULD BE STUPID ENOUGH TO THINK THIS WOULD WORK?
ASK A SILLY QUESTION...
I DON'T BELIEVE IT!
WHAT? THAT YOU'RE A PUSH-OVER?
NO, THAT THAT LITTLE TWERP SISTER OF YOURS KNEW YOU WOULDN'T FALL FOR MY TRAP.
DAWN?!
WHERE IS SHE?
SPIKE!
SHE'S WITH SPIKE!
HEY! I'M NOT LETTING YOU GET AWAY WITH THAT!

HARMONY'S ROLE AS comic relief, not to mention as Spike's girlfriend, warranted her introduction into the comics series.

 Above and opposite: Script by Tom Fassbender and Jim Pascoe, pencils by Cliff Richards, inks by Joe Pimentel and Will Conrad, colors by Dave McCaig, letters by Clem Robins. Interiors, *BTVS* #36 and #38, August and November 2001.

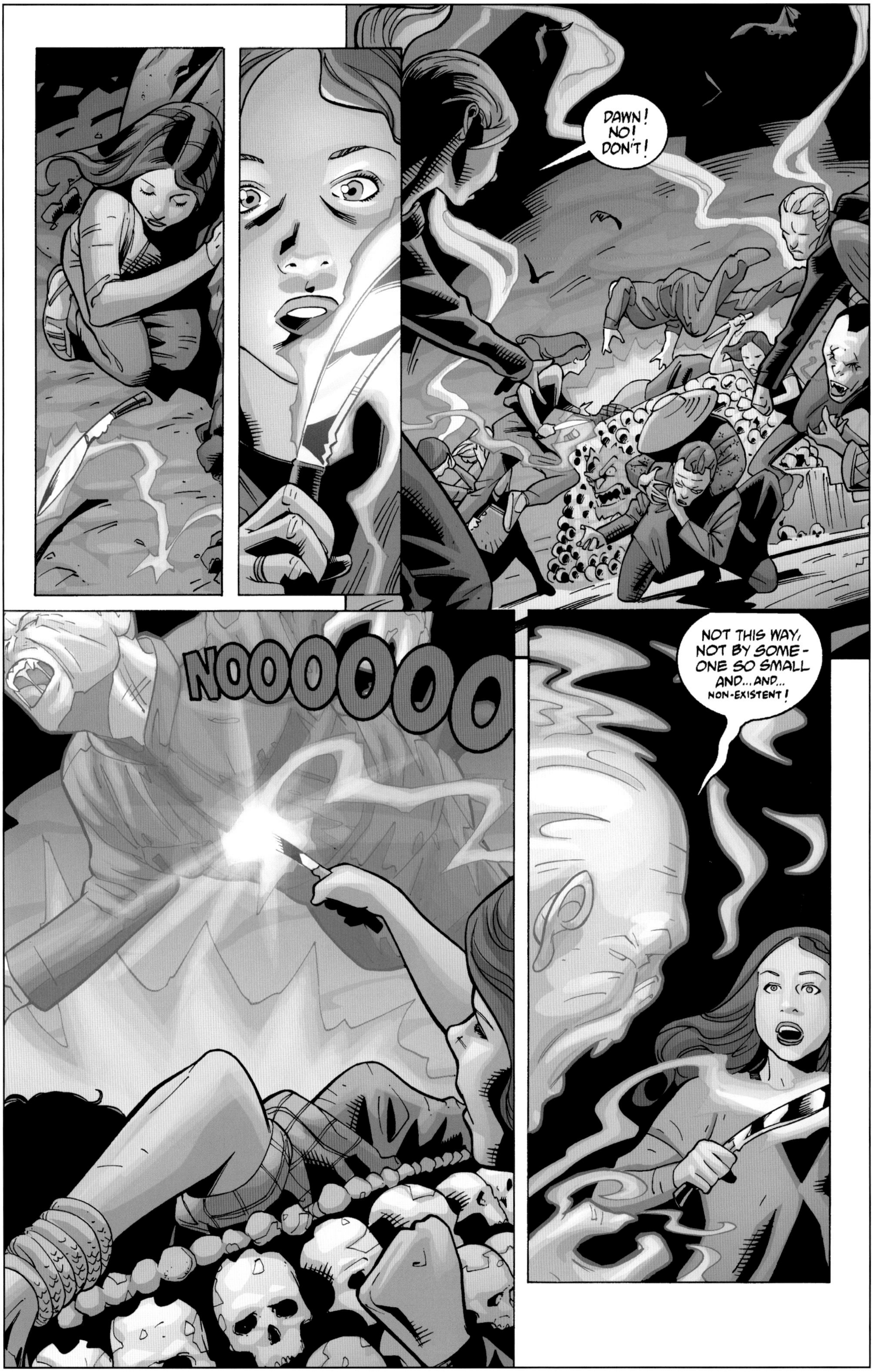
DAWN! NO! DON'T!
NOOOOOOO
NOT THIS WAY, NOT BY SOME-ONE SO SMALL AND... AND... NON-EXISTENT!

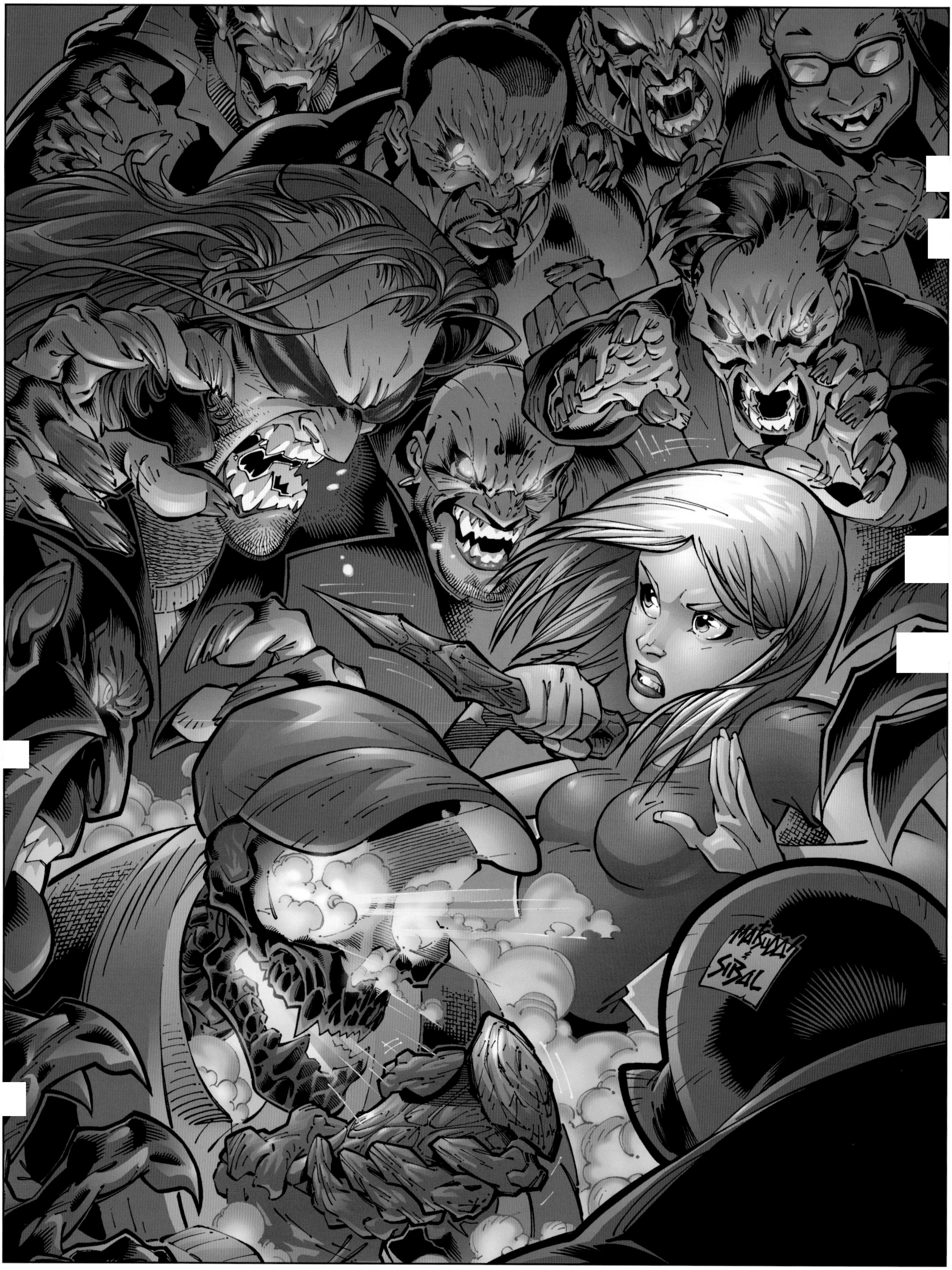
MATSUDA & SIBAL

TRYING TO GET AHEAD of scheduling snafus had led me to commission an inventory cover from Jeff Matsuda—a cover we could use if we got into a tight spot. This cover sat in a drawer for over a year before I realized that we'd licked our scheduling problems, and decided to slot the cover in. I gave the drawing to Tom Fassbender and Jim Pascoe, who'd been writing the monthly series, and asked them to write a story around it. They included a panel where a vampire stakes himself in despair.

 Pencils by Matsuda, inks by Jon Sibal, colors by Guy Major. Cover, *BTVS* #39, November 2001.

JUST AS DOUG PETRIE had set *Ring of Fire* a couple of seasons into the past, Jane Espenson chose to set her first miniseries, *Haunted*, immediately after Season Three, with Faith manipulated by the ghost of the Mayor. Because of the drastic changes Faith went though on the show, it was hard for us to write her into the comic without making the story irrelevant by the time it came out. This was Faith's only appearance in the comics until her story in Season Eight.

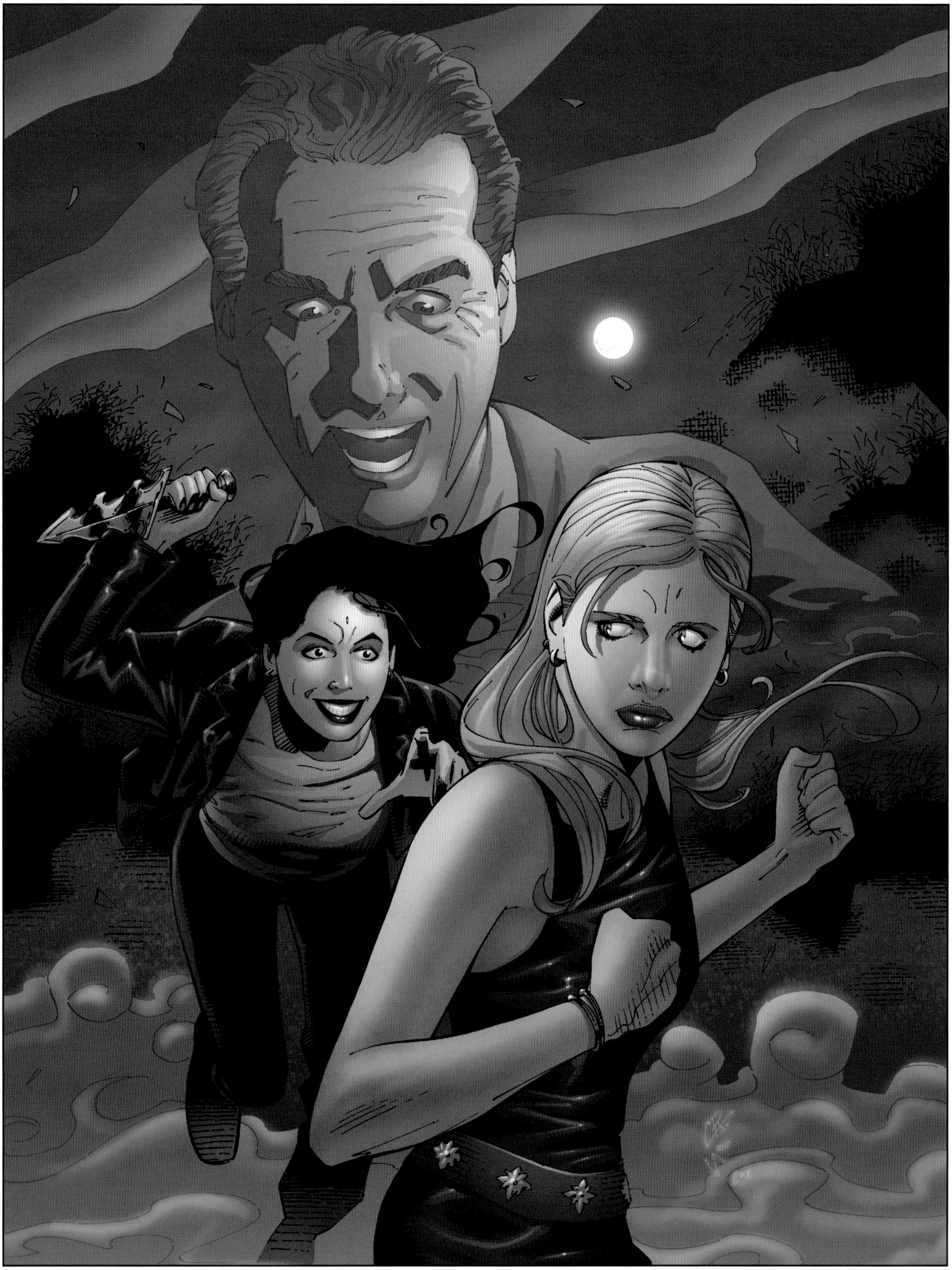

Above and following two pages: Pencils by Cliff Richards, inks by Julio Ferreira, colors by Jeromy Cox. Covers, *BTVS: Haunted* #1–3, December 2001–February 2002.

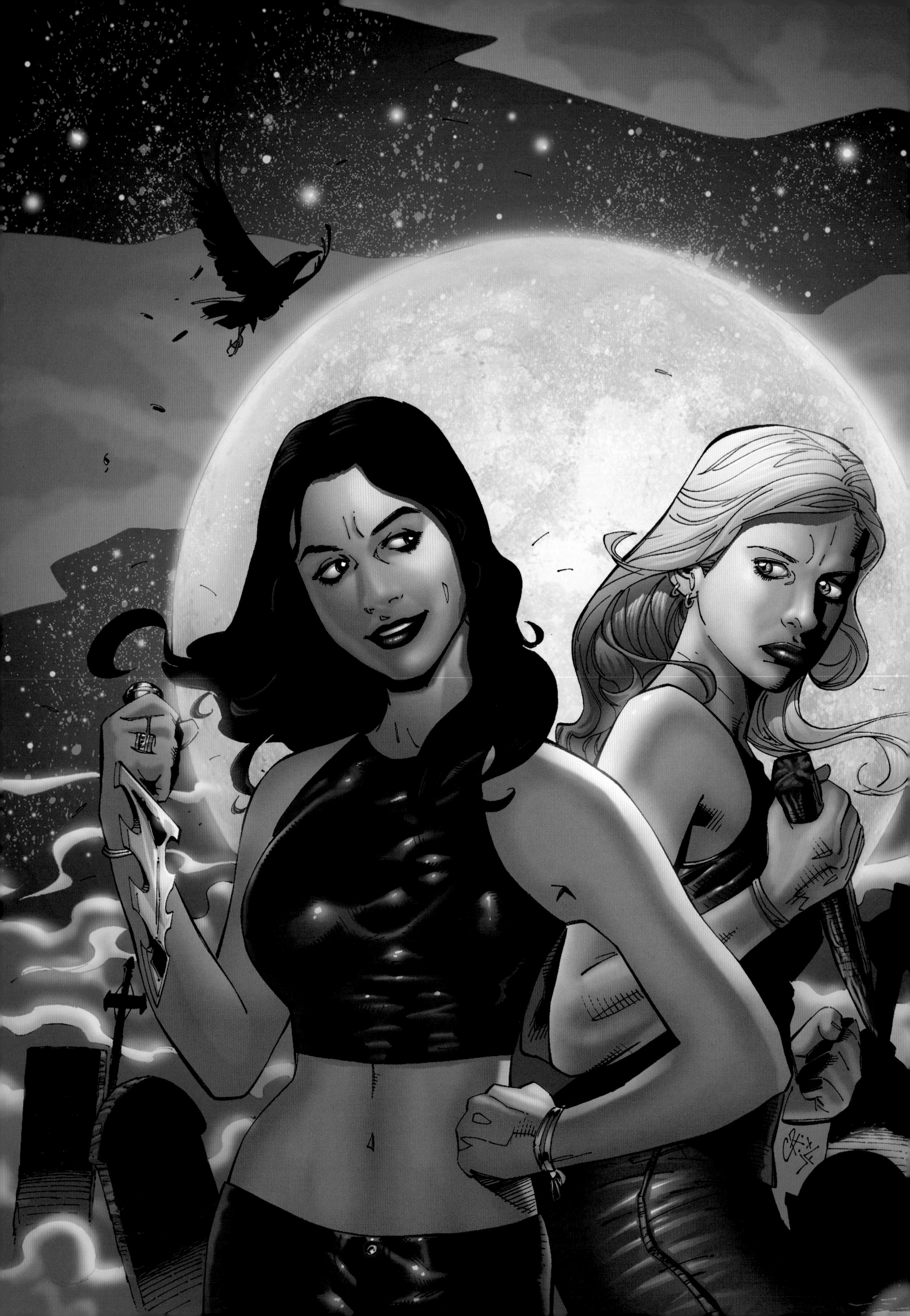

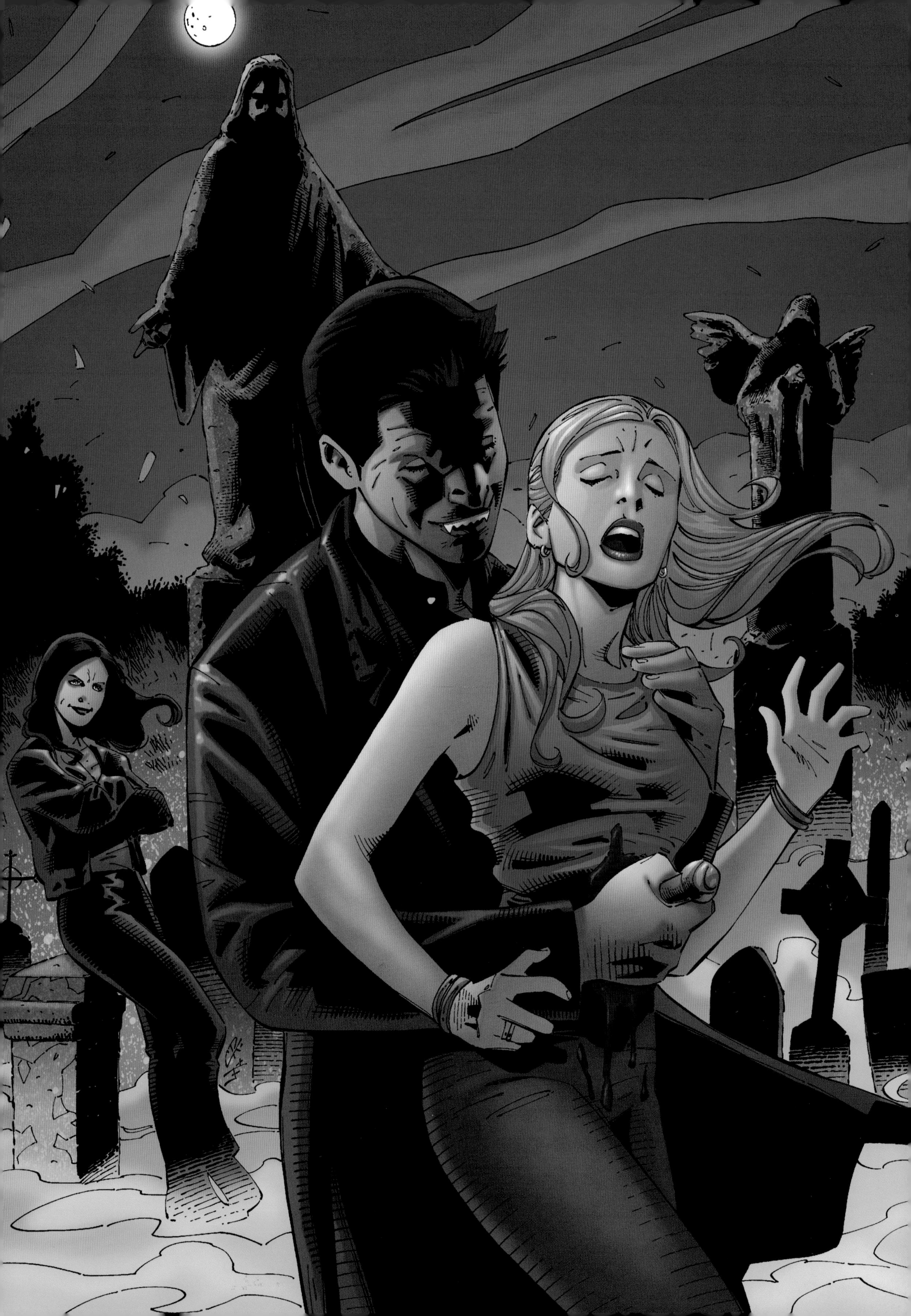

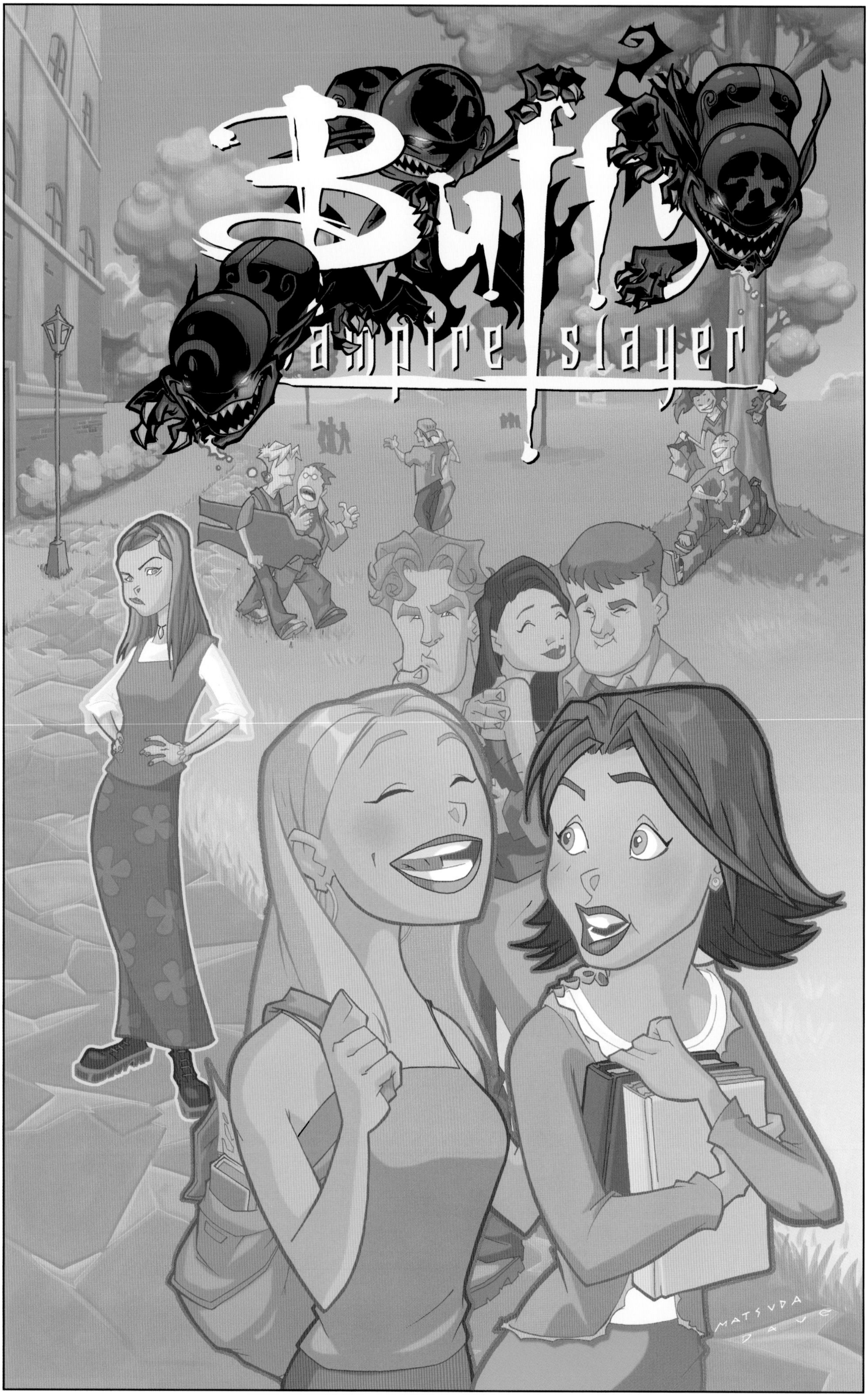
Buffy
the vampire slayer
MATSUDA
DAVE

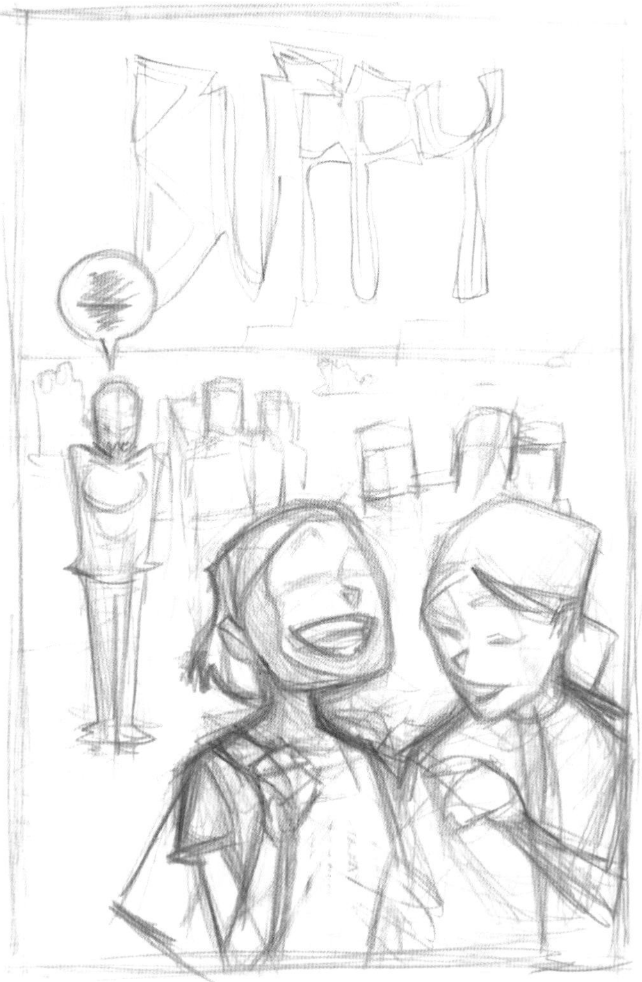

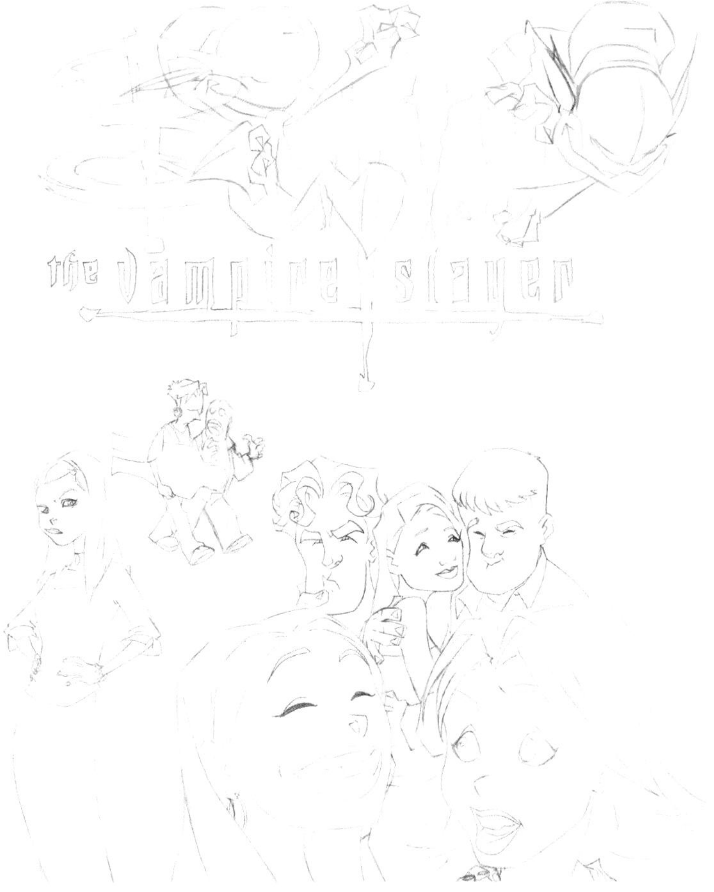
the vampire slayer

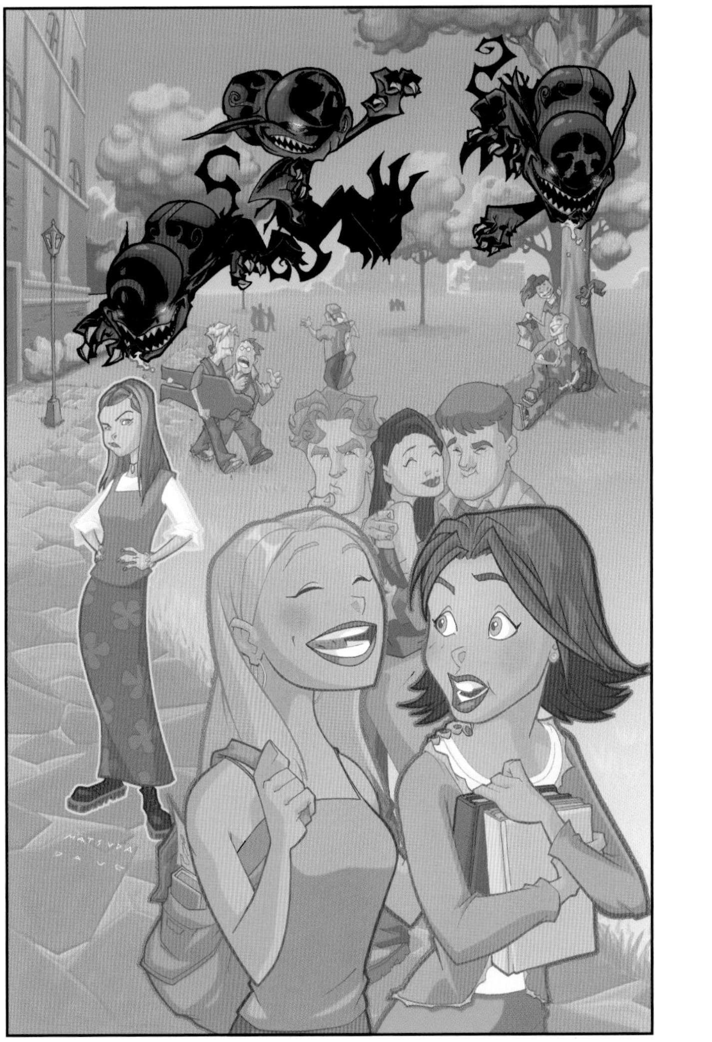

THE NEXT SERIES in the monthly was partly concocted over a dinner at the San Diego Comic-Con, with Tom Fassbender, Jim Pascoe, Dave McCaig, Jeff Matsuda, and Brian Horton all present. We became fixated with the number three, leading to a three-issue story with a three-word title, *Ugly Little Monsters.* Interior pages had three panels, triangular compositions, and triadic color schemes. Covers featured three main characters, as well as the three little uglies. Matsuda's style had evolved a lot from his earlier, more mainstream comics style. I think that if he'd auditioned with this style in the first place, he may not have met with approval from some of the actresses. But the condition for artist approval was that any given artist only need be approved once. As Jeff's style changed, he was able to bring a very different feel to the covers. Over the phone, we came up with the idea to suspend the monsters from the logo. Jeff drew them without the logo there, and the book's designer, Keith Wood—now Dark Horse's Design and Production Coordinator—had to match the figures to the logo. Having Jeff design these creatures, as he'd designed the monsters in *Blood of Carthage*, gave Cliff Richards something to draw that he probably wouldn't have come up with on his own.

Sketch and pencils by Matsuda, colors by McCaig. Cover, *BTVS* #40, December 2001.

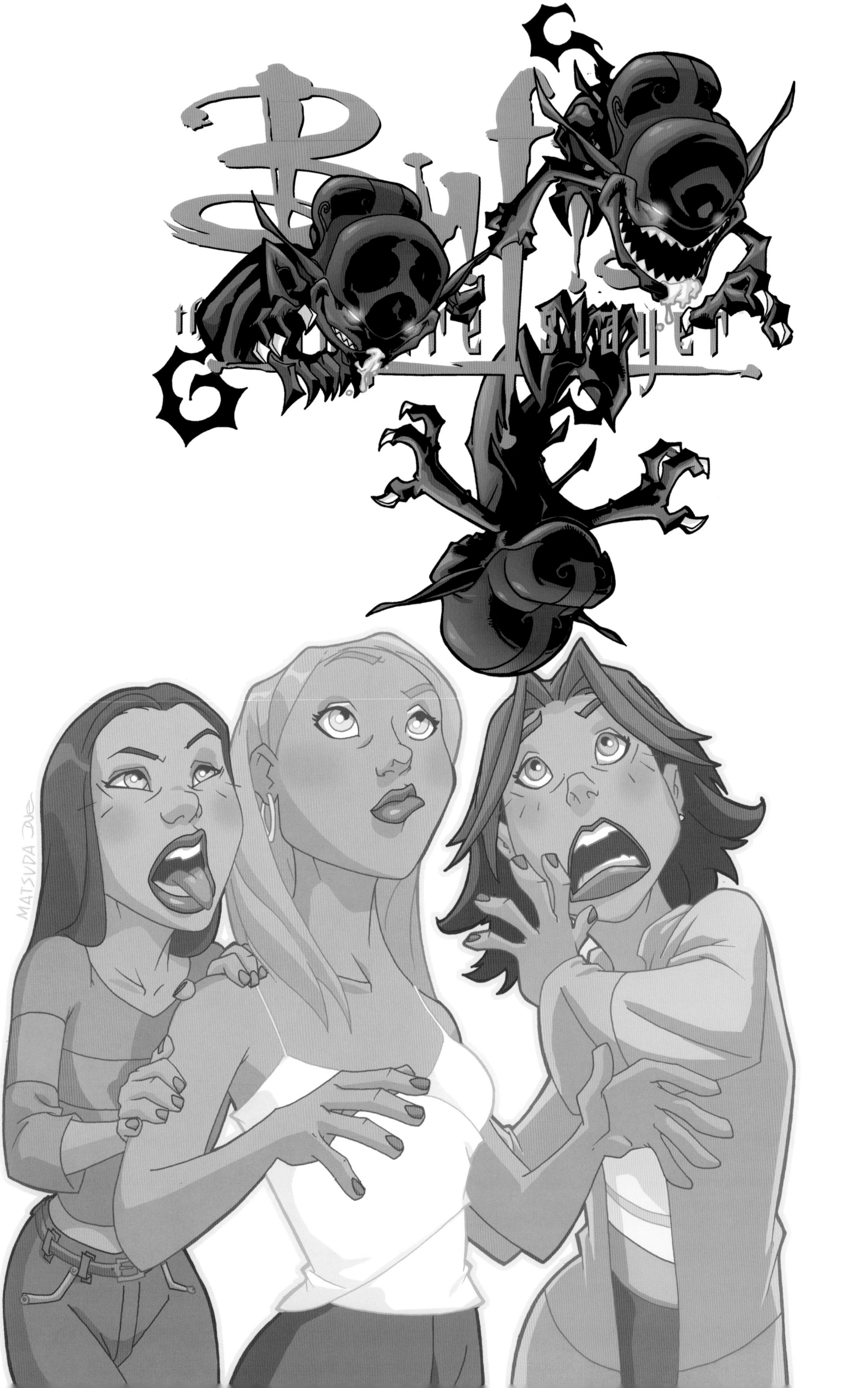

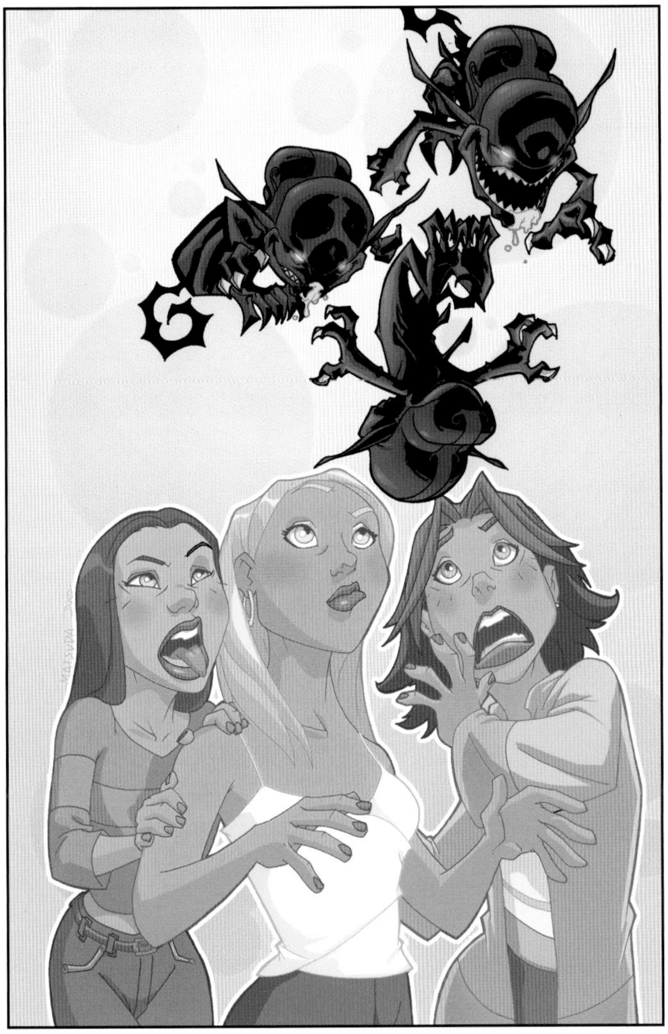

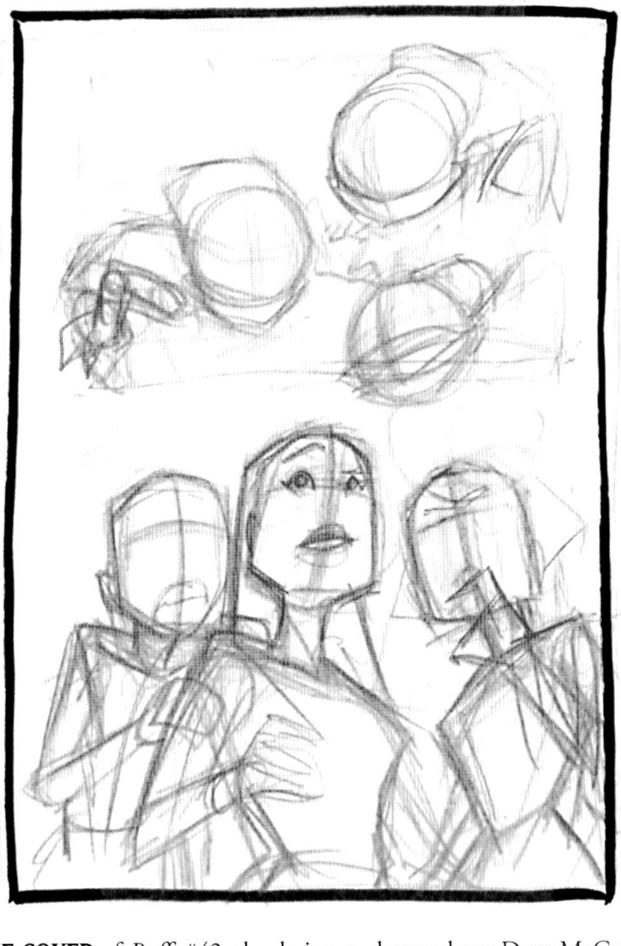

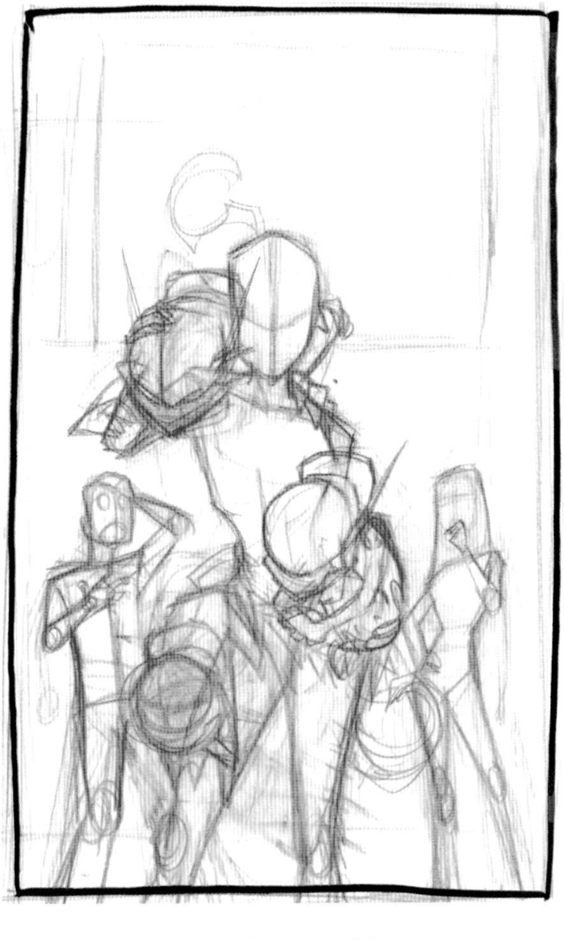

FOR THE COVER of *Buffy* #42, the designers dropped out Dave McCaig's colored background in order to simplify the image.

Sketch and pencils by Jeff Matsuda, colors by Dave McCaig. Cover, *BTVS* #41 and #42, January and February 2002.

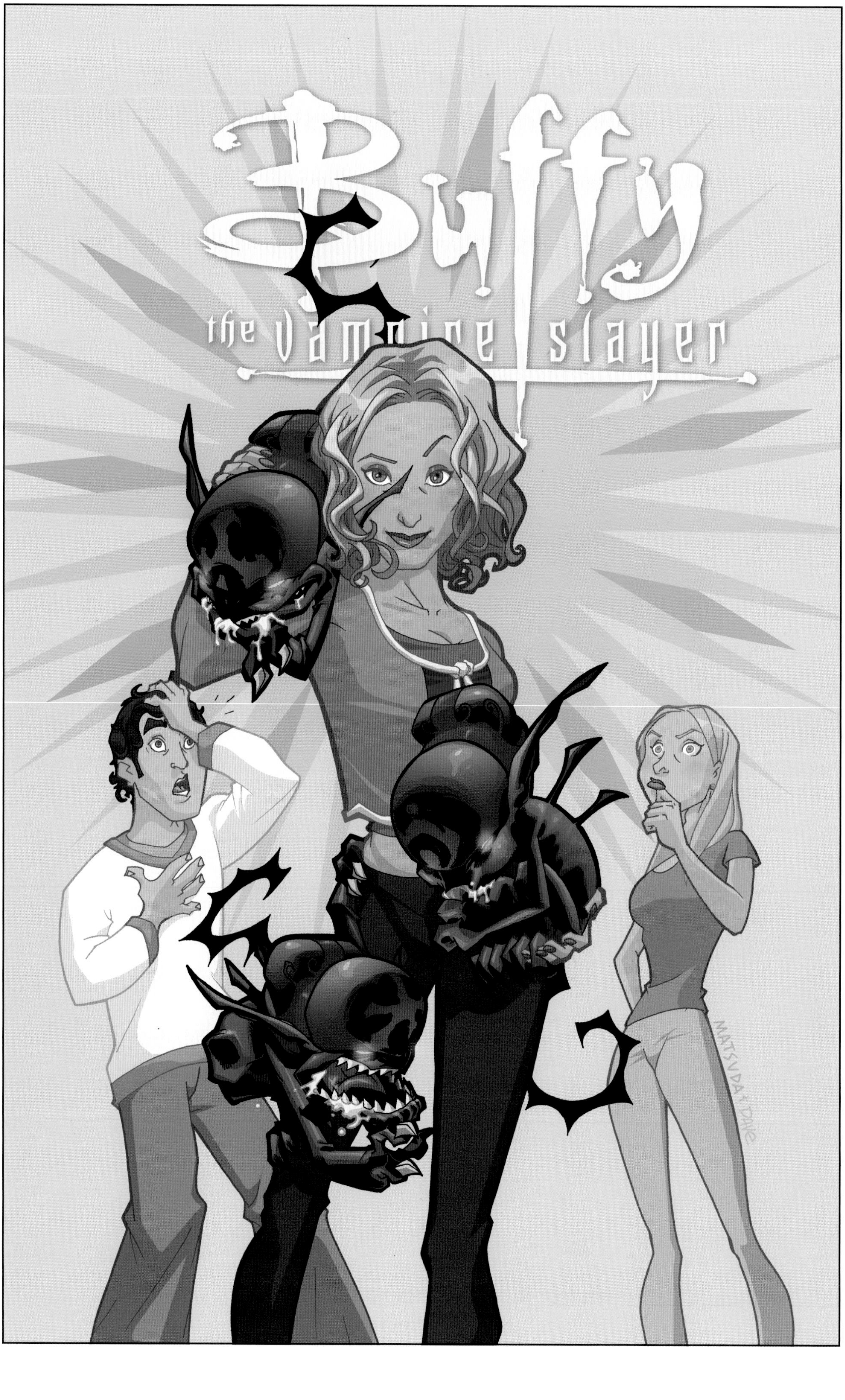
Buffy
the vampire slayer
MATSUDA & DAVE

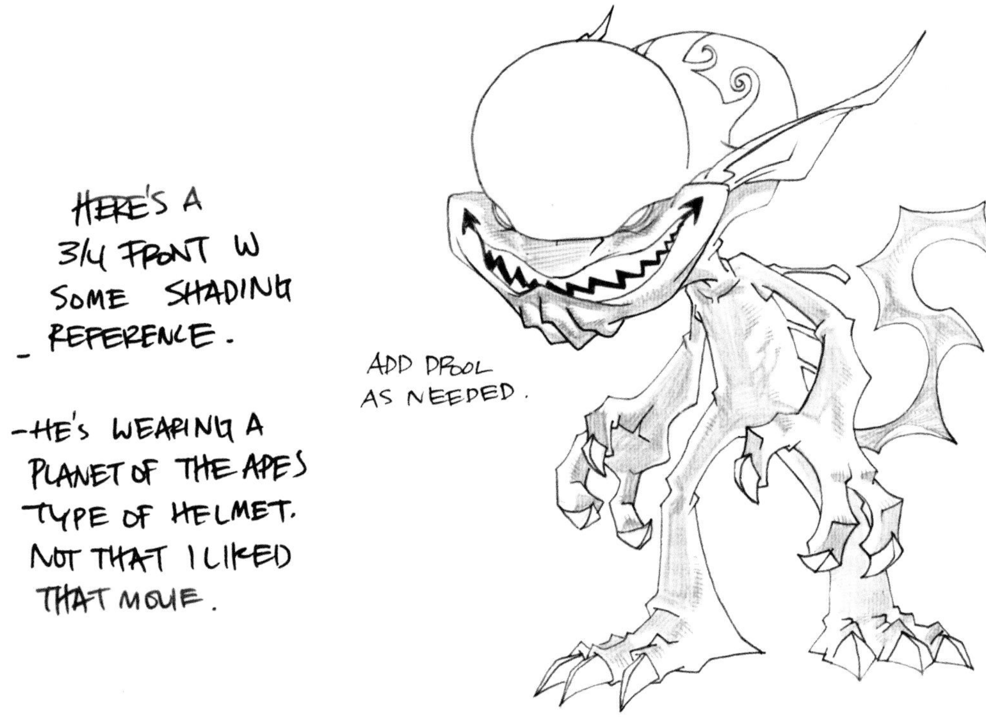
HERE'S A 3/4 FRONT W SOME SHADING REFERENCE.
-HE'S WEARING A PLANET OF THE APES TYPE OF HELMET. NOT THAT I LIKED THAT MOVIE.
ADD DROOL AS NEEDED.

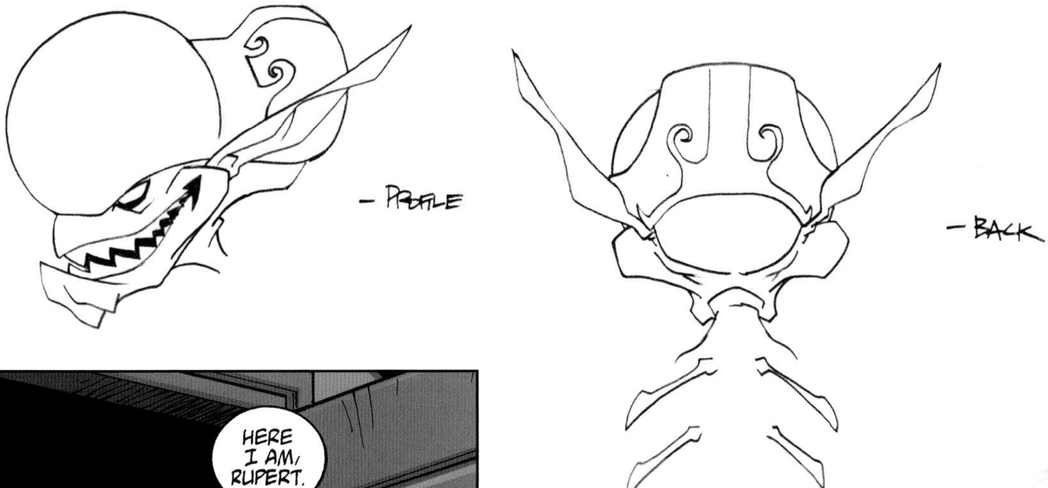
- PROFILE
- BACK

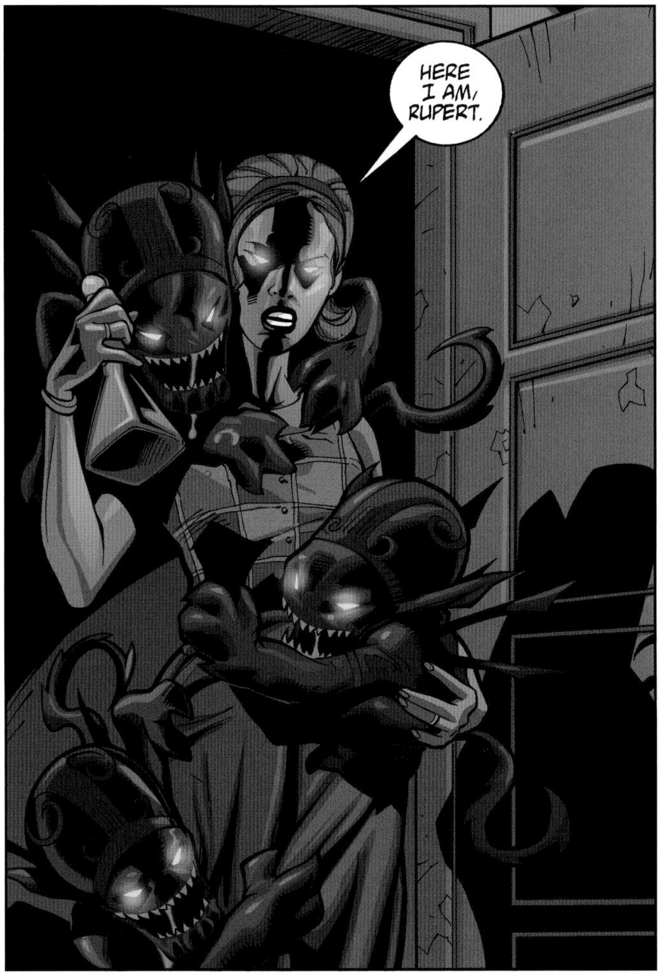
HERE I AM, RUPERT.

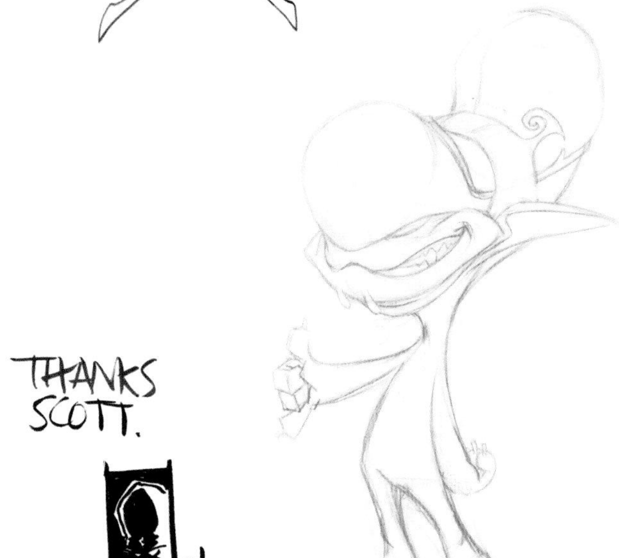
THANKS SCOTT.

CLIFF RICHARDS WAS so fast drawing the series that we settled into a schedule where covers were drawn before scripts were even written. This allowed the writers to sometimes borrow details from covers in the stories. The script for *Buffy* #42 directed Cliff to base this panel on the cover for that issue, as the crew become possessed.

Character designs and cover pencils by Jeff Matsuda. Cover colors by Dave McCaig. Script by Tom Fassbender and Jim Pascoe, pencils by Richards, inks by Joe Pimentel and Will Conrad, colors by McCaig. Cover and interiors, *BTVS* #42, February 2002.

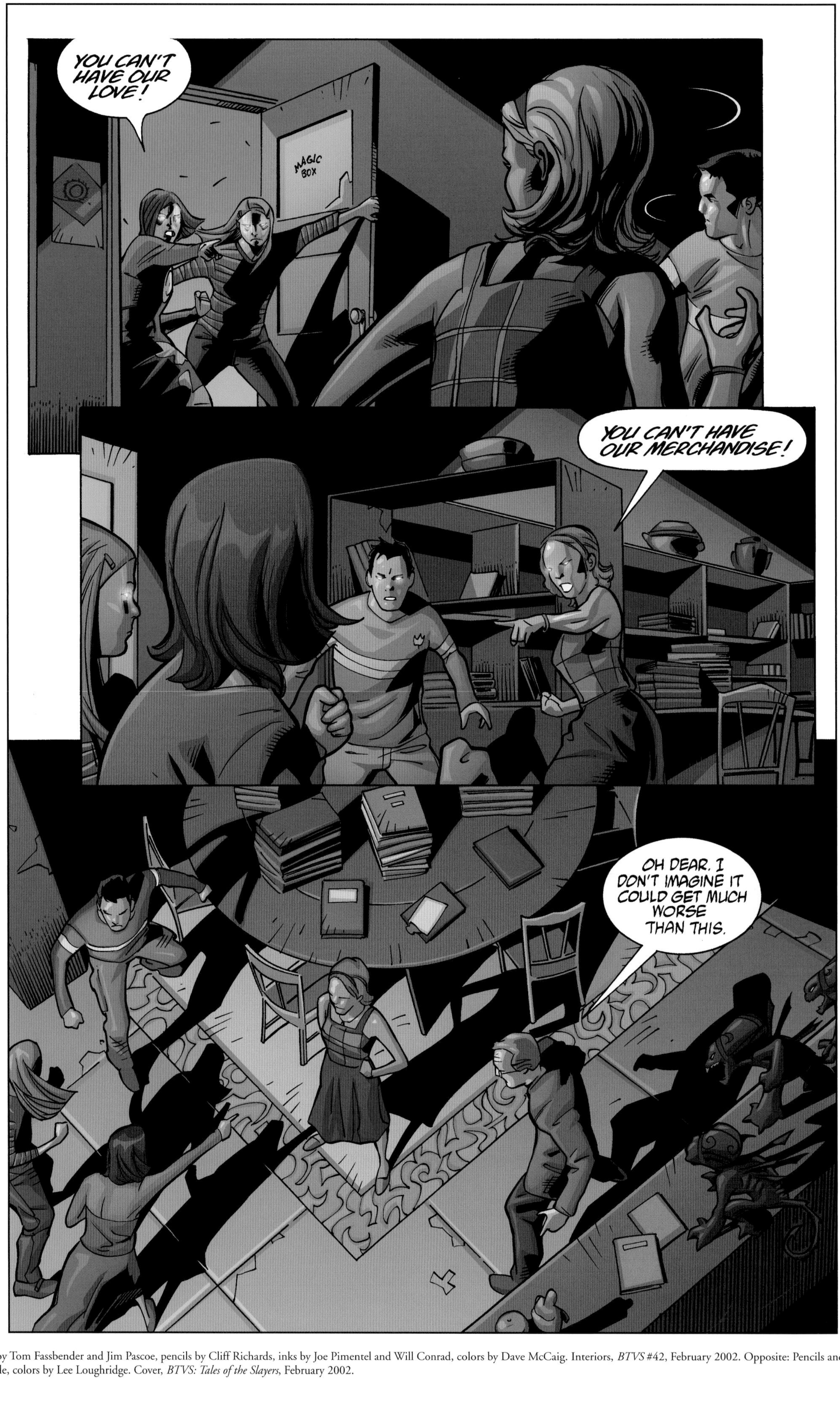
YOU CAN'T HAVE OUR LOVE!
MAGIC BOX
YOU CAN'T HAVE OUR MERCHANDISE!
OH DEAR. I DON'T IMAGINE IT COULD GET MUCH WORSE THAN THIS.

 Script by Tom Fassbender and Jim Pascoe, pencils by Cliff Richards, inks by Joe Pimentel and Will Conrad, colors by Dave McCaig. Interiors, *BTVS* #42, February 2002. Opposite: Pencils and inks by Tim Sale, colors by Lee Loughridge. Cover, *BTVS: Tales of the Slayers*, February 2002.

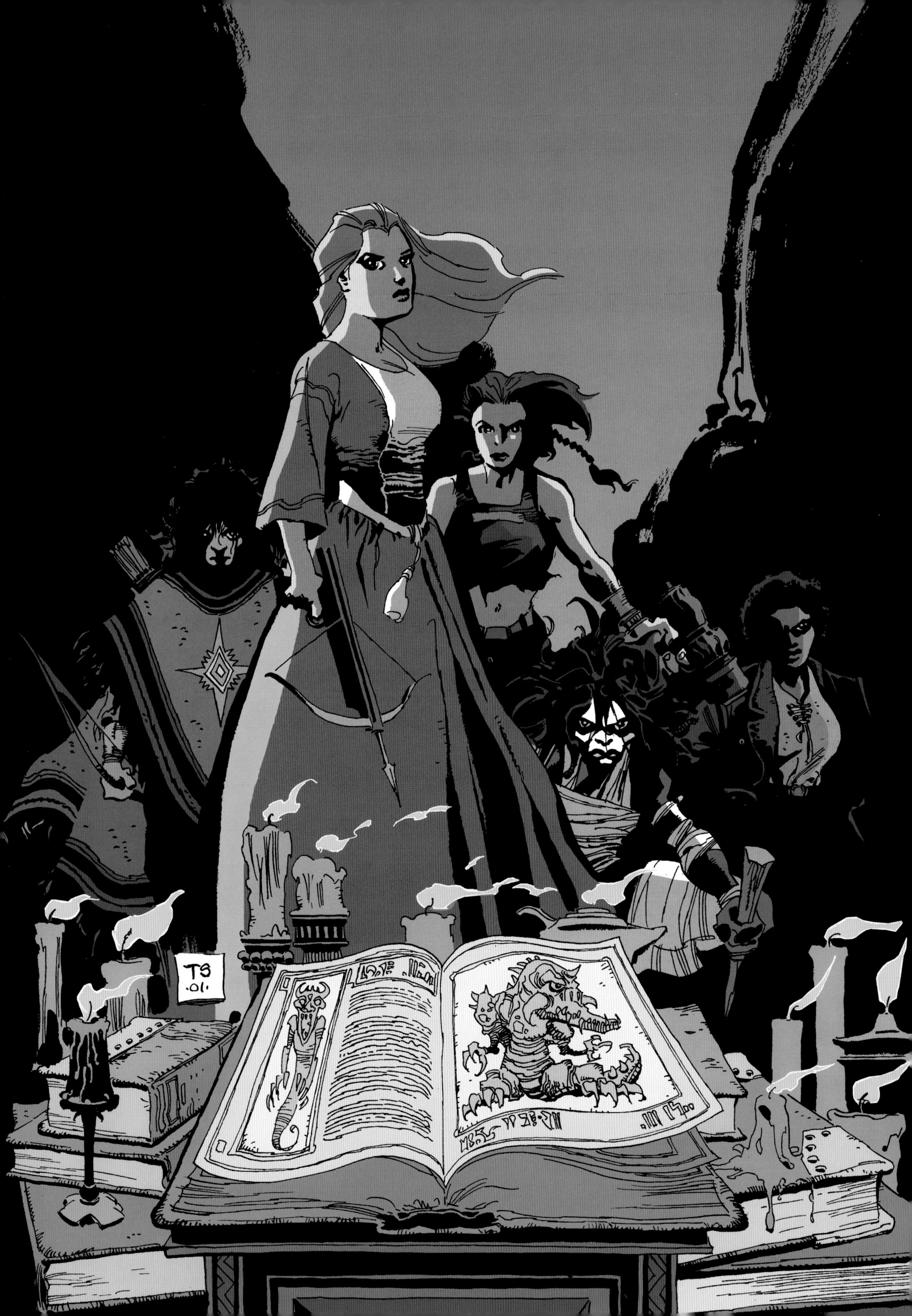
TS
.01.

JOSS AND I had been working on *Fray* for a while when he pitched me the idea of doing an anthology of stories about Slayers, done by writers from the show and featuring an all-star cast of artists. Ironically, *Tales of the Slayers* was an idea I'd pitched early on, before I was talking directly to Joss. The idea had been shot down. It's just as well, because we did it better with Joss than we could have without. I'd also talked to Pocket Books about teaming up and making a cross-company project out of it. When they heard that Joss was going to be involved with ours, they moved ahead on theirs. Eventually, I'd wind up writing stories for their second and fourth volumes of the series. *Tales of the Slayers* was Dark Horse's third original graphic novel in the *Buffy* line, after *The Dust Waltz* and *Ring of Fire*. The first story in our book featured the original Slayer, as an introduction to the history of the Slayers. We teamed Joss with Leinil Francis Yu, who'd go on to be a production artist on the film *Serenity*.

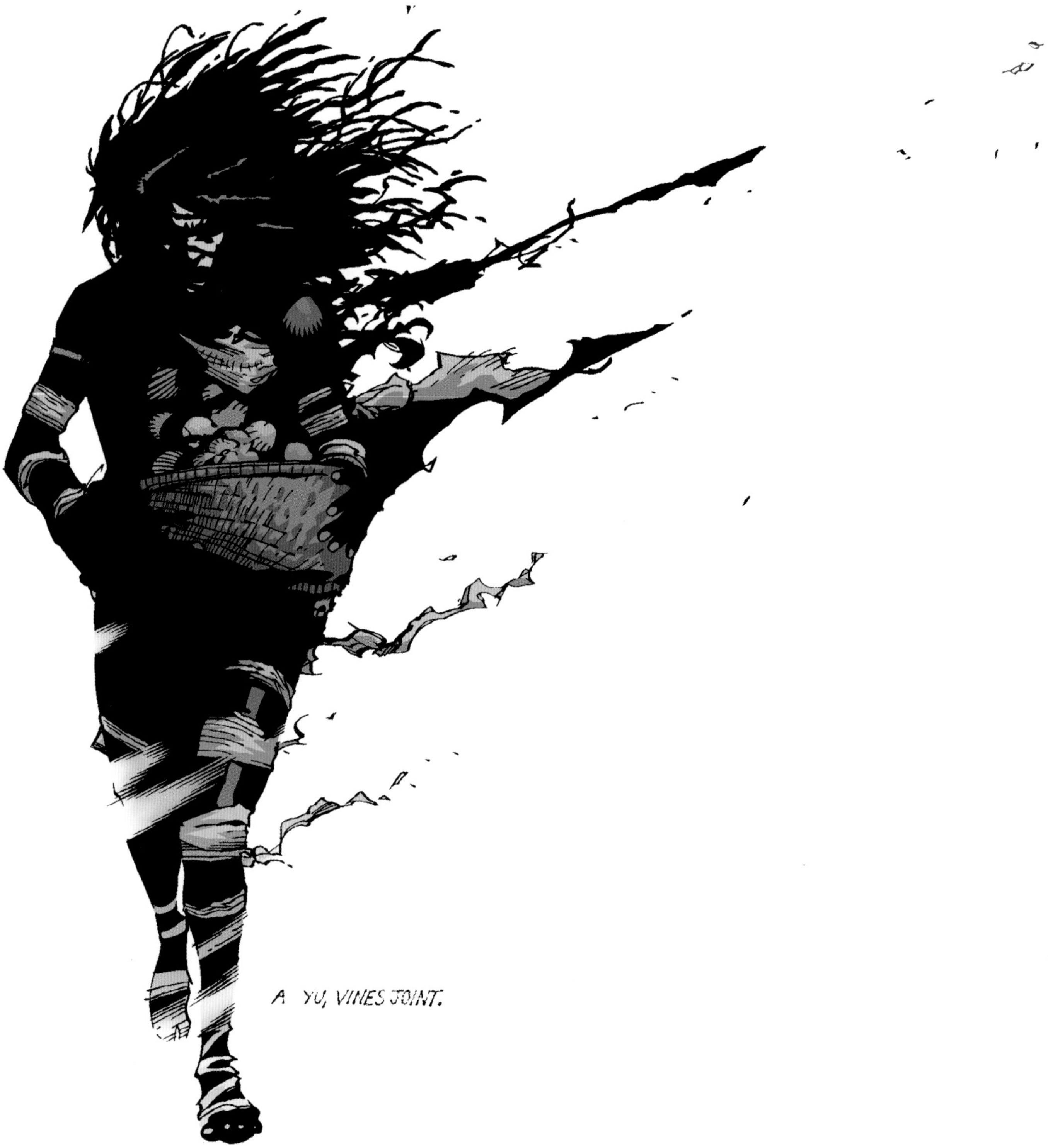
A YU, VINES JOINT.

 Script by Whedon, pencils by Yu, inks by Dexter Vines, colors by Dave Stewart, letters by Michelle Madsen. Interiors, "Prologue," *Tales of the Slayers*, February 2002.

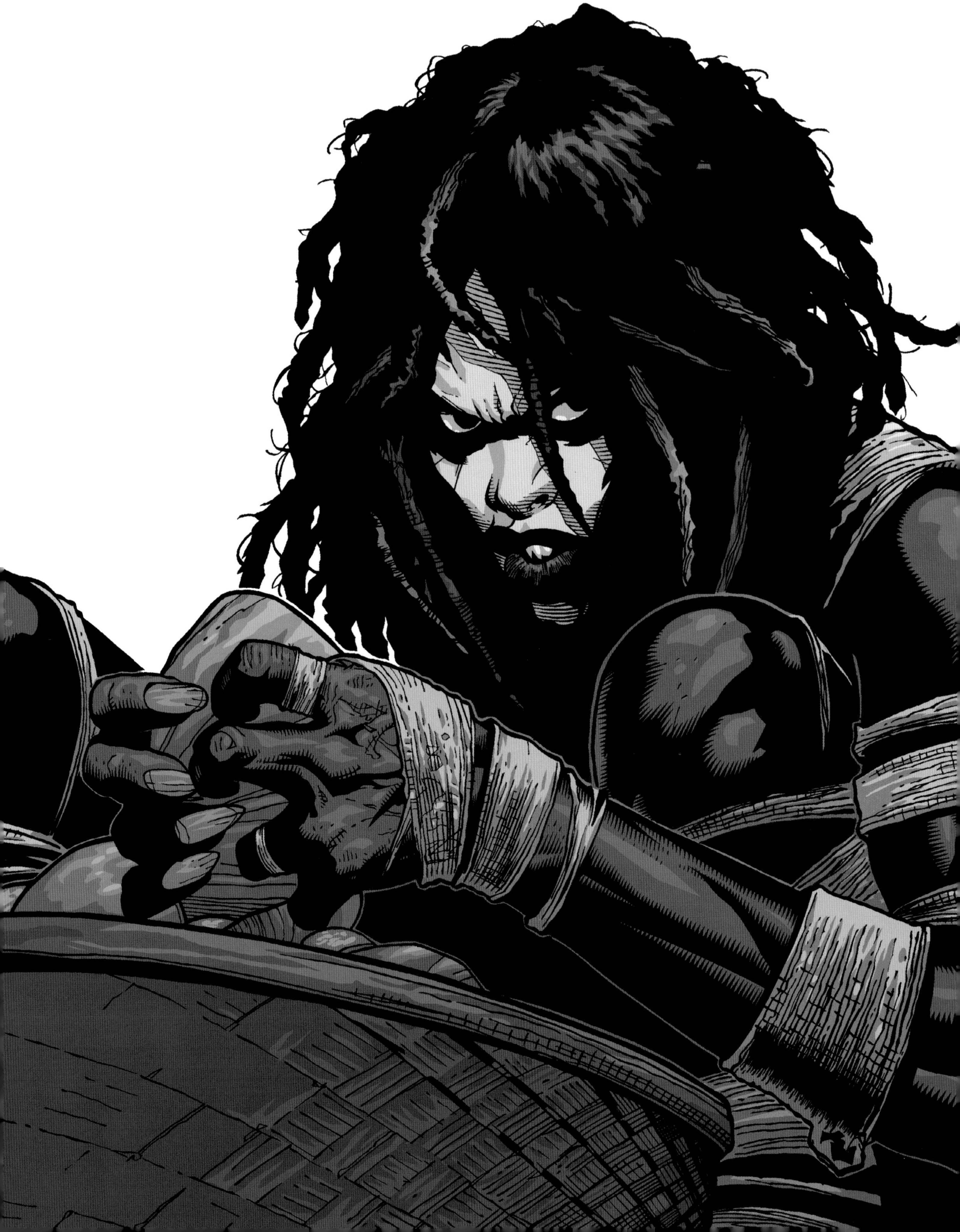

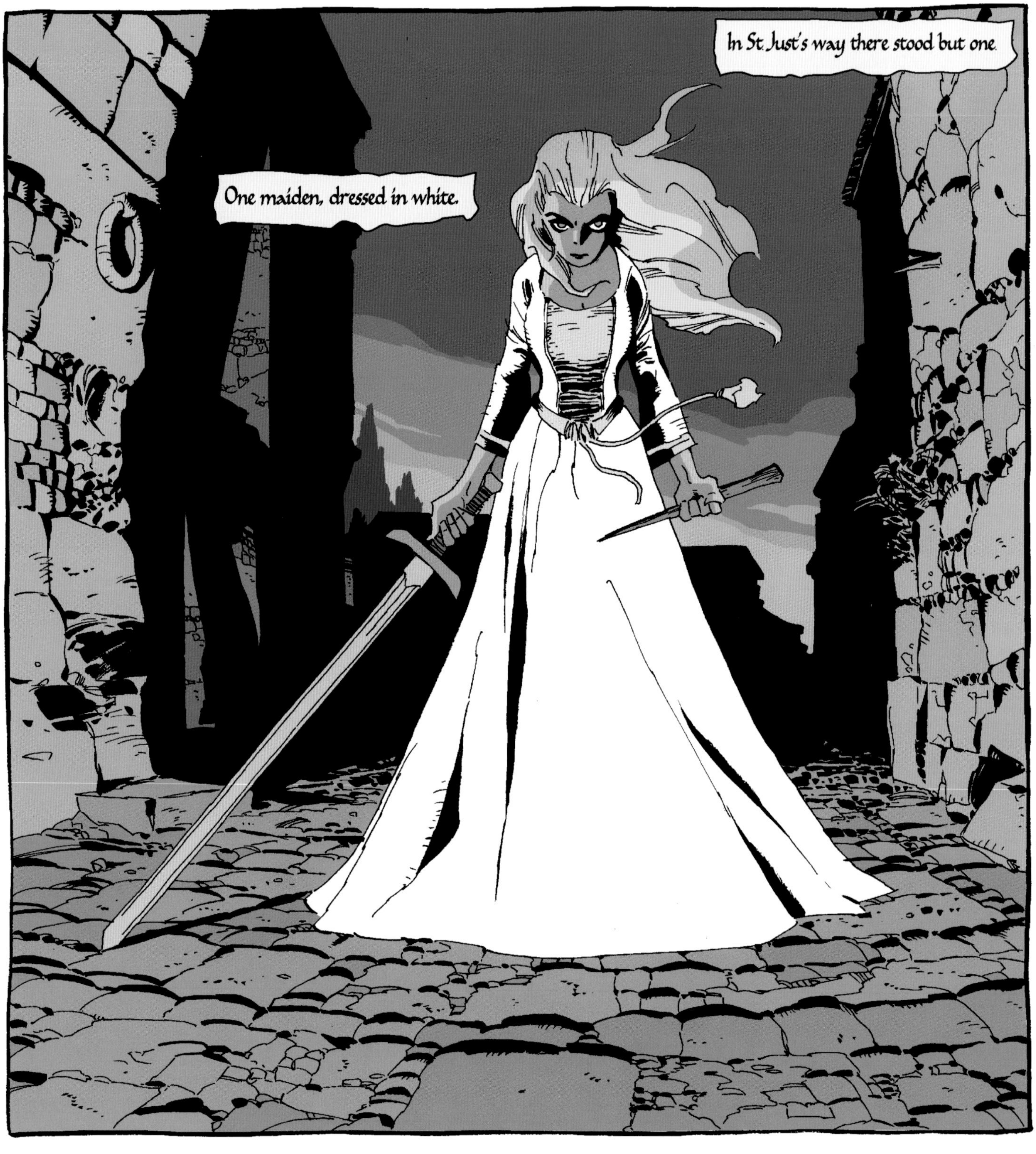
In St Just's way there stood but one.
One maiden, dressed in white.

JOSS ALSO WROTE the second story in the book, teaming with Tim Sale, who did the cover on page 107 featuring an assortment of Slayers. Sale is the only artist other than Karl Moline to draw Fray. Joss and Sale had met through mutual friend/collaborator Jeph Loeb, who makes almost as many introductions in the world of comics as he writes books.

Jane Espenson had only written a few comics for me when she dove into *Tales of the Slayers*, and she hadn't grown up on comics the way Joss and Doug Petrie had. She made a great comics writer, though, and stuck to some very simple guidelines I'd given her about the number of panels on a page and number of words in a panel. These are decent rules of thumb that always work, but don't leave a lot of room for inventive direction. For her story in *Slayers*, I teamed her with P. Craig Russell, an absolute master of the form who'd previously only done a little inking on *Buffy* projects. Russell is well known for adapting prose, opera, and fairy tales to comics. I asked him to handle Espenson's script the same way. Her five-panel pages were transformed into nine-, ten-, eleven-panel pages, by someone who always makes that sort of thing work. The musical nature of this particular scene played to Russell's strengths, and made it one of the most sophisticated bits of comics in the book.

 Above: Script by Whedon, pencils and inks by Sale, colors by Lee Loughridge, letters by Richard Starkings. Interiors, "Righteous." Opposite: Script by Espenson, pencils and inks by Russell, colors by Lovern Kindzierski, letters by Galen Showman. Interiors, "Presumption." Both from *Tales of the Slayers*, February 2002.

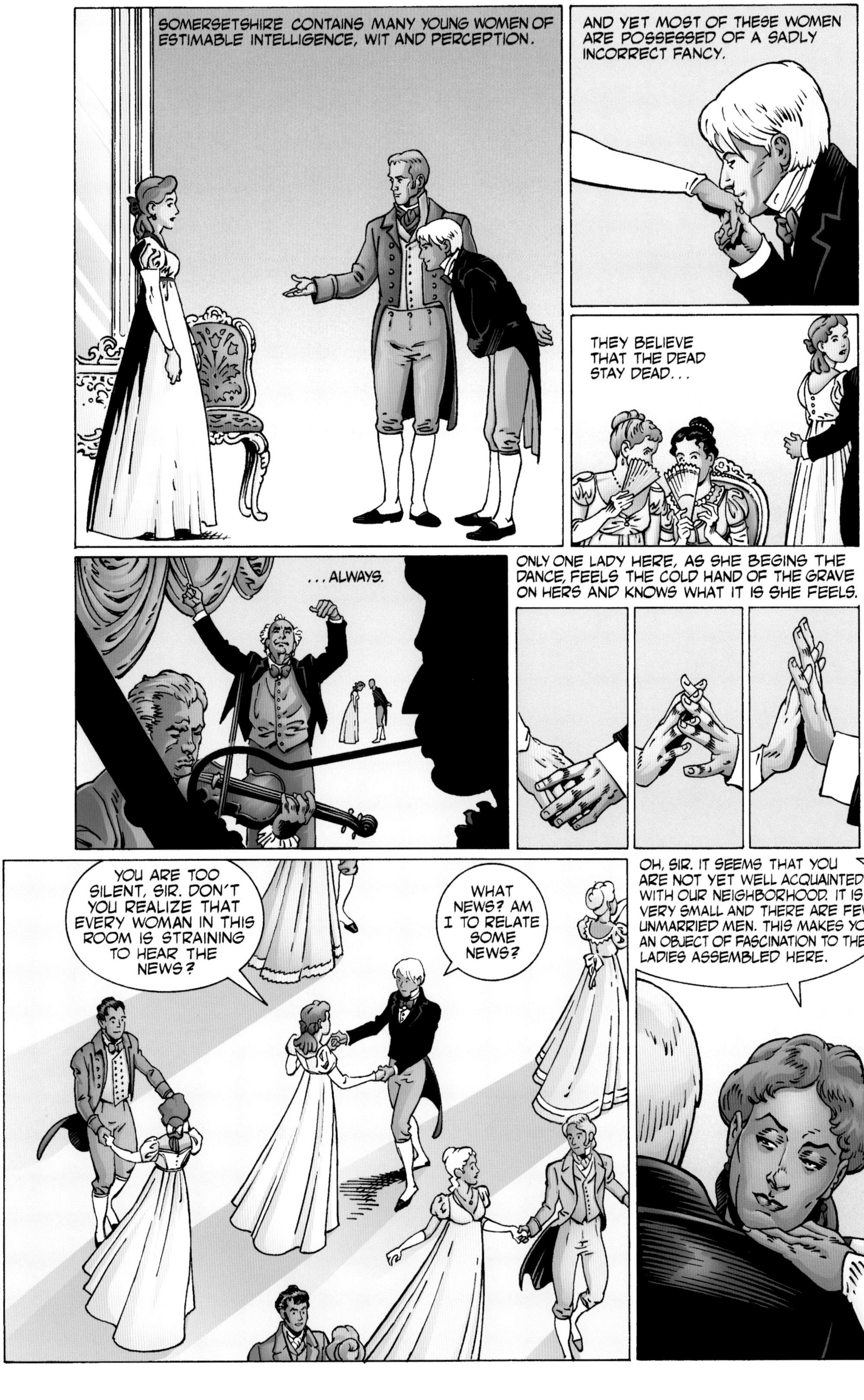
SOMERSETSHIRE CONTAINS MANY YOUNG WOMEN OF ESTIMABLE INTELLIGENCE, WIT AND PERCEPTION.
AND YET MOST OF THESE WOMEN ARE POSSESSED OF A SADLY INCORRECT FANCY.
THEY BELIEVE THAT THE DEAD STAY DEAD...
...ALWAYS.
ONLY ONE LADY HERE, AS SHE BEGINS THE DANCE, FEELS THE COLD HAND OF THE GRAVE ON HERS AND KNOWS WHAT IT IS SHE FEELS.
YOU ARE TOO SILENT, SIR. DON'T YOU REALIZE THAT EVERY WOMAN IN THIS ROOM IS STRAINING TO HEAR THE NEWS?
WHAT NEWS? AM I TO RELATE SOME NEWS?
OH, SIR. IT SEEMS THAT YOU ARE NOT YET WELL ACQUAINTED WITH OUR NEIGHBORHOOD. IT IS VERY SMALL AND THERE ARE FEW UNMARRIED MEN. THIS MAKES YOU AN OBJECT OF FASCINATION TO THE LADIES ASSEMBLED HERE.

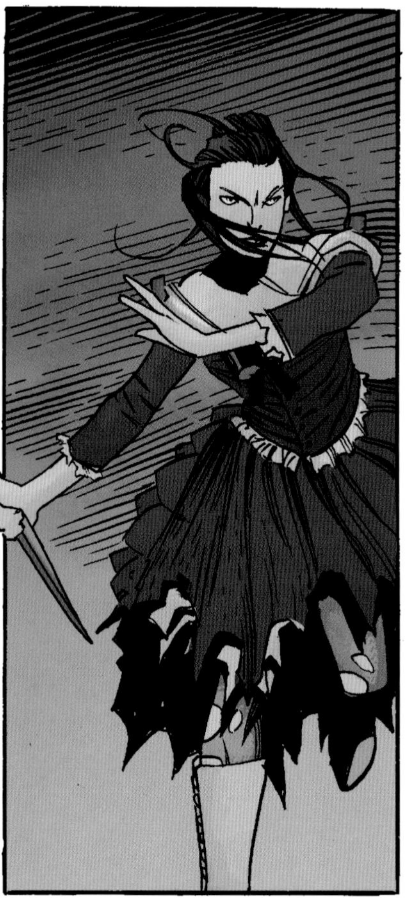

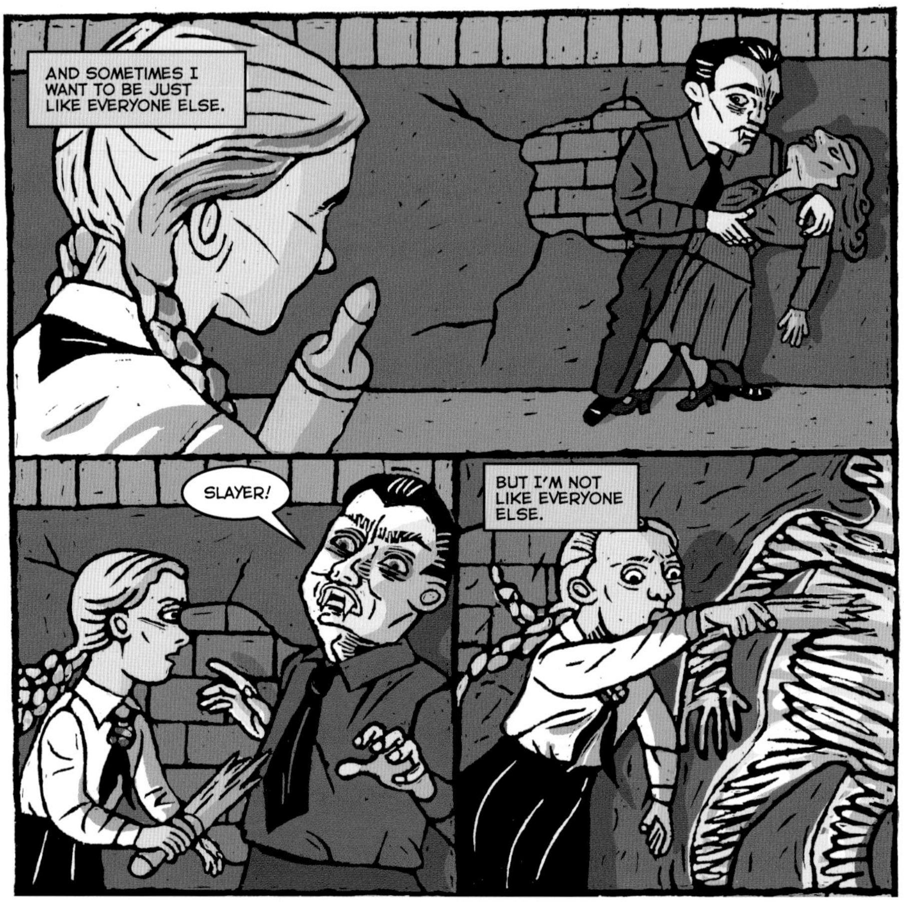
AND SOMETIMES I WANT TO BE JUST LIKE EVERYONE ELSE.
SLAYER!
BUT I'M NOT LIKE EVERYONE ELSE.

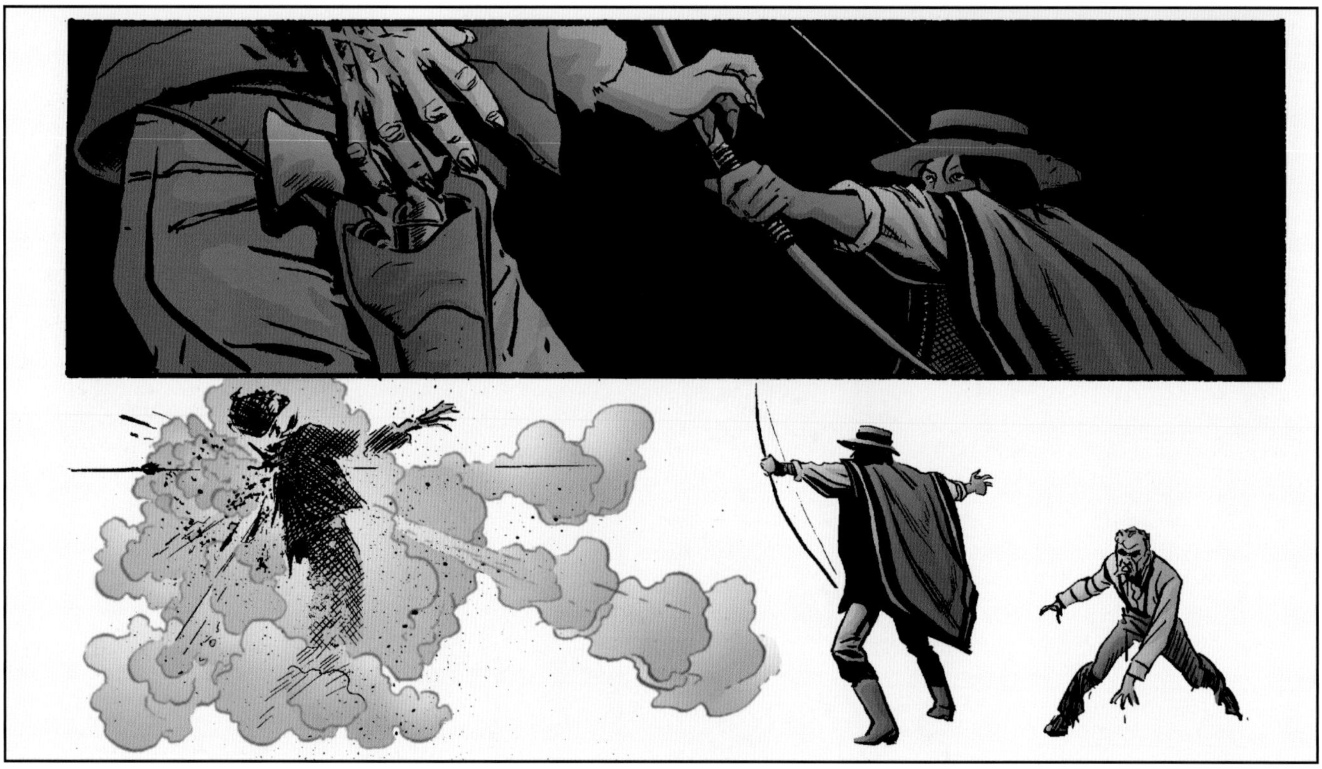

WHEN PUTTING TOGETHER anthologies, I always shoot for variety. Points go to Rebecca Rand Kirshner, a *Buffy* television writer with whom I'd never worked before, whose only exposure to comics was less mainstream fare. Her first suggestion for a collaborator was Daniel Clowes, creator of the comic book *Ghost World*. I got a hold of Clowes, but he turned me down, saying he only works on comics he writes. I actually love to get turned down for reasons like that, because I'm glad someone as good as he is, with such a bizarre aesthetic, gets to call his own shots. Kirshner's next suggestion was an Israeli artist I'd never heard of. Mira Friedmann's part of a group of artists called Actus Tragicus. While working on this story, I got Friedmann to contribute a strip to a 9/11 benefit book Dark Horse published in mid-2002.

One of the most gratifying things about the book was pairing Doug Petrie with Gene Colan on a story about Robin Wood's mom, the Slayer from the 1970s that Spike killed. It was a dream come true for Petrie, to work with one of his heroes, and Colan said that Petrie's script was one of the best-conceived scripts he'd seen in years, easy to visualize, easy to draw.

Top left: Script by Amber Benson, pencils and inks by Ted Naifeh, colors by Dave Stewart, letters by Michelle Madsen. Interiors, "The Innocent." Top right: Script by Rebecca Rand Kirshner, pencils, inks, and colors by Mira Friedmann, letters by Jason Hvam. Interiors, "Sonnenblue." Below: Script by David Fury, pencils, inks, and letters by Steve Lieber, colors by Matt Hollingsworth. "The Glittering World." Opposite: Script by Petrie, pencils by Colan, colors by Stewart, letters by Madsen. "Nikki Goes Down." All from *Tales of the Slayers,* February 2002.

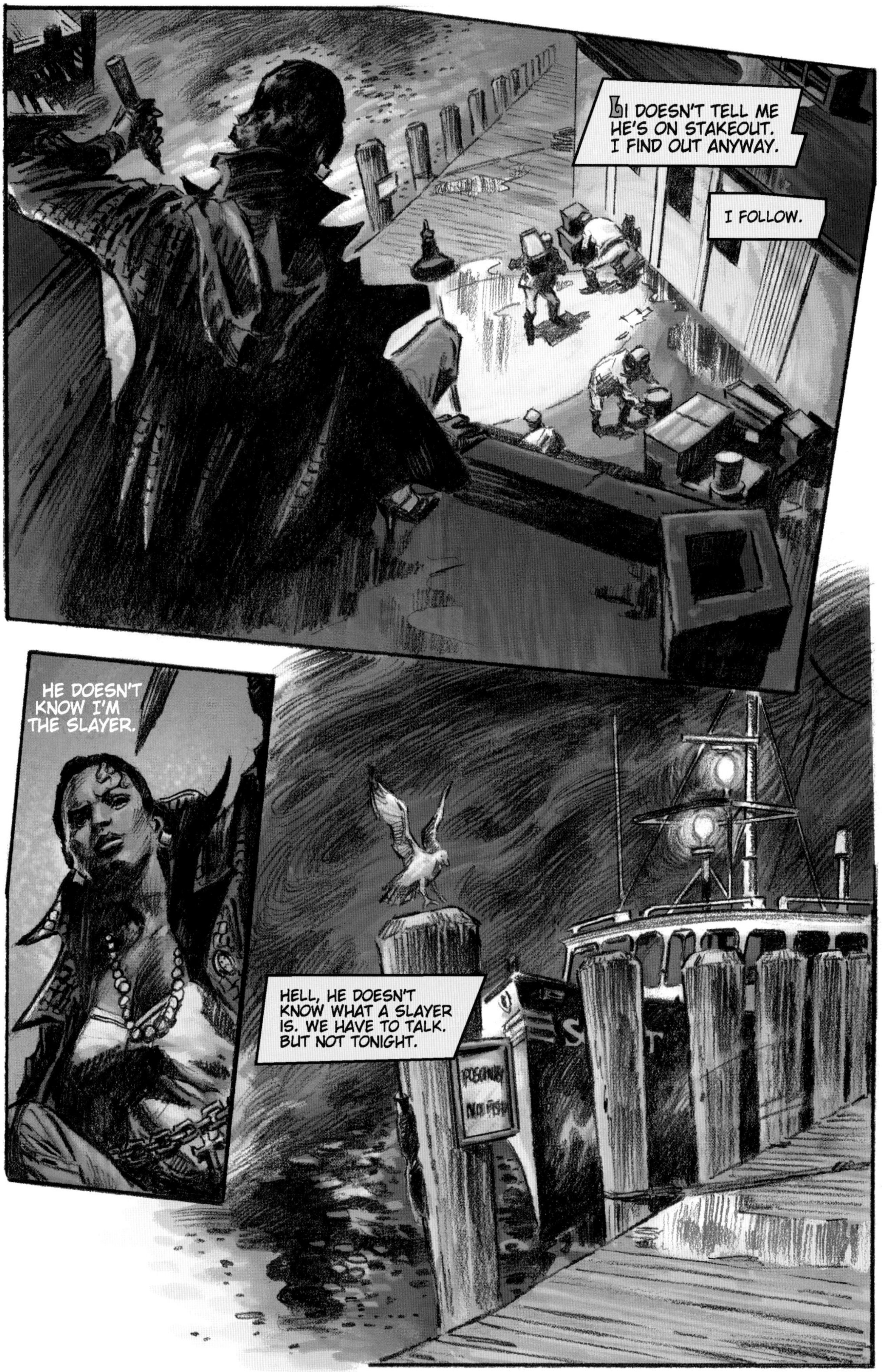
LI DOESN'T TELL ME HE'S ON STAKEOUT. I FIND OUT ANYWAY.
I FOLLOW.
HE DOESN'T KNOW I'M THE SLAYER.
HELL, HE DOESN'T KNOW WHAT A SLAYER IS. WE HAVE TO TALK. BUT NOT TONIGHT.

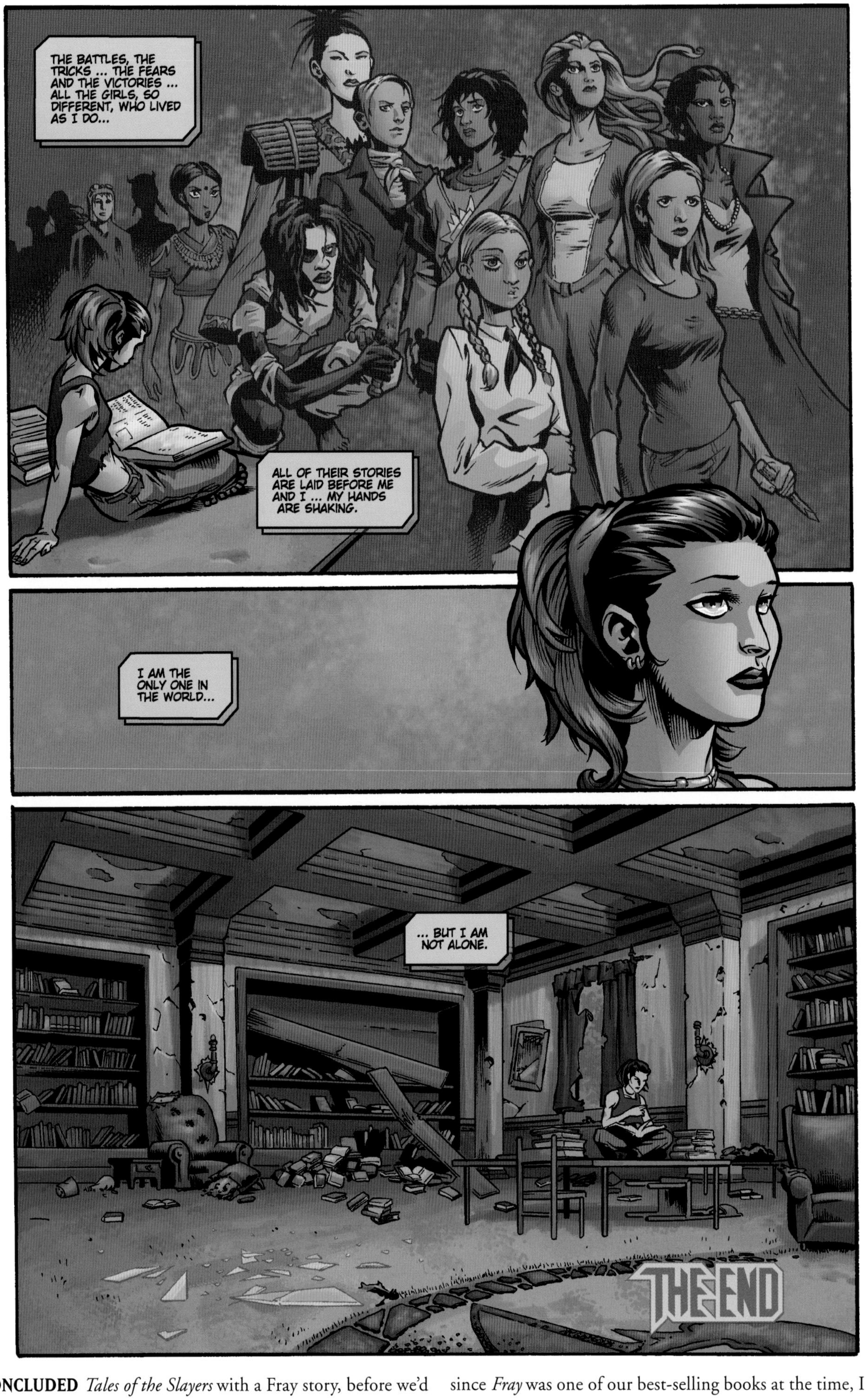
THE BATTLES, THE TRICKS ... THE FEARS AND THE VICTORIES ... ALL THE GIRLS, SO DIFFERENT, WHO LIVED AS I DO...
ALL OF THEIR STORIES ARE LAID BEFORE ME AND I ... MY HANDS ARE SHAKING.
I AM THE ONLY ONE IN THE WORLD...
... BUT I AM NOT ALONE.
THE END

JOSS CONCLUDED *Tales of the Slayers* with a Fray story, before we'd managed to wrap up the *Fray* miniseries. Karl Moline had to audition to draw Sarah Michelle Gellar in that one panel, alongside a mix of Slayers from the show and the comics. Since he got approved, and since *Fray* was one of our best-selling books at the time, I asked Karl to do some covers for the monthly *Buffy* series. But the schedule on *Fray* was such a mess it never happened. He *is* approved to draw our main girl, though.

 Script by Whedon, pencils by Moline, inks by Andy Owens, colors by Dave Stewart, letters by Michelle Madsen. Interiors, "Tales," *Tales of the Slayers*, February 2002.

IN THE MONTHLY, thanks to a fast pair of writers and a faster artist, we were able to be more timely about the continuity of the comic matching up with that of the show. This resulted in a change in how we did the comics, with fewer stories set in other periods of the show's history. Having caught up to the end of Season Five of the show, we wanted to deal with Buffy's death. We'd realized by then that setting stories in the summers between seasons of the show gave us a certain amount of freedom. A one-shot comic called *Lost and Found* and three issues of the monthly series followed, with evocative covers by Paul Lee and Brian Horton. This was their first cover work on the series, and the response was so good they continued on until the end.

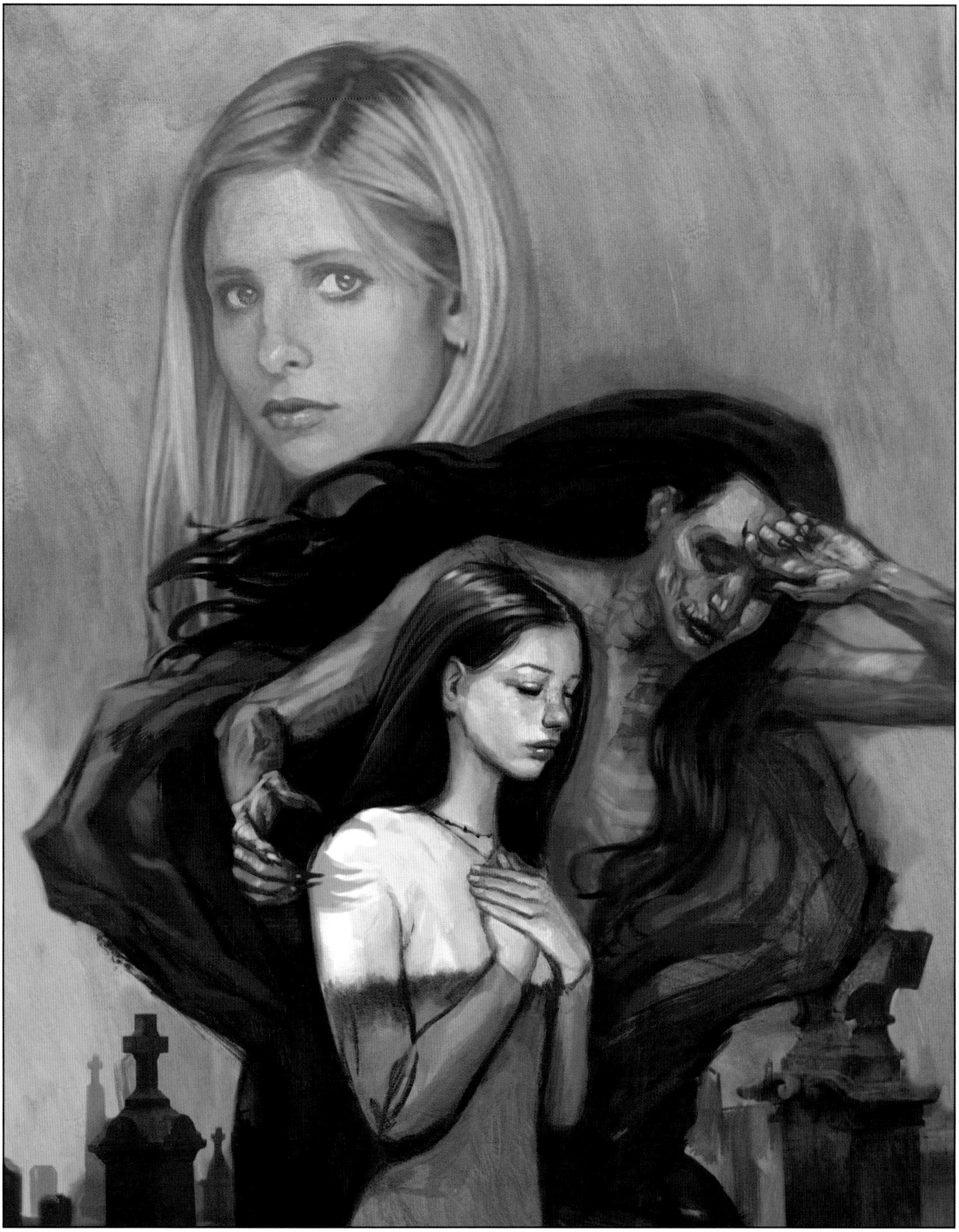

Painting by Lee and Horton. Cover, *BTVS: Lost and Found*, March 2002.

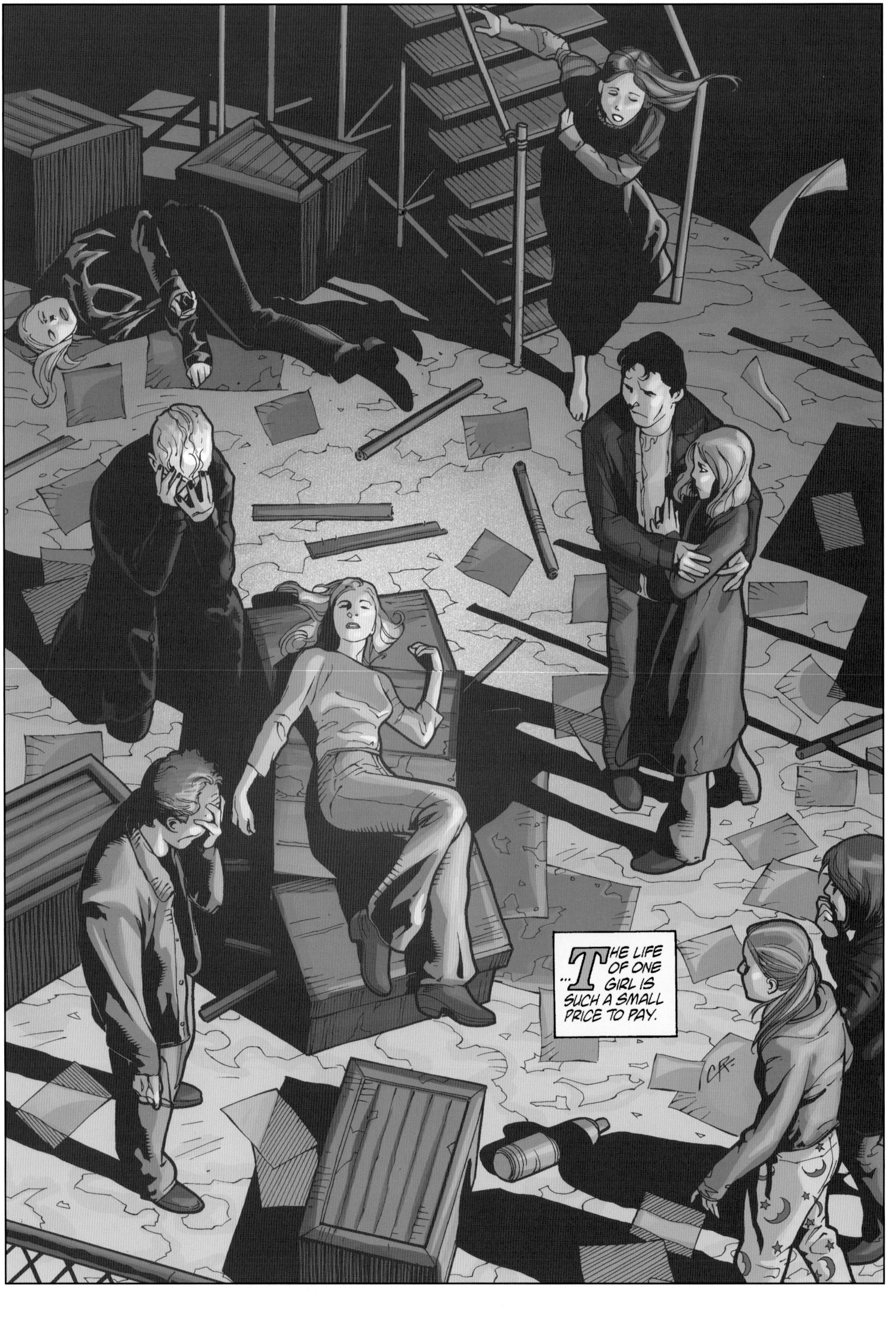
...THE LIFE OF ONE GIRL IS SUCH A SMALL PRICE TO PAY.

THE DEATH OF BUFFY started at the moment of Buffy's death and continued through her resurrection—which gave us one of the creepiest covers of the entire series (page 122). Note the dead Buffybot in the background of the facing page. Until this time, *Buffy* trade paperbacks had always featured photo covers, at the behest of our marketing department. When they saw Paul Lee and Brian Horton's covers, they said we should use these on the collections. This cover became the first art cover on a Buffy collection, for *The Death of Buffy*.

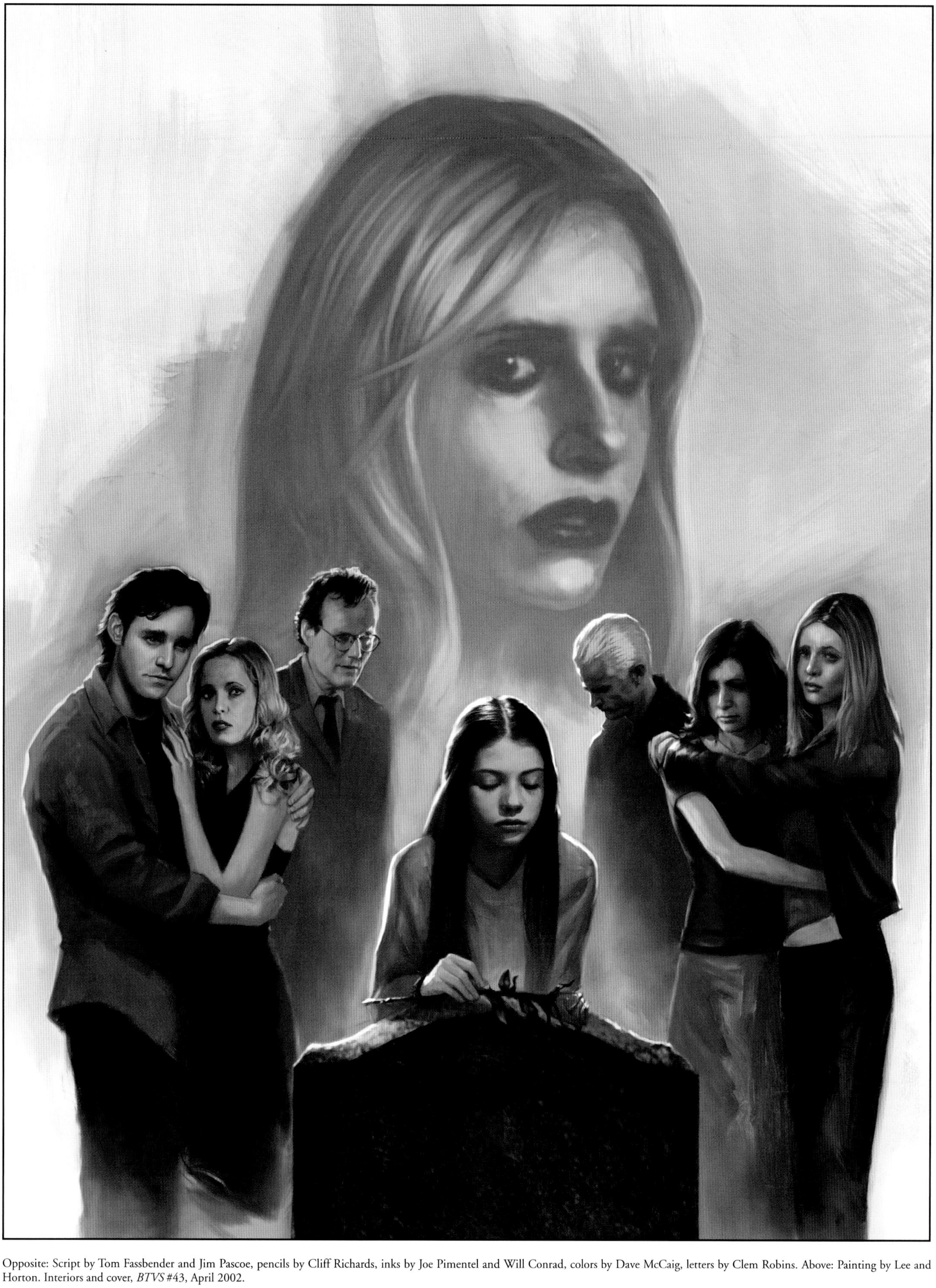

Opposite: Script by Tom Fassbender and Jim Pascoe, pencils by Cliff Richards, inks by Joe Pimentel and Will Conrad, colors by Dave McCaig, letters by Clem Robins. Above: Painting by Lee and Horton. Interiors and cover, *BTVS* #43, April 2002.

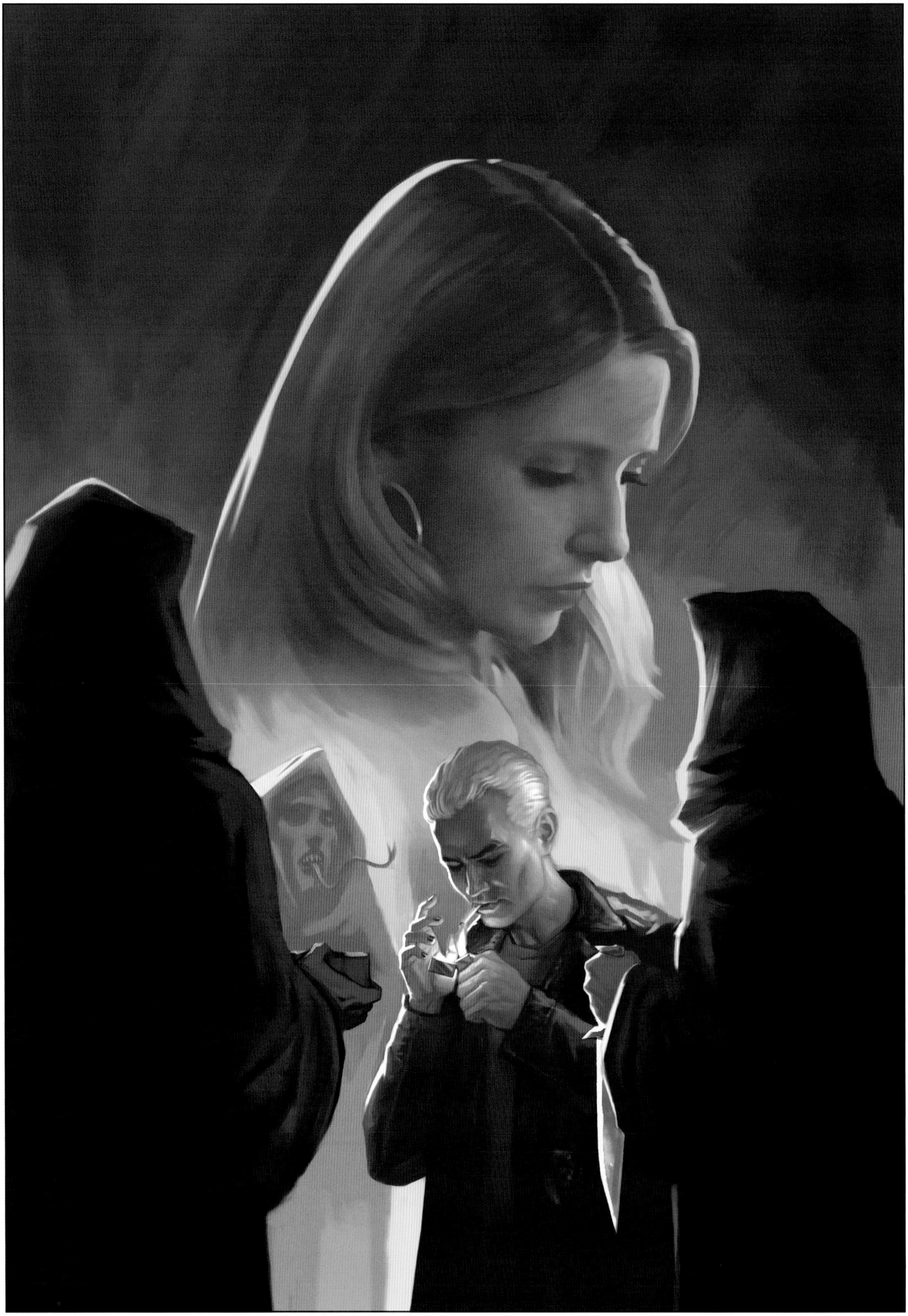

 Painting by Paul Lee and Brian Horton. Cover, *BTVS* #44, May 2002. Opposite: Script by Fabian Nicieza, pencils by Cliff Richards, inks by Joe Pimentel and Will Conrad, colors by Dave McCaig, letters by Clem Robins. Interiors, *BTVS: Lost and Found*, March 2002.

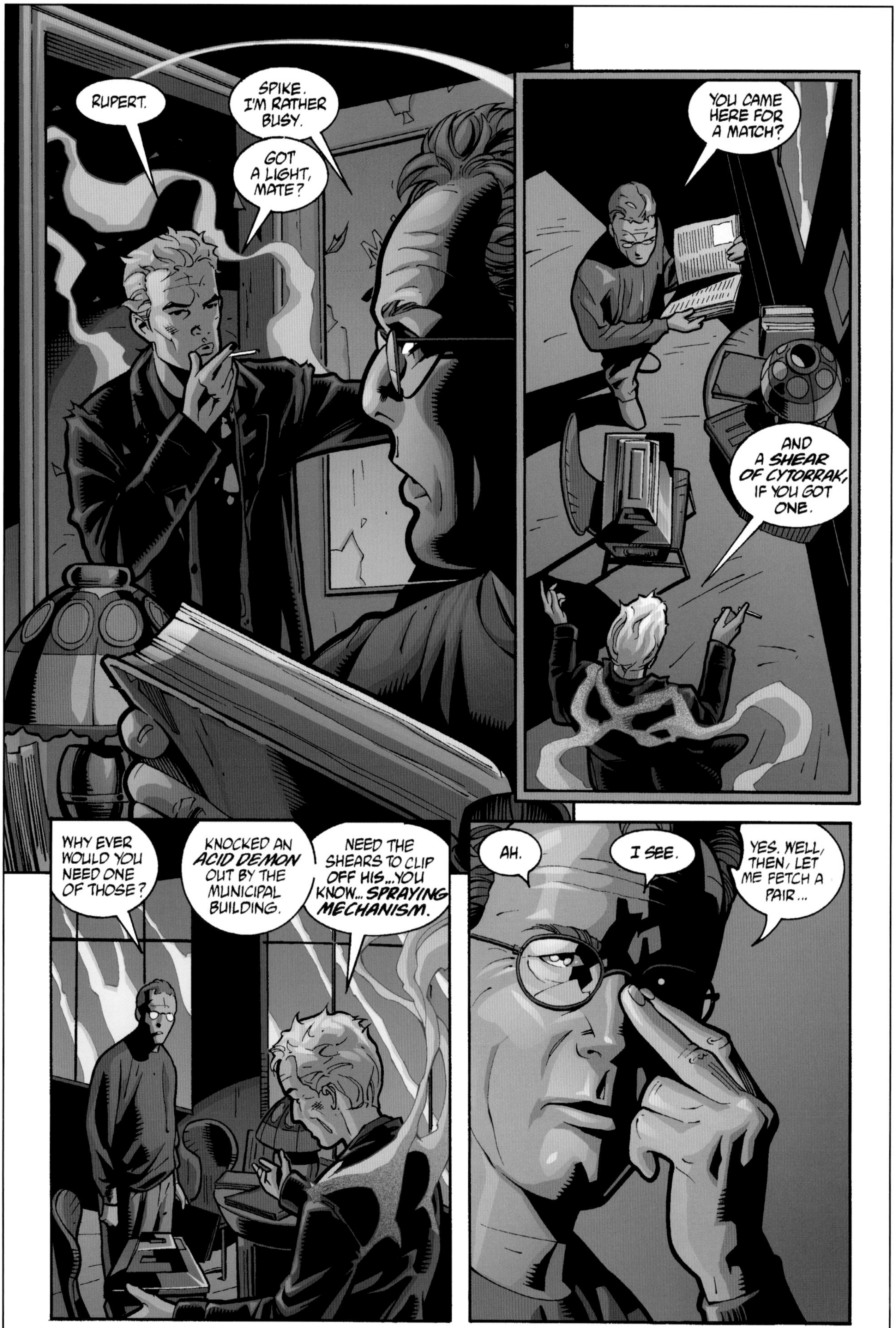
RUPERT.
SPIKE. I'M RATHER BUSY.
GOT A LIGHT, MATE?
YOU CAME HERE FOR A MATCH?
AND A SHEAR OF CYTORRAK, IF YOU GOT ONE.
WHY EVER WOULD YOU NEED ONE OF THOSE?
KNOCKED AN ACID DEMON OUT BY THE MUNICIPAL BUILDING.
NEED THE SHEARS TO CLIP OFF HIS...YOU KNOW... SPRAYING MECHANISM.
AH.
I SEE.
YES. WELL, THEN, LET ME FETCH A PAIR...

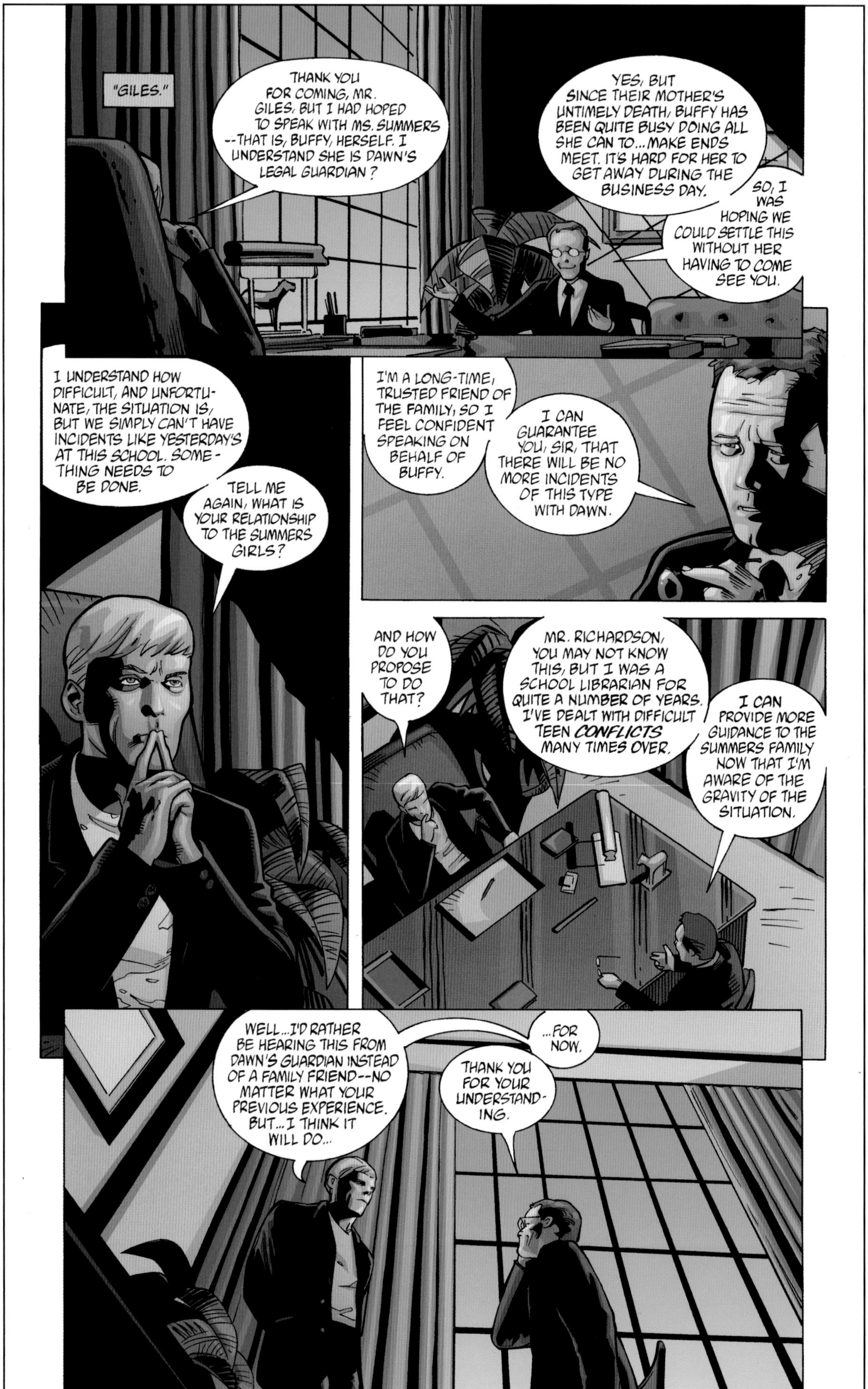
"GILES."
THANK YOU FOR COMING, MR. GILES, BUT I HAD HOPED TO SPEAK WITH MS. SUMMERS --THAT IS, BUFFY, HERSELF. I UNDERSTAND SHE IS DAWN'S LEGAL GUARDIAN?
YES, BUT SINCE THEIR MOTHER'S UNTIMELY DEATH, BUFFY HAS BEEN QUITE BUSY DOING ALL SHE CAN TO...MAKE ENDS MEET. IT'S HARD FOR HER TO GET AWAY DURING THE BUSINESS DAY.
SO, I WAS HOPING WE COULD SETTLE THIS WITHOUT HER HAVING TO COME SEE YOU.
I UNDERSTAND HOW DIFFICULT, AND UNFORTUNATE, THE SITUATION IS, BUT WE SIMPLY CAN'T HAVE INCIDENTS LIKE YESTERDAY'S AT THIS SCHOOL. SOMETHING NEEDS TO BE DONE.
TELL ME AGAIN, WHAT IS YOUR RELATIONSHIP TO THE SUMMERS GIRLS?
I'M A LONG-TIME, TRUSTED FRIEND OF THE FAMILY, SO I FEEL CONFIDENT SPEAKING ON BEHALF OF BUFFY.
I CAN GUARANTEE YOU, SIR, THAT THERE WILL BE NO MORE INCIDENTS OF THIS TYPE WITH DAWN.
AND HOW DO YOU PROPOSE TO DO THAT?
MR. RICHARDSON, YOU MAY NOT KNOW THIS, BUT I WAS A SCHOOL LIBRARIAN FOR QUITE A NUMBER OF YEARS. I'VE DEALT WITH DIFFICULT TEEN CONFLICTS MANY TIMES OVER.
I CAN PROVIDE MORE GUIDANCE TO THE SUMMERS FAMILY NOW THAT I'M AWARE OF THE GRAVITY OF THE SITUATION.
WELL...I'D RATHER BE HEARING THIS FROM DAWN'S GUARDIAN INSTEAD OF A FAMILY FRIEND--NO MATTER WHAT YOUR PREVIOUS EXPERIENCE. BUT...I THINK IT WILL DO...
...FOR NOW.
THANK YOU FOR YOUR UNDERSTANDING.

WITH THE BUFFYBOT standing in for Buffy, Giles ran interference with the new Sunnydale principal when Dawn started having trouble at the end of the school year. Tom Fassbender and Jim Pascoe dropped in the name Richardson in the scene in *Buffy* #43, and I asked Cliff Richards to draw him as my boss, the 6'9"–tall Mike Richardson, founder of Dark Horse Comics.

THE BOYS BROUGHT the principal back a couple issues later. Maybe this is what golfers wear in Brazil, where Cliff lives.

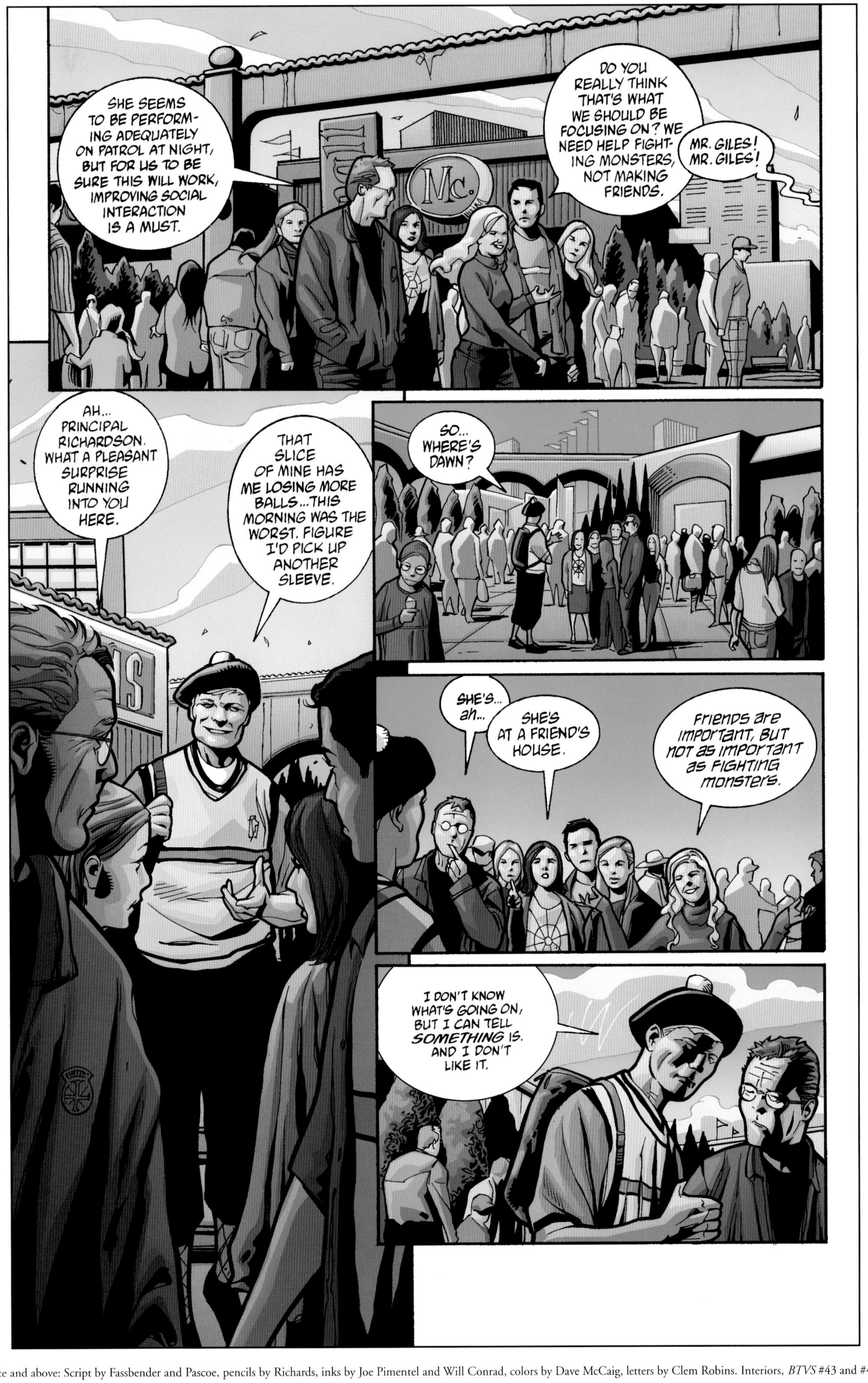
SHE SEEMS TO BE PERFORMING ADEQUATELY ON PATROL AT NIGHT, BUT FOR US TO BE SURE THIS WILL WORK, IMPROVING SOCIAL INTERACTION IS A MUST.
DO YOU REALLY THINK THAT'S WHAT WE SHOULD BE FOCUSING ON? WE NEED HELP FIGHTING MONSTERS, NOT MAKING FRIENDS.
MR. GILES! MR. GILES!
AH... PRINCIPAL RICHARDSON. WHAT A PLEASANT SURPRISE RUNNING INTO YOU HERE.
THAT SLICE OF MINE HAS ME LOSING MORE BALLS...THIS MORNING WAS THE WORST. FIGURE I'D PICK UP ANOTHER SLEEVE.
SO... WHERE'S DAWN?
SHE'S... ah...
SHE'S AT A FRIEND'S HOUSE.
Friends are important, but not as important as fighting monsters.
I DON'T KNOW WHAT'S GOING ON, BUT I CAN TELL SOMETHING IS. AND I DON'T LIKE IT.

Opposite and above: Script by Fassbender and Pascoe, pencils by Richards, inks by Joe Pimentel and Will Conrad, colors by Dave McCaig, letters by Clem Robins. Interiors, *BTVS* #43 and #45, April and June 2002.

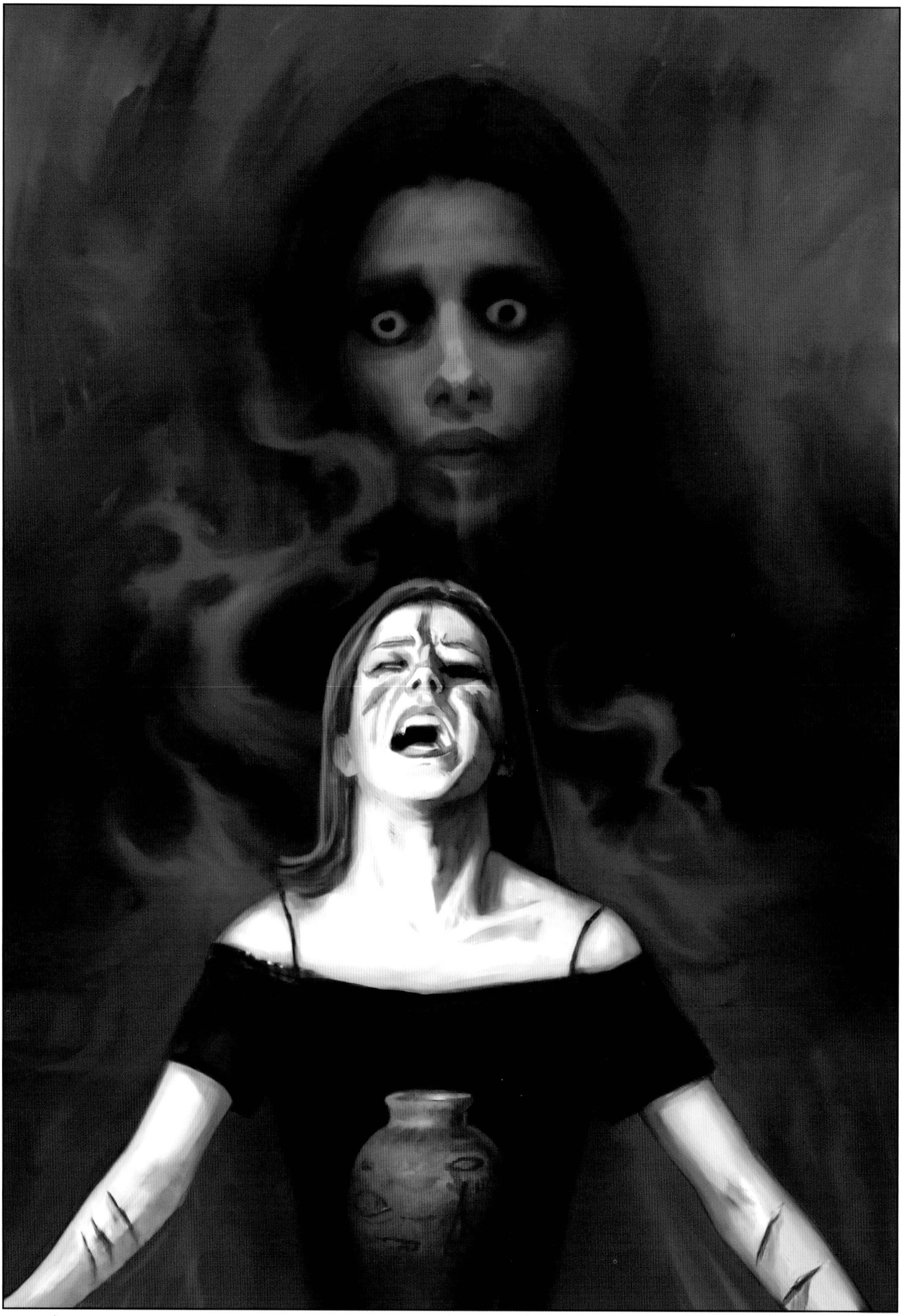

IN THE SEASON SIX EPISODE "Life Serial," the newly resurrected Buffy goes to meet Angel halfway between L.A. and Sunnydale. Buffy reveals nothing of the meeting, and Angel keeps quiet in the corresponding episode of his show. Jane Espenson, who co-wrote the *Buffy* episode, wrote the one-shot *Reunion* for me, in which Buffy's friends speculate on the meeting. The different points of view allowed for a who's who of *Buffy* comics artists, including cover artist Jeff Matsuda.

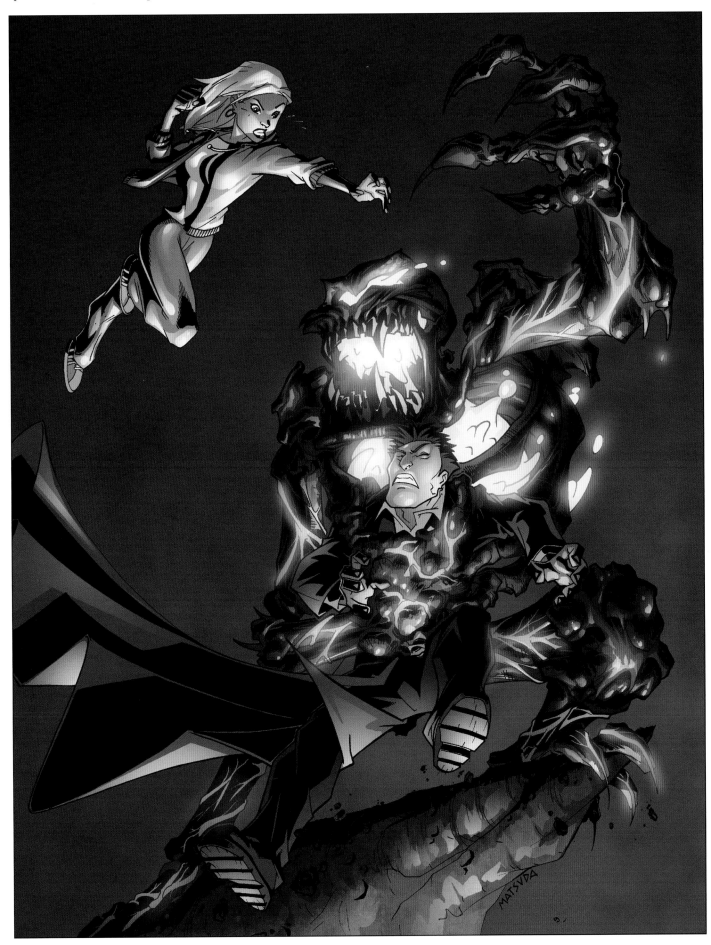

Opposite: Painting by Paul Lee and Brian Horton. Cover, *BTVS* #45, June 2002. Above: Art by Matsuda, colors by Guy Major. Cover, *BTVS: Reunion*, June 2002.

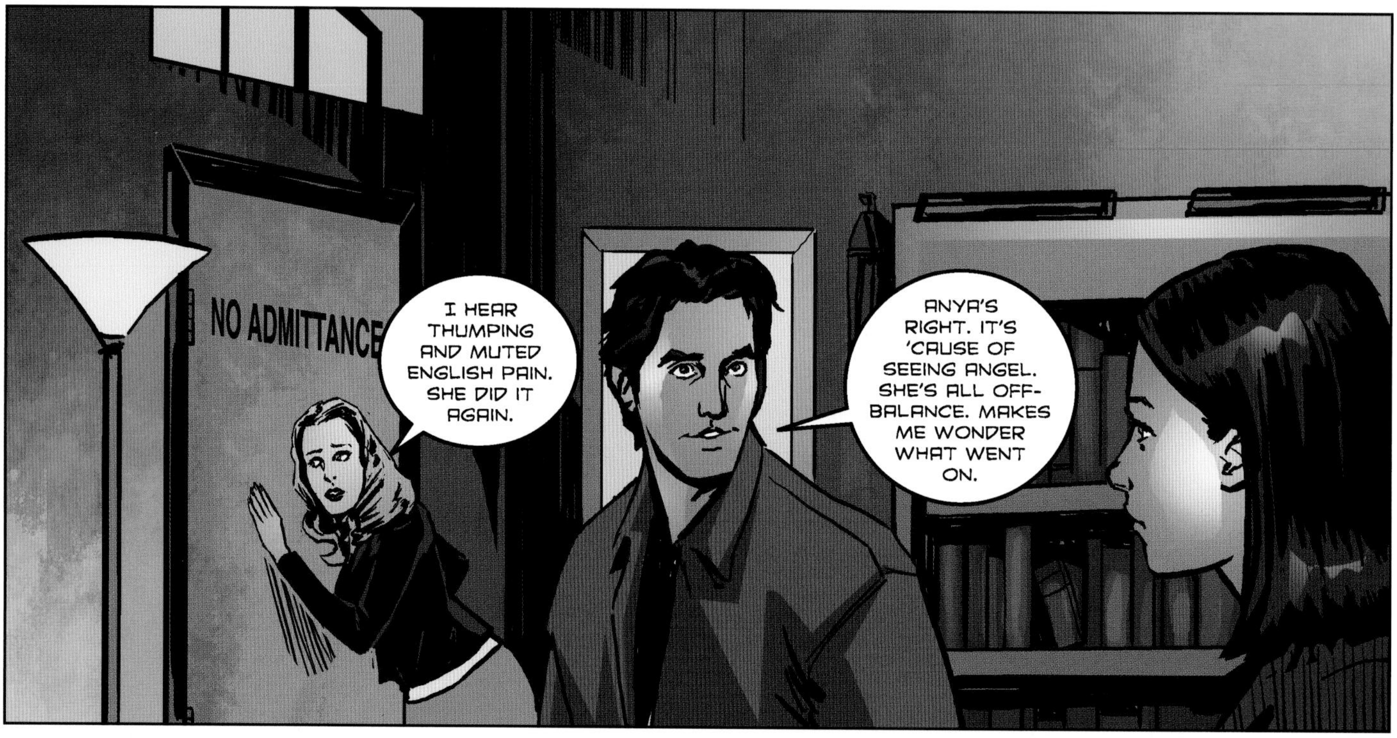
NO ADMITTANCE
I HEAR THUMPING AND MUTED ENGLISH PAIN. SHE DID IT AGAIN.
ANYA'S RIGHT. IT'S 'CAUSE OF SEEING ANGEL. SHE'S ALL OFF-BALANCE. MAKES ME WONDER WHAT WENT ON.

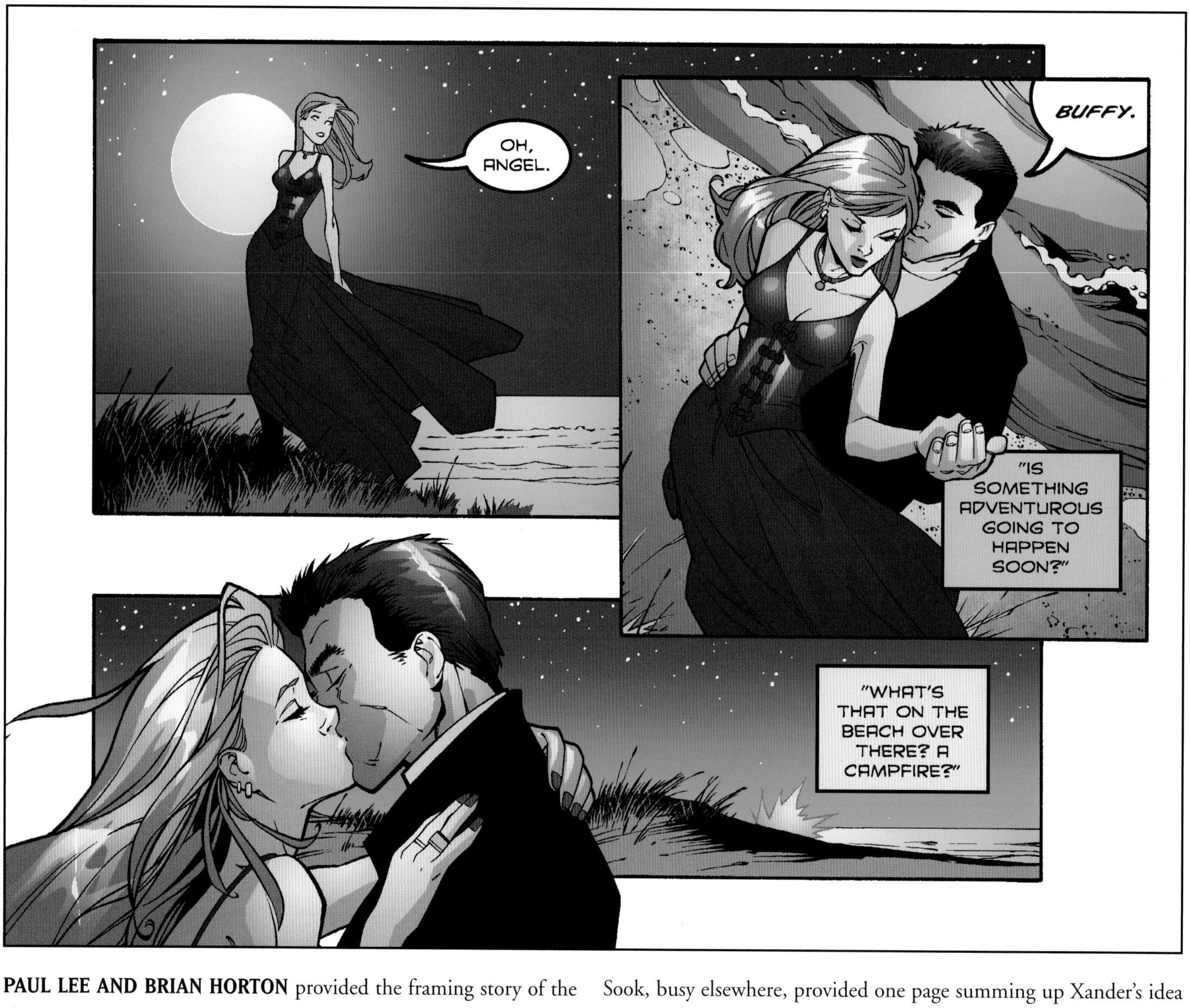
OH, ANGEL.
BUFFY.
"IS SOMETHING ADVENTUROUS GOING TO HAPPEN SOON?"
"WHAT'S THAT ON THE BEACH OVER THERE? A CAMPFIRE?"

PAUL LEE AND BRIAN HORTON provided the framing story of the characters hanging out in the Magic Box, and Randy Green, four years after dropping out of issue #1, finally drew his first pages of *Buffy*—dramatizing Dawn's idea of what went on during the reunion. Ryan Sook, busy elsewhere, provided one page summing up Xander's idea of what happened. The colored captions indicate the off-panel speculators—Anya in yellow, Xander in blue, and Dawn in pink.

 Top: Pencils and inks by Lee and Horton. Bottom: Pencils by Green, inks by Rick Ketcham. Opposite: Pencils and inks by Sook. Script by Jane Espenson, colors by Guy Major, letters by Pat Brosseau. Interiors, *BTVS: Reunion*, June 2002.

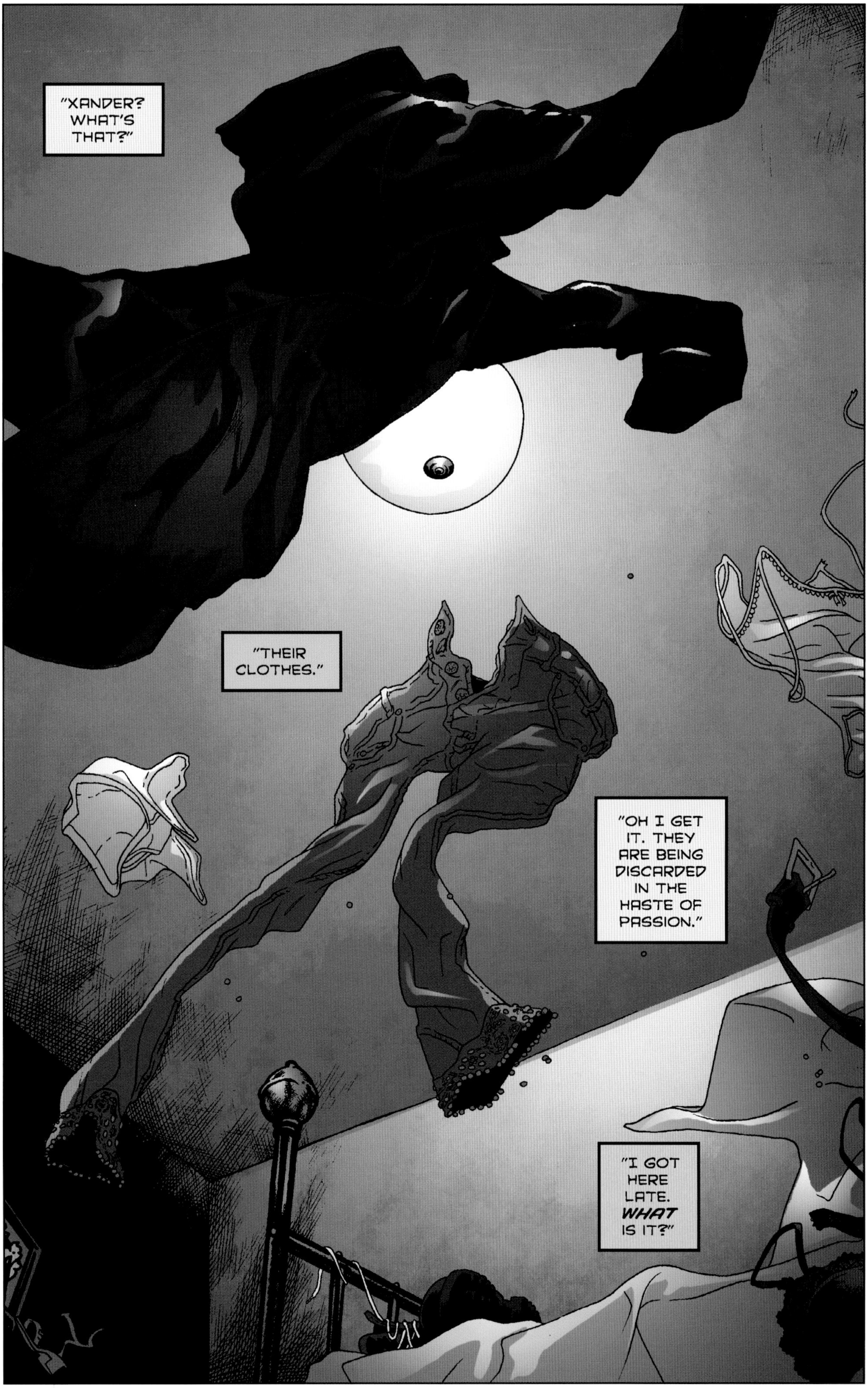
"XANDER? WHAT'S THAT?"
"THEIR CLOTHES."
"OH I GET IT. THEY ARE BEING DISCARDED IN THE HASTE OF PASSION."
"I GOT HERE LATE. ***WHAT*** IS IT?"

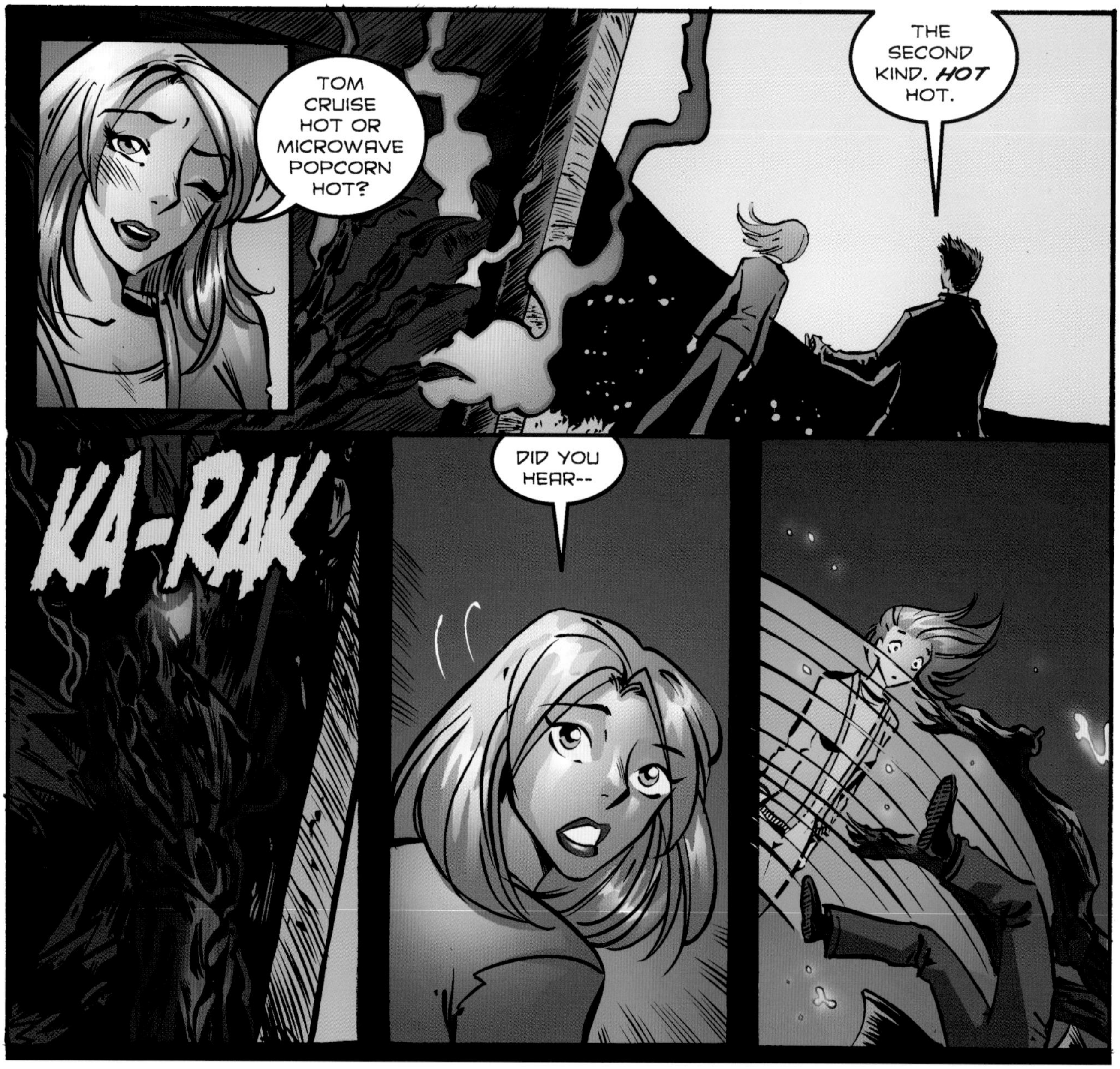
TOM CRUISE HOT OR MICROWAVE POPCORN HOT?
THE SECOND KIND. *HOT* HOT.
KA-RAK
DID YOU HEAR--

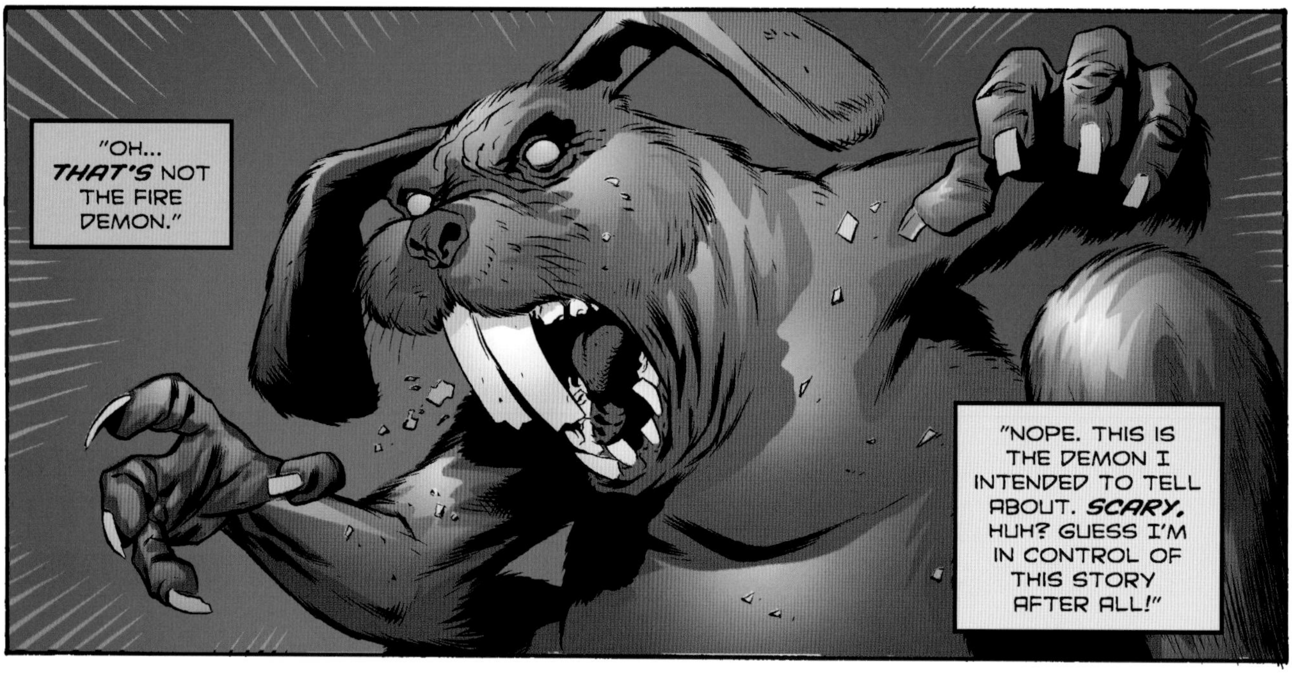
"OH... *THAT'S* NOT THE FIRE DEMON."
"NOPE. THIS IS THE DEMON I INTENDED TO TELL ABOUT. *SCARY,* HUH? GUESS I'M IN CONTROL OF THIS STORY AFTER ALL!"

CHYNNA CLUGSTON, a big *Buffy* fan who'd done a pinup for us, drew Xander's revised take on the reunion, and Eric Powell drew Anya's. Only Powell could accurately bring Anya's deepest fears to life.

 Top: Pencils and inks by Clugston. Bottom: Pencils and inks by Powell. Script by Jane Espenson, colors by Guy Major, letters by Pat Brosseau. Interiors, *BTVS: Reunion*, June 2002.

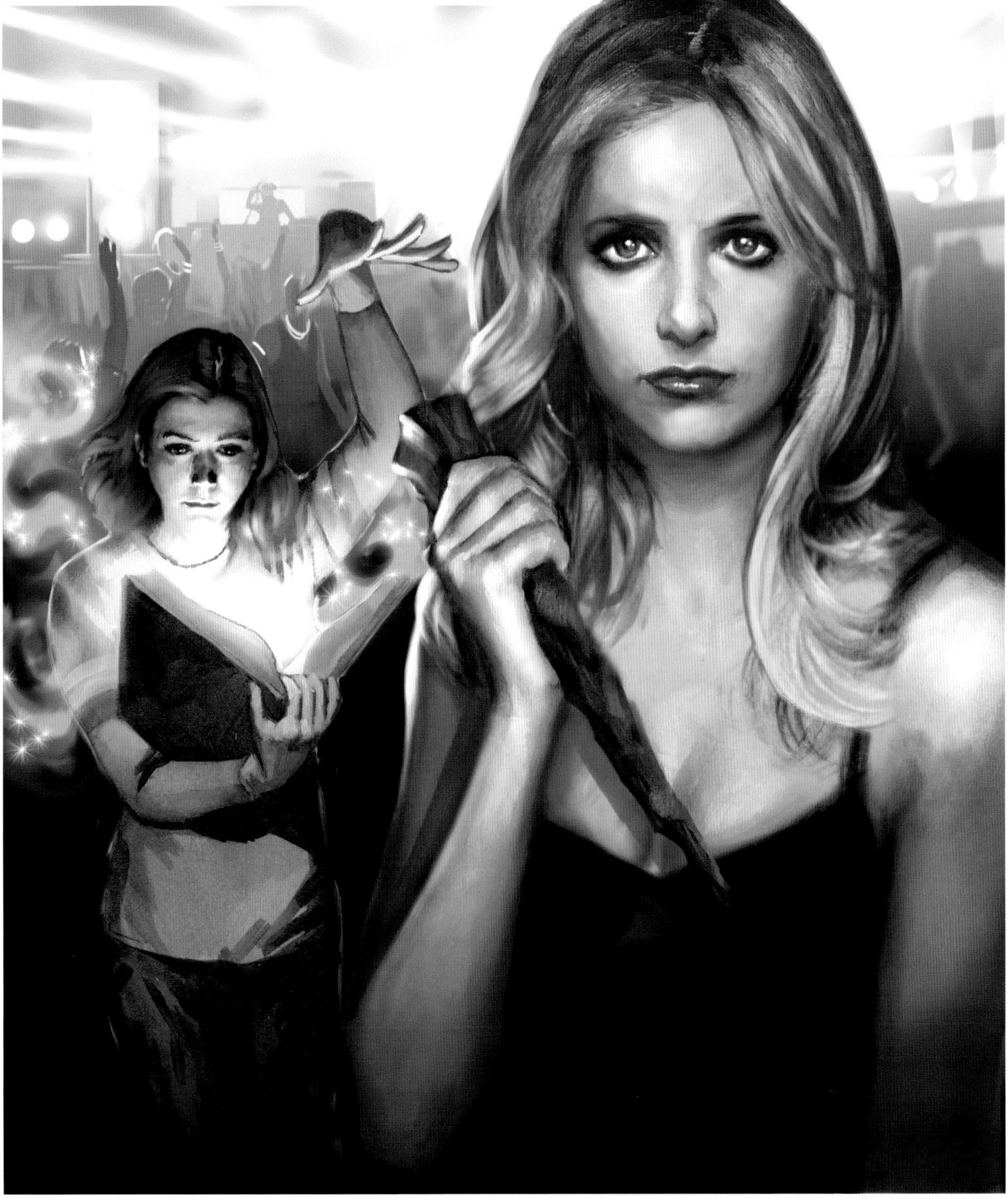

WHILE THE NOVEL LICENSE for *Buffy* remained with Pocket Books, there was room in our license to do illustrated prose. I commissioned the monthly series writers Tom Fassbender and Jim Pascoe to write it, since it was their prose on their co-written novel *By the Balls* that had led me to hire them for the comic in the first place. The art was created by the Lee-Horton team. The book was called *Creatures of Habit*, playing off the Season Six metaphor of magic as drug addiction, and mixing in vampirism. Our first meeting about the book took place at night at the San Diego Comic-Con, with my wife present, and the artists' agent falling asleep.

Above and following four pages: Paintings and pencils and inks by Paul Lee and Brian Horton. Cover and interiors, *BTVS: Creatures of Habit*, May 2002.

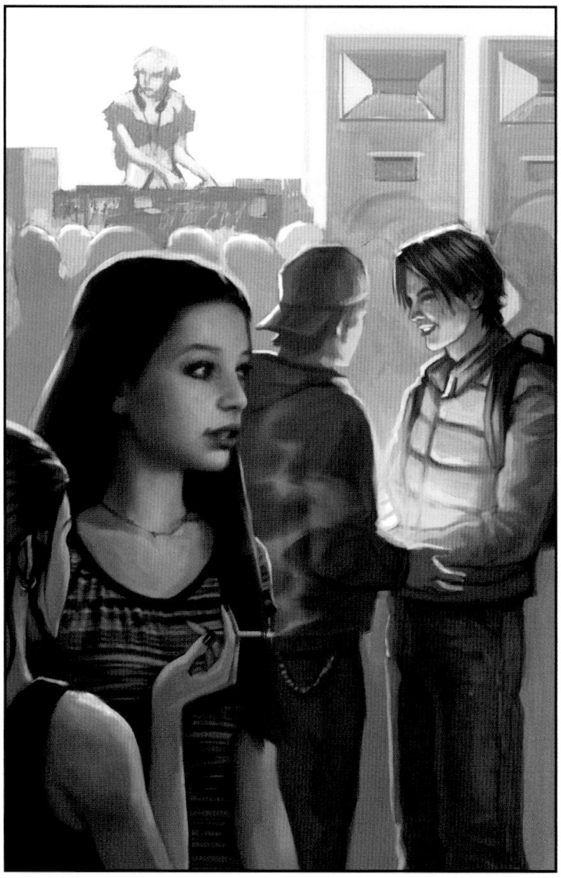
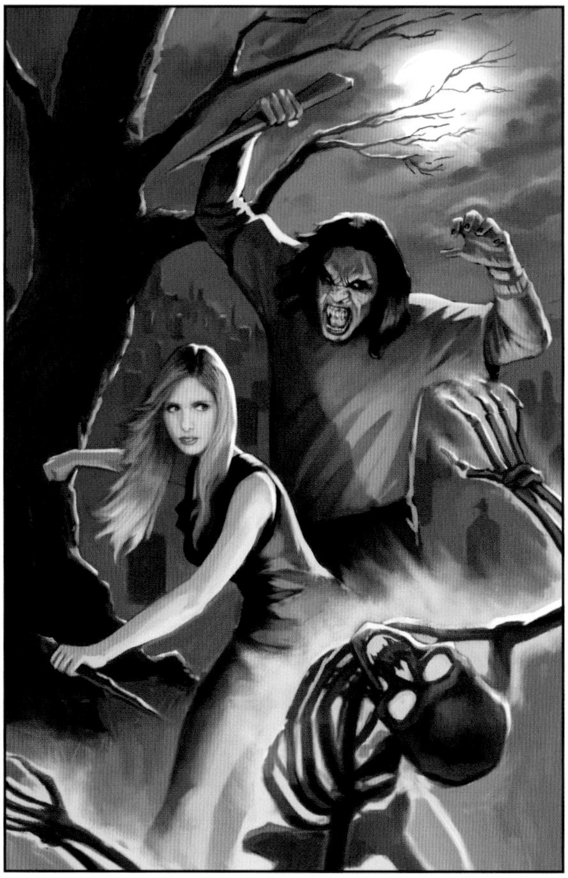
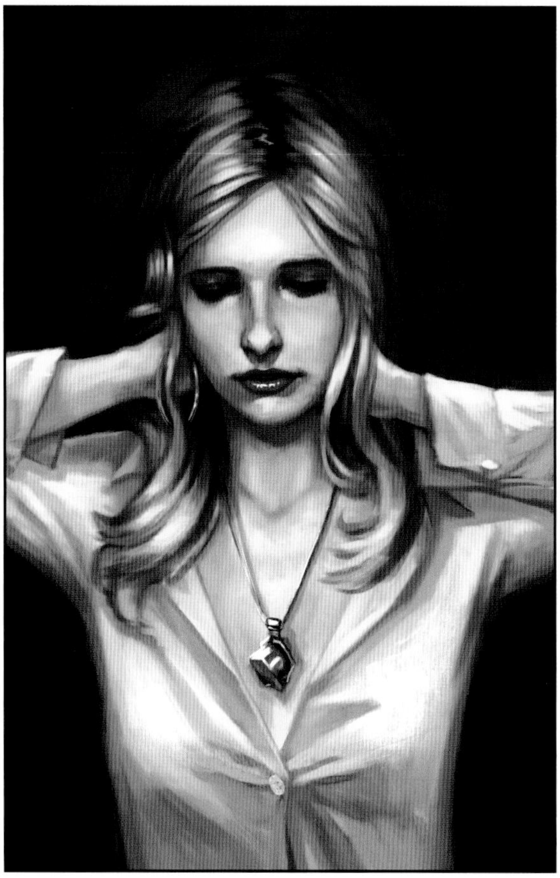
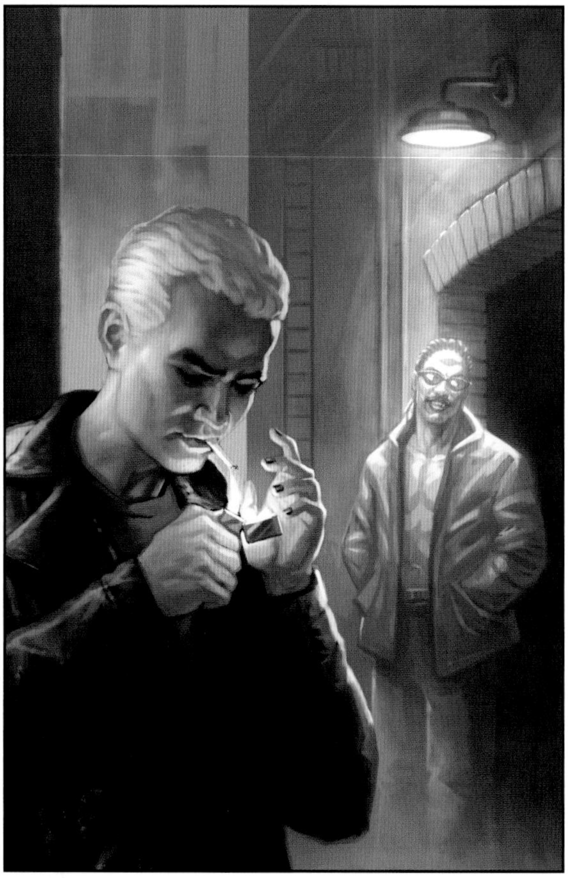

WITH THE WHOLE creative team in L.A., I flew down for a follow-up meeting to work out the story and talk about how the art and the text would interact. Since we were coming from comics, we didn't want the art to just be tacked on to the story, but to serve story purposes, to be planned as part of the reading experience—something we can't recreate on these pages, and you can only appreciate by reading the novel. We met for breakfast in a typically trendy outdoor restaurant. We sat at a big table, with all Paul and Brian's previous *Buffy* art scattered before us. In one of the most ironic and unlikely moments of my career, Sarah Michelle Gellar walked in, passed us, and sat two tables away.

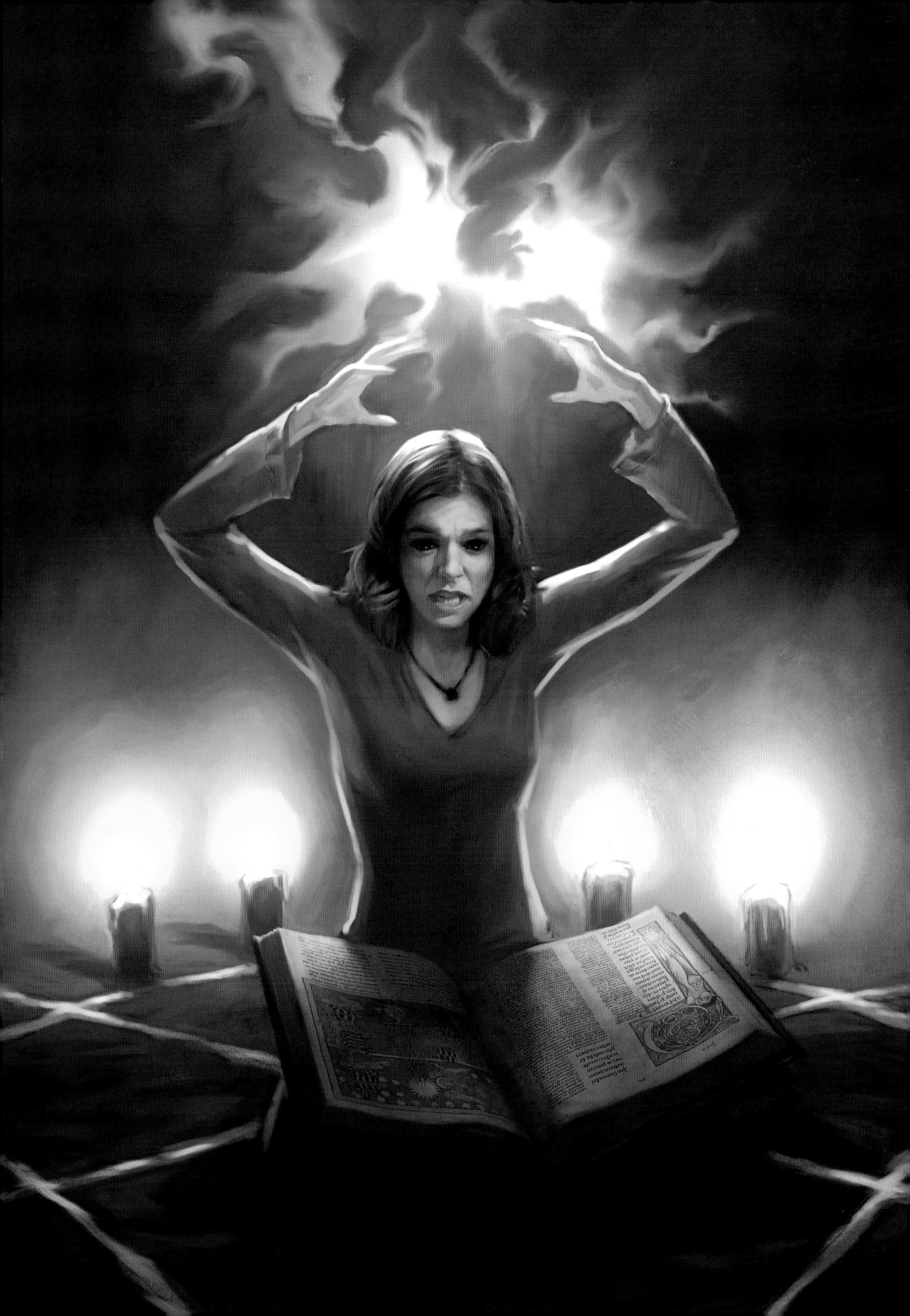

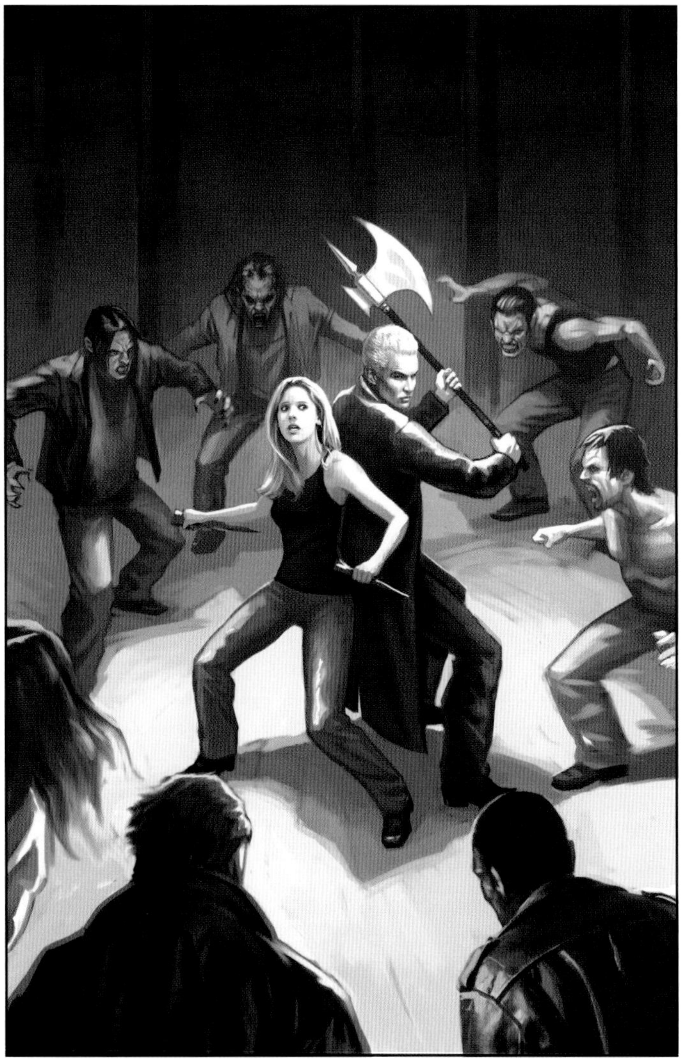

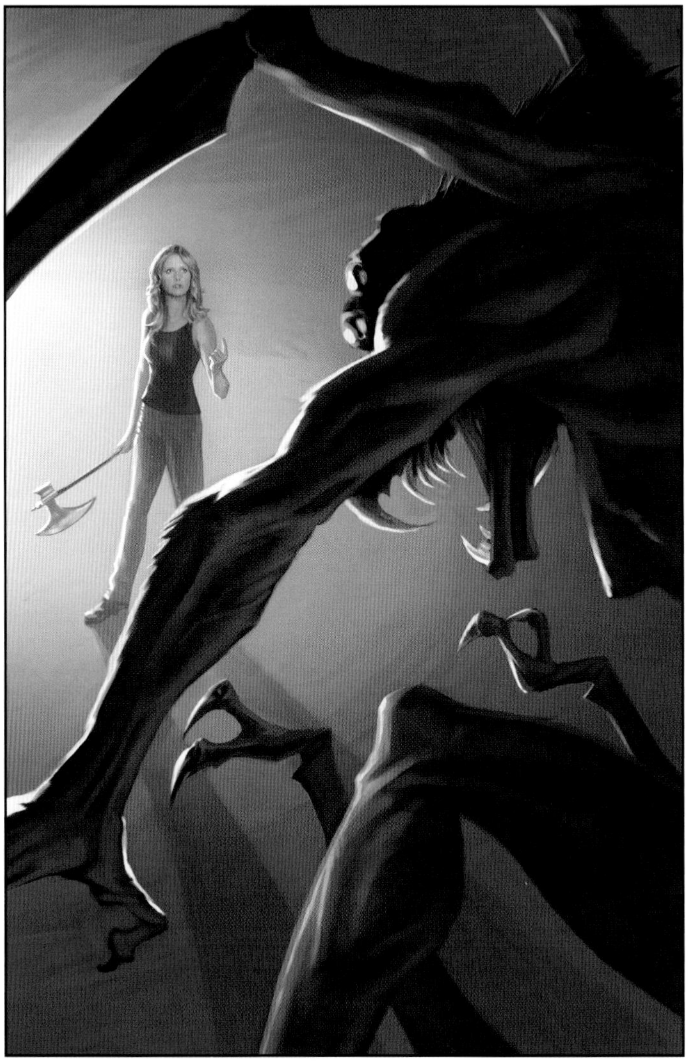

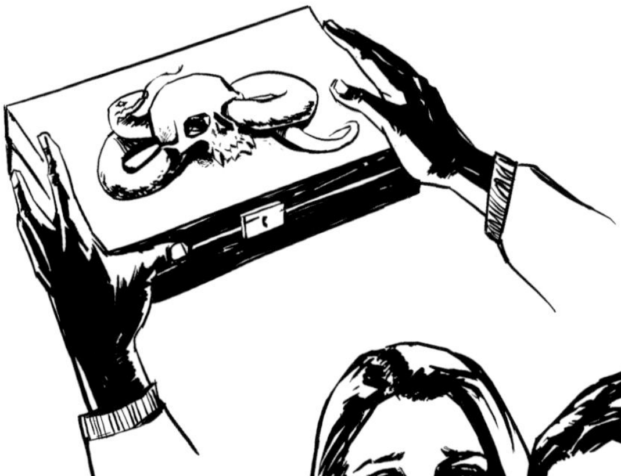

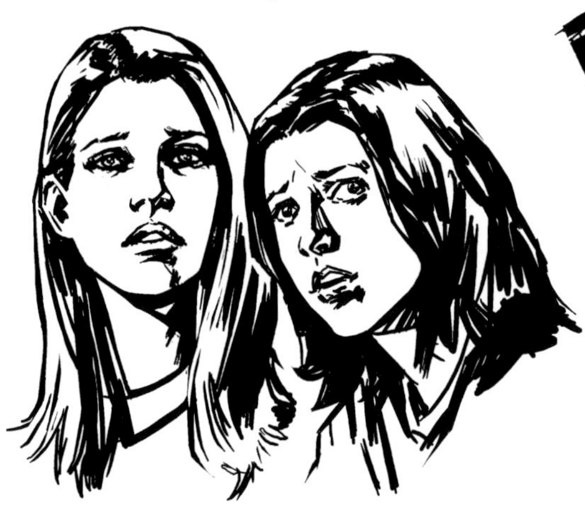

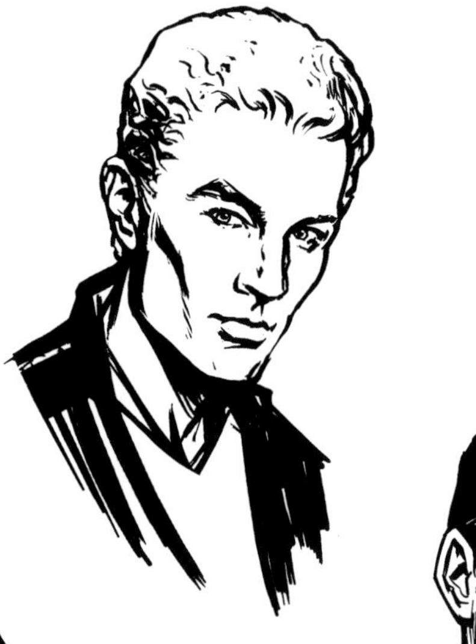

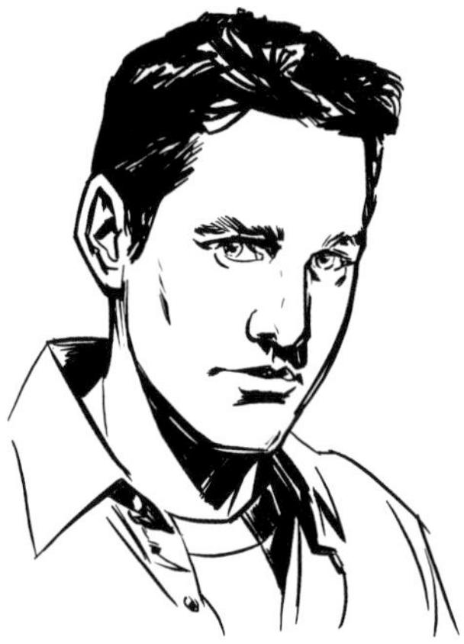

WE ALL FROZE, trying to wrap our heads around the synchronicity. I stood up and flipped all of the paintings face-down. Paul and Brian looked at each other, looked at me, and started flipping them all back over. The meeting was derailed by an argument over whether or not to go over to her to show her the art, with me exercising executive veto privilege. To Brian in particular, it was a god-given opportunity we shouldn't ignore. When I saw Joss the next day, I told him what had happened, and he said I'd probably spared us stalking charges.

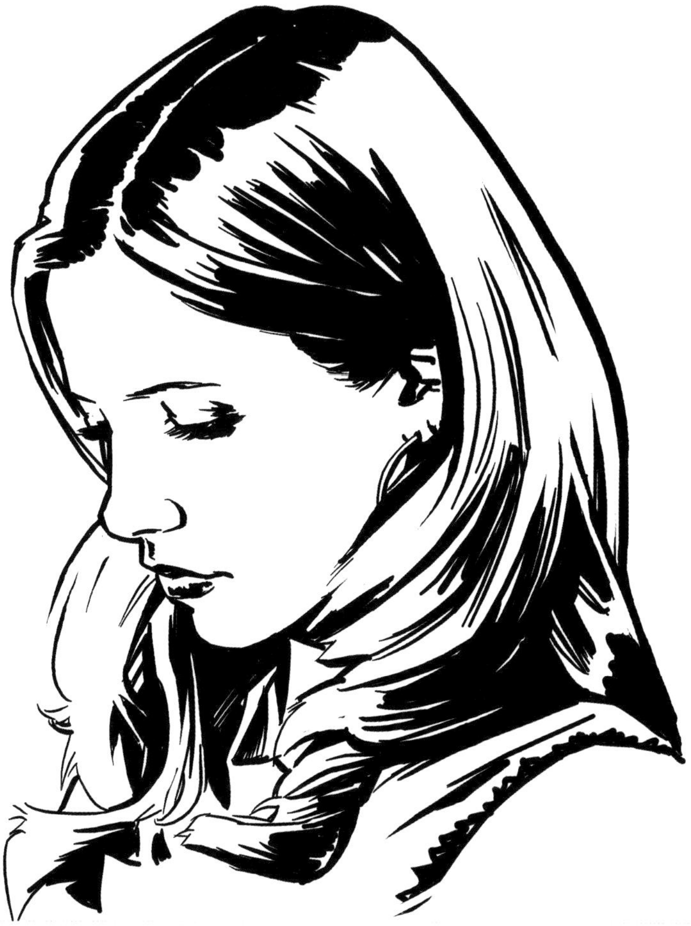

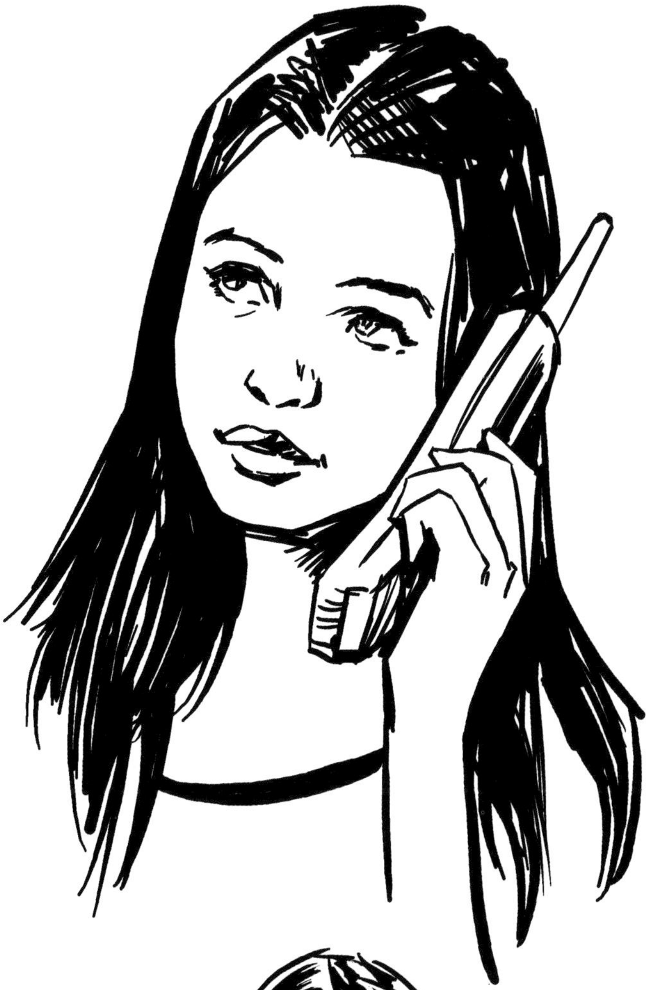

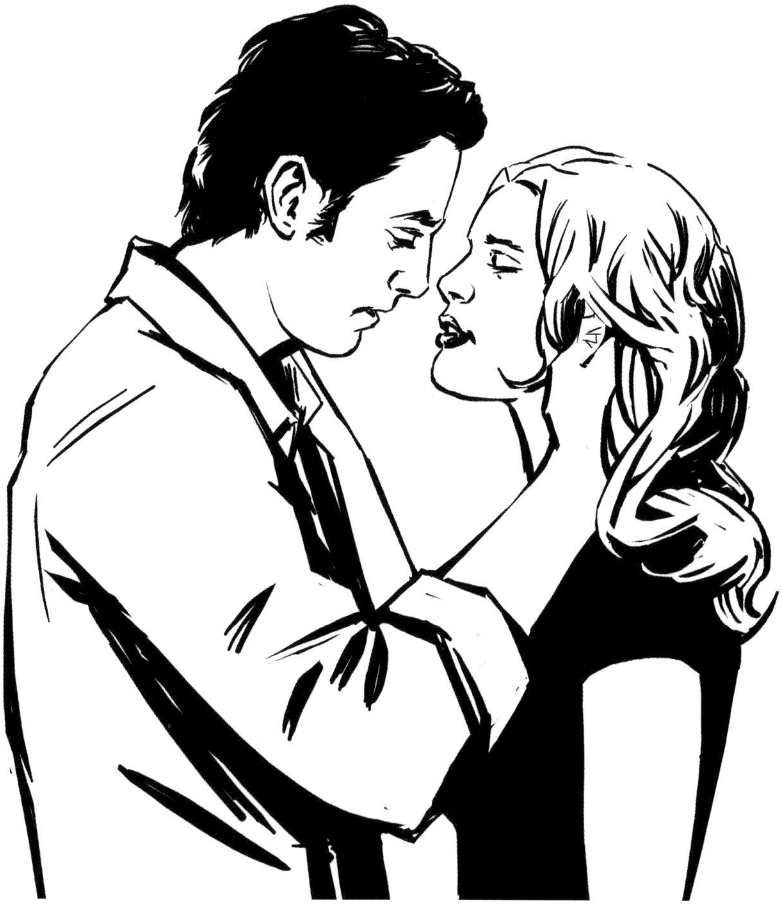

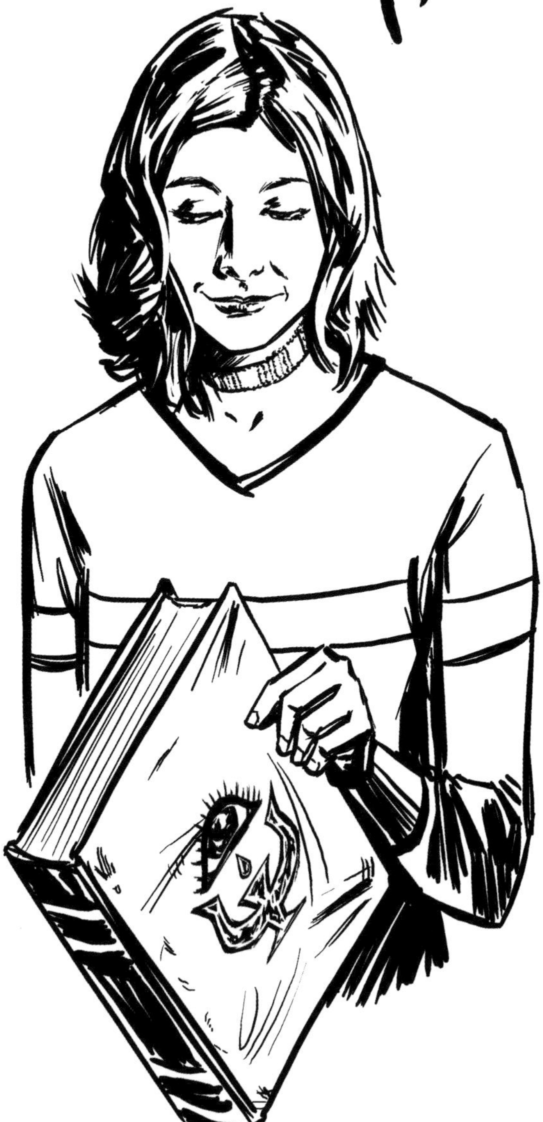

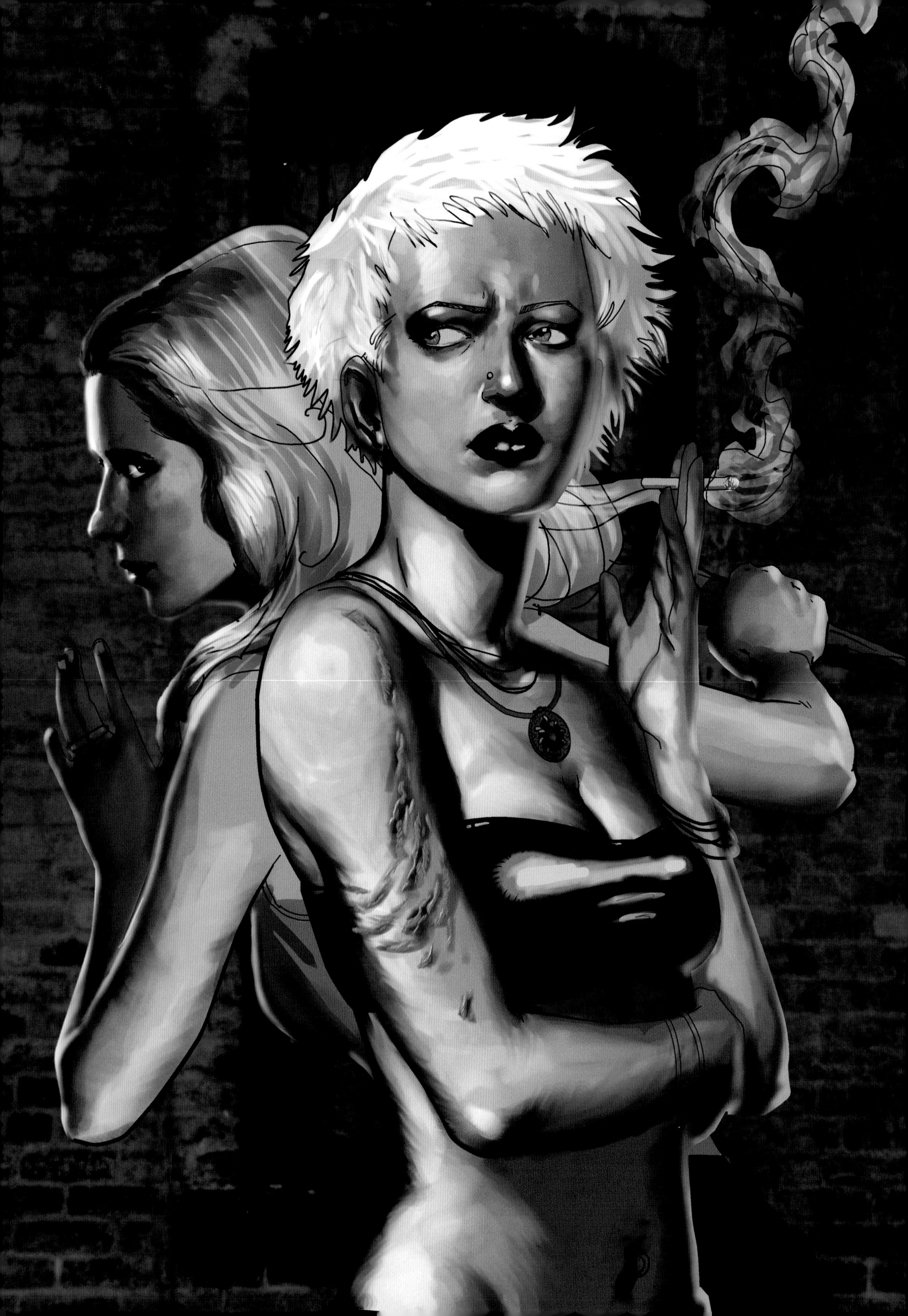

WILL, YOU BELIEVE ME, RIGHT?
IT'S LIKE, YOU KNOW HOW YOU CAN LOVE SOMETHING SO MUCH THAT IT KINDA SCARES YOU?
YEAH. I DO.
YOU'RE WHAT? A SEXUALLY LIBERATED FEMALE? PLEASE. COME TO GRIPS WITH WHO YOU ARE ... WITH WHAT YOU ARE.
YOU CAN RISE ABOVE ALL THIS, YOU KNOW. I MEAN, LOOK AT YOU, YOU WORK AT DOUBLEMEAT PALACE, FOR BLOODY SAKE! YOU'RE BETTER--
I'D KICK YOU, BUT ALL THE STRENGTH HAS GONE OUT OF MY LEGS.
OKAY, GO THEN. YOU BEST LOOK AFTER THE LITTLE BIT AND ALL. GET SOME QUALITY TIME, SIS TO SIS.
DAWN'S FINE, SHE DOESN'T NEED ME CROWDING HER.
I SENSE A PLAN COMING TOGETHER. YOU KNOW WHAT TO DO?
UG.

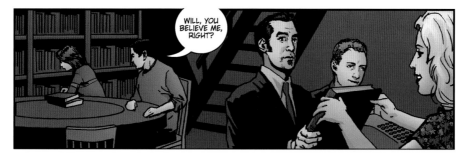

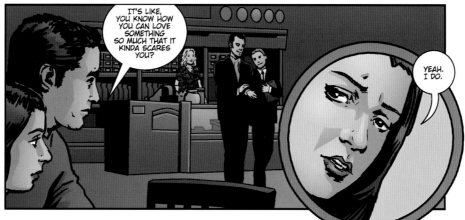

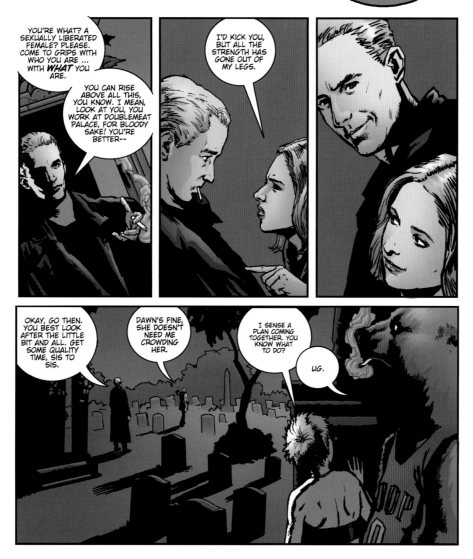

THE WORK ON *CREATURES OF HABIT* was grueling, and took a toll on the creative team. However, we somehow pulled off a follow-up the month after. Tom Fassbender, Jim Pascoe, and Paul Lee teamed up for *Buffy* #46, a rare issue not drawn by Cliff. It wrapped up the story of one of the villains who survived the novel. The giant bear, Hoopy, was Paul's idea. Fassbender and Pascoe wrote themselves into the scene in the Magic Box—Pascoe had green hair at the time; Fassbender, a soul patch—but Paul offered his own take on their partnership.

Opposite: Painting by Lee. Above: Script by Fassbender and Pascoe, pencils and inks by Lee, colors and letters by Michelle Madsen. Cover and interiors, *BTVS* #46, June 2002.

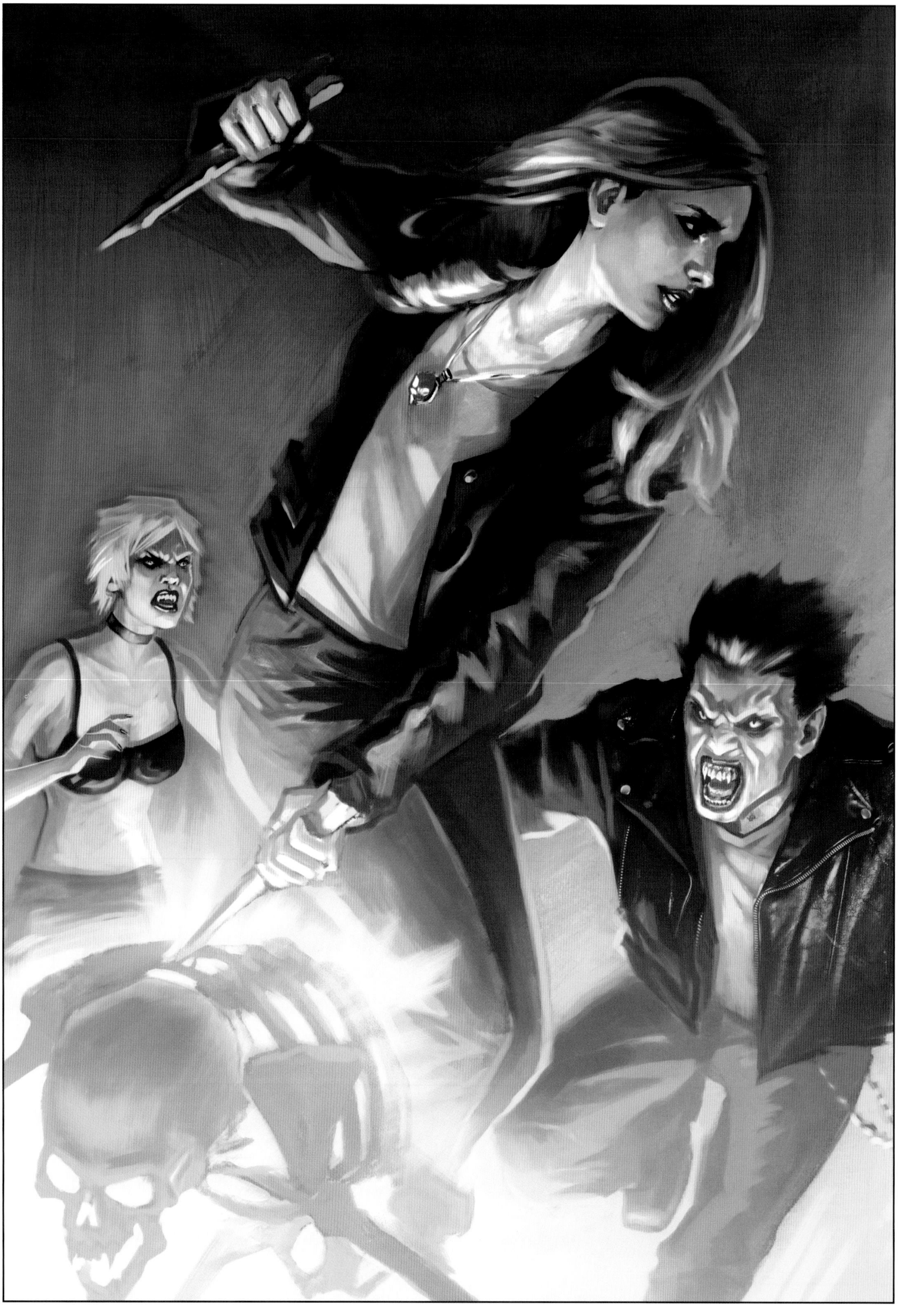

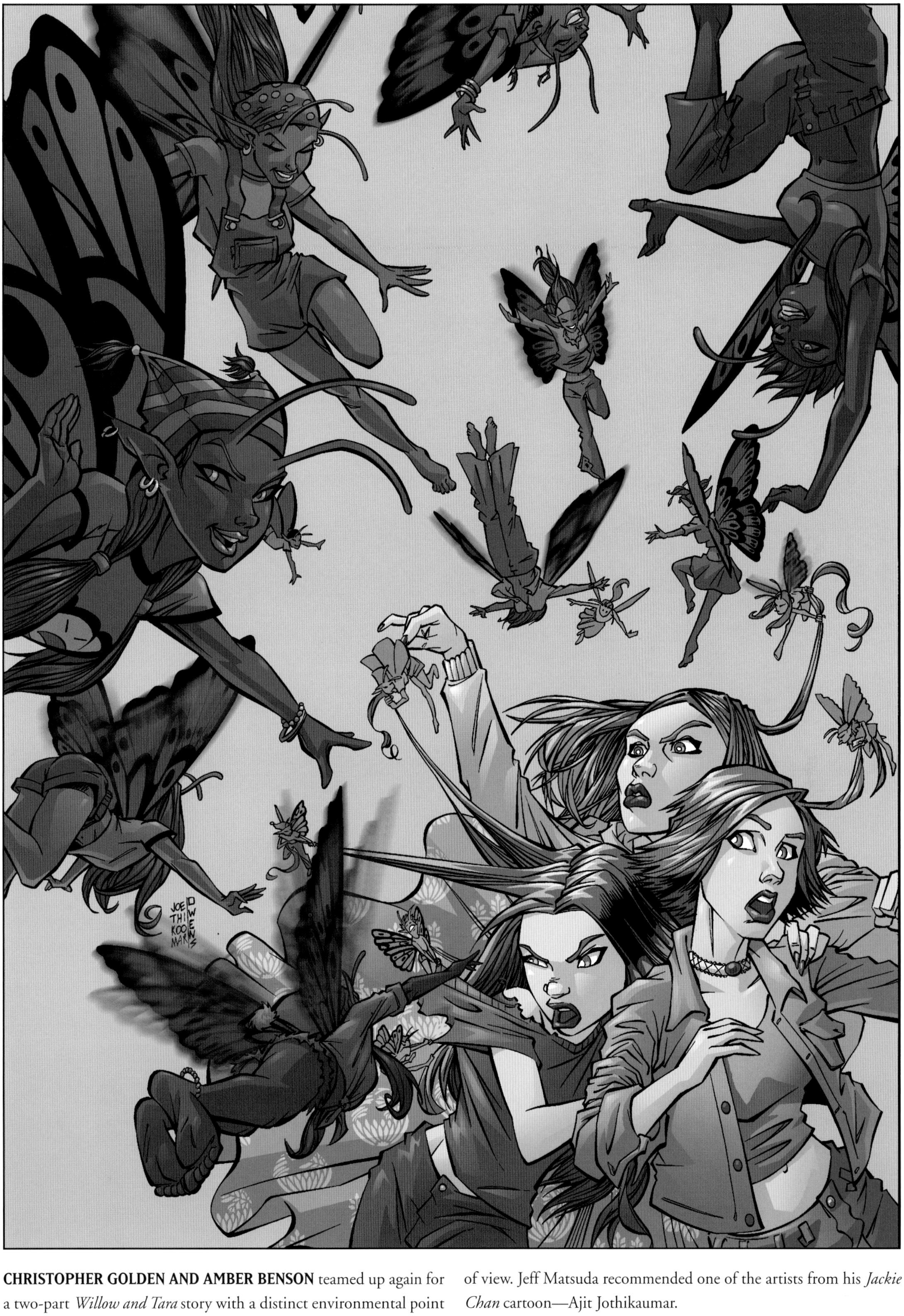

CHRISTOPHER GOLDEN AND AMBER BENSON teamed up again for a two-part *Willow and Tara* story with a distinct environmental point of view. Jeff Matsuda recommended one of the artists from his *Jackie Chan* cartoon—Ajit Jothikaumar.

Opposite: Art by Paul Lee and Brian Horton. Interiors, *BTVS: Creatures of Habit*, May 2002. Above: Pencils by Ajit Jothikaumar, inks by Andy Owens, colors by Dave Stewart. Cover, *Willow and Tara: Wilderness* #1, July 2006.

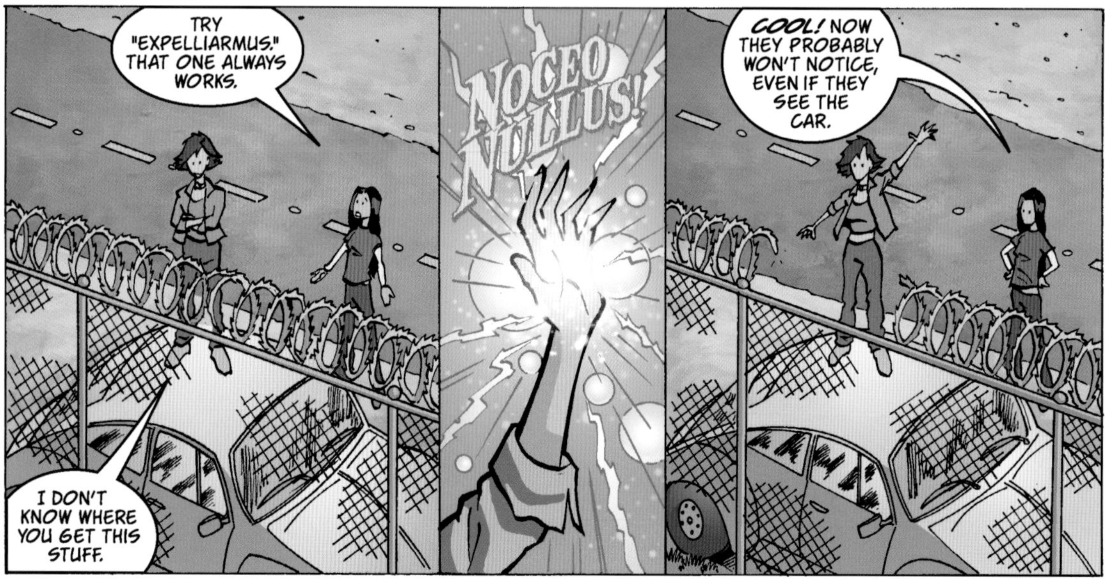
TRY "EXPELLIARMUS." THAT ONE ALWAYS WORKS.
I DON'T KNOW WHERE YOU GET THIS STUFF.
NOCEO NULLUS!
COOL! NOW THEY PROBABLY WON'T NOTICE, EVEN IF THEY SEE THE CAR.

A TERRIFIC ARTIST, Ajit Jothikaumar couldn't keep up with the schedule, and was replaced in the middle of issue two by Klebs Junior, who did a great job of matching the style—but the second issue was still a month late. Christopher Golden was disappointed that he needed to explain to me that the first panel, above, was a Harry Potter reference. "Don't you think you should pay attention to these things?" he asked.

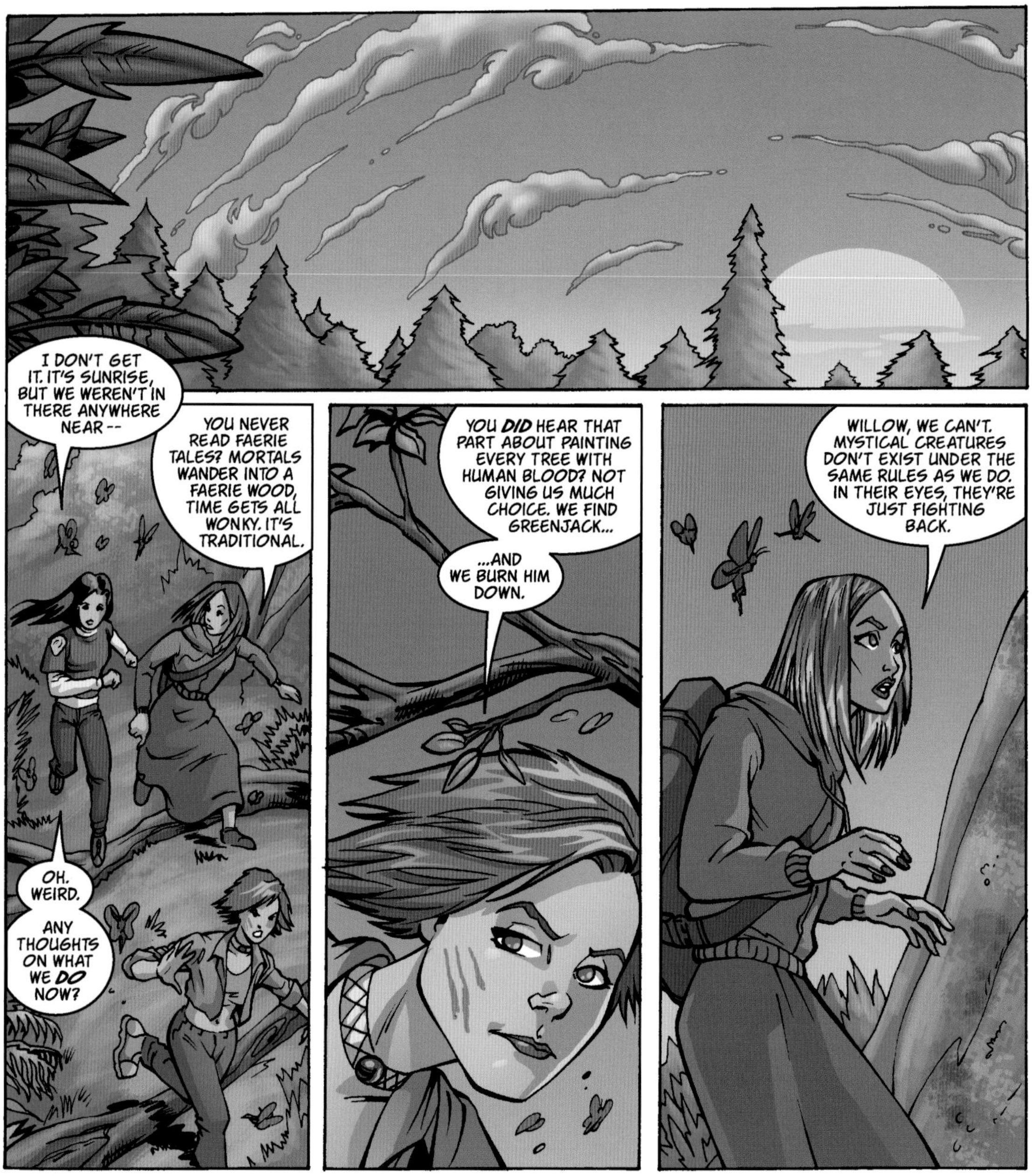
I DON'T GET IT. IT'S SUNRISE, BUT WE WEREN'T IN THERE ANYWHERE NEAR --
YOU NEVER READ FAERIE TALES? MORTALS WANDER INTO A FAERIE WOOD, TIME GETS ALL WONKY. IT'S TRADITIONAL.
OH. WEIRD.
ANY THOUGHTS ON WHAT WE *DO* NOW?
YOU *DID* HEAR THAT PART ABOUT PAINTING EVERY TREE WITH HUMAN BLOOD? NOT GIVING US MUCH CHOICE. WE FIND GREENJACK...
...AND WE BURN HIM DOWN.
WILLOW, WE CAN'T. MYSTICAL CREATURES DON'T EXIST UNDER THE SAME RULES AS WE DO. IN THEIR EYES, THEY'RE JUST FIGHTING BACK.

 Top: Pencils by Jothikaumar, inks by Derek Fridolfs. Middle and bottom: Pencils by Klebs Jr., inks by Fabio Laguna. Script by Amber Benson and Golden, colors by Michelle Madsen, letters by Michael Heisler. Interiors, *Willow and Tara: Wilderness* #1 and #2, July and September 2002. Opposite: Pencils by Jothikaumar, inks by Andy Owens, colors by Dave Stewart. Cover, *Willow and Tara: Wilderness* #2, September 2002.

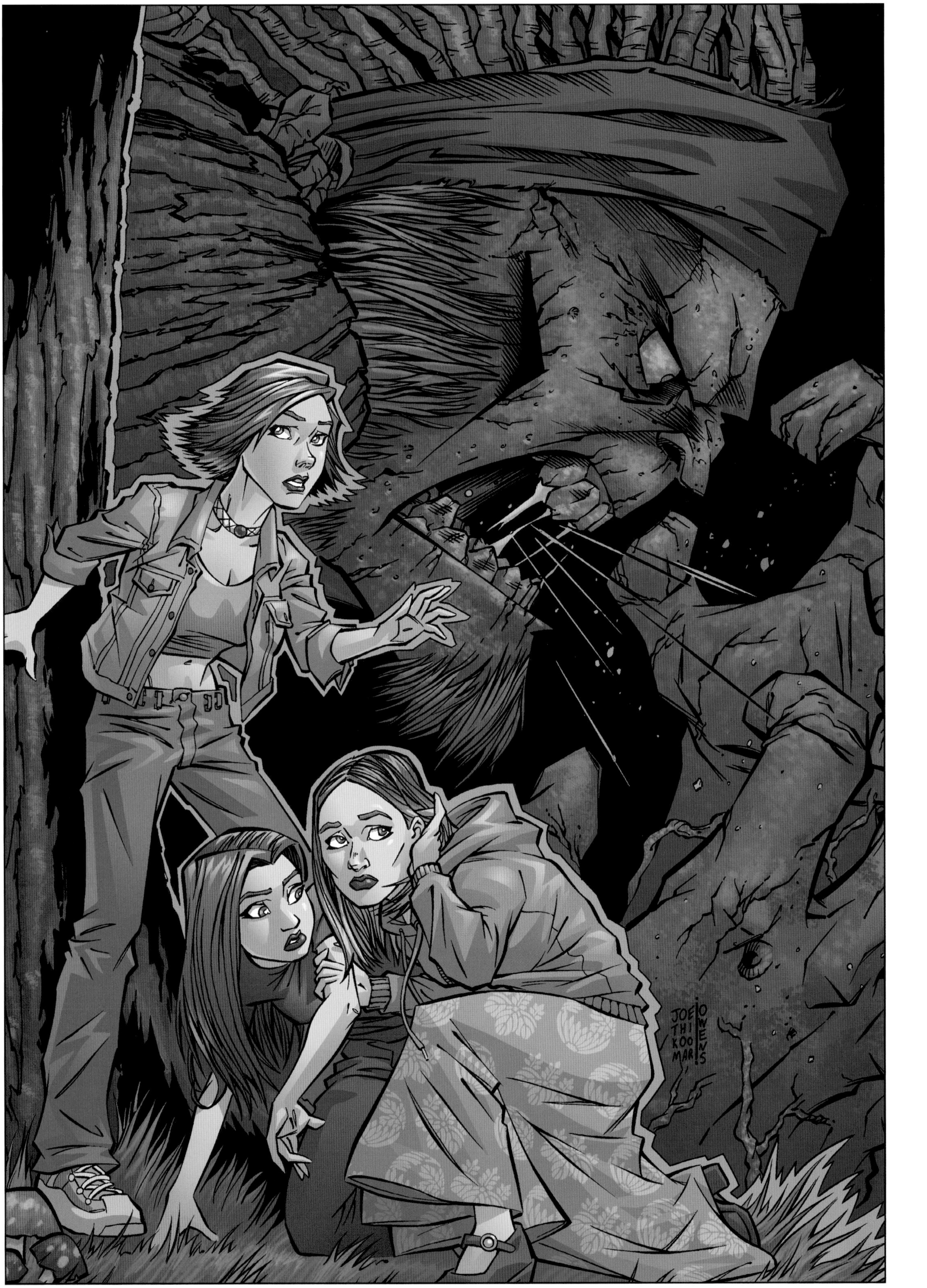
JOE THI KOO MAR
OWENS

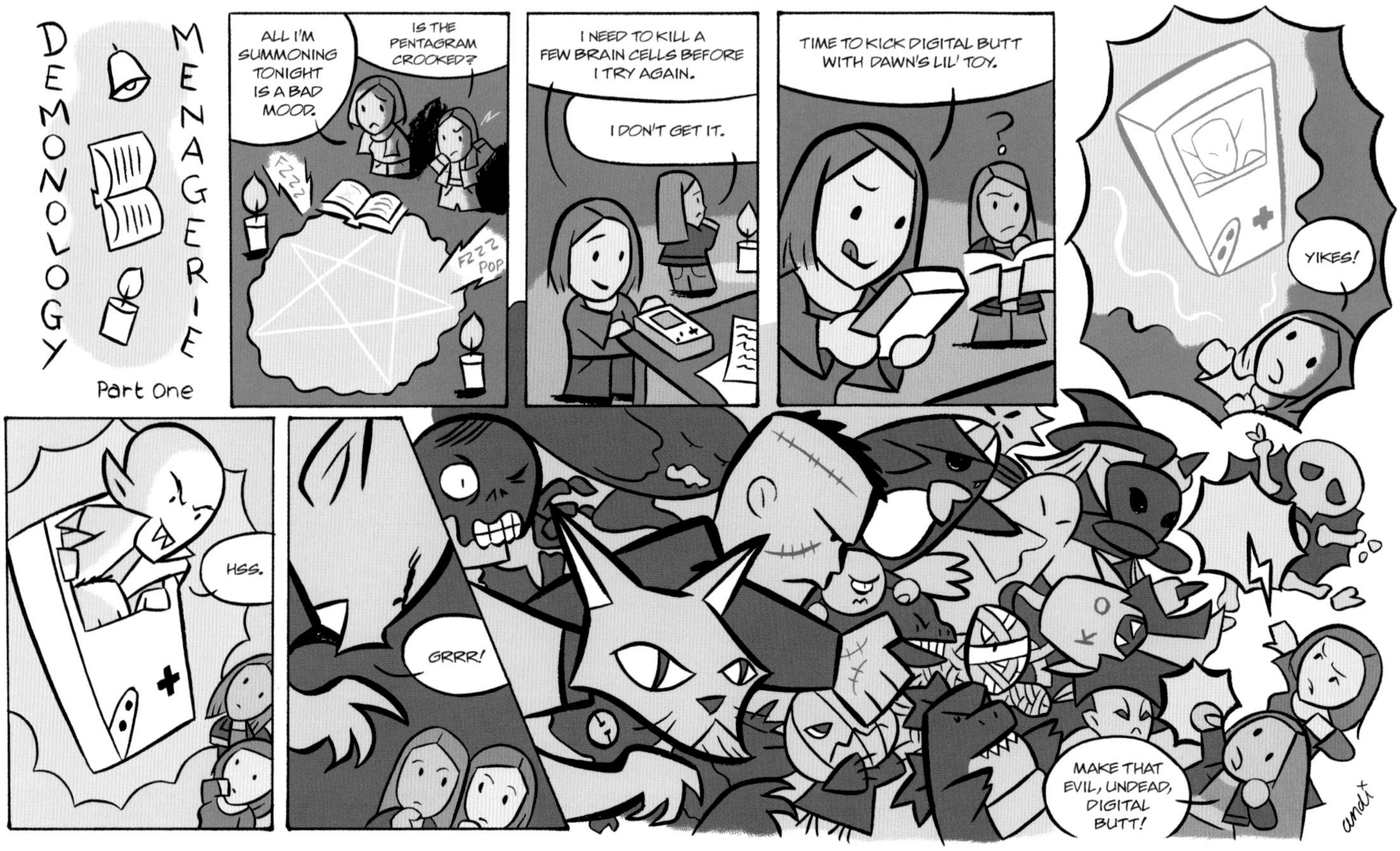
DEMONOLOGY MENAGERIE
Part One
ALL I'M SUMMONING TONIGHT IS A BAD MOOD.
IS THE PENTAGRAM CROOKED?
ZZZ
FZZZ POP
I NEED TO KILL A FEW BRAIN CELLS BEFORE I TRY AGAIN.
I DON'T GET IT.
TIME TO KICK DIGITAL BUTT WITH DAWN'S LIL' TOY.
?
YIKES!
HSS.
GRRR!
MAKE THAT EVIL, UNDEAD, DIGITAL BUTT!

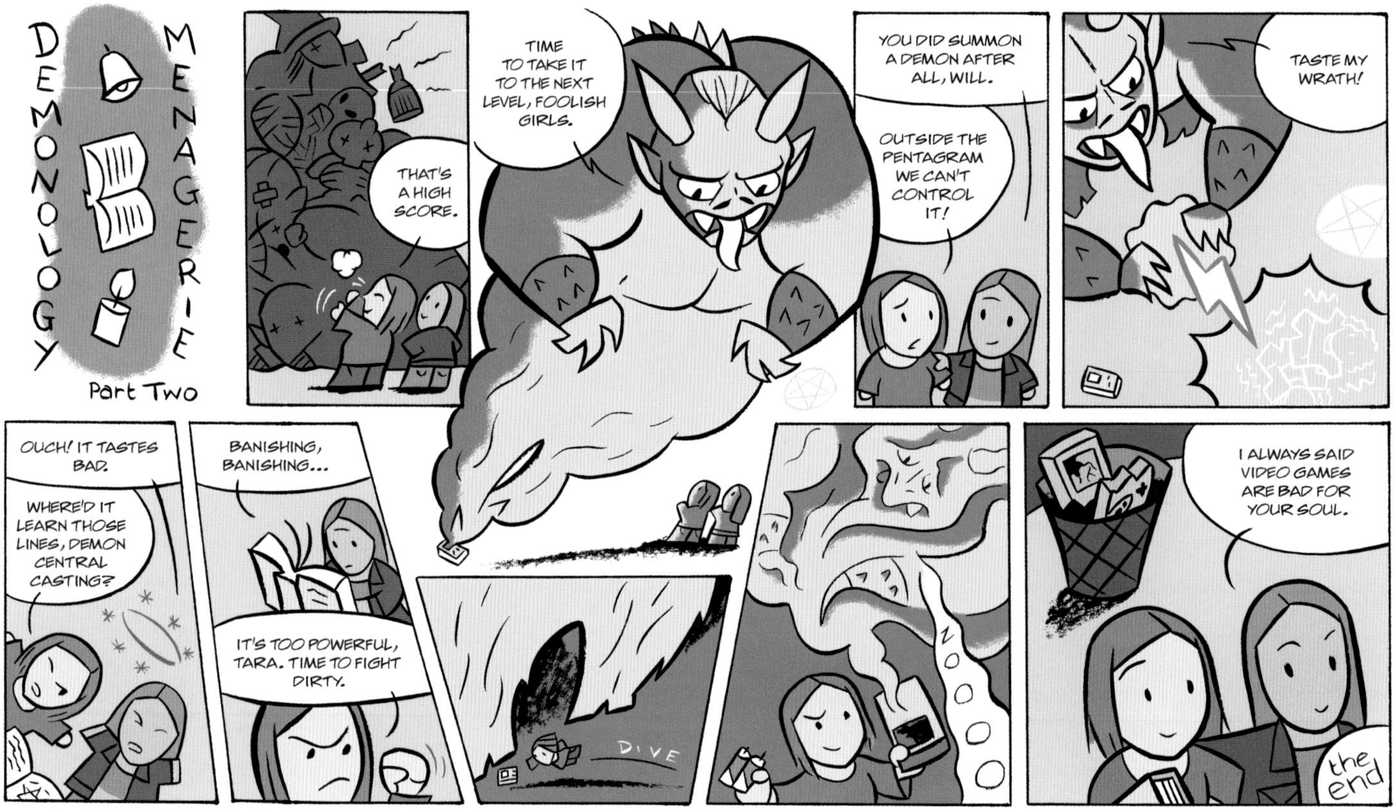
DEMONOLOGY MENAGERIE
Part Two
THAT'S A HIGH SCORE.
TIME TO TAKE IT TO THE NEXT LEVEL, FOOLISH GIRLS.
YOU DID SUMMON A DEMON AFTER ALL, WILL.
OUTSIDE THE PENTAGRAM WE CAN'T CONTROL IT!
TASTE MY WRATH!
OUCH! IT TASTES BAD.
WHERE'D IT LEARN THOSE LINES, DEMON CENTRAL CASTING?
BANISHING, BANISHING...
IT'S TOO POWERFUL, TARA. TIME TO FIGHT DIRTY.
DIVE
NOOOOO
I ALWAYS SAID VIDEO GAMES ARE BAD FOR YOUR SOUL.
the end

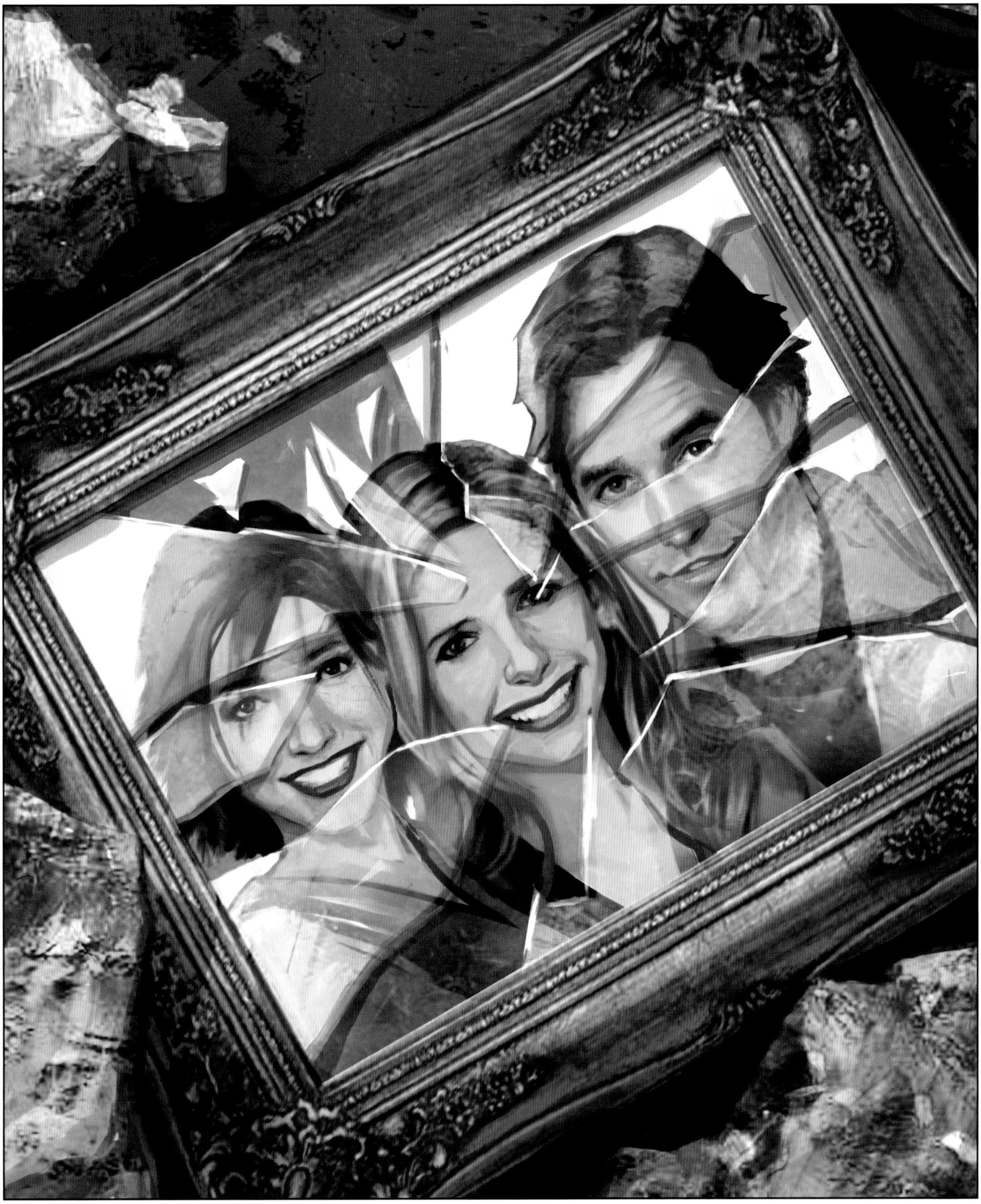

FOR A FEW YEARS starting in the late nineties, Dark Horse published a newspaper-format promotional item called *Dark Horse Extra*, which featured exclusive strips, usually timed to highlight upcoming releases. I wanted to do something with Willow and Tara to promote the Benson-Golden book, but didn't want to make a bad schedule worse. I went to the original *Buffy* comics writer Andi Watson. This is the only *Buffy* piece he both wrote and drew—and of course she's not even in it.

Creatures of Habit had been such a scheduling challenge that it soon led Tom Fassbender and Jim Pascoe to leave the series. They quit at a bad time, and it got worse quick. I hired Scott Lobdell to take over the series. His first pitch for a post–Season Six story was initially approved by Fox, but ultimately shot down by Joss, for being too close to his Season Seven plans. This cover was commissioned based off that plot before it got rejected. We then had to hustle to come up with a story that would pass muster and still fit the cover. Lobdell brought Fabian Nicieza in to co-write.

Opposite: Script, pencils, inks, color, and letters by Watson. "Demonology Menagerie," *Dark Horse Extra* #47 and #48, May and June 2002. Above: Painting by Paul Lee and Brian Horton. Cover, *BTVS* #47, August 2002.

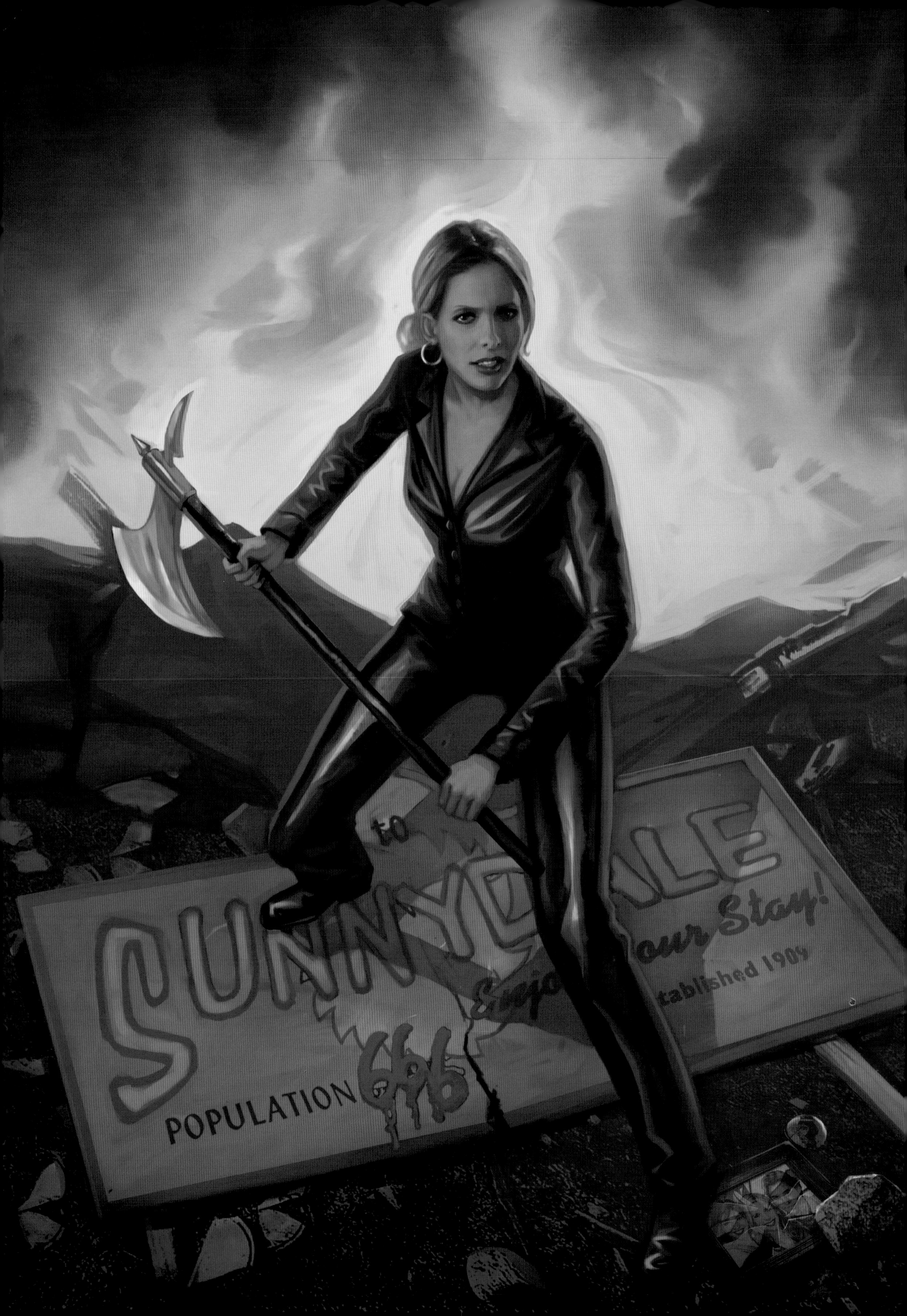
to
POPULATION 666

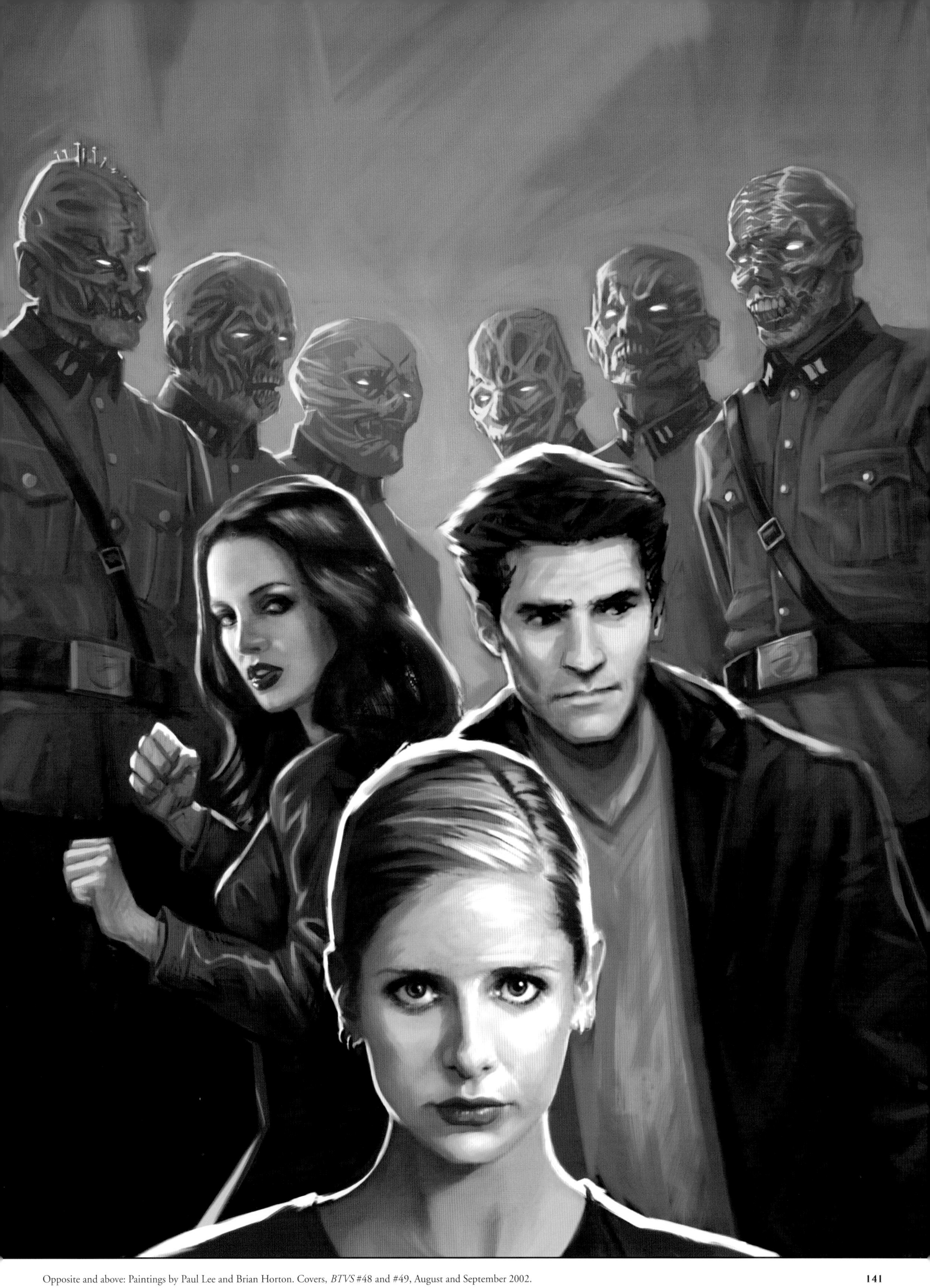

Opposite and above: Paintings by Paul Lee and Brian Horton. Covers, *BTVS* #48 and #49, August and September 2002.

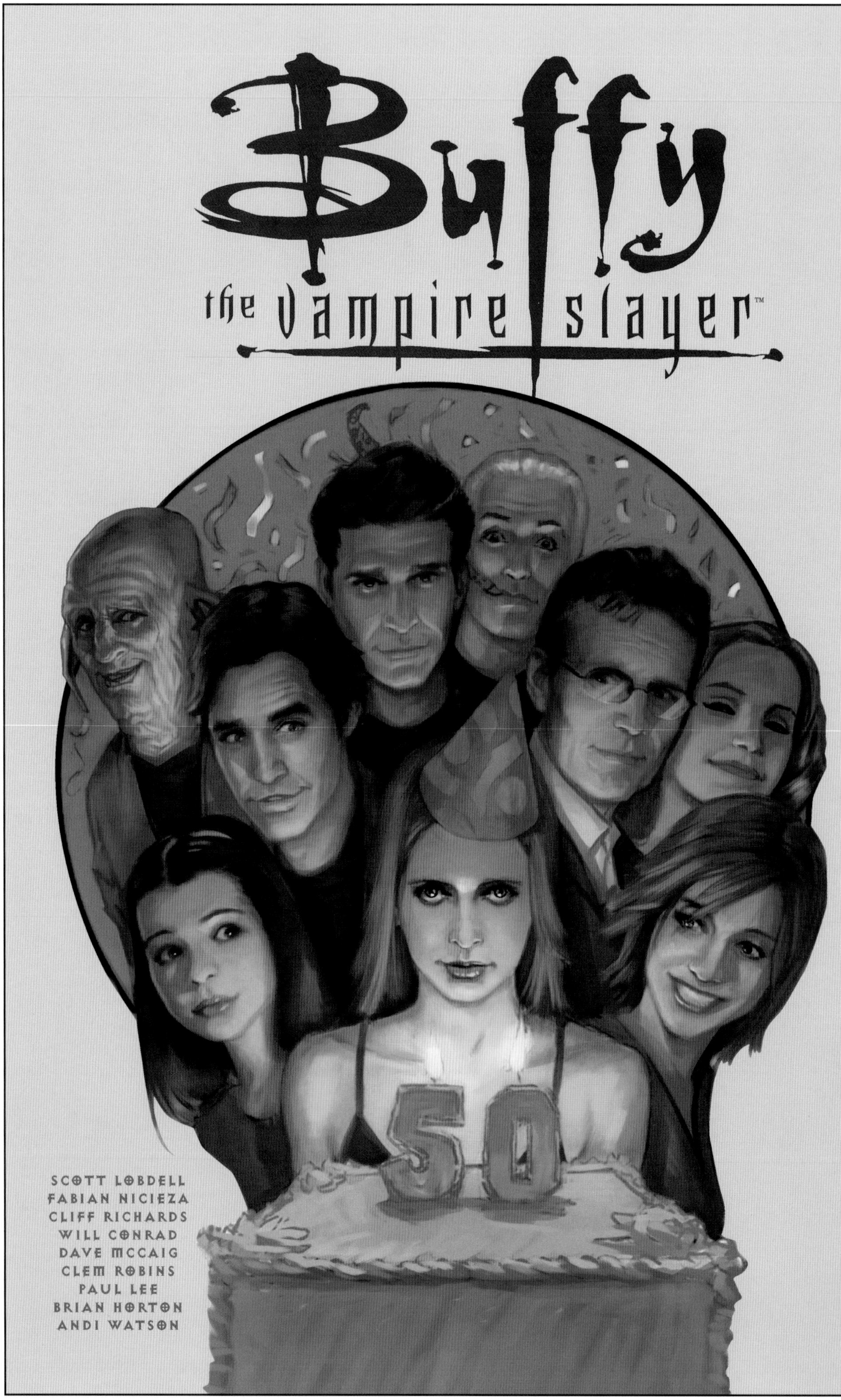

Buffy the vampire slayer™
50
SCOTT LOBDELL
FABIAN NICIEZA
CLIFF RICHARDS
WILL CONRAD
DAVE McCAIG
CLEM ROBINS
PAUL LEE
BRIAN HORTON
ANDI WATSON

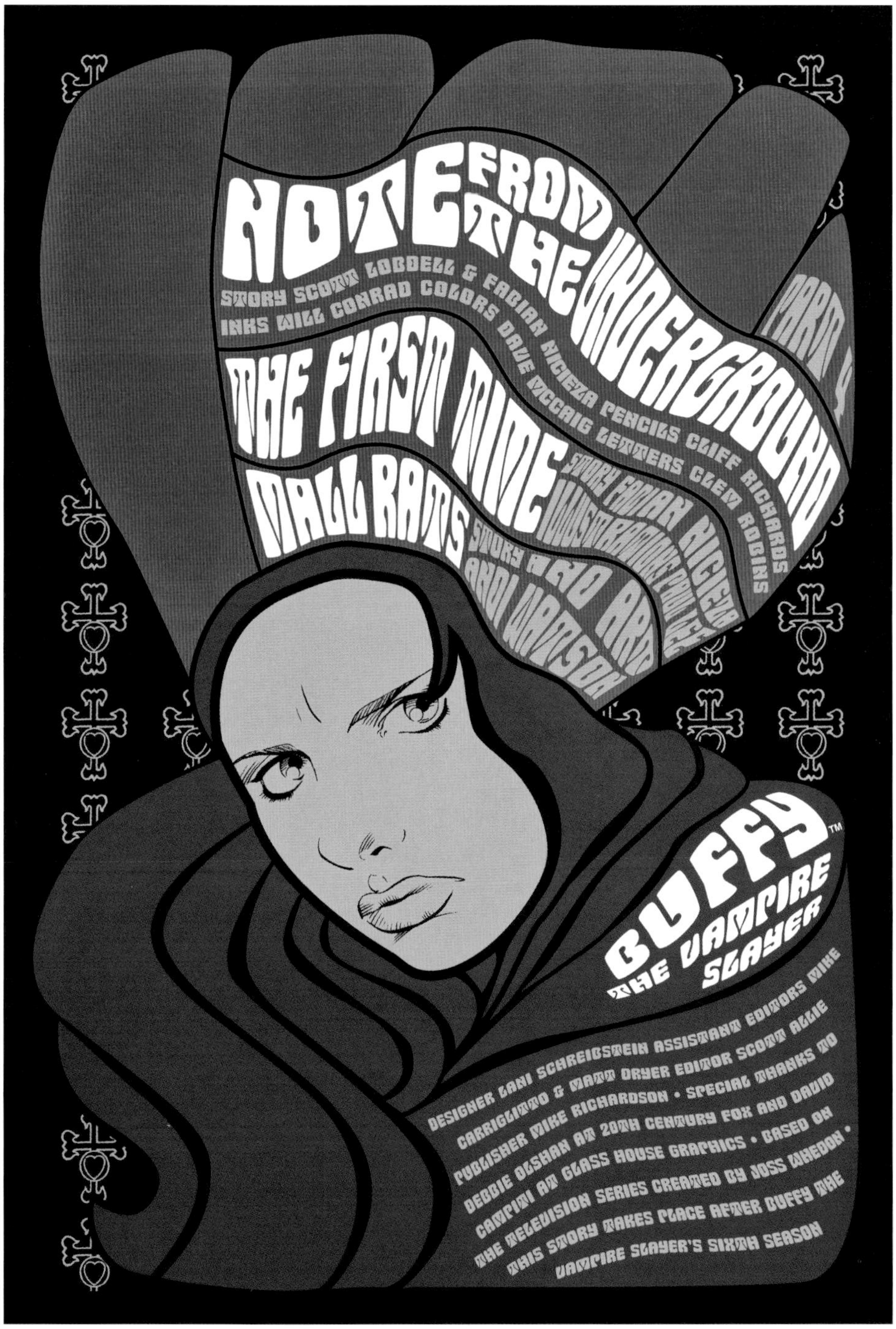
NOTE FROM THE UNDERGROUND
PART 4
STORY SCOTT LOBDELL & FABIAN NICIEZA PENCILS CLIFF RICHARDS
INKS WILL CONRAD COLORS DAVE MCCAIG LETTERS CLEM ROBINS
THE FIRST TIME
STORY FABIAN NICIEZA
MALL RATS
STORY AND ART ANDI WATSON
BUFFY™ THE VAMPIRE SLAYER
DESIGNER LANI SCHREIBSTEIN ASSISTANT EDITORS MIKE CARRIGLITTO & MATT DRYER EDITOR SCOTT ALLIE PUBLISHER MIKE RICHARDSON • SPECIAL THANKS TO DEBBIE OLSHAN AT 20TH CENTURY FOX AND DAVID CAMPITI AT GLASS HOUSE GRAPHICS • BASED ON THE TELEVISION SERIES CREATED BY JOSS WHEDON • THIS STORY TAKES PLACE AFTER BUFFY THE VAMPIRE SLAYER'S SIXTH SEASON

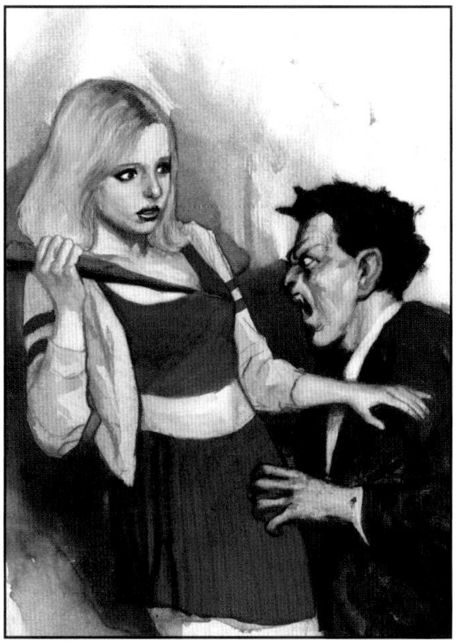

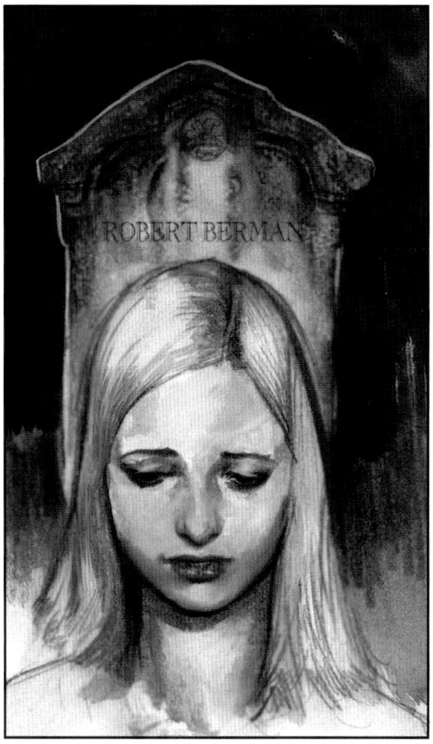
ROBERT BERMAN

FOR THE FIFTIETH ISSUE, we threw in some extras. Front and back covers paid tribute to Norman Rockwell—only because Paul Lee and I were really into him at the time. Spike, with the noisemaker, is based on Rockwell and his ever-present pipe. See page 190 for the back cover. A special inside-cover credits page was influenced by vintage rock posters, and the issue was rounded out by an illustrated prose piece by Fabian Nicieza and Lee.

Opposite: Painting by Paul Lee and Brian Horton. Above, left: Pencils by Cliff Richards, inks by Will Conrad, design by Lani Schreibstein. Above, right: Paintings by Lee. All from *BTVS* #50, October 2002.

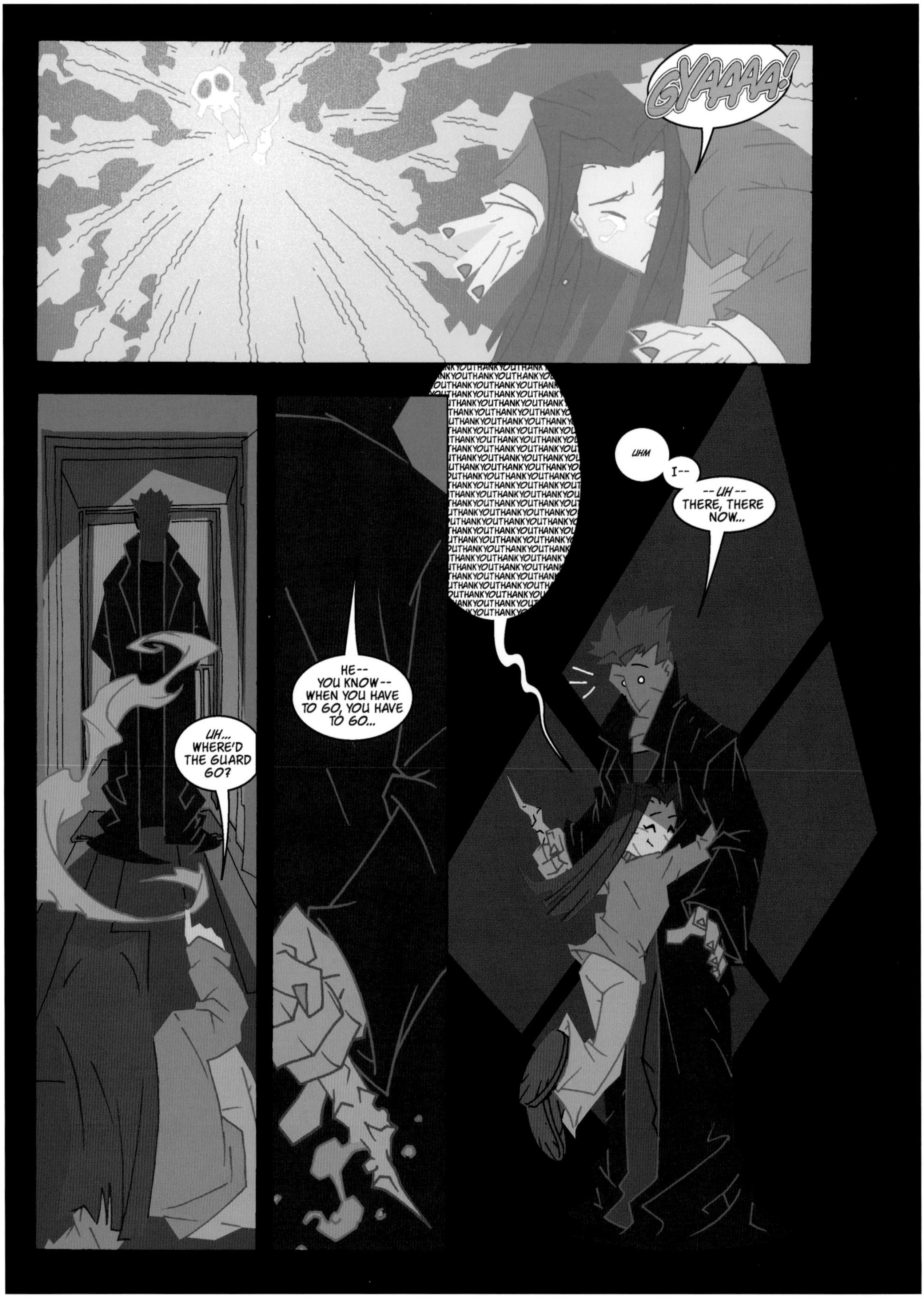
GYAAAA!
UH... WHERE'D THE GUARD GO?
HE-- YOU KNOW-- WHEN YOU HAVE TO GO, YOU HAVE TO GO...
UHM
I--
--UH-- THERE, THERE NOW...

AFTER THREE YEARS of asking, I finally got Jeff Matsuda to do some interiors—twice in two months, but neither time a full issue. Both times he gave me a style we'd never seen in the *Buffy* comics. Matsuda teamed with Scott Lobdell and Fabian Nicieza for the anthology *Reveal*, which began as my attempt to relaunch our flagship title *Dark Horse Presents*. Earlier, Doug Petrie had pitched me the idea of a *Tales of the Slayers* one-shot by him and Gene Colan. The project wound up a collaboration with Jane Espenson and Matsuda telling the story of Buffy facing off against a djinn that had been shut up in a locker for decades, and Petrie and Colan showing how it had wound up there. The two radically different art styles came together on the cover. Matsuda would later hire both Petrie and Espenson to write episodes of his cartoon *The Batman* in 2007.

Above: Plot by Lobdell, dialogue by Nicieza, characters by Matsuda, backgrounds by Hakjoon Kang and Nolan Obena, colors by Dave McCaig, letters by Michael Heisler. Interiors, "Angels We Have Seen on High," *Reveal* #1, November 2002. Opposite: Pencils by Matsuda and Colan, colors by Dave Stewart. Cover, *BTVS: Tales of the Slayers: Broken Bottle of Djinn*, October 2002.

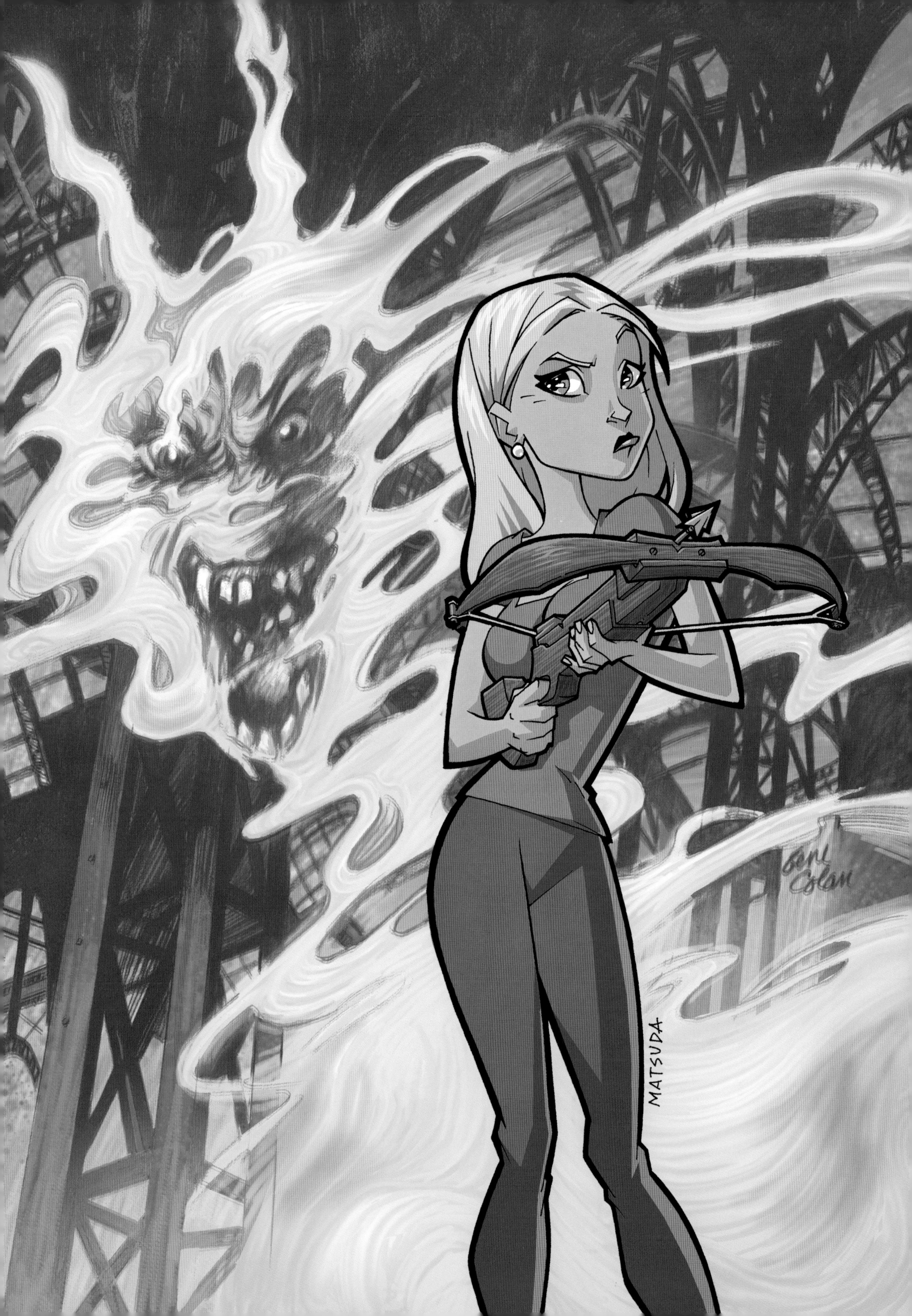
Gene Colan
MATSUDA

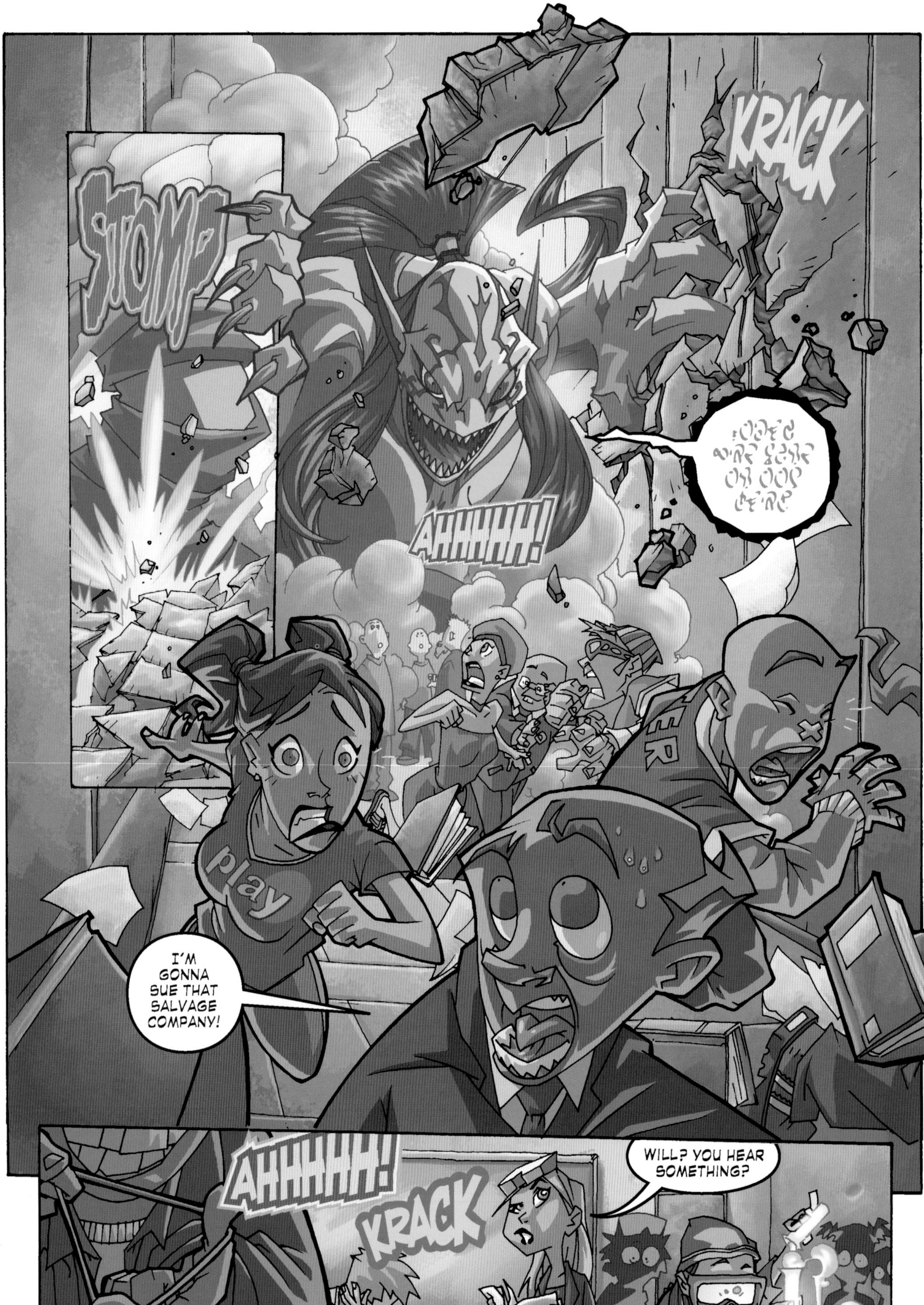
STOMP
KRACK
AHHHHH!
I'M GONNA SUE THAT SALVAGE COMPANY!
AHHHHH!
KRACK
WILL? YOU HEAR SOMETHING?

 Above: Script by Jane Espenson, pencils by Jeff Matsuda. Opposite: Script by Doug Petrie, pencils by Gene Colan. Colors by Dave Stewart, letters by Pat Brosseau. Interiors, *Tales of the Slayers: Broken Bottle of Djinn*, October 2002.

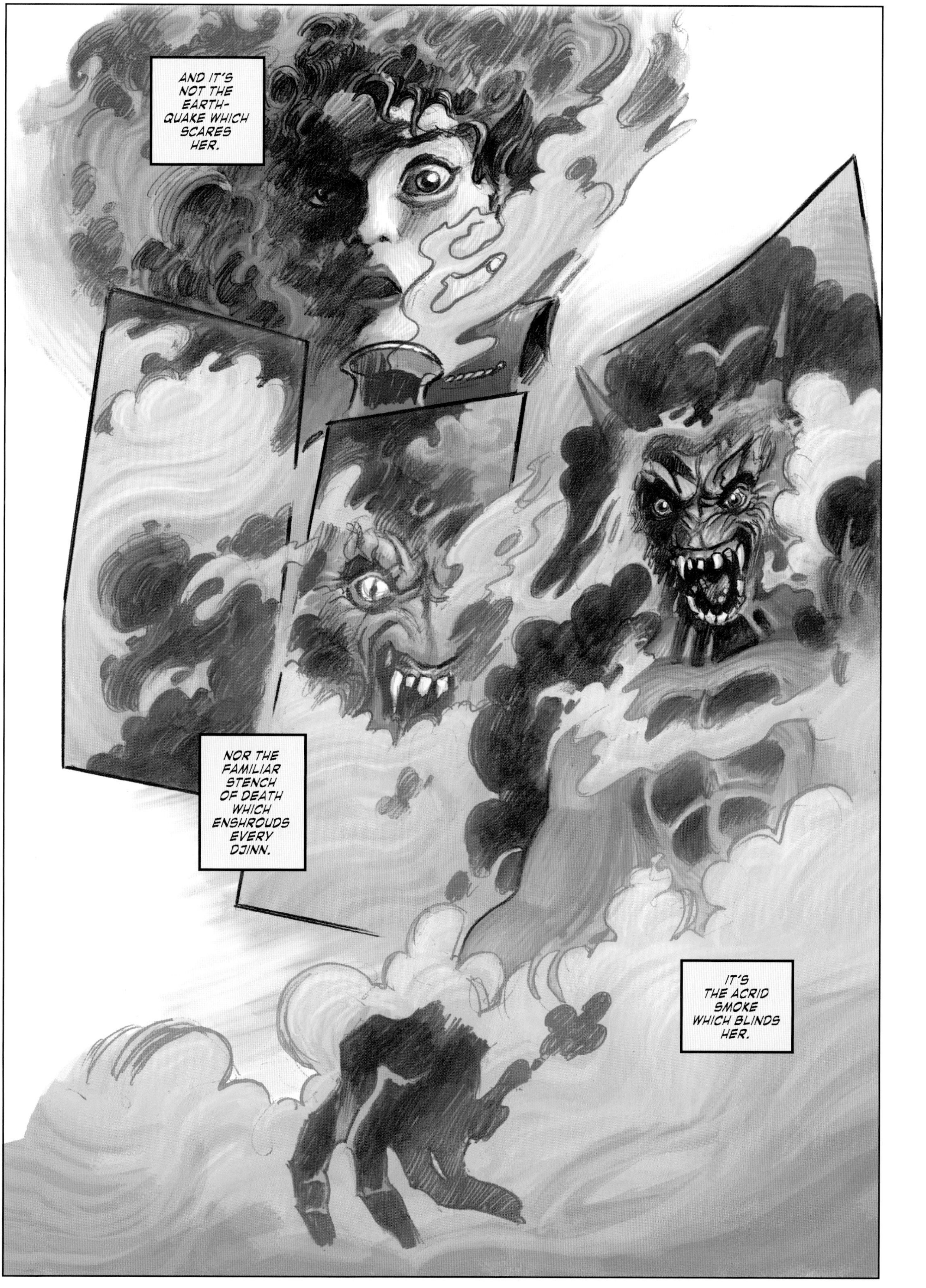
AND IT'S NOT THE EARTH-QUAKE WHICH SCARES HER.
NOR THE FAMILIAR STENCH OF DEATH WHICH ENSHROUDS EVERY DJINN.
IT'S THE ACRID SMOKE WHICH BLINDS HER.

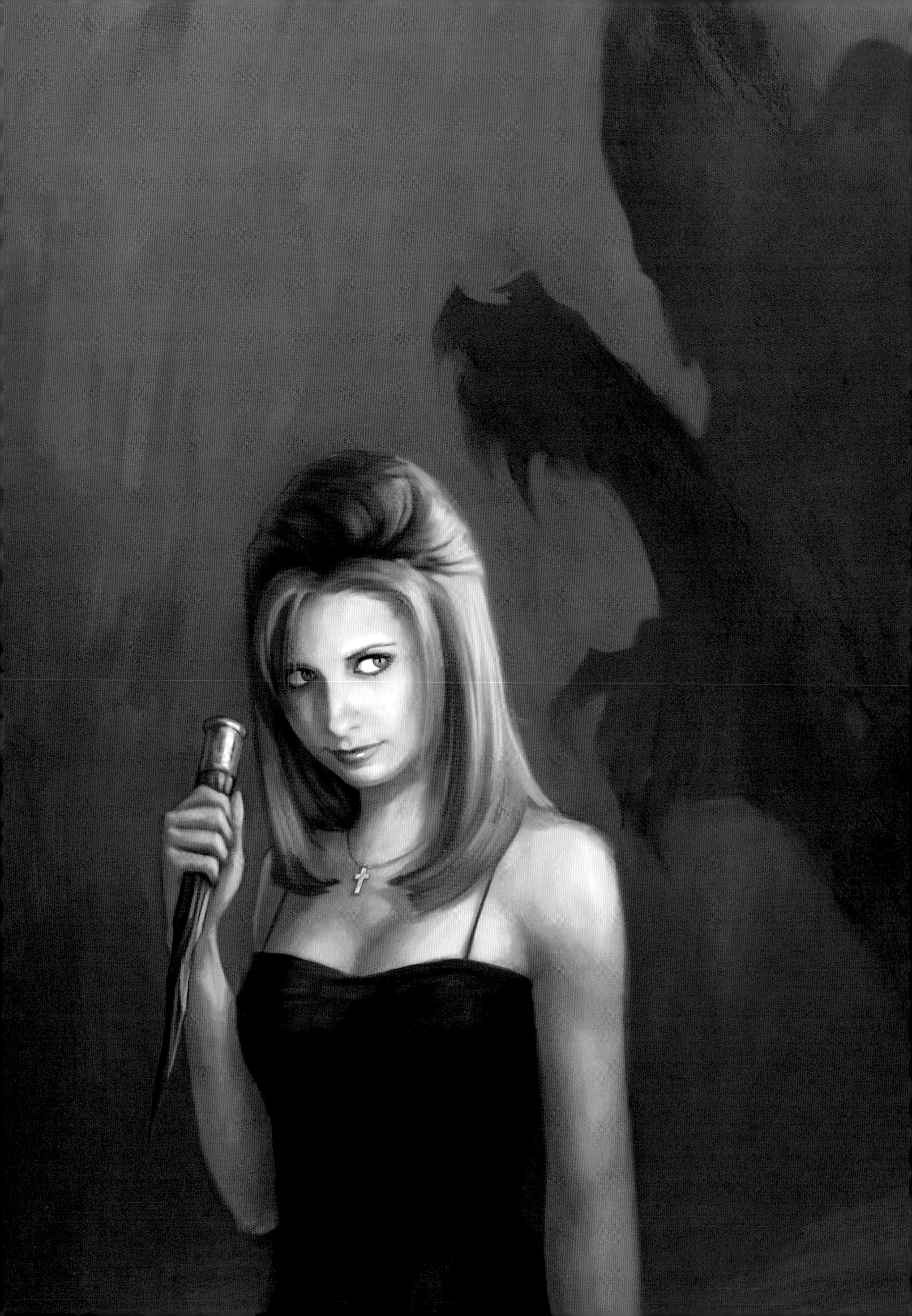

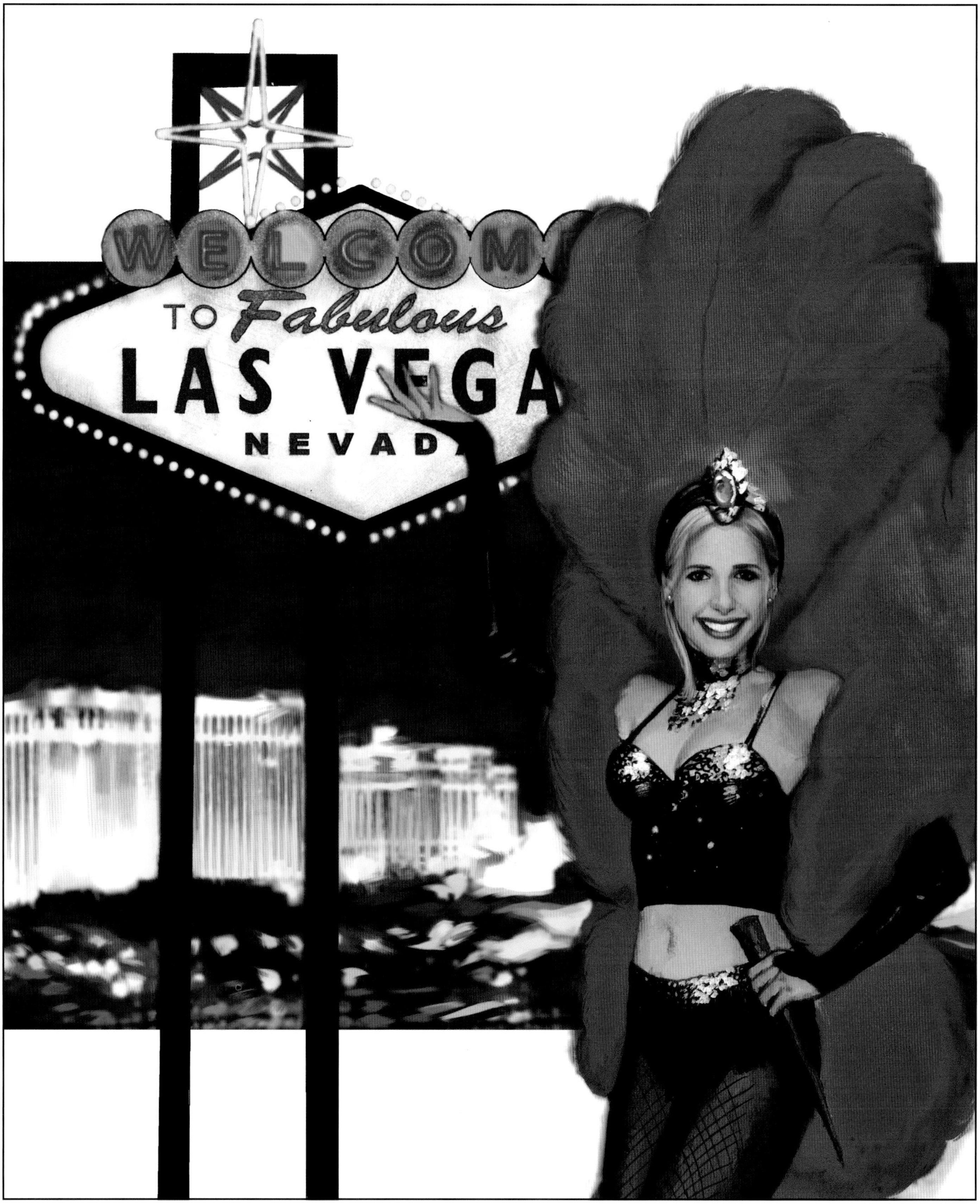
WELCOM
TO Fabulous
LAS VEGA
NEVAD

TOM FASSBENDER AND JIM PASCOE had been eager to catch up with the television continuity, but after they left and the pitch for our post–Season Six story was shot down for being too close to the TV show, I remembered why we wanted a safe distance between us and the show. So I took Scott Lobdell up on his idea to do a Year One story. That phrase comes from Frank Miller's *Batman: Year One*, and refers to a story not necessarily dealing with a character's origin, but her earliest adventures. At the end of *The Origin* comic and the film, Pike and Buffy were headed to Las Vegas. We viewed *Buffy* #51 as a new starting point, and plotted twelve issues between the original screenplay and the first episode of the TV show. Since Dawn had been in the comic, and was currently in the TV show, we decided to feature her in the Year One stories. While she hadn't been there, Buffy would *remember* her being there—and this stuff's all made up anyway. The Buffy showgirl cover is not exactly the version that was printed on *Buffy* #52. The face on that cover was never quite right, so the artists reworked it for the cover of the trade paperback, and it's that version presented here.

Opposite and above: Paintings by Lee and Horton. Covers, *BTVS* #51 and #52, November and December 2002.

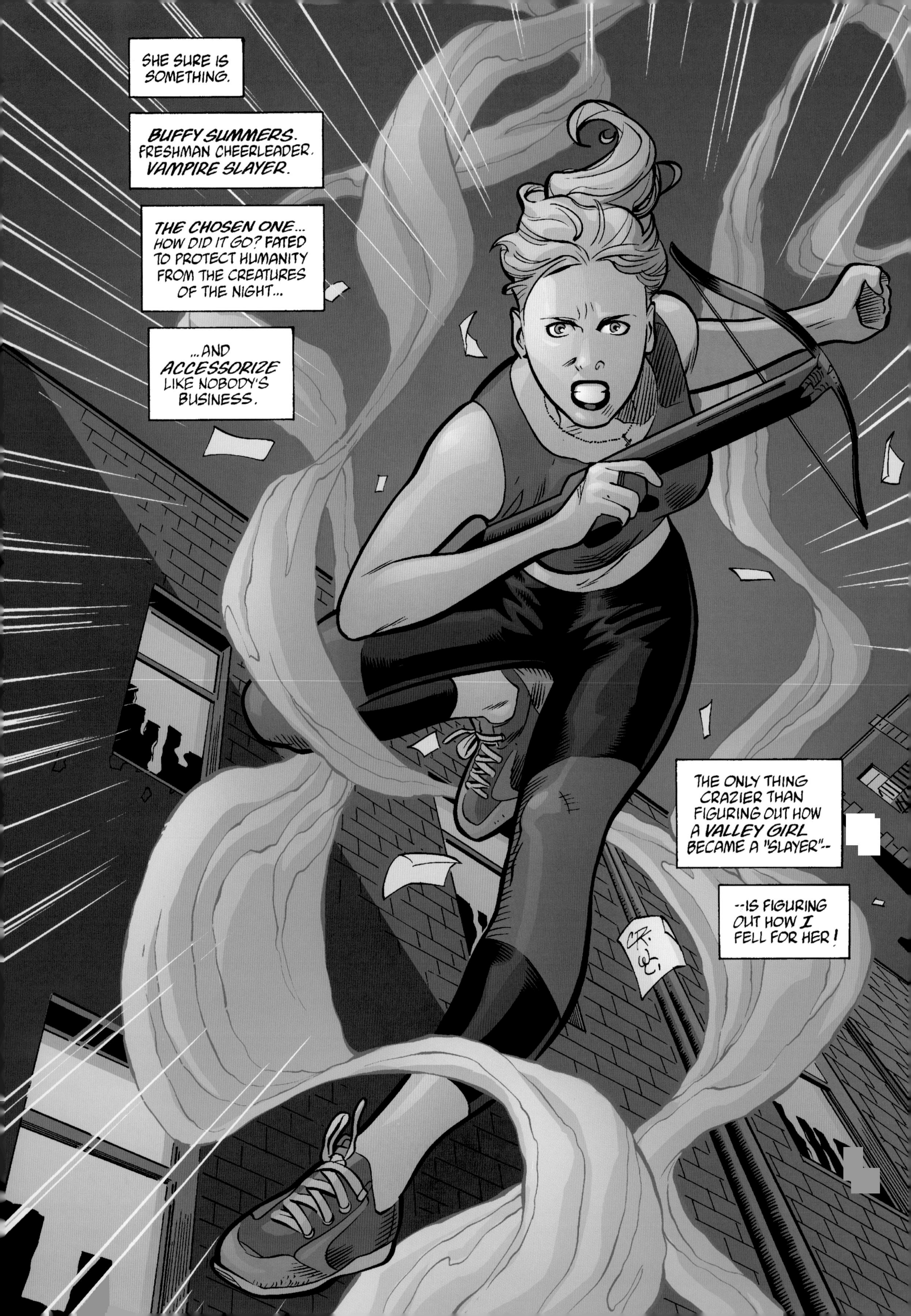
SHE SURE IS SOMETHING.
BUFFY SUMMERS. FRESHMAN CHEERLEADER. VAMPIRE SLAYER.
THE CHOSEN ONE... HOW DID IT GO? FATED TO PROTECT HUMANITY FROM THE CREATURES OF THE NIGHT...
...AND ACCESSORIZE LIKE NOBODY'S BUSINESS.
THE ONLY THING CRAZIER THAN FIGURING OUT HOW A VALLEY GIRL BECAME A "SLAYER"--
--IS FIGURING OUT HOW I FELL FOR HER!

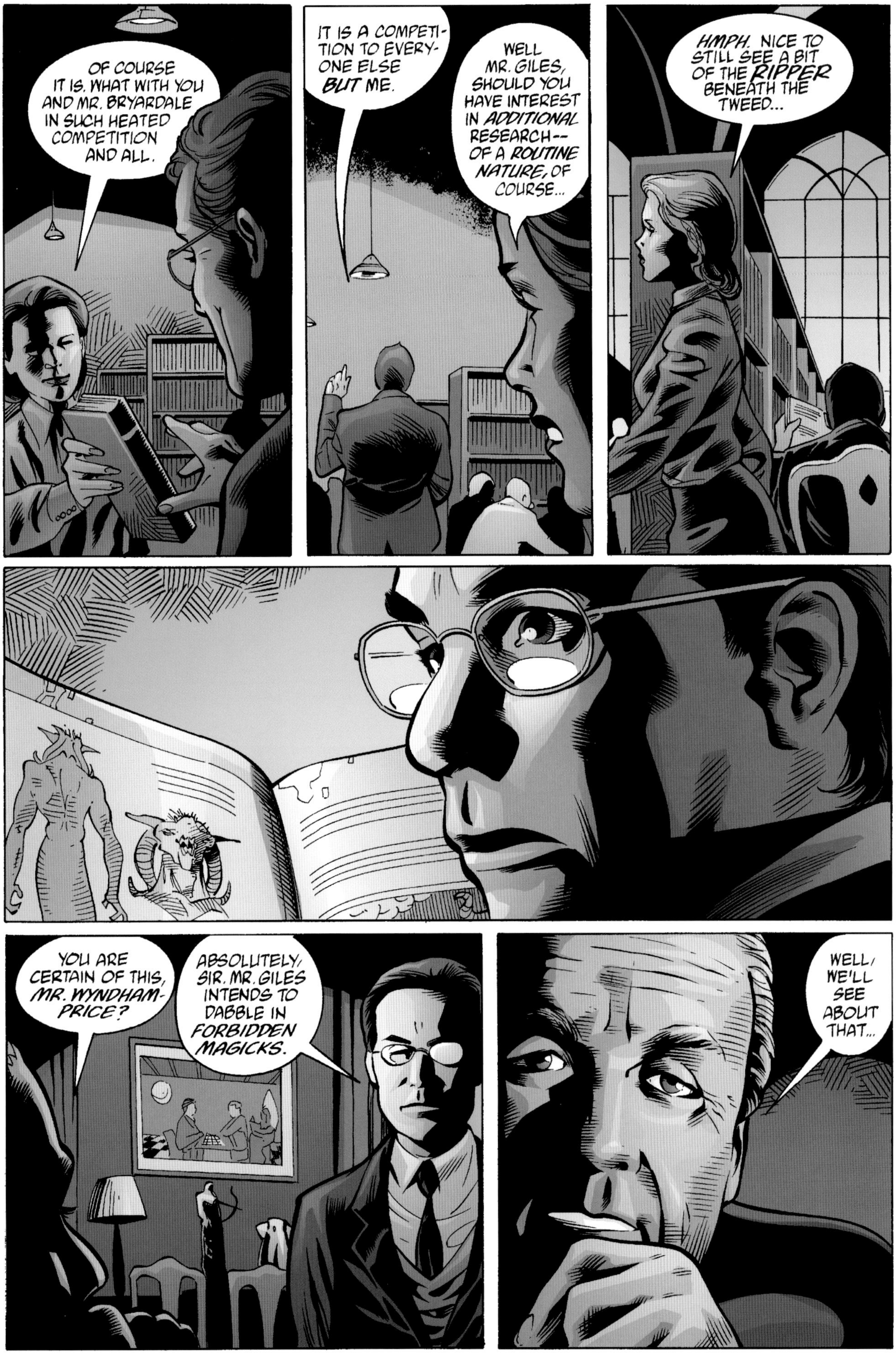
OF COURSE IT IS. WHAT WITH YOU AND MR. BRYARDALE IN SUCH HEATED COMPETITION AND ALL.
IT IS A COMPETITION TO EVERYONE ELSE *BUT* ME.
WELL MR. GILES, SHOULD YOU HAVE INTEREST IN *ADDITIONAL* RESEARCH-- OF A *ROUTINE NATURE,* OF COURSE...
HMPH. NICE TO STILL SEE A BIT OF THE *RIPPER* BENEATH THE TWEED...
YOU ARE CERTAIN OF THIS, *MR. WYNDHAM-PRICE?*
ABSOLUTELY, SIR. MR. GILES INTENDS TO DABBLE IN *FORBIDDEN MAGICKS.*
WELL, WE'LL SEE ABOUT THAT...

PIKE CONSIDERS BUFFY, and readers get their earliest view of Wesley. At this point, Cliff Richards was constantly inserting inside references into the pages. The picture in Wesley's book is Cliff's version of Brian Horton's demon designs for our book *The Devil's Footprints*; the painting on the wall behind him refers to Arturo Pérez Reverte's novel *The Flanders Panel*.

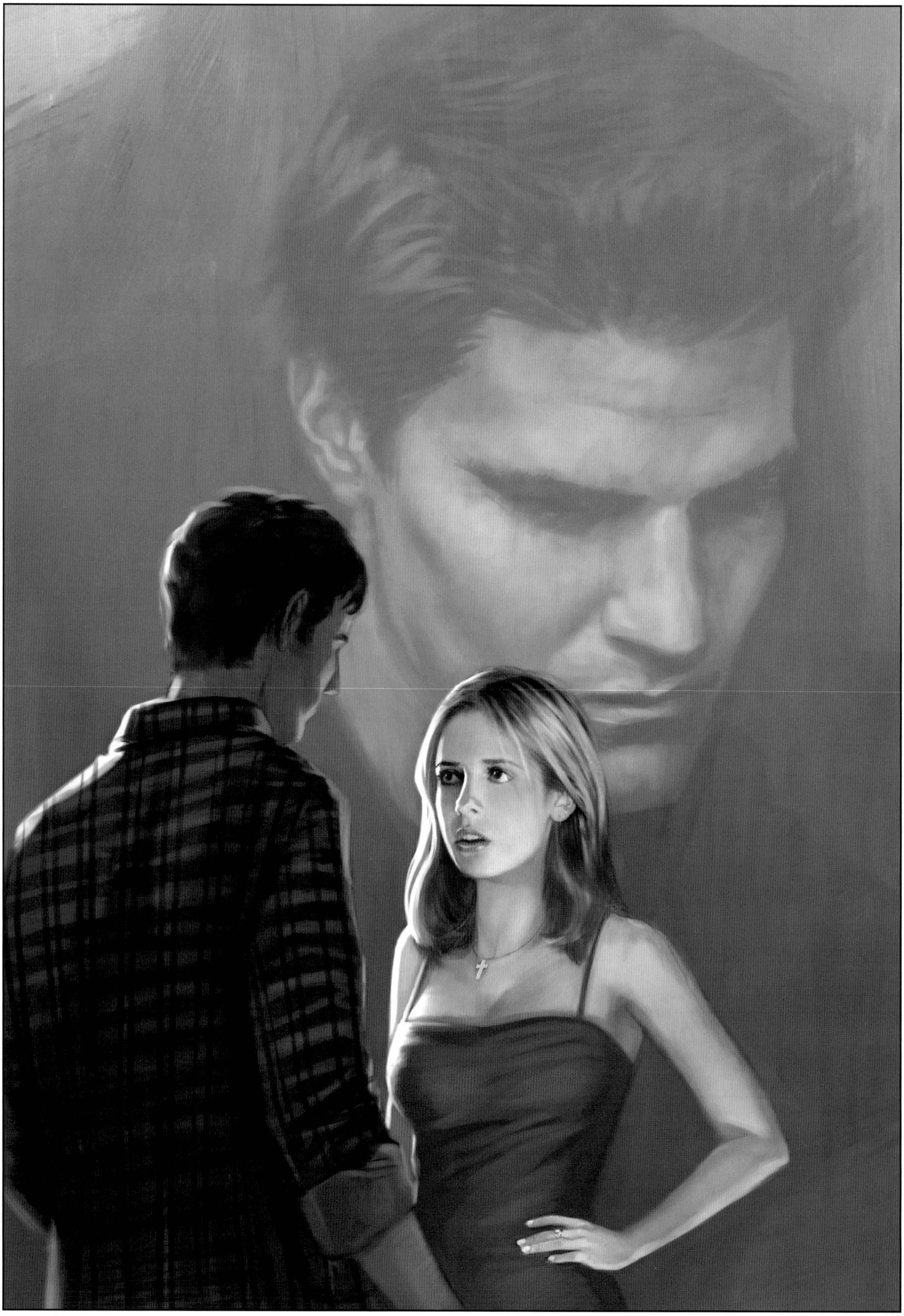

Above and opposite: Paintings by Paul Lee and Brian Horton. Covers, *BTVS* #53 and #54, January and February 2002. Following: Script by Scott Lobdell and Fabian Nicieza, pencils by Cliff Richards, inks by Will Conrad, colors by Dave McCaig, letters by Clem Robins. Interiors, *BTVS* #54, February 2002.

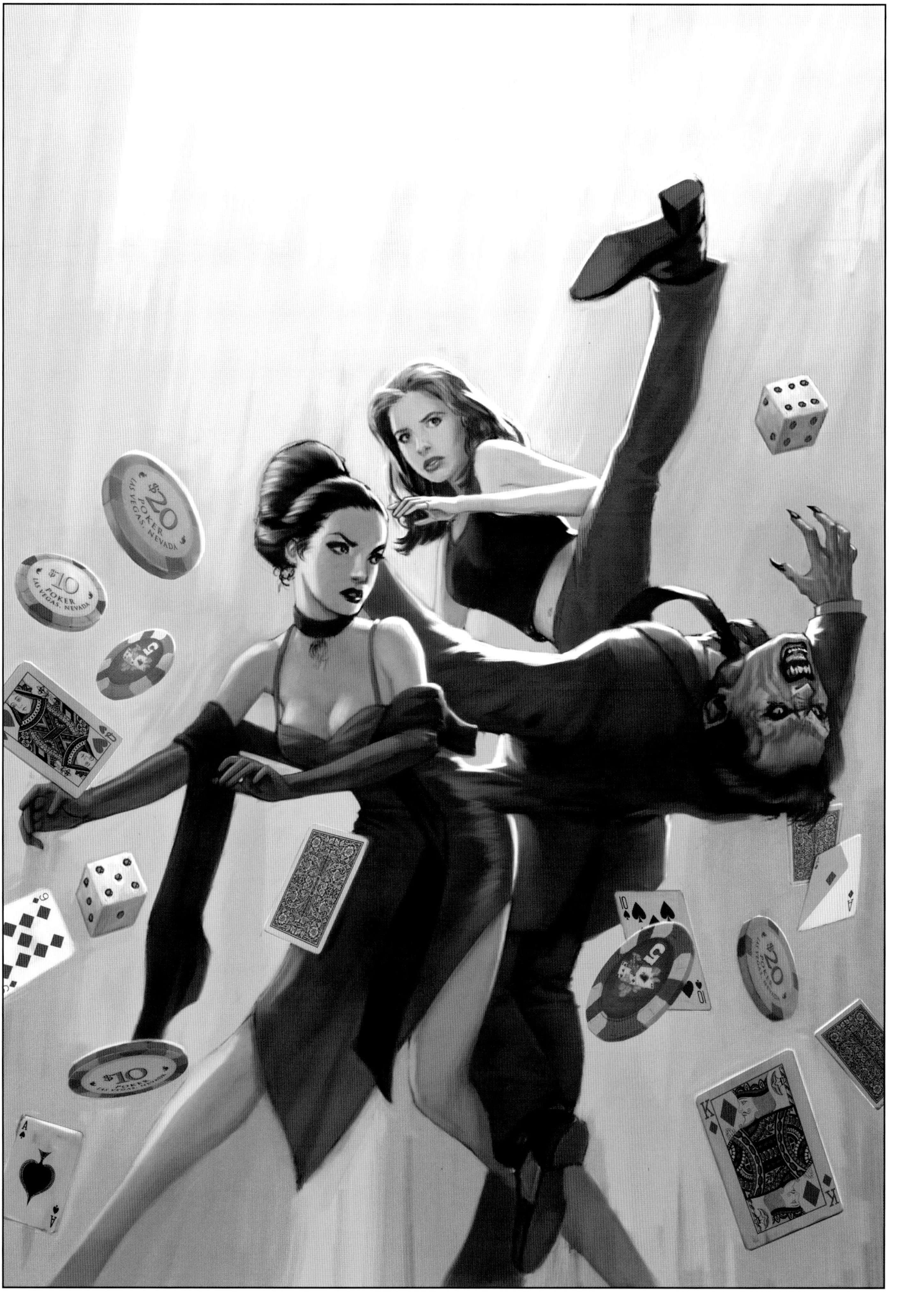
$20
POKER
LAS VEGAS, NEVADA
$10
POKER
LAS VEGAS, NEVADA

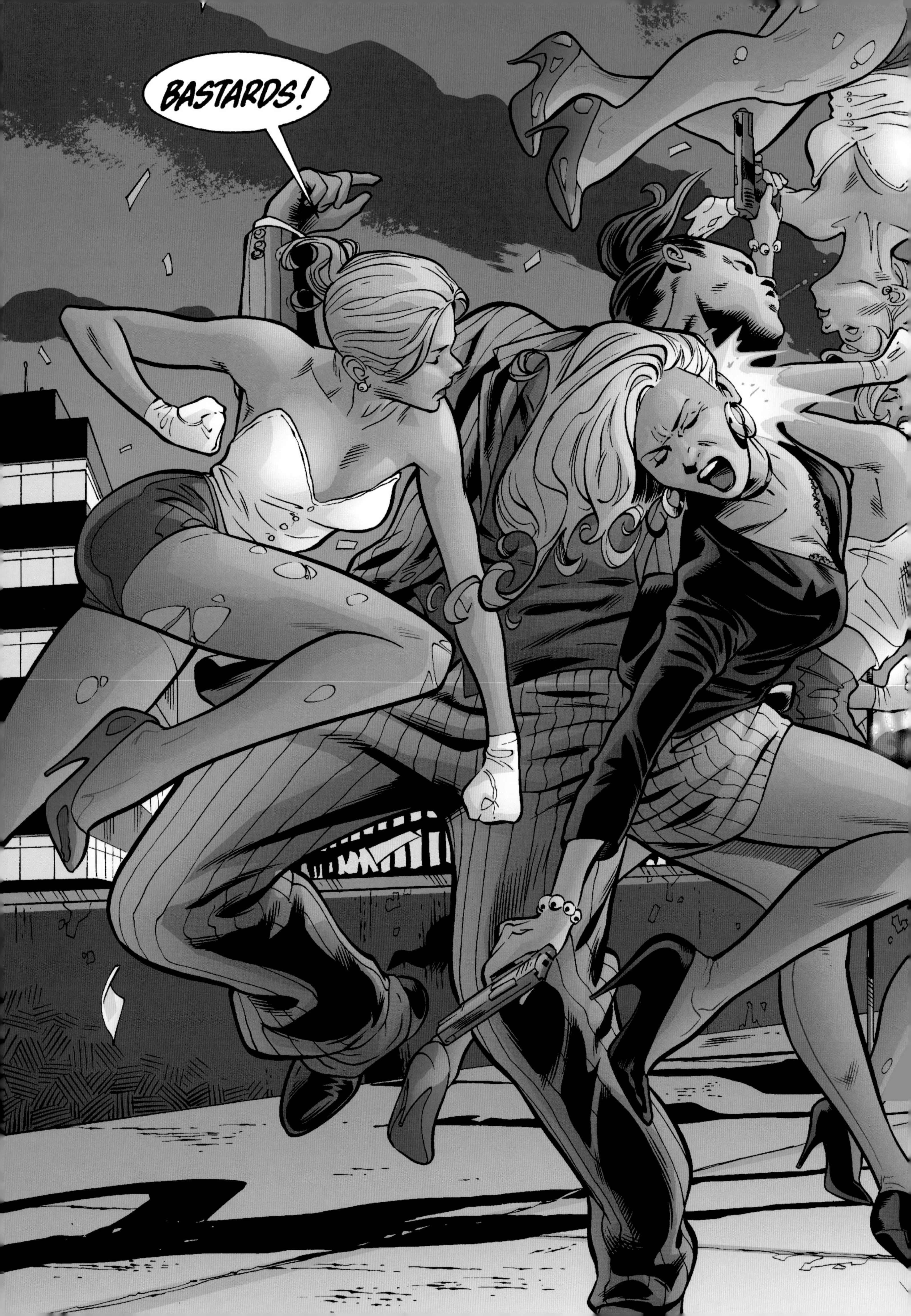
BASTARDS!

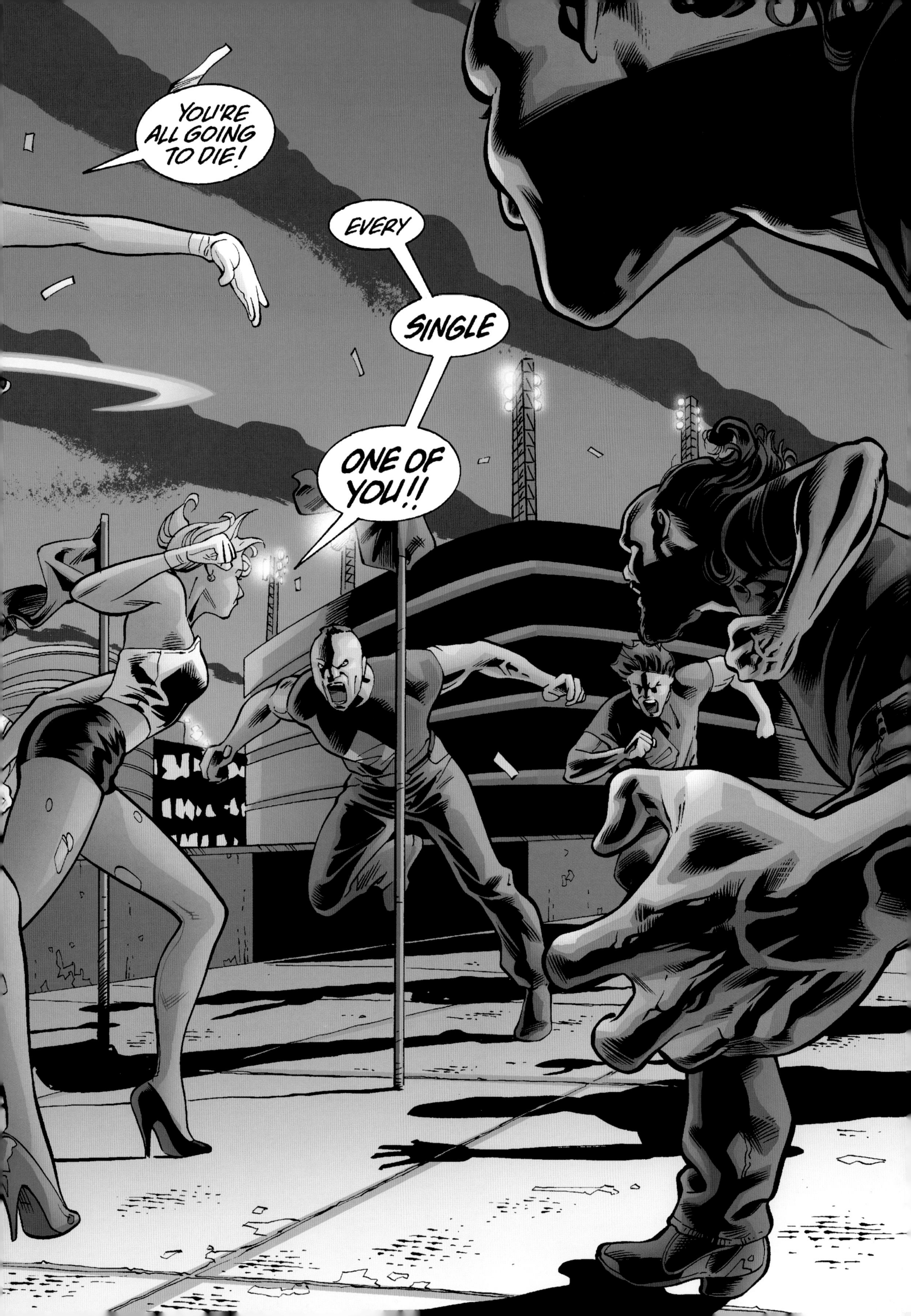
YOU'RE ALL GOING TO DIE!
EVERY
SINGLE
ONE OF YOU!!

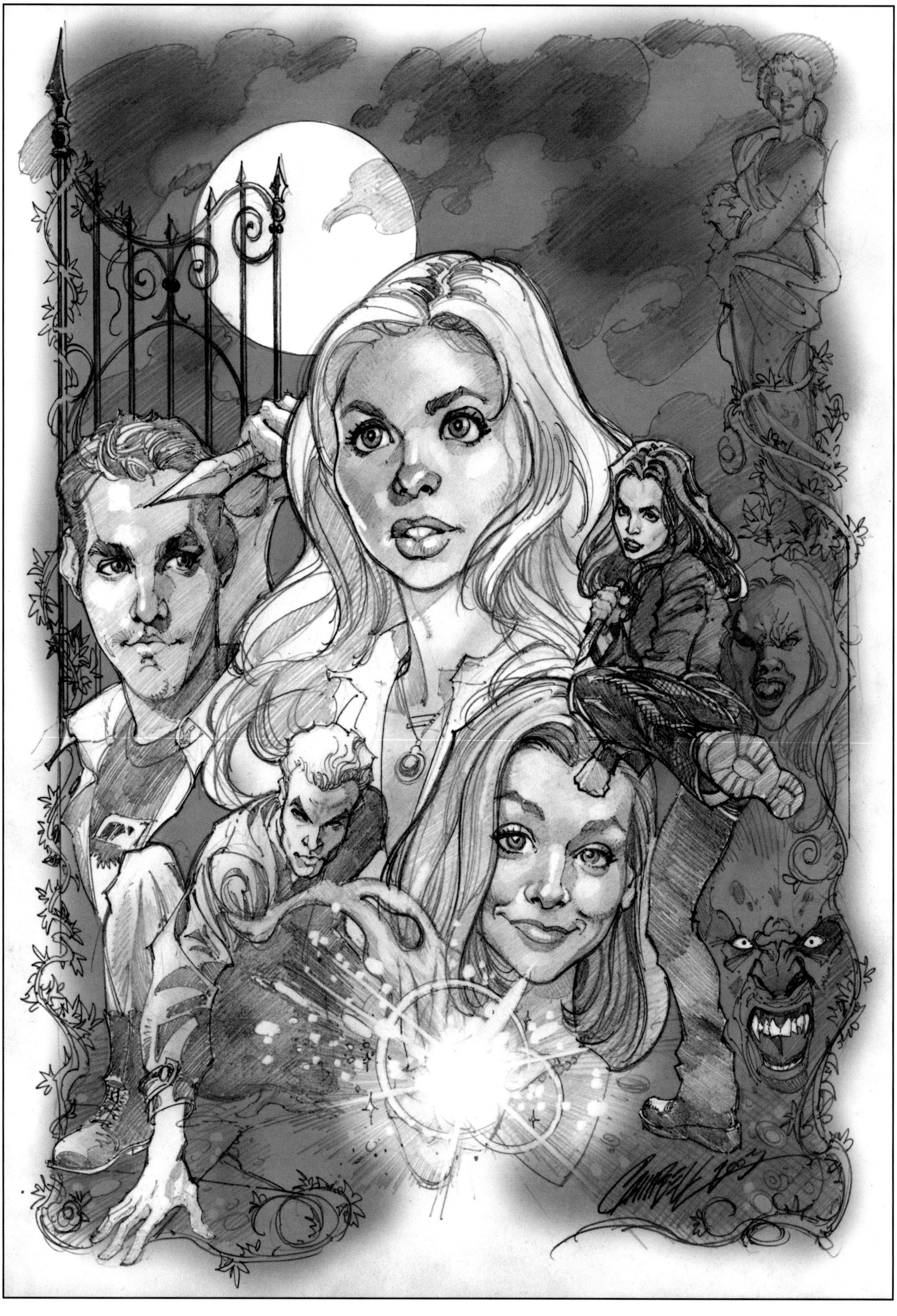

CHRISTOPHER GOLDEN AND TOM SNIEGOSKI co-wrote the Buffy video game *Chaos Bleeds*, and came to us to do a comic tie-in. Golden helped to arrange for us to use the promotional poster for the game, drawn by J. Scott Campbell, as the cover of the comic. This gave me my second Campbell cover for the series, although Dark Horse was not responsible for commissioning the piece. Sid the ventriloquist dummy from Season One of the TV show was featured in the game, as well as the comic.

 Art by Campbell. Cover, *BTVS: Chaos Bleeds*, June 2003.

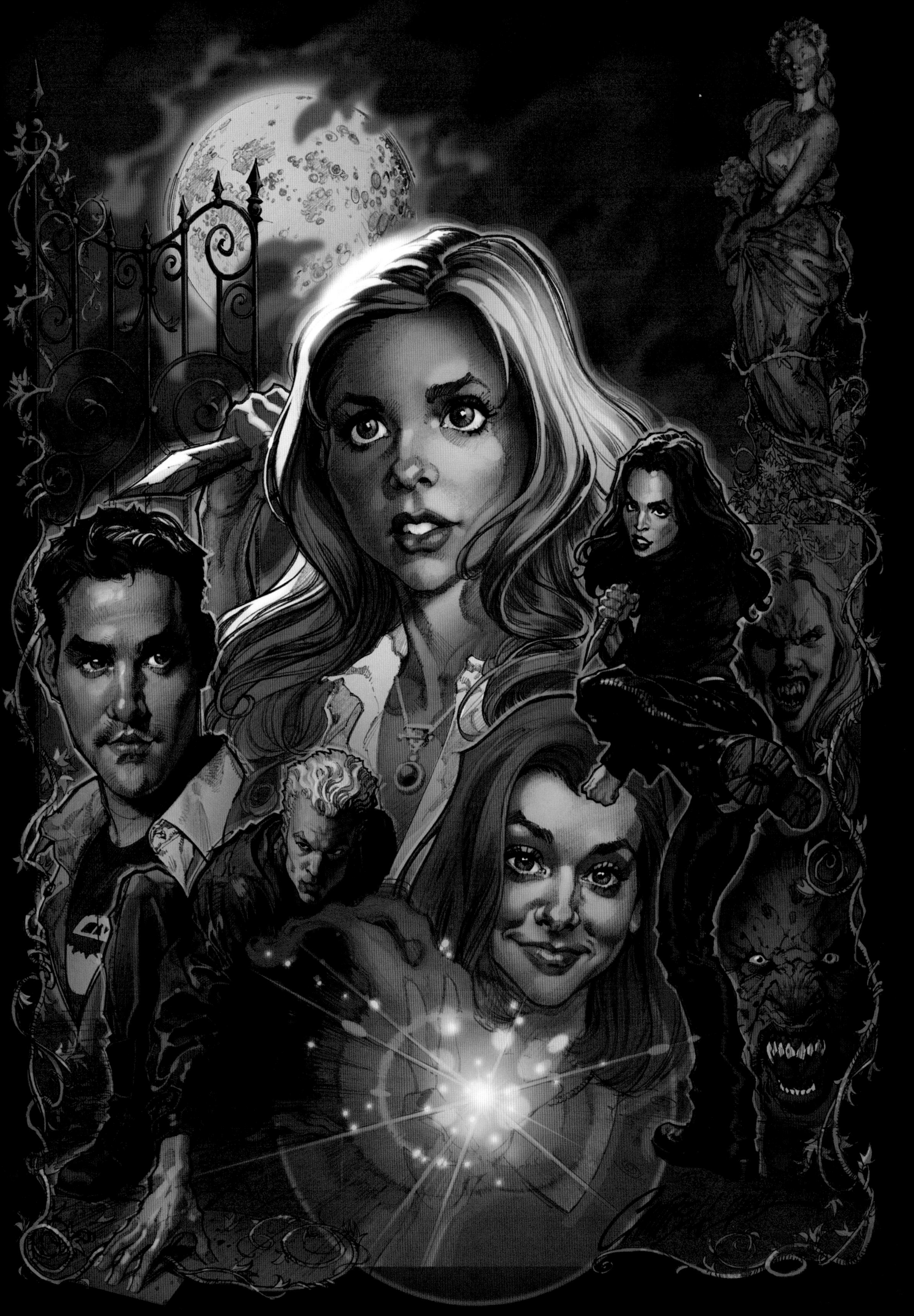

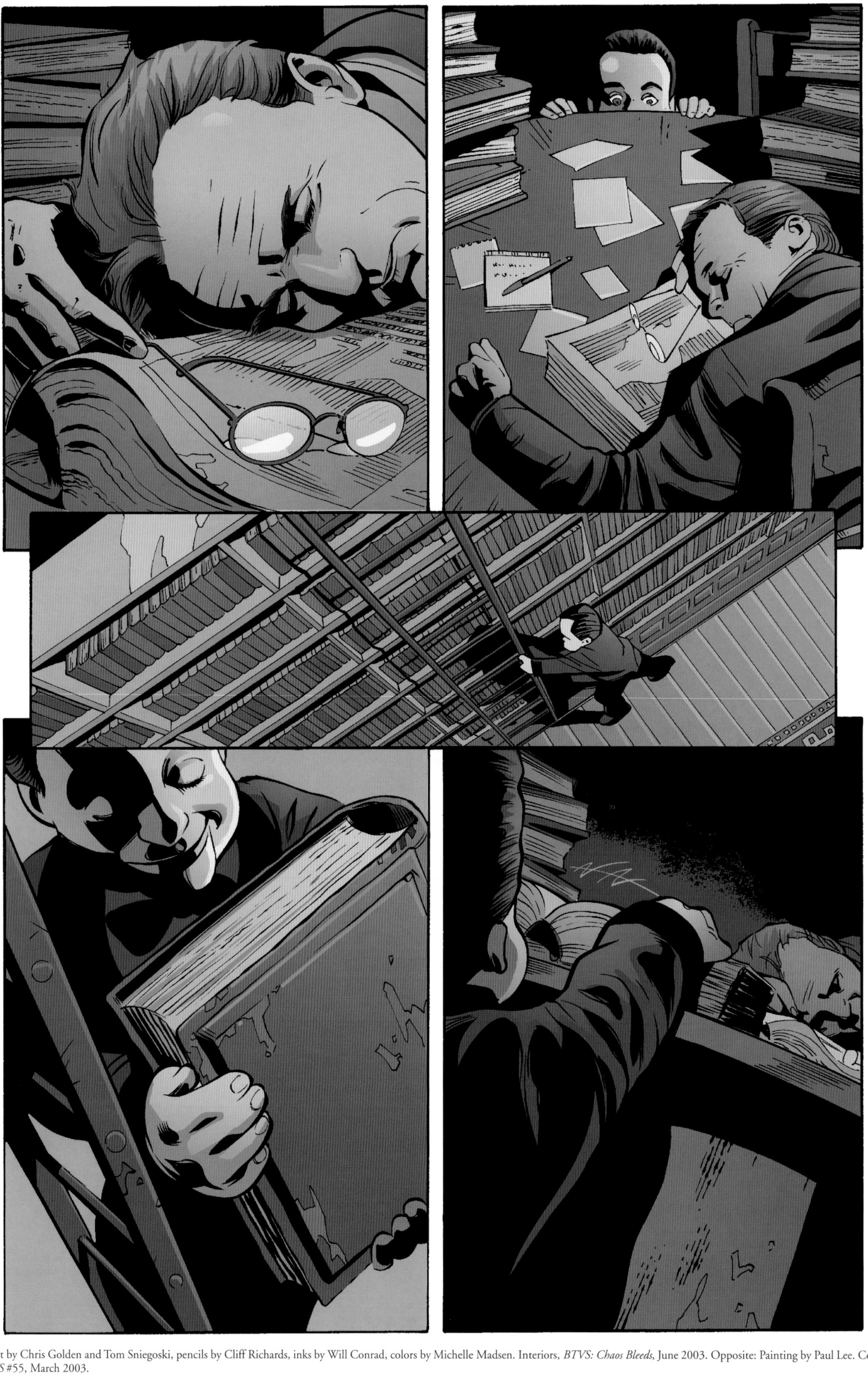

 Script by Chris Golden and Tom Sniegoski, pencils by Cliff Richards, inks by Will Conrad, colors by Michelle Madsen. Interiors, *BTVS: Chaos Bleeds*, June 2003. Opposite: Painting by Paul Lee. Cover, *BTVS* #55, March 2003.

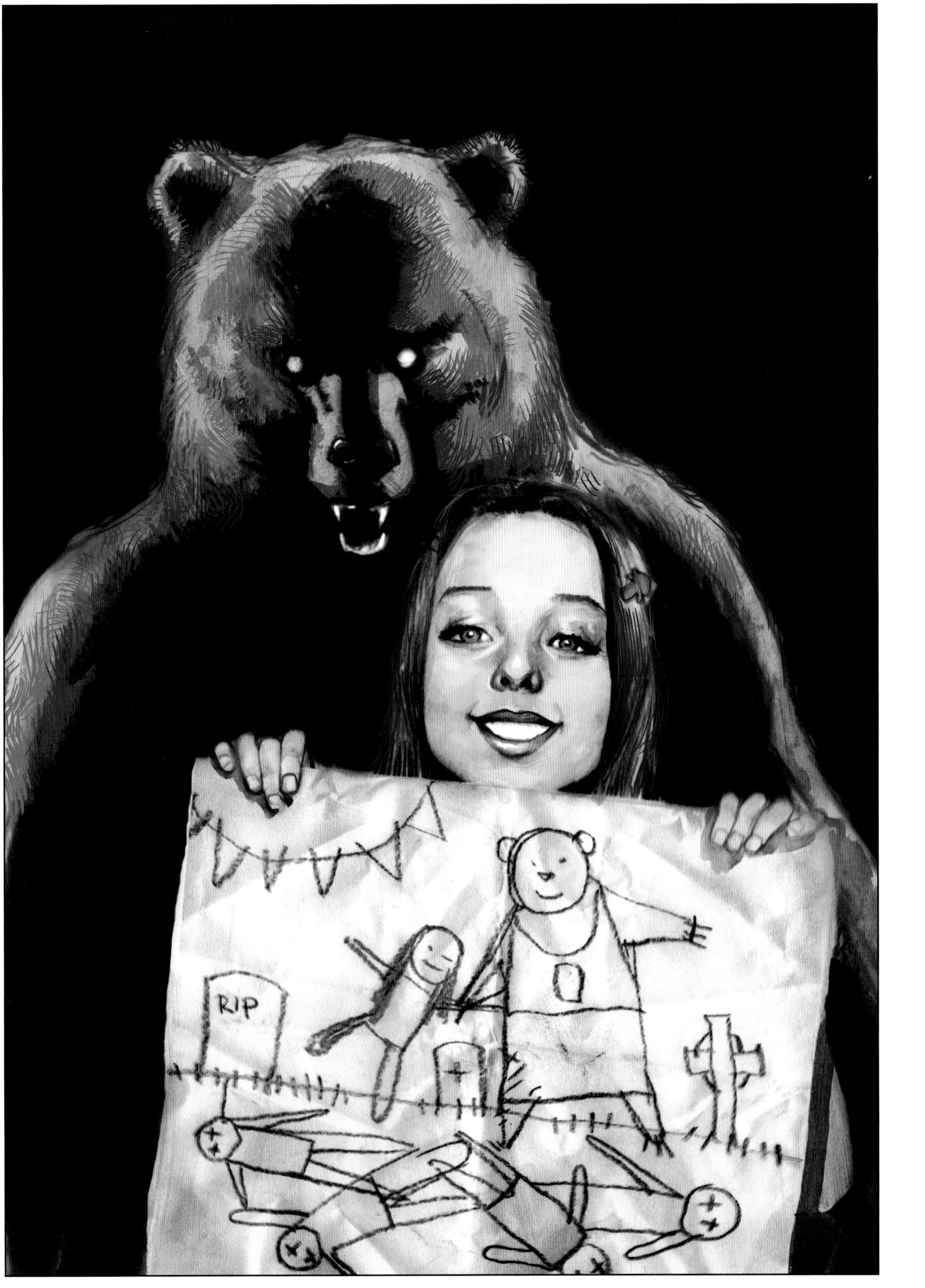
RIP

IN THE MIDDLE of our Year One story, which had been taken over by Fabian Nicieza after Scott Lobdell became too busy, the whole interior team took an issue off. Paul Lee and I had talked a lot about the assembly-line nature of work-for-hire comics, as opposed to books like *Strangers in Paradise* or *Usagi Yojimbo*, where one person does everything. So for *Buffy* #55, Paul did everything on the book, including designing the inside cover and answering letters. He brought back Hoopy, the bear from his previous issue of the series. Since there was still demand for photo covers, Lee took a picture of his son Ethan's teddy bear and married it to a photo of Michelle Trachtenberg. This story also set up the next arc, in which Dawn discovers Buffy's diary, leading to the Slayer's stint in a mental ward, as referenced briefly in the Season Six episode "Normal Again."

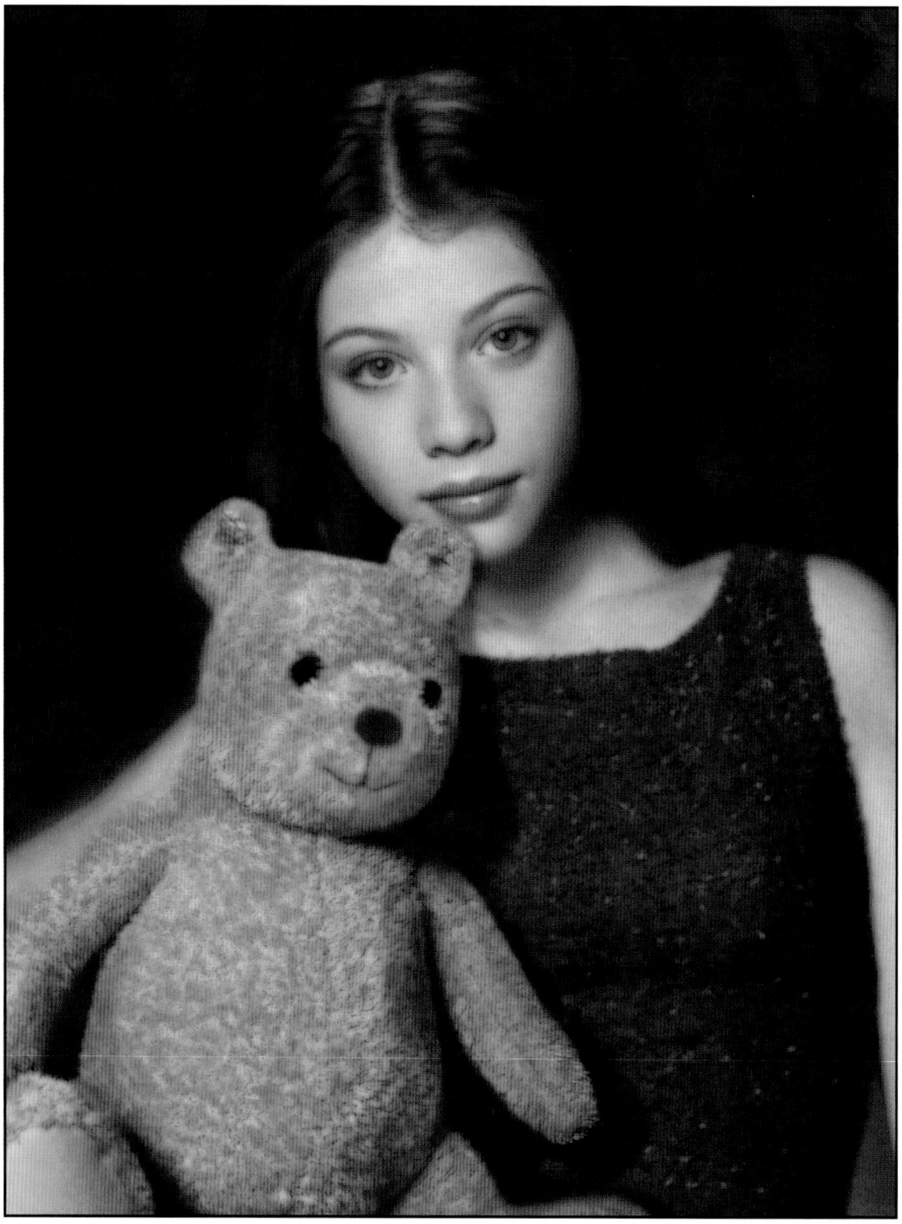

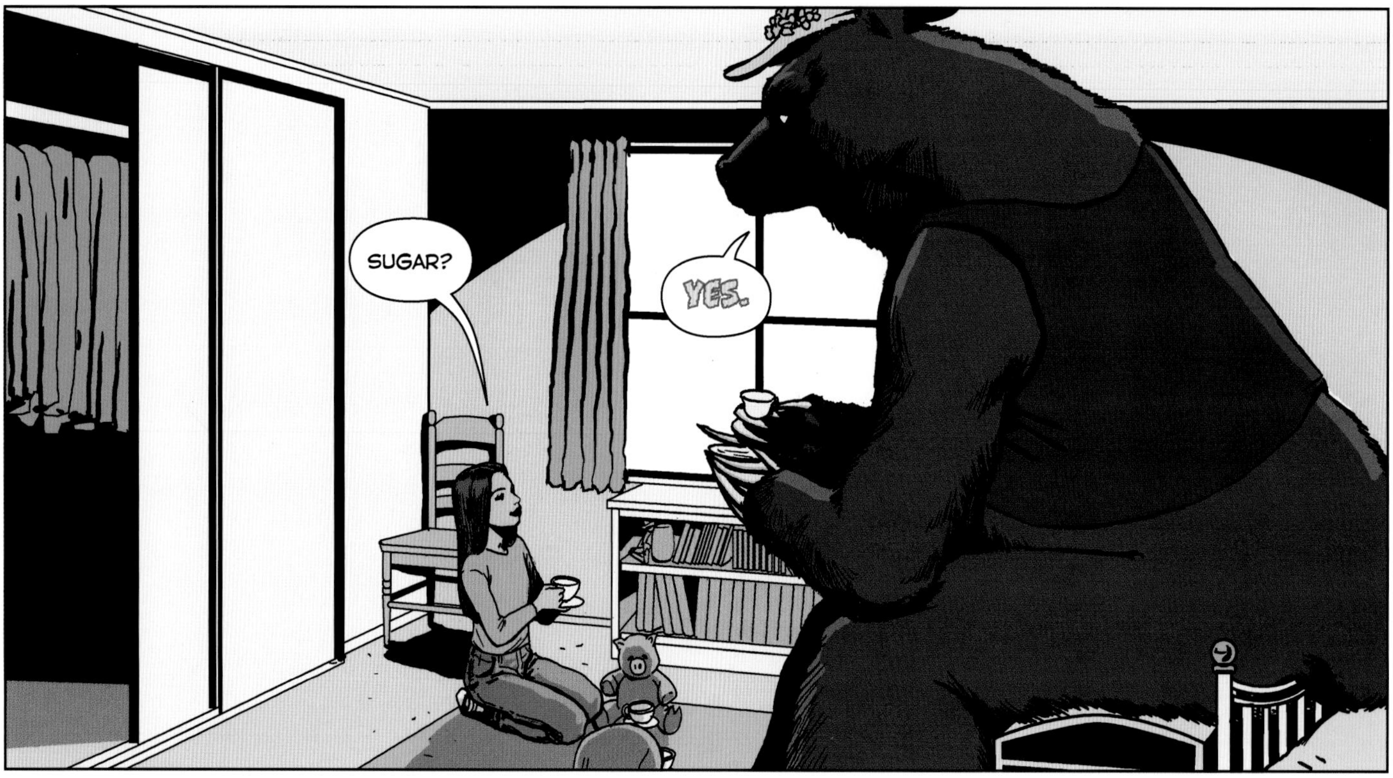
SUGAR?
YES.

Above: Script, pencils, inks, colors, letters, and montage by Lee. Cover and interiors, *BTVS* #55, March 2003. Opposite and following two pages: Paintings by Lee and Brian Horton. Covers, *BTVS* #56–58, April–June 2003.

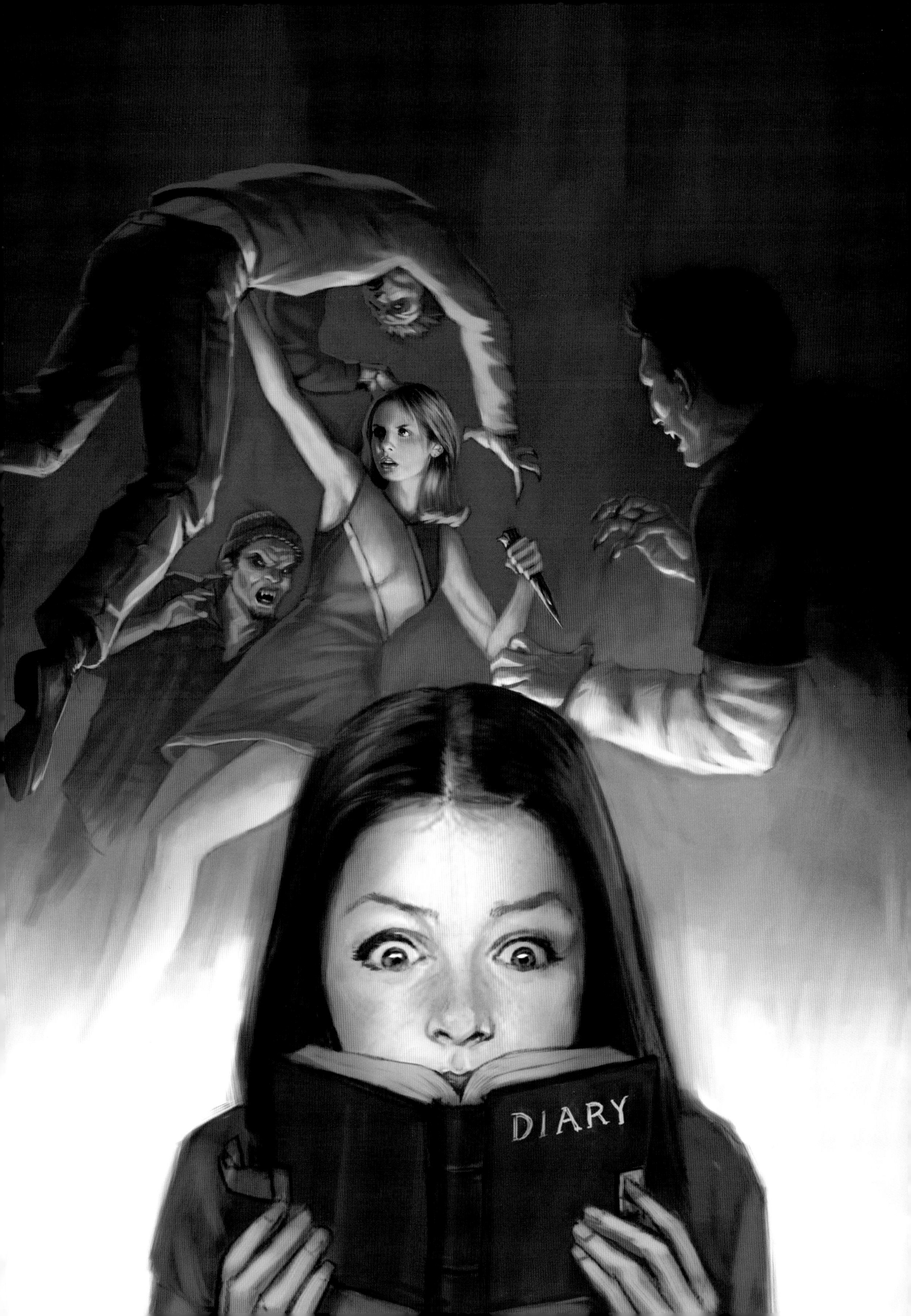
DIARY

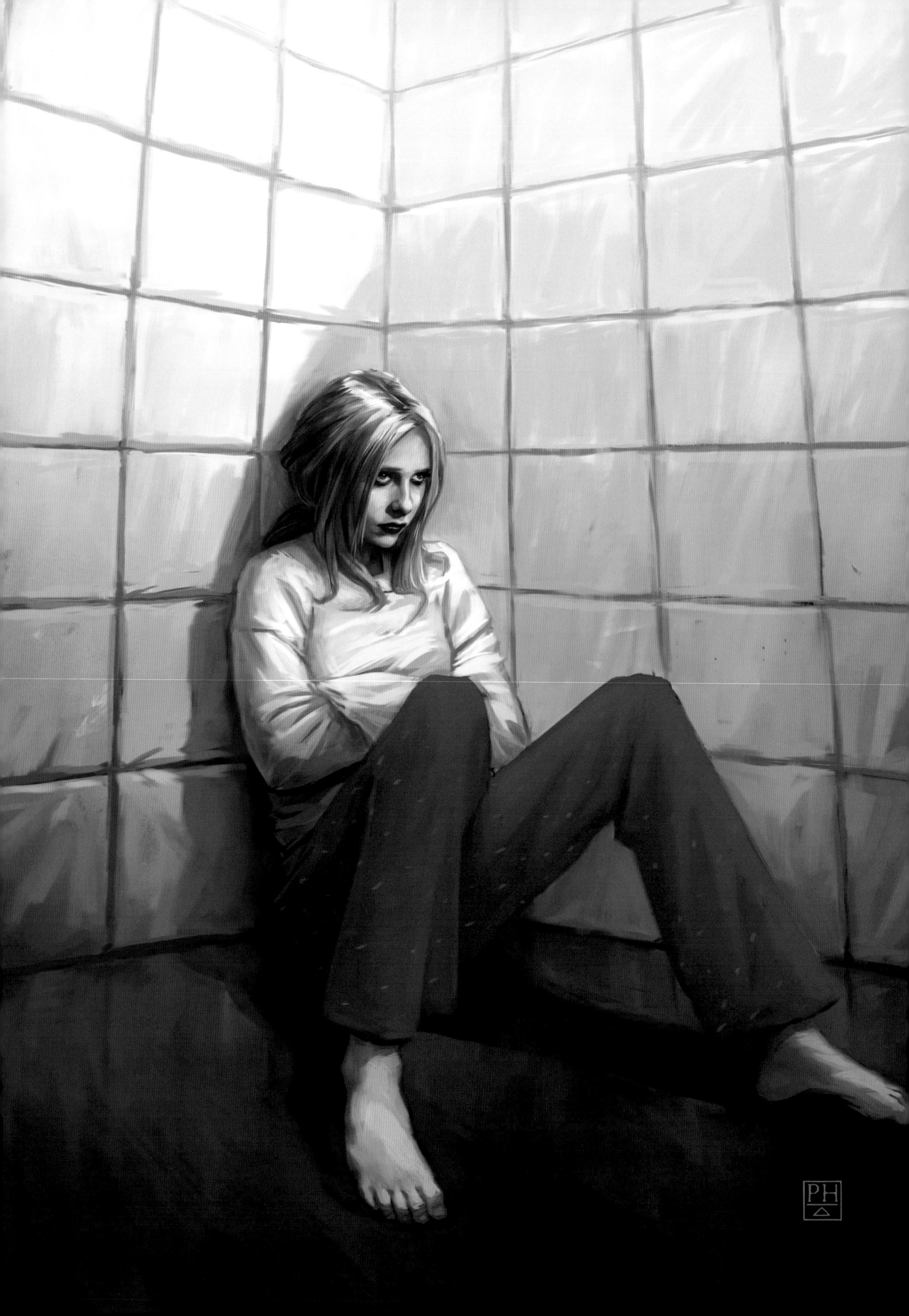

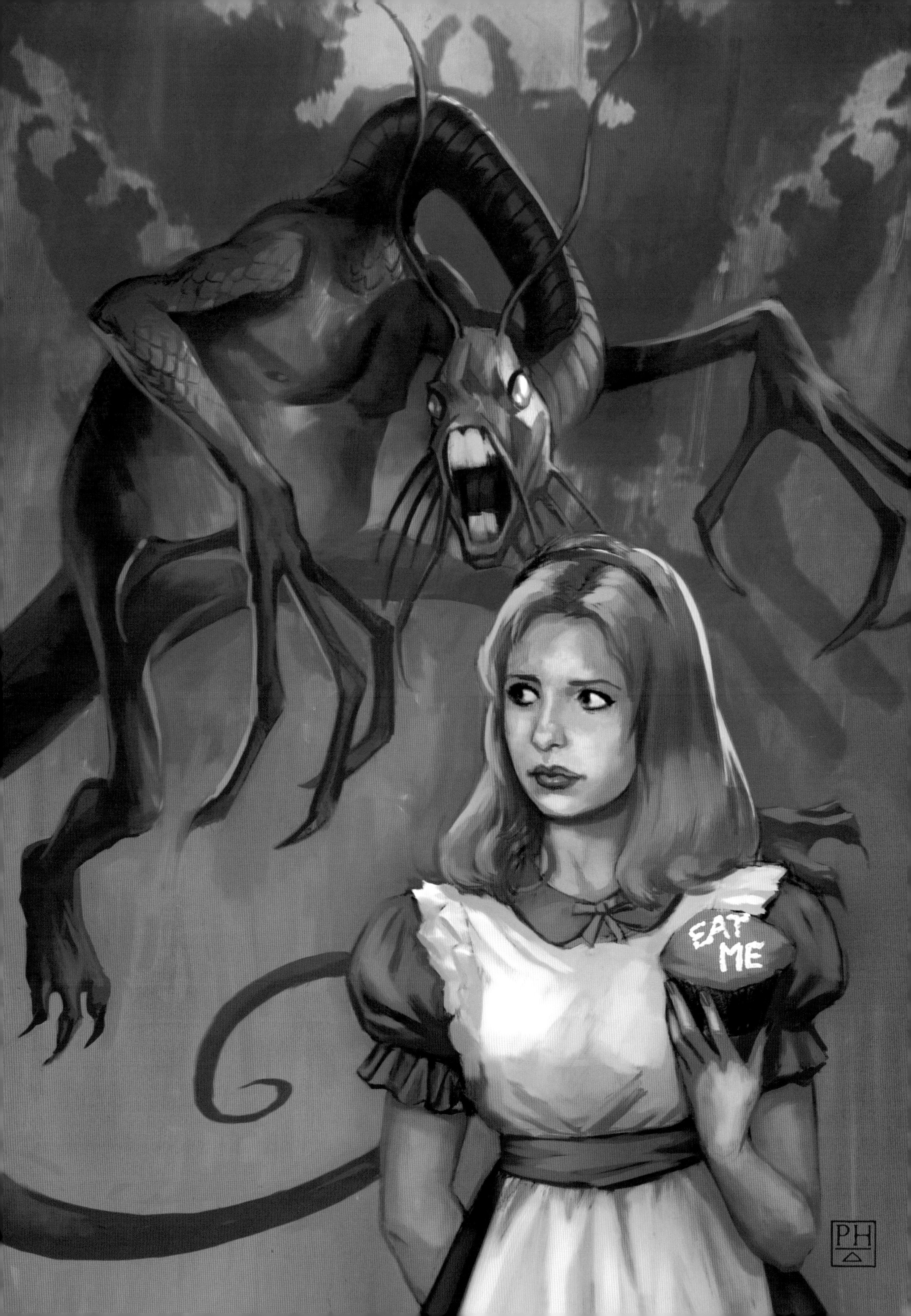
EAT ME
PH

BUFFY FACED OFF with a harsh psychiatrist in the series, leading to psychedelic sequences like the one below.

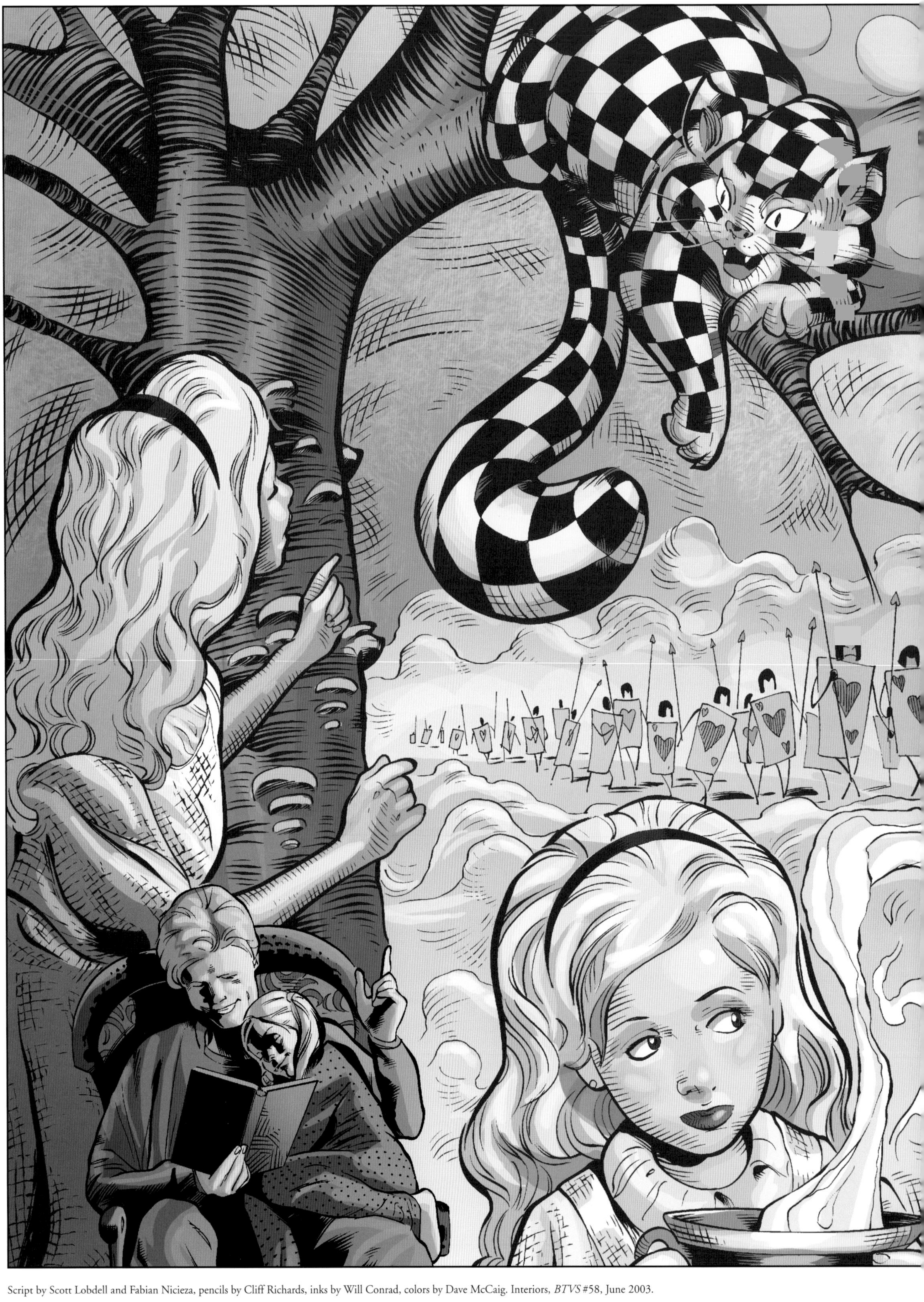

 Script by Scott Lobdell and Fabian Nicieza, pencils by Cliff Richards, inks by Will Conrad, colors by Dave McCaig. Interiors, *BTVS* #58, June 2003.

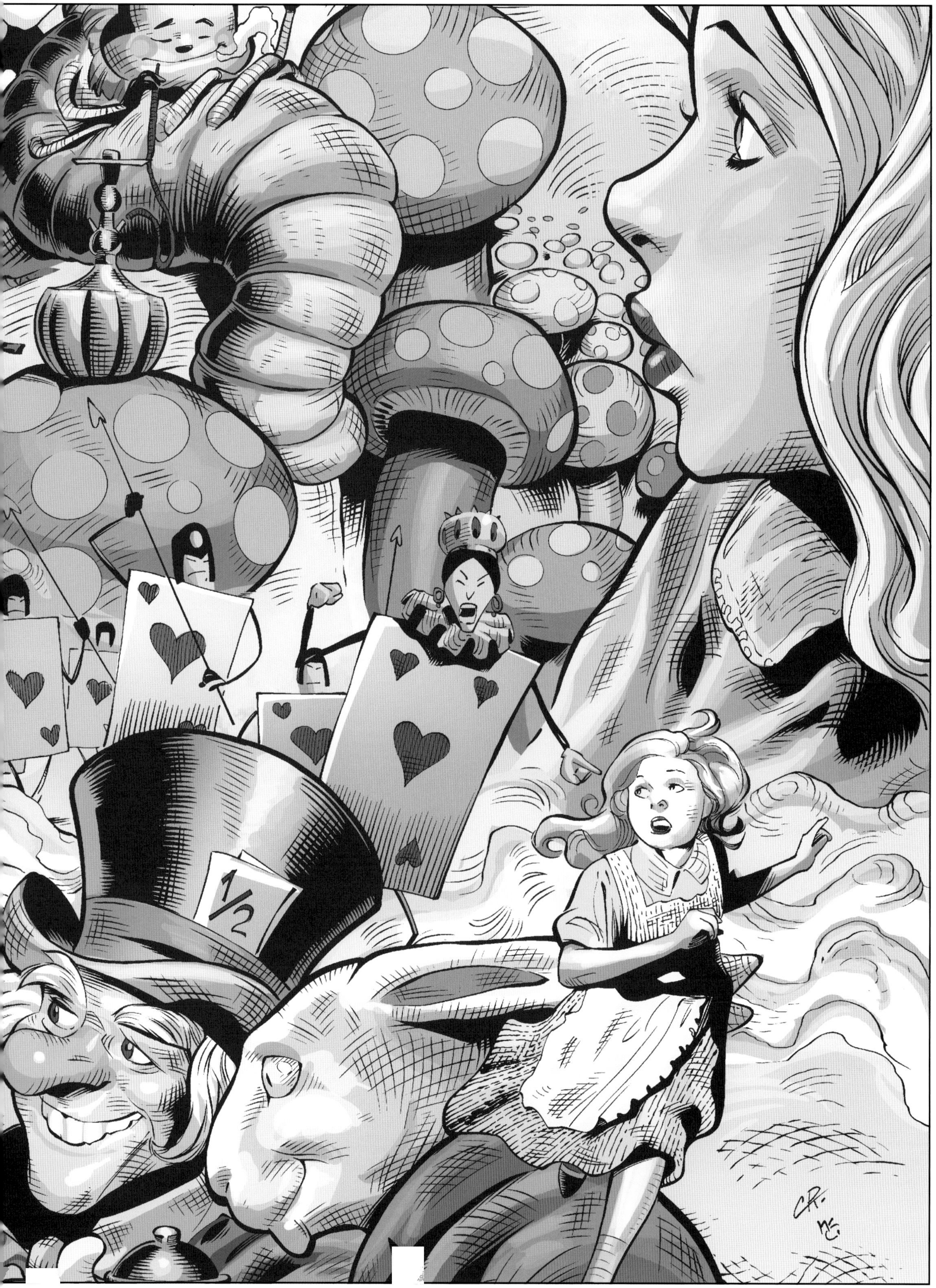
1/2

THE FINAL PART OF THE YEAR ONE storyline was called *A Stake to the Heart*, beginning in *Buffy* #60. We entered into it knowing it was going to be the end of the monthly series. The TV show was ending, we'd just done a series in a mental institution, and we all felt we were doing the best work the monthly had seen. Our disappointment with having the book end was reflected in the extremely dark storyline.

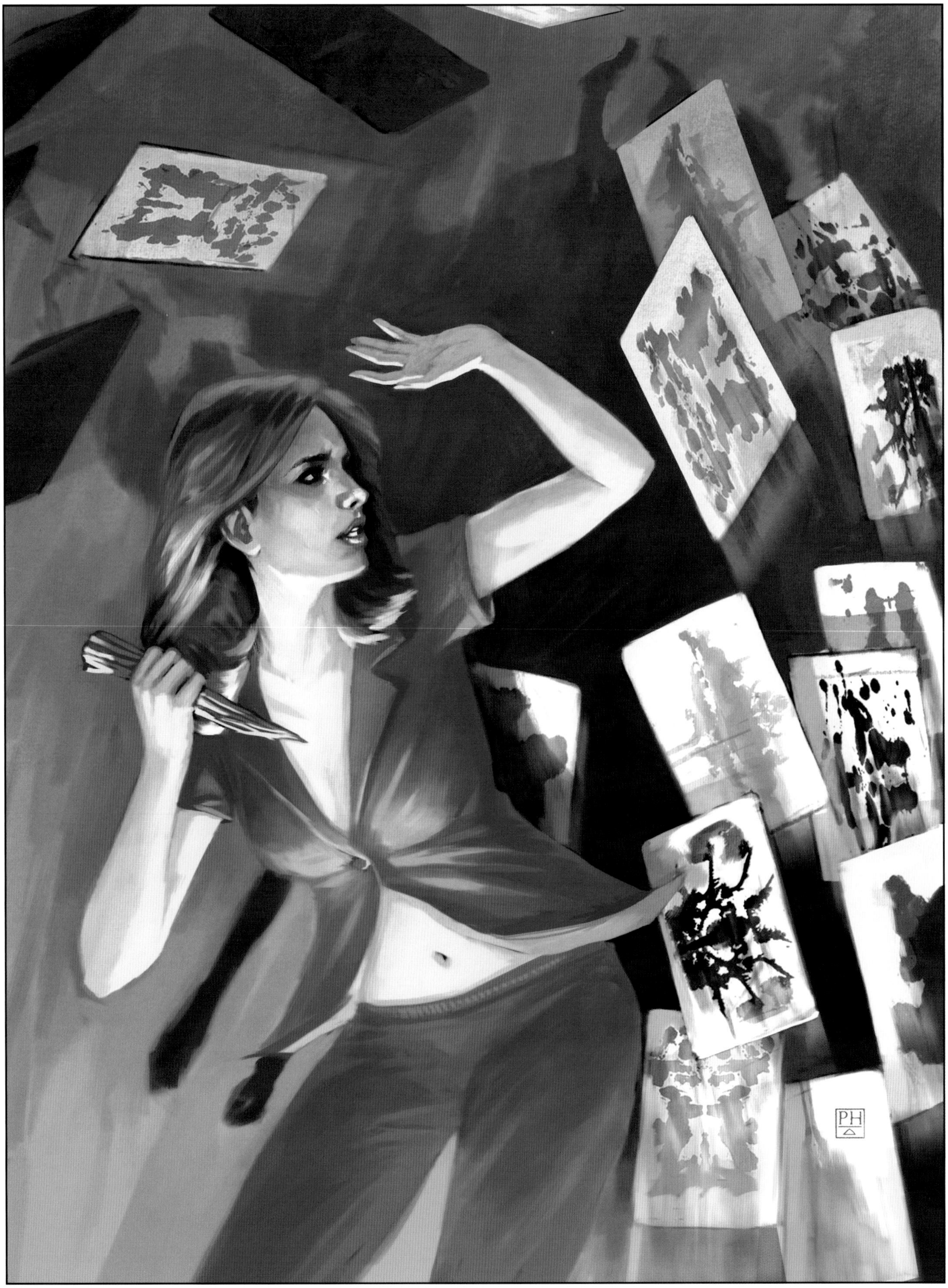
PH

 Above: Painting by Paul Lee and Brian Horton. Opposite: Painting by Horton. Covers, *BTVS* #59 and #60, July and August 2003.

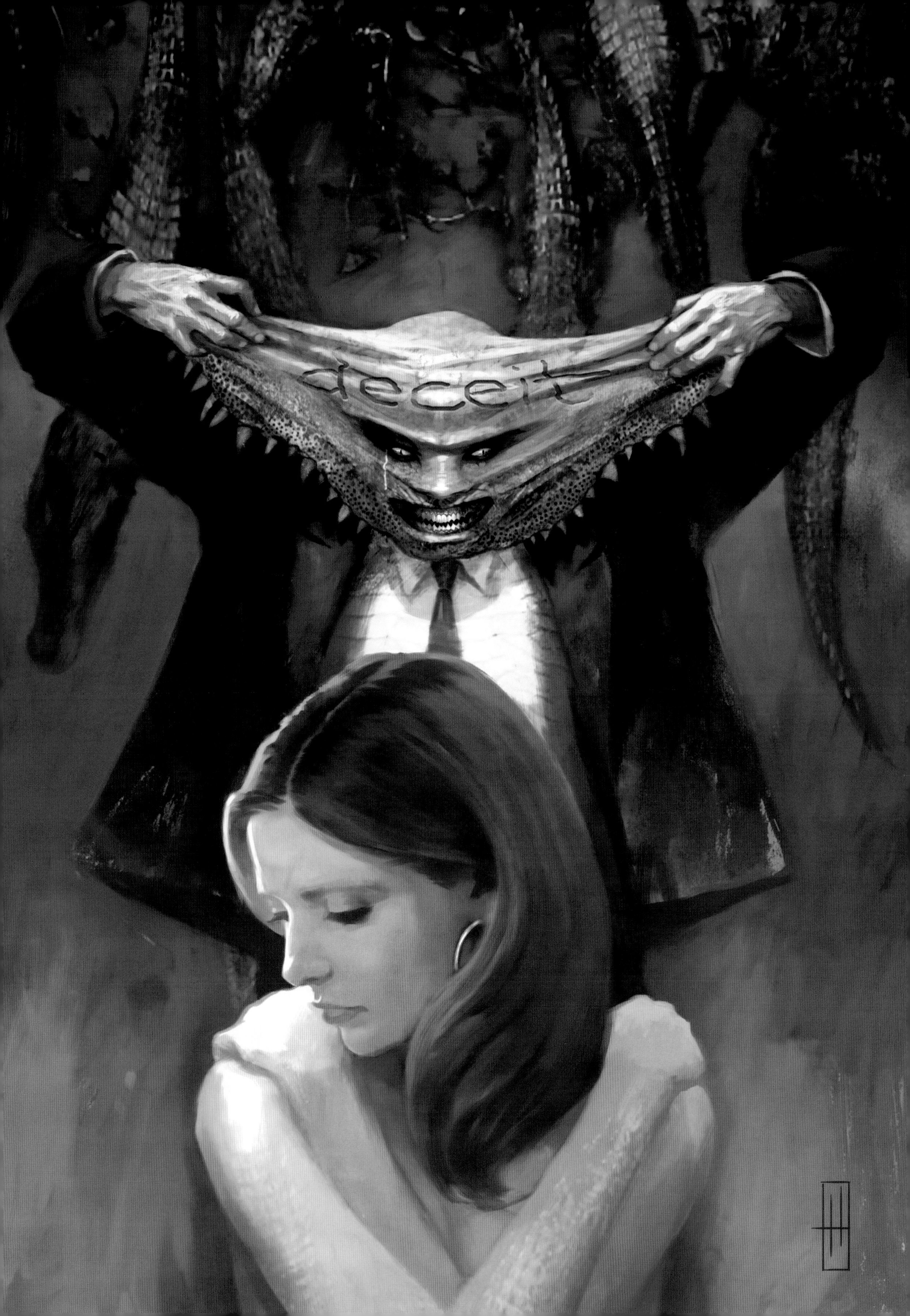
deceit

BRIAN HORTON HAD BEEN ITCHING to do some covers on his own, and we took this opportunity. Fabian Nicieza proposed a story, involving demonic manifestations of human weakness—or demons that fed on human weakness, depending on your perspective. We wanted these things to have distinct and horrible appearances, and Brian's background as a character designer working in video games and with Clive Barker made him ideal for this. Between Fabian and Brian and me, we worked out a set of symbols for the emotions in question, including totemic animals.

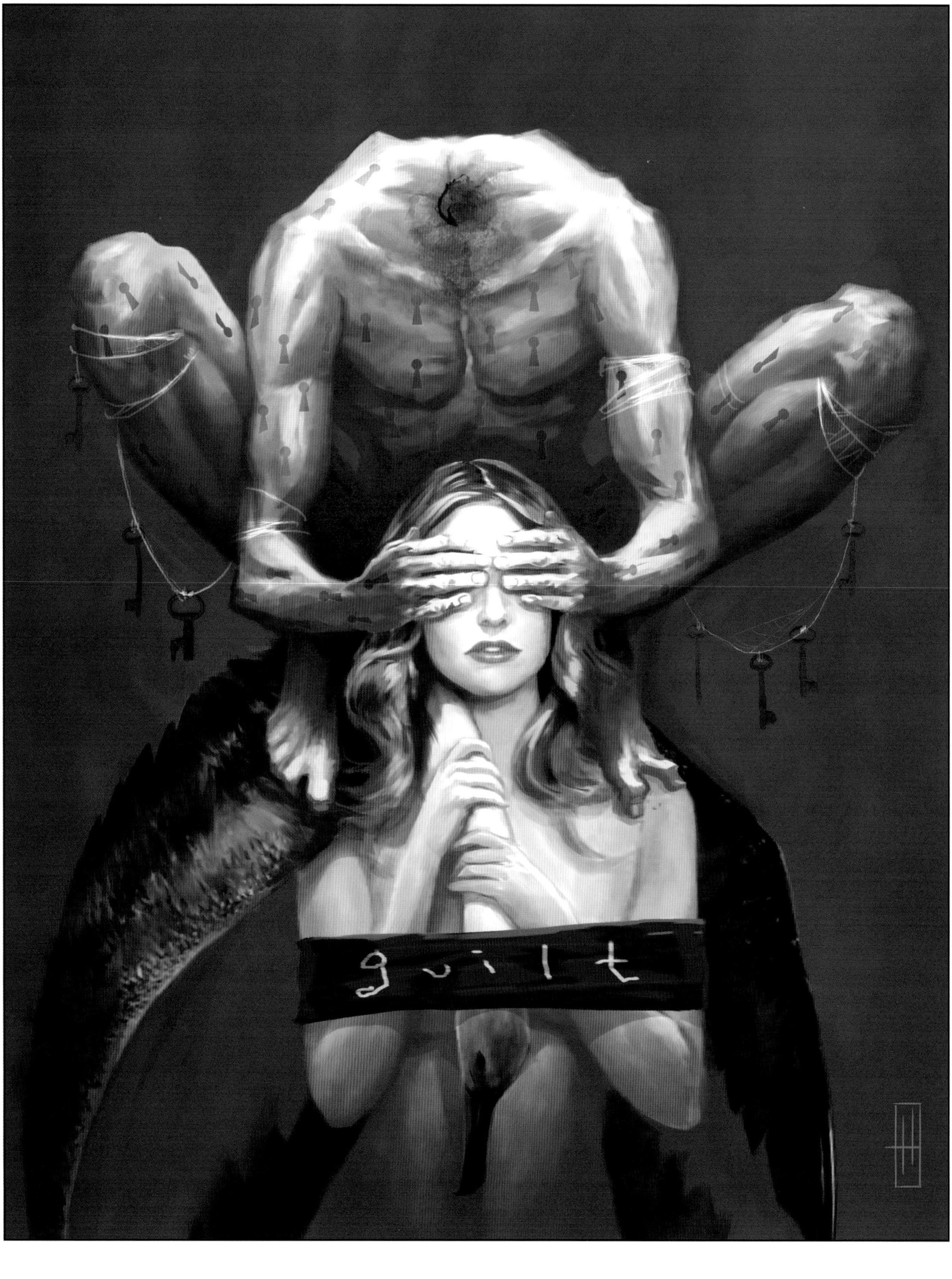
guilt

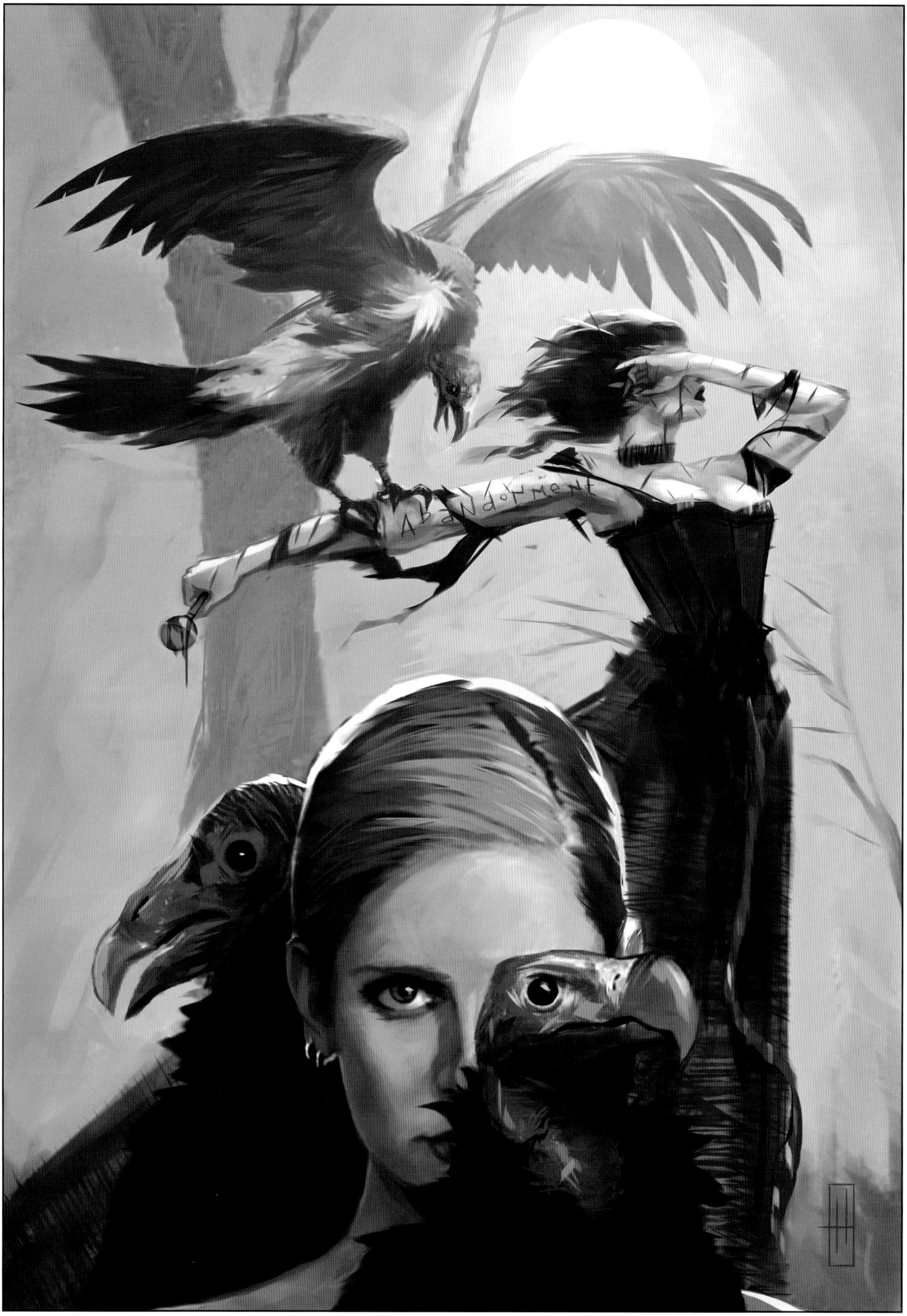
ABANDONMENT

Opposite, above and following page: Paintings by Horton. Covers, *BTVS* #61–63, September–November 2003.

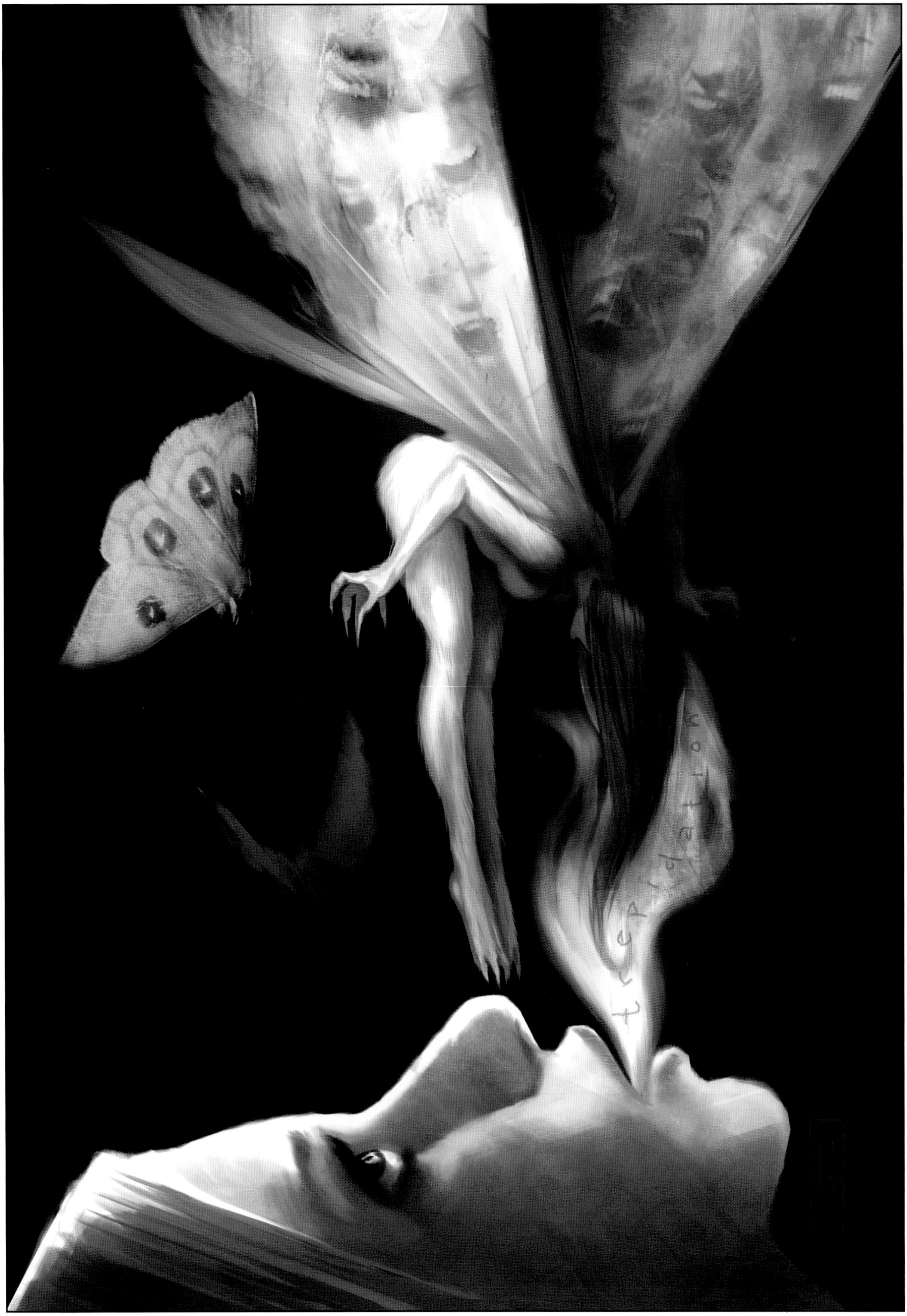
trepidation

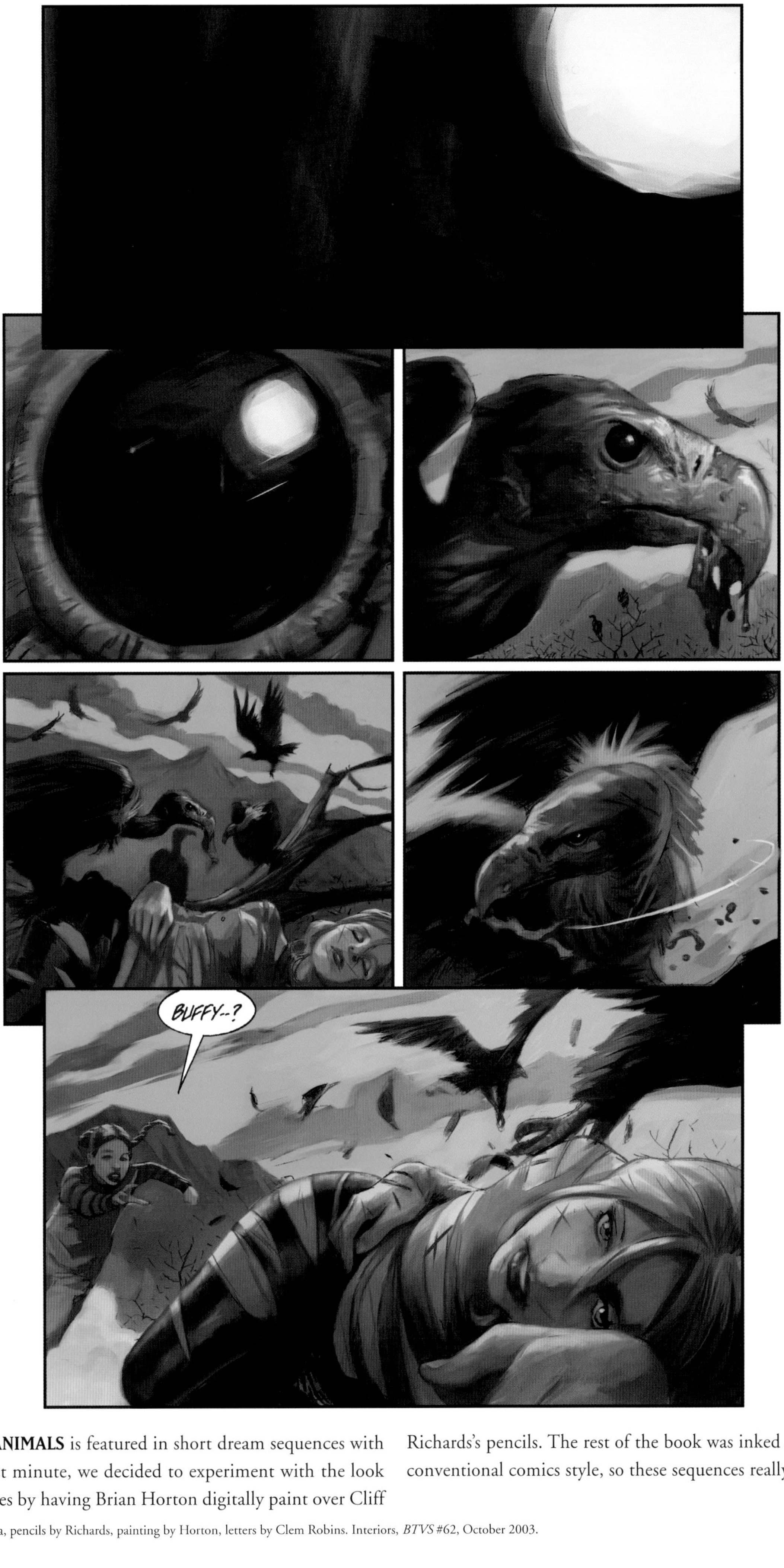
BUFFY--?

EACH OF THE ANIMALS is featured in short dream sequences with Buffy. At the last minute, we decided to experiment with the look of these sequences by having Brian Horton digitally paint over Cliff Richards's pencils. The rest of the book was inked and colored in a conventional comics style, so these sequences really stood out.

Script by Fabian Nicieza, pencils by Richards, painting by Horton, letters by Clem Robins. Interiors, *BTVS* #62, October 2003.

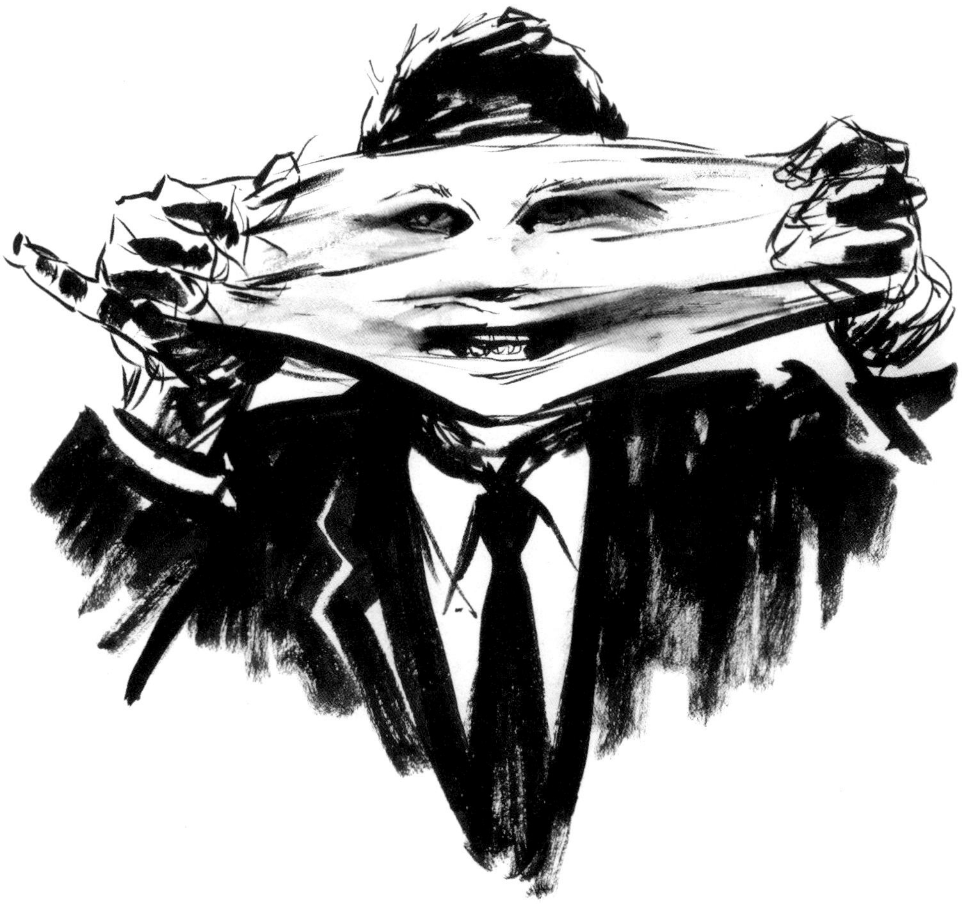

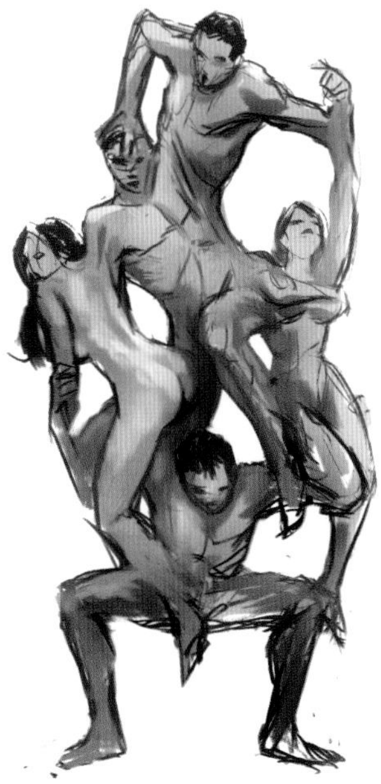

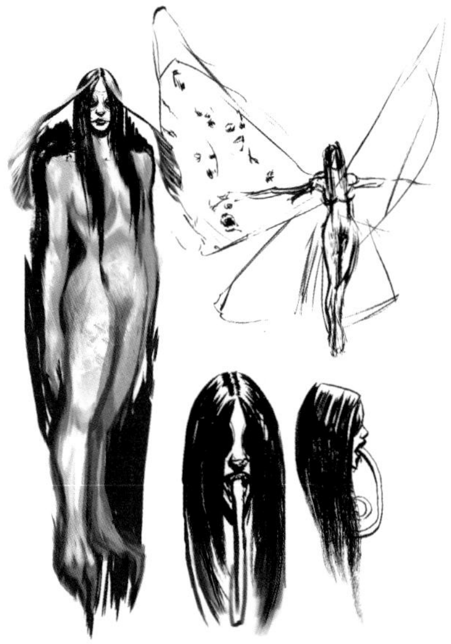

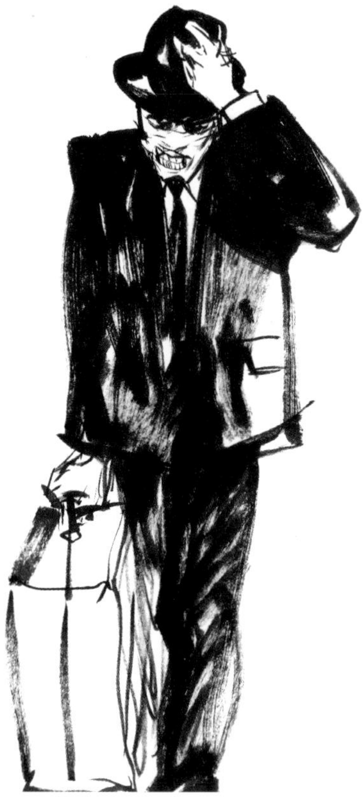

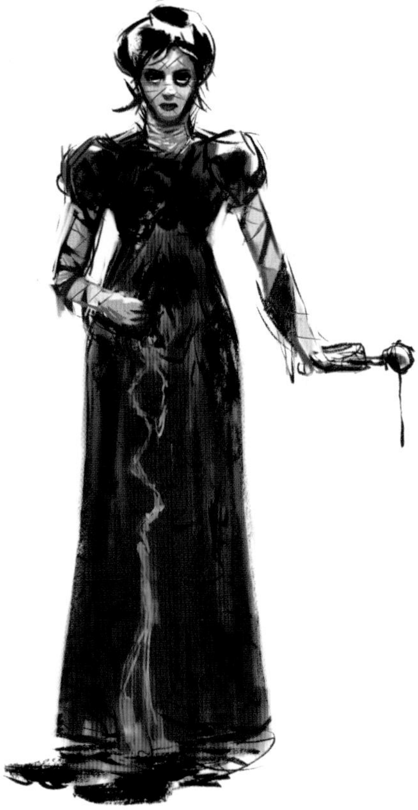

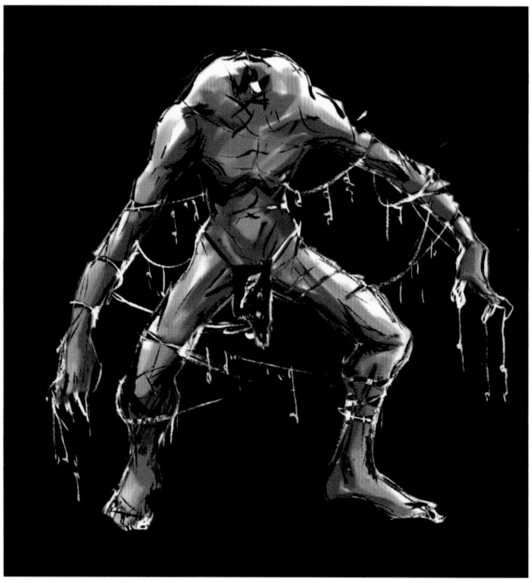

BRIAN HORTON DESIGNED the demons with a lot of input from Fabian Nicieza and me, including sketches from Fabian. The pile of melded bodies was based on a drawing from Fabian for the character of Trepidation, but as we moved more into the idea of the totem animals, Brian came up with the butterfly concept.

Since starting to use Brian and Paul's covers on the trade paperbacks, w simply reuse a cover from the monthly series. We realized we couldn't that here, because each cover only represented one chapter of the story, a we wanted a cover to bring them all together. Brian dashed out the pie on the right without showing me a sketch. I wanted Buffy featured mc prominently, so he created the piece on the following page.

 Above: Sketches by Horton, 2003. Opposite: Painting by Horton. Unused cover, *BTVS: A Stake to the Heart* trade paperback, April 2004.

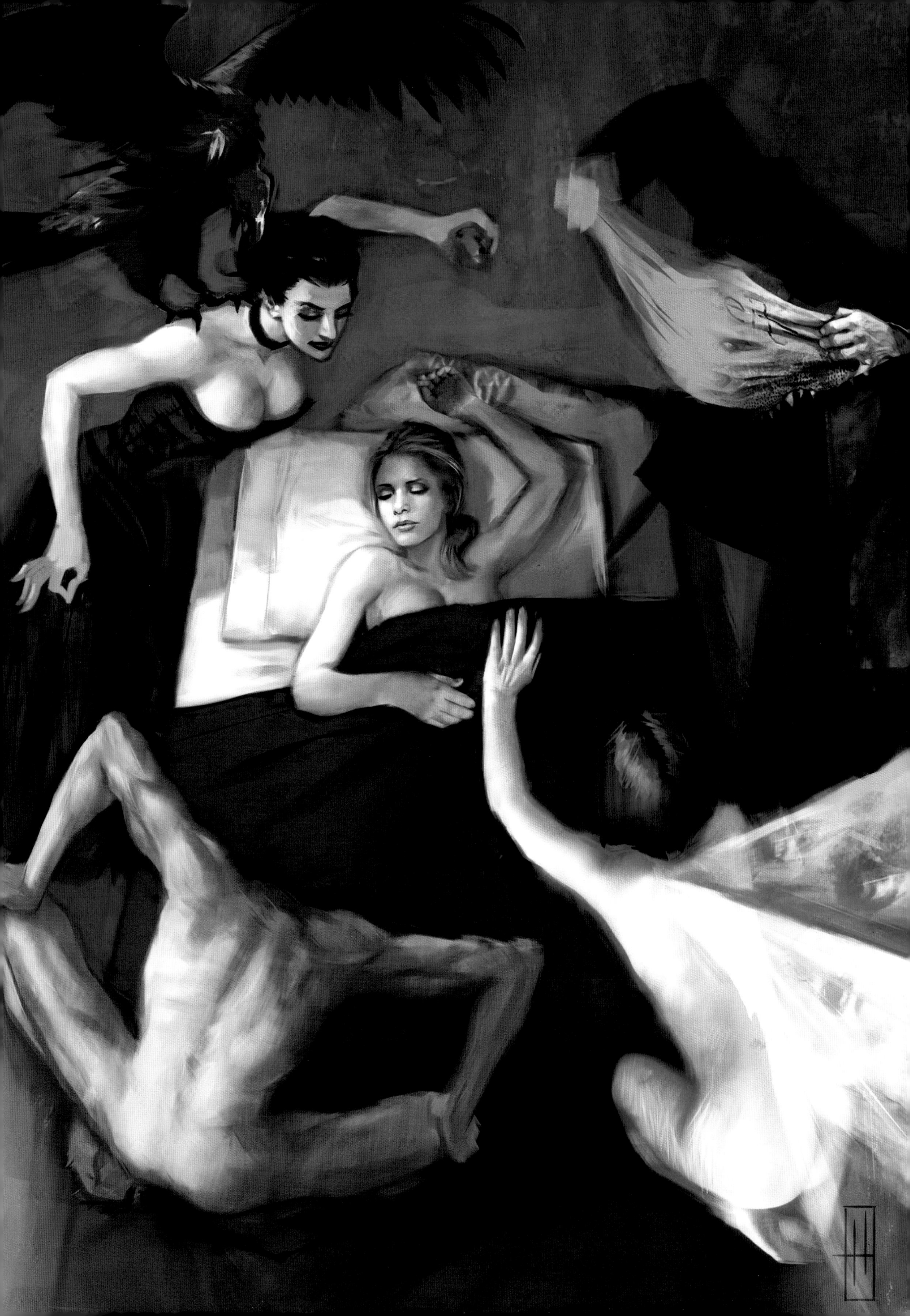

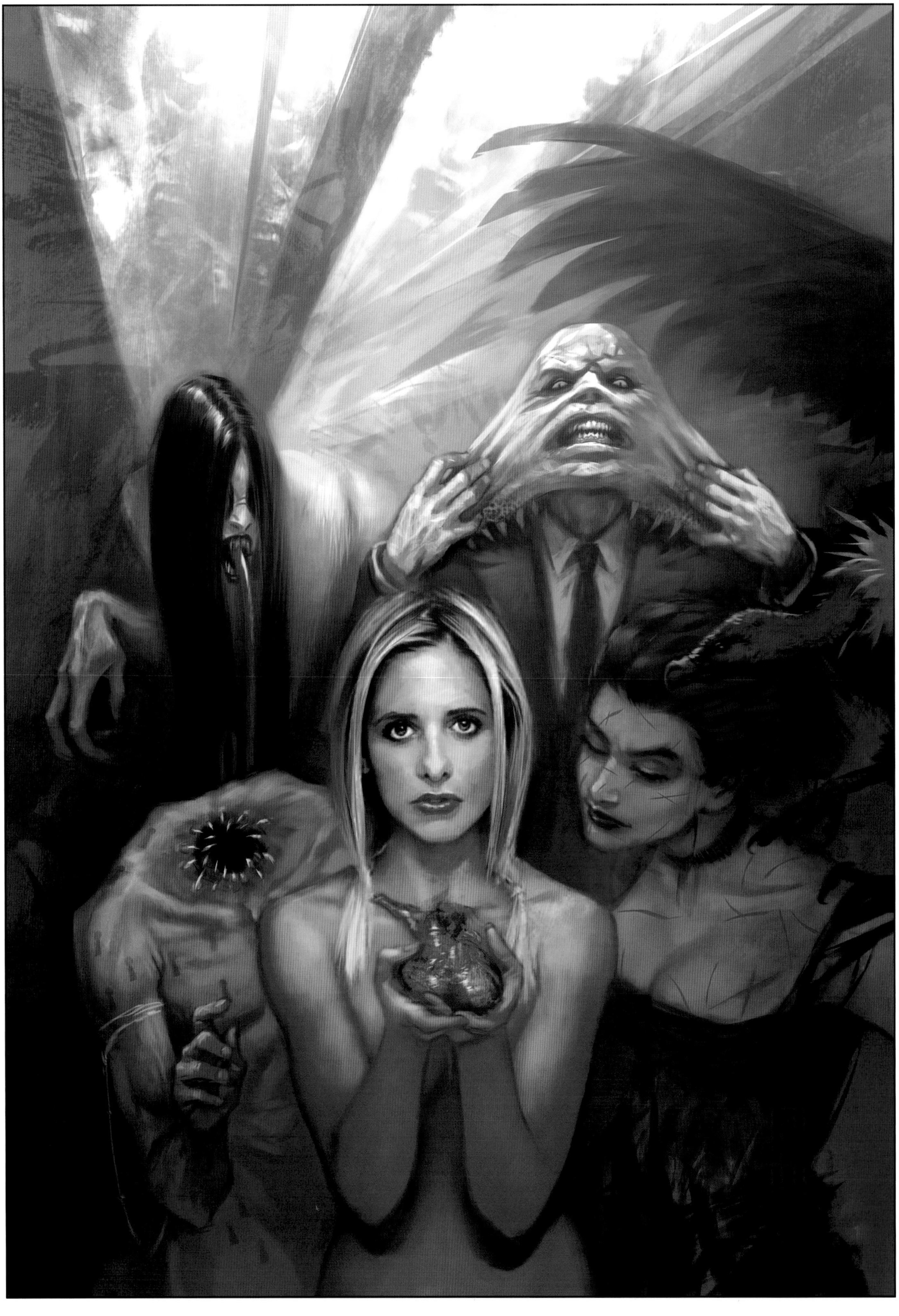

FOLLOWING ON THE SUCCESS of *Tales of the Slayers*, and staring down the end of the TV series, Joss came back with *Tales of the Vampires*. Once again he brought along writers from the show, but this time we did the stories spread over five issues. Eric Powell returned to *Buffy* for this cover featuring Dracula's first appearance in the comics.

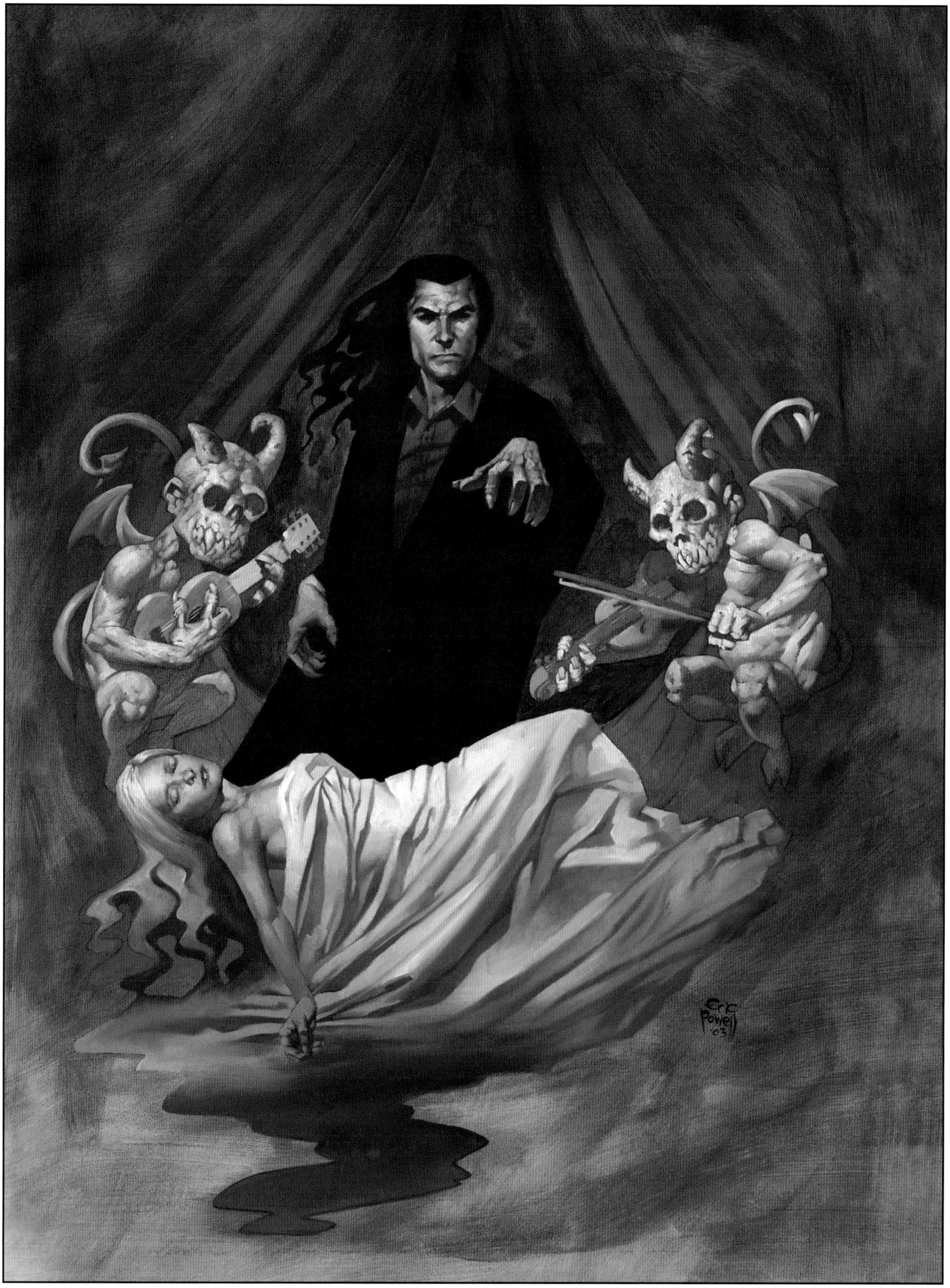
Eric Powell '03

Opposite: Painting by Brian Horton. Cover, *BTVS: A Stake to the Heart* trade paperback, April 2004. Above: Painting by Powell. Cover, *BTVS: Tales of the Vampires* #3, February 2004.

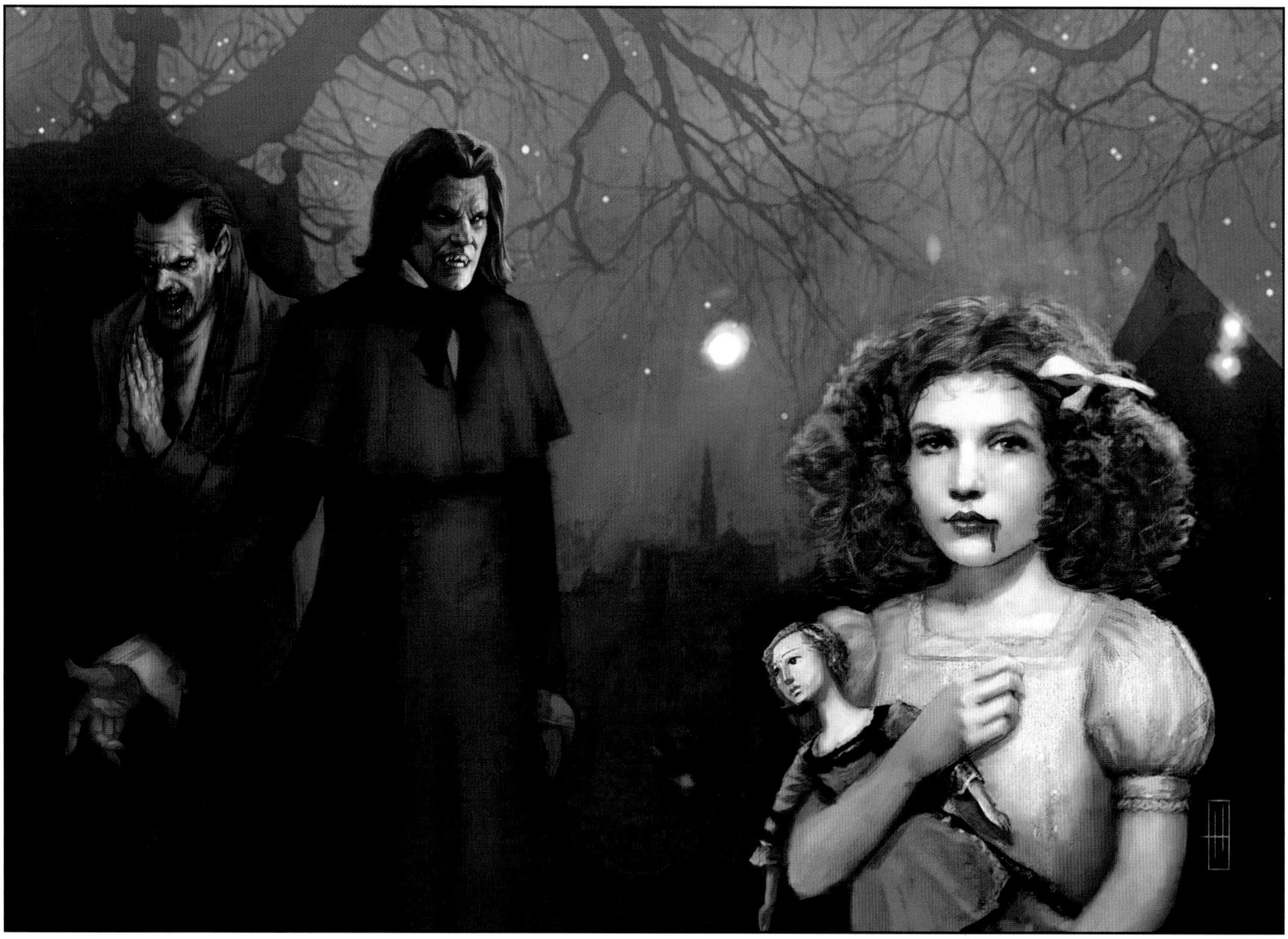

TALES OF THE VAMPIRES tied a little more directly into the television show than *Tales of the Slayers*, with stories featuring Angel (the little girl below is reminding him of things he did as Angelus) and Spike and Dru, and a hilarious story by Drew Goddard featuring Xander once more in the thrall of Dracula. The book also featured a story by Joss told one chapter at a time in each issue.

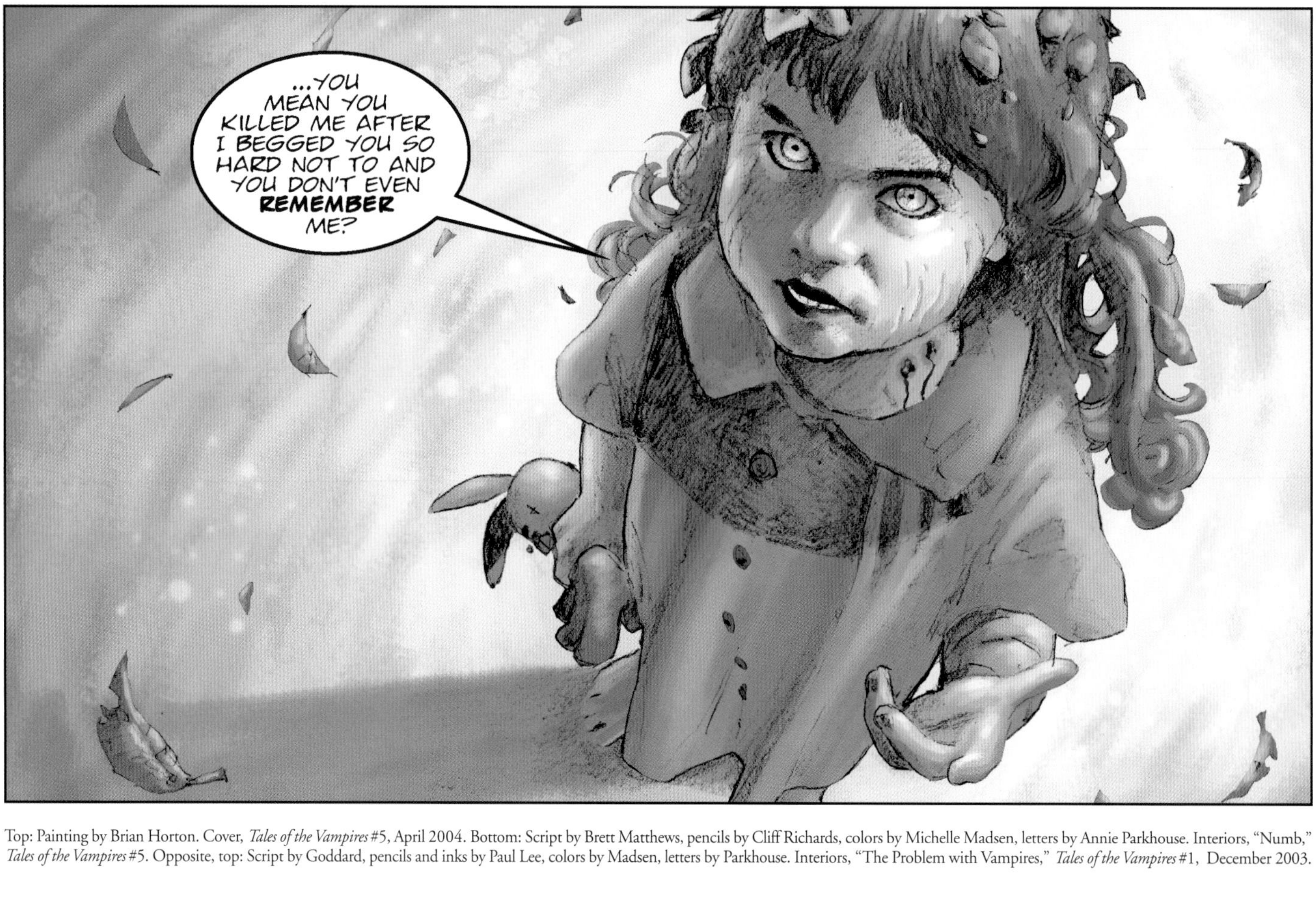
...YOU MEAN YOU KILLED ME AFTER I BEGGED YOU SO HARD NOT TO AND YOU DON'T EVEN **REMEMBER** ME?

 Top: Painting by Brian Horton. Cover, *Tales of the Vampires* #5, April 2004. Bottom: Script by Brett Matthews, pencils by Cliff Richards, colors by Michelle Madsen, letters by Annie Parkhouse. Interiors, "Numb," *Tales of the Vampires* #5. Opposite, top: Script by Goddard, pencils and inks by Paul Lee, colors by Madsen, letters by Parkhouse. Interiors, "The Problem with Vampires," *Tales of the Vampires* #1, December 2003.

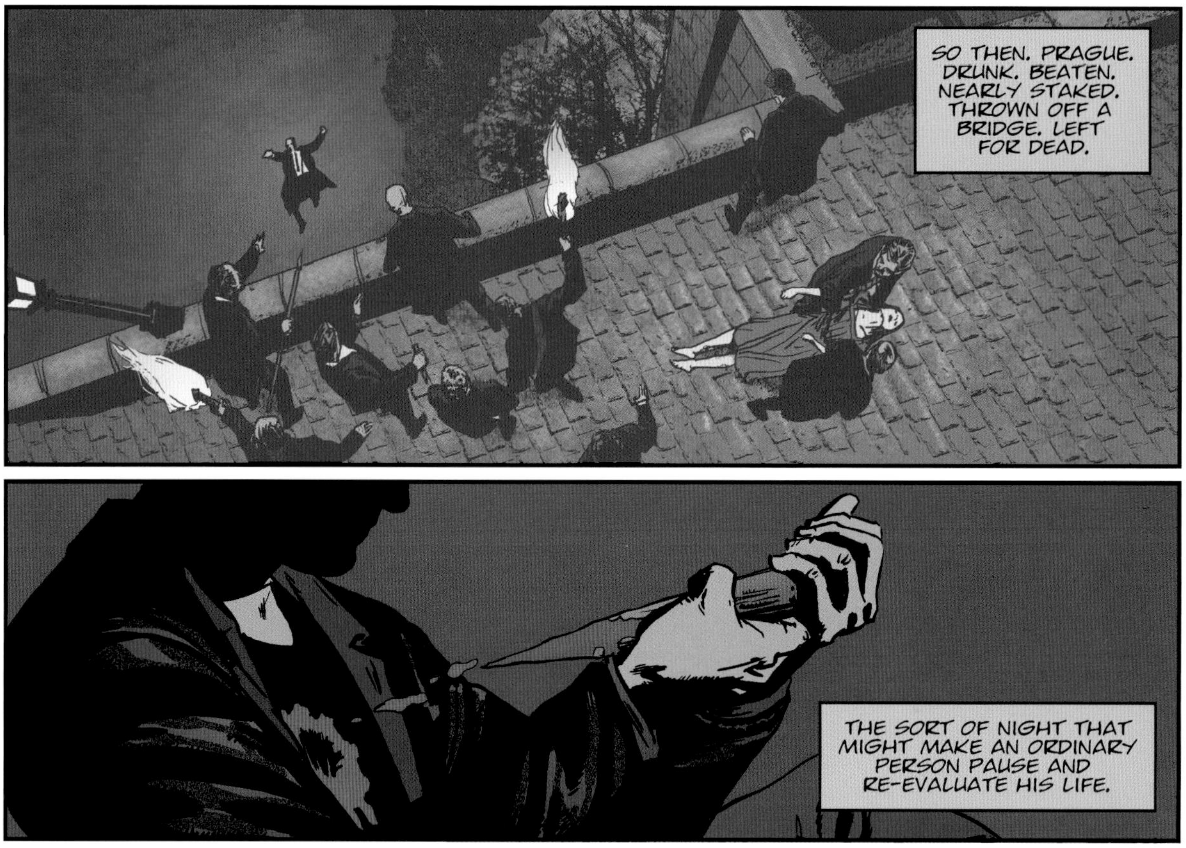
SO THEN. PRAGUE. DRUNK. BEATEN. NEARLY STAKED. THROWN OFF A BRIDGE. LEFT FOR DEAD.
THE SORT OF NIGHT THAT MIGHT MAKE AN ORDINARY PERSON PAUSE AND RE-EVALUATE HIS LIFE.

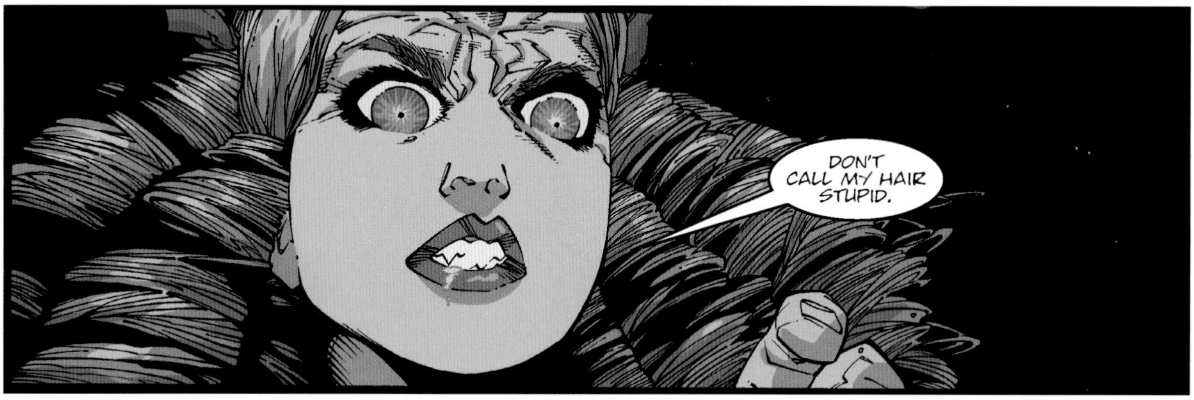
DON'T CALL MY HAIR STUPID.

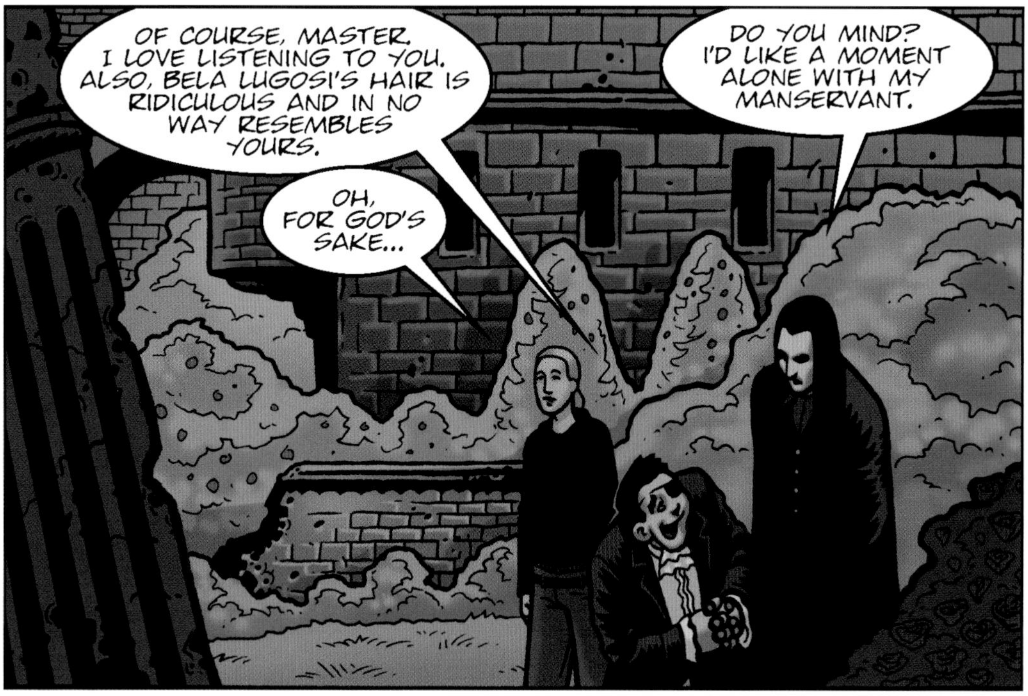
DO YOU MIND? I'D LIKE A MOMENT ALONE WITH MY MANSERVANT.
OF COURSE, MASTER. I LOVE LISTENING TO YOU. ALSO, BELA LUGOSI'S HAIR IS RIDICULOUS AND IN NO WAY RESEMBLES YOURS.
OH, FOR GOD'S SAKE...

Above, middle: Script by Whedon, pencils by Alex Sanchez, inks by Derek Fridolfs, colors by Madsen, letters by Parkhouse. Interiors, "Tales of the Vampires," *Tales of the Vampires* #5. Above, bottom: Script by Goddard; pencils, inks, and colors by Ben Stenbeck; letters by Parkhouse. Interiors, "Antique," *Tales of the Vampires* #3, February 2004.

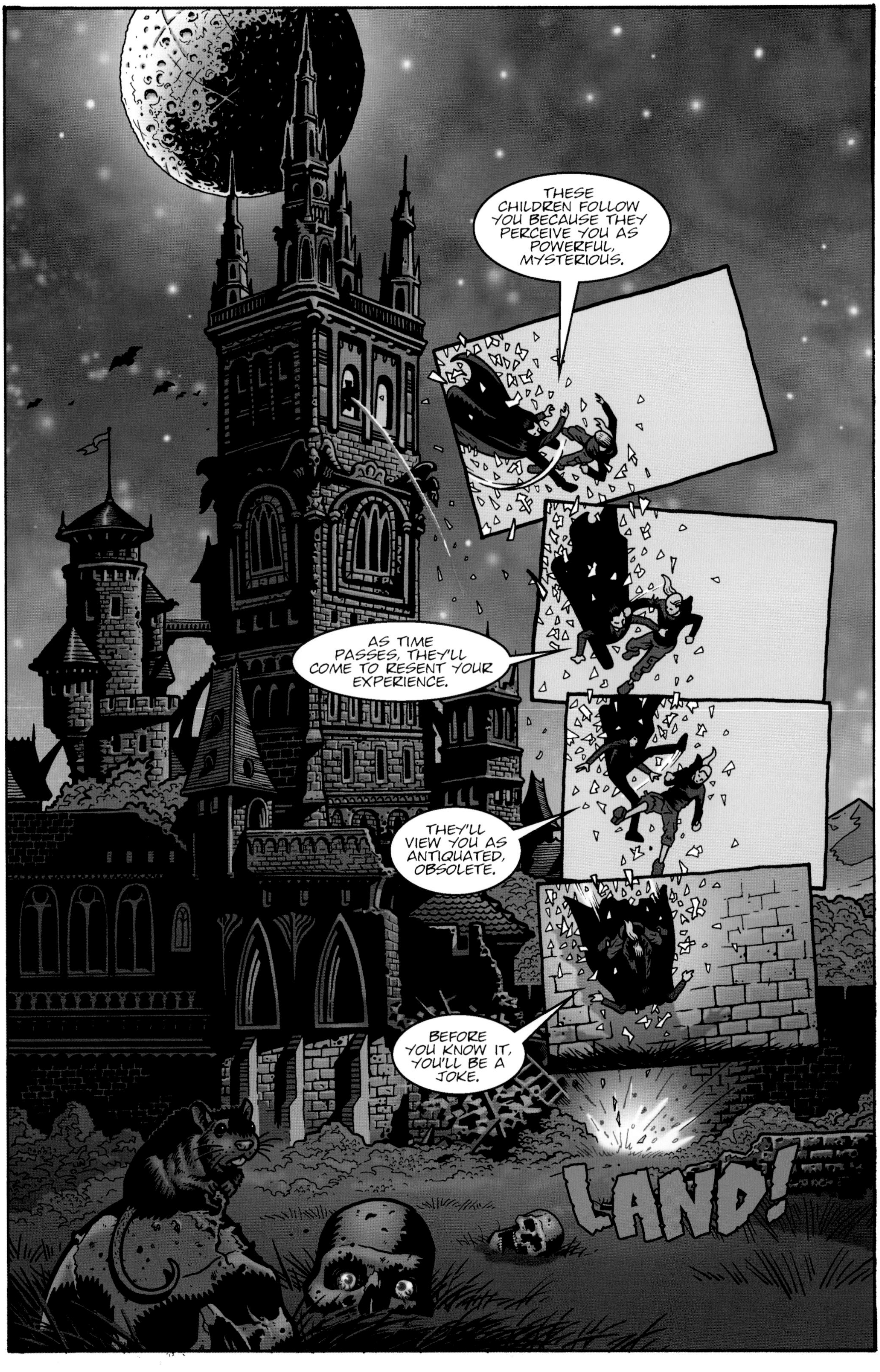
THESE CHILDREN FOLLOW YOU BECAUSE THEY PERCEIVE YOU AS POWERFUL, MYSTERIOUS.
AS TIME PASSES, THEY'LL COME TO RESENT YOUR EXPERIENCE.
THEY'LL VIEW YOU AS ANTIQUATED, OBSOLETE.
BEFORE YOU KNOW IT, YOU'LL BE A JOKE.
LAND!

DREW GODDARD AND ARTIST BEN STENBECK—a Dark Horse discovery via the Internet—made great use of the comics page, with something you could only do in this medium. And I don't just mean the "Land!" sound effect. Since the series fell in the first year of Dark Horse's horror line, I used the opportunity to go after great horror artists, one of my favorites being John Totleben.

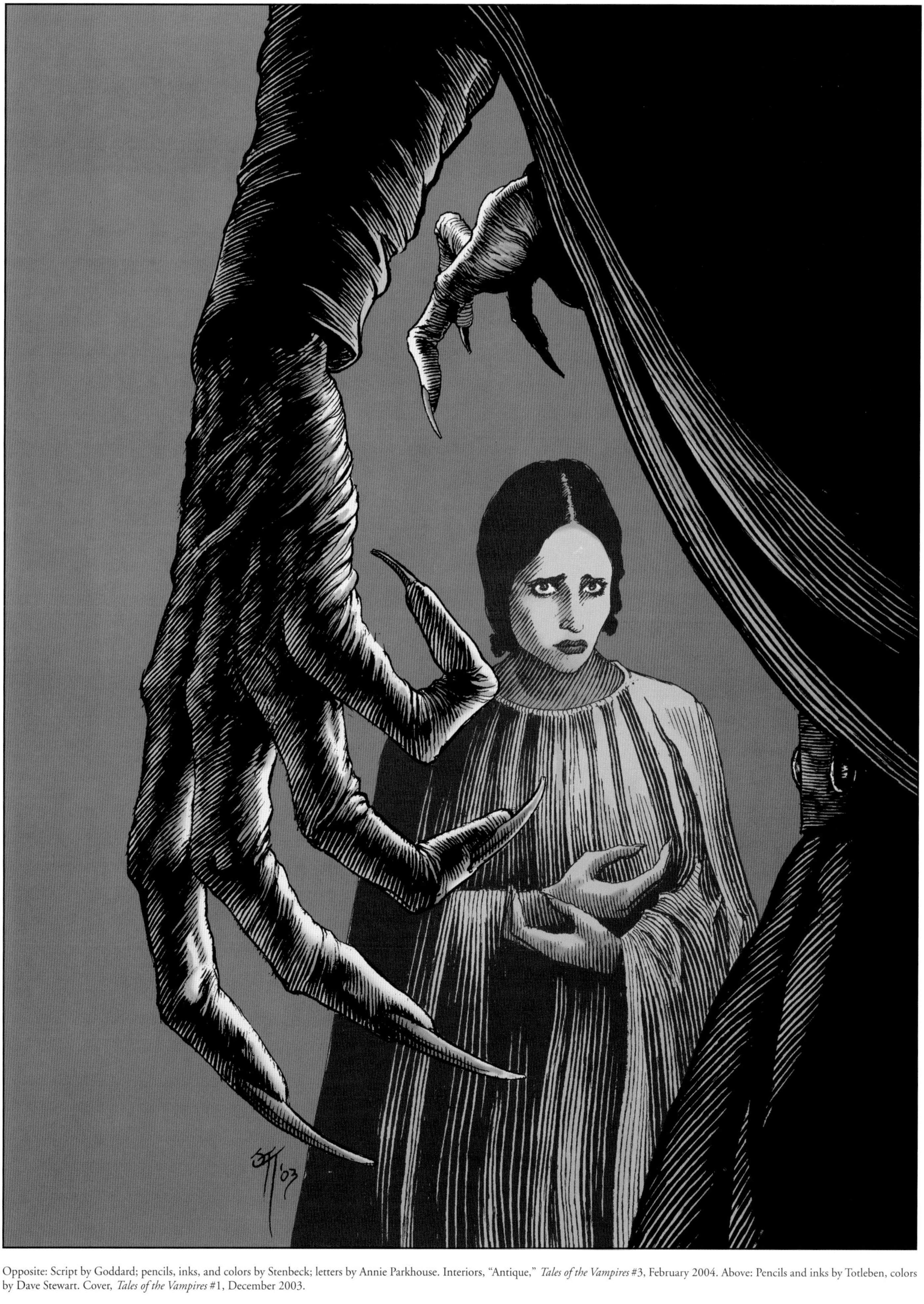

Opposite: Script by Goddard; pencils, inks, and colors by Stenbeck; letters by Annie Parkhouse. Interiors, "Antique," *Tales of the Vampires* #3, February 2004. Above: Pencils and inks by Totleben, colors by Dave Stewart. Cover, *Tales of the Vampires* #1, December 2003.

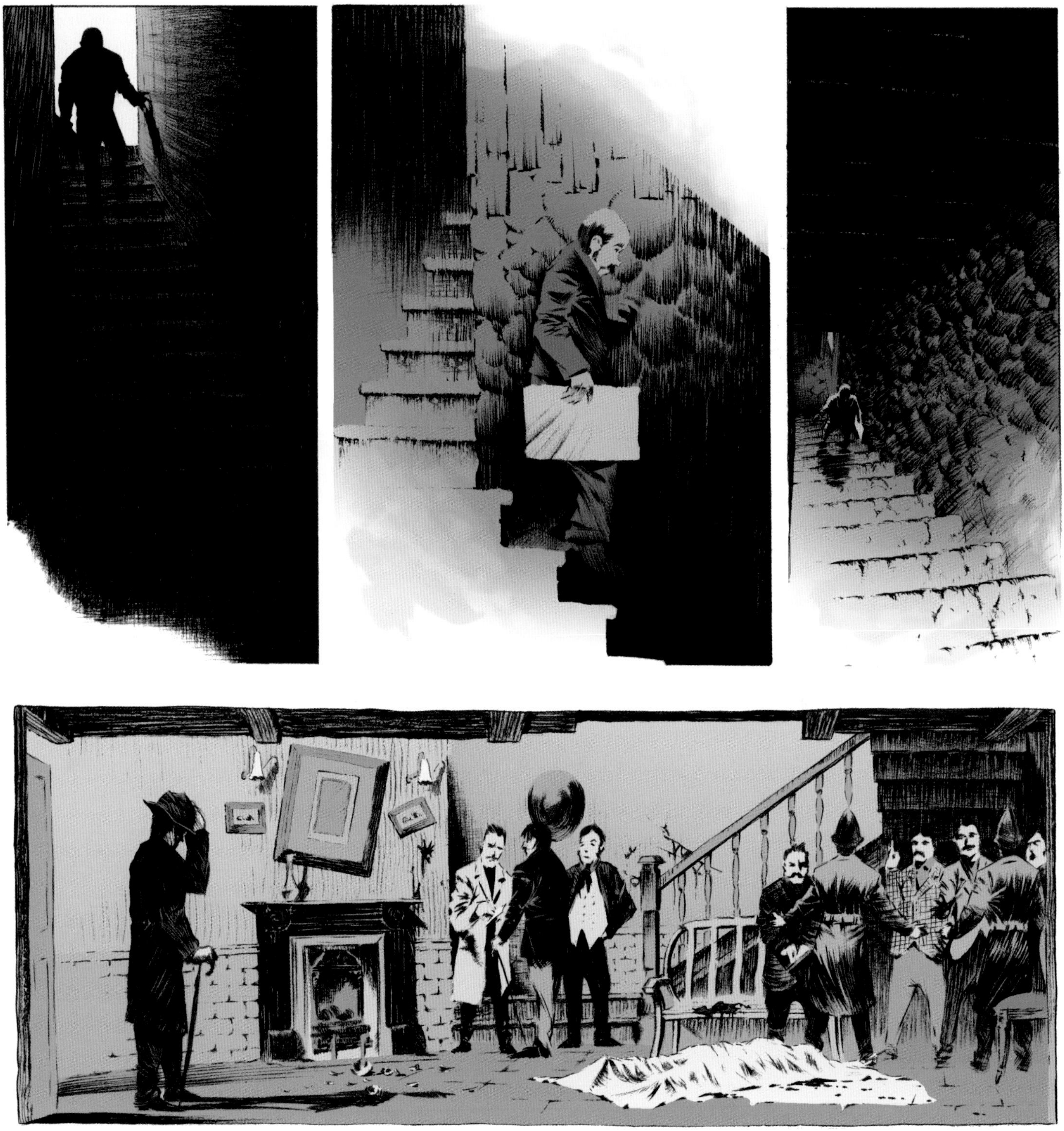

 Script by Brett Matthews, pencils and inks by Vatche Mavlian, colors by Michelle Madsen, letters by Annie Parkhouse. Opposite: Painting by Ben Templesmith. Interiors from "Jack," and cover, *Tales of the Vampires* #2, January 2004.

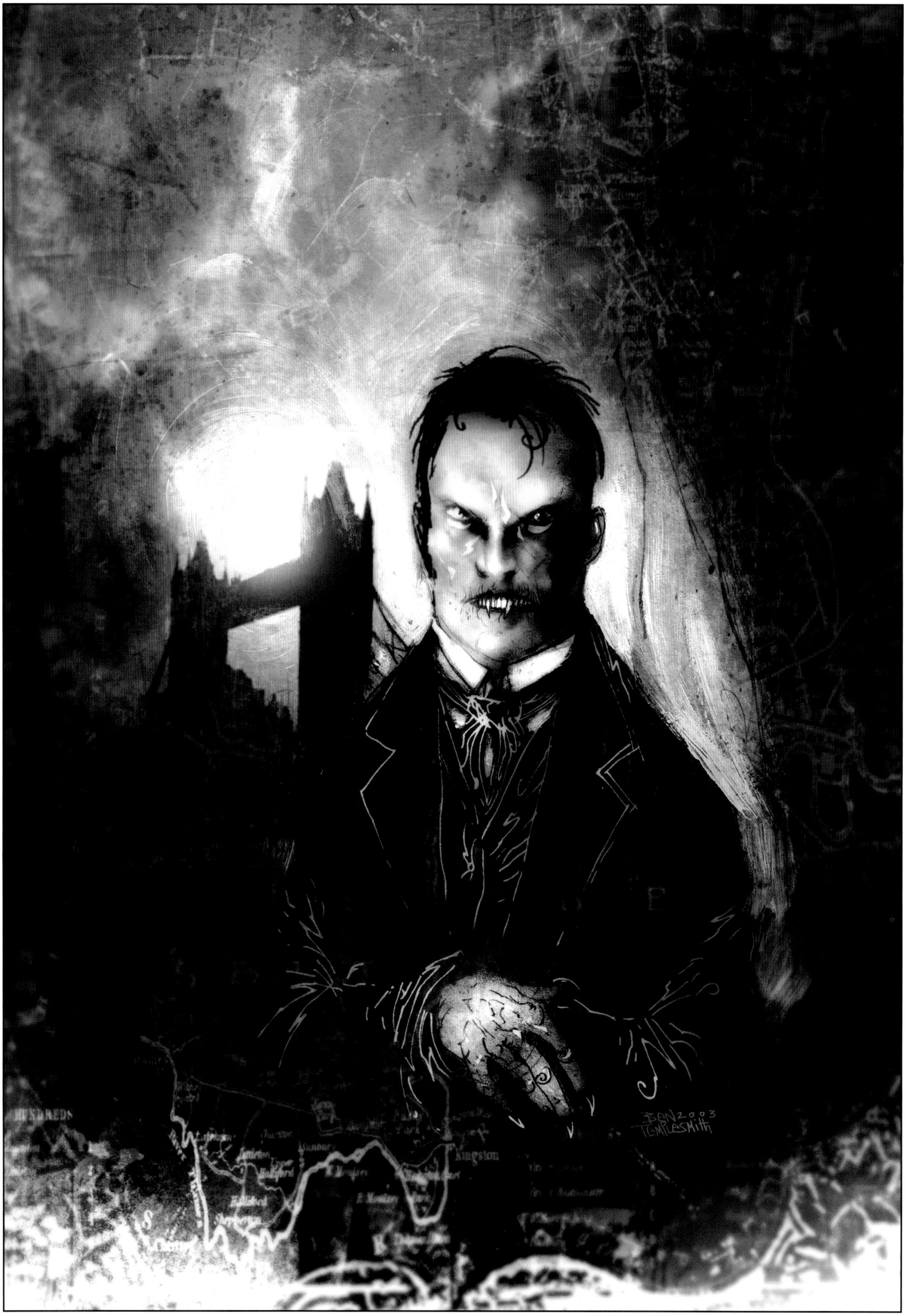
HUNDREDS
Kingston
BEN2003
TEMPLESMITH

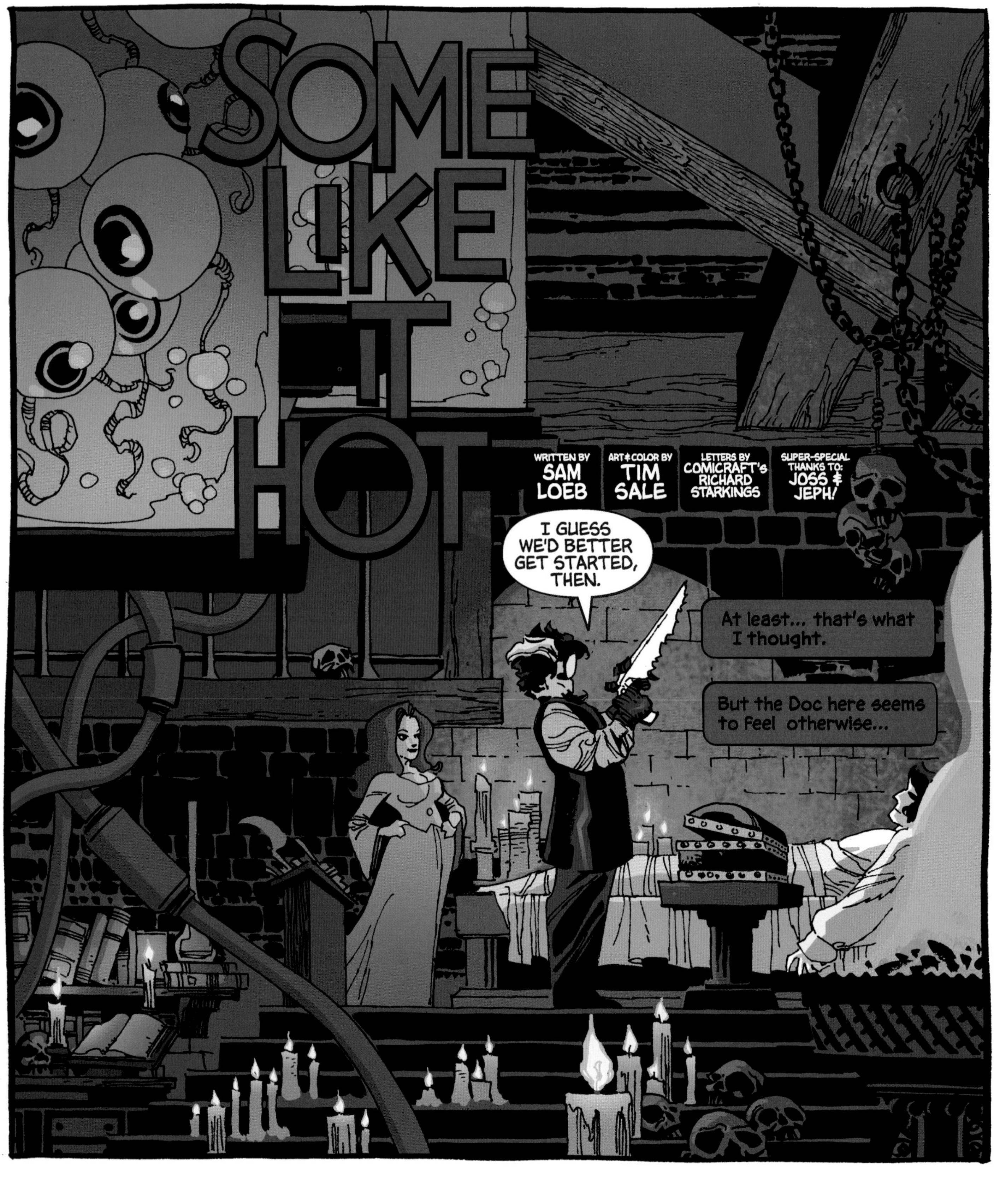
SOME LIKE IT HOT
WRITTEN BY SAM LOEB
ART & COLOR BY TIM SALE
LETTERS BY COMICRAFT'S RICHARD STARKINGS
SUPER-SPECIAL THANKS TO: JOSS & JEPH!
I GUESS WE'D BETTER GET STARTED, THEN.
At least... that's what I thought.
But the Doc here seems to feel otherwise...

TIM SALE WAS THE ONLY returning artist from *Tales of the Slayers*. He came back to draw the first published story by Jeph Loeb's son, Sam. Scott Morse teamed with Jane Espenson for a nursery rhyme about looking for a vampire in a picture, only to realize too late that the picture is actually a mirror, and so you'd never see it coming.

Above and opposite, bottom: Script by Sam Loeb, pencils and inks by Tim Sale, colors by Lee Loughridge, letters by Richards Starkings. Interiors, "Some Like It Hot," *Tales of the Vampires* #5, April 2004. Opposite, top: Script by Espenson, paints and letters by Morse. Interiors, "Spot the Vampire," *Tales of the Vampires* #2, January 2004.

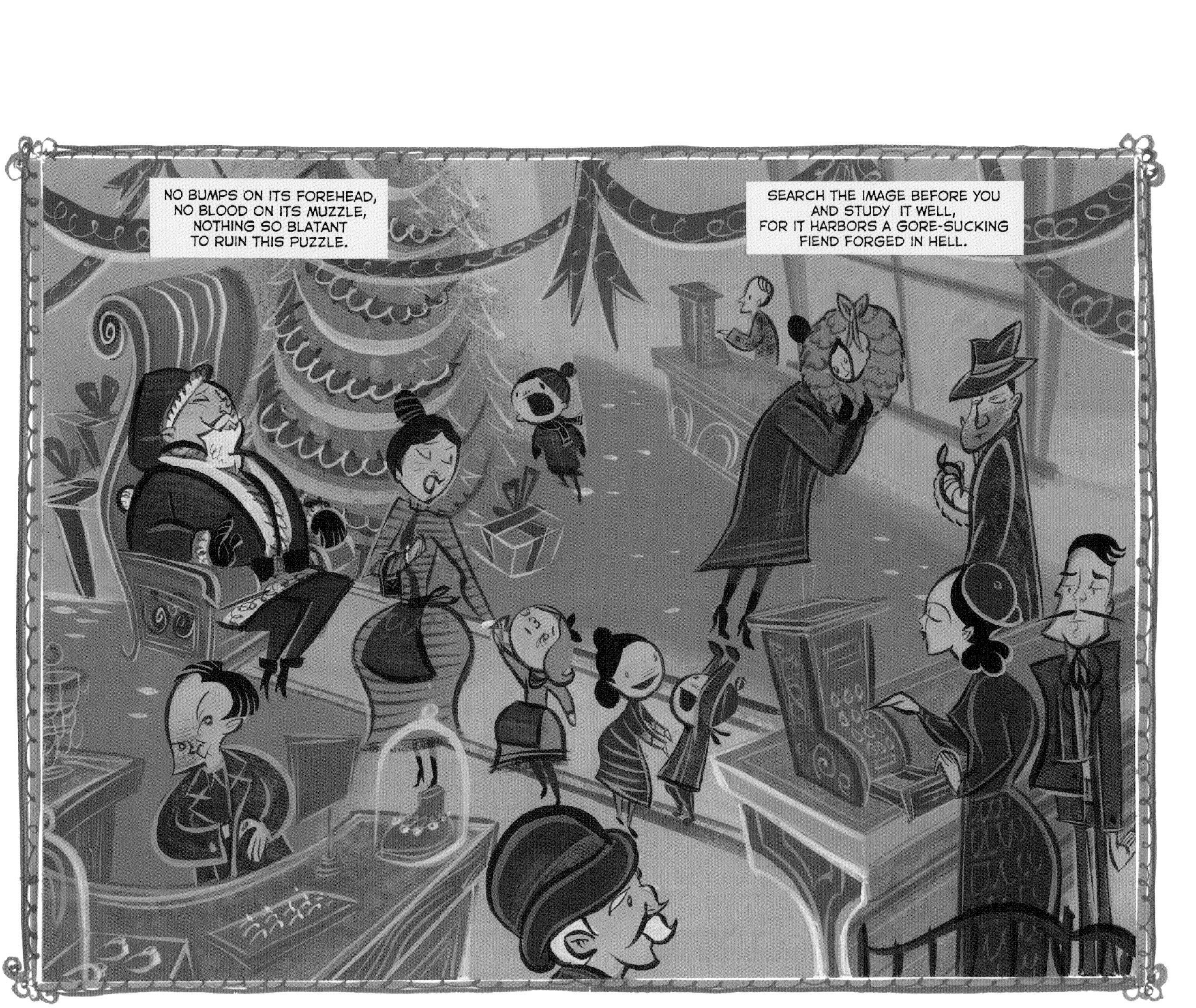
NO BUMPS ON ITS FOREHEAD, NO BLOOD ON ITS MUZZLE, NOTHING SO BLATANT TO RUIN THIS PUZZLE.
SEARCH THE IMAGE BEFORE YOU AND STUDY IT WELL, FOR IT HARBORS A GORE-SUCKING FIEND FORGED IN HELL.

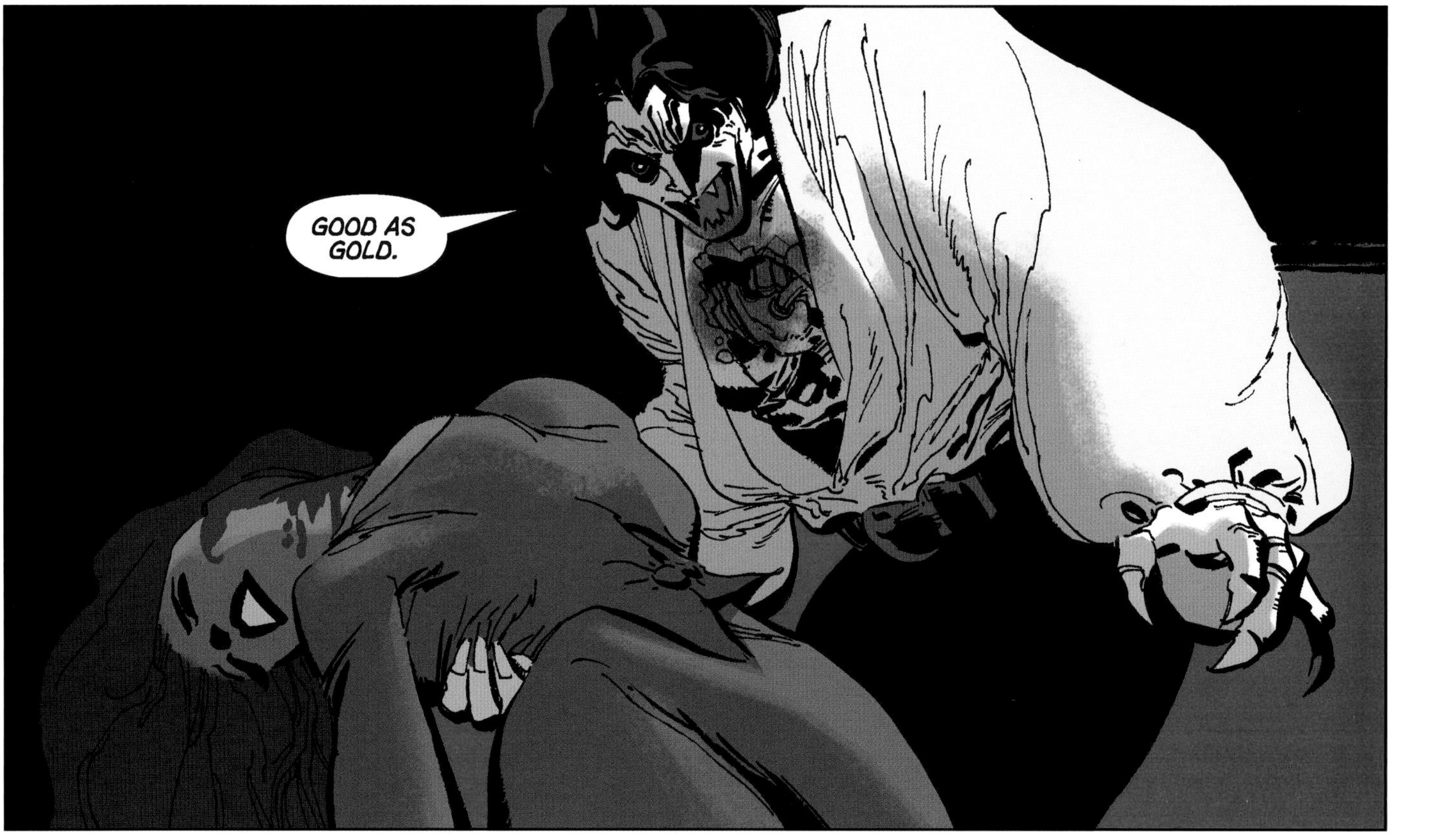
GOOD AS GOLD.

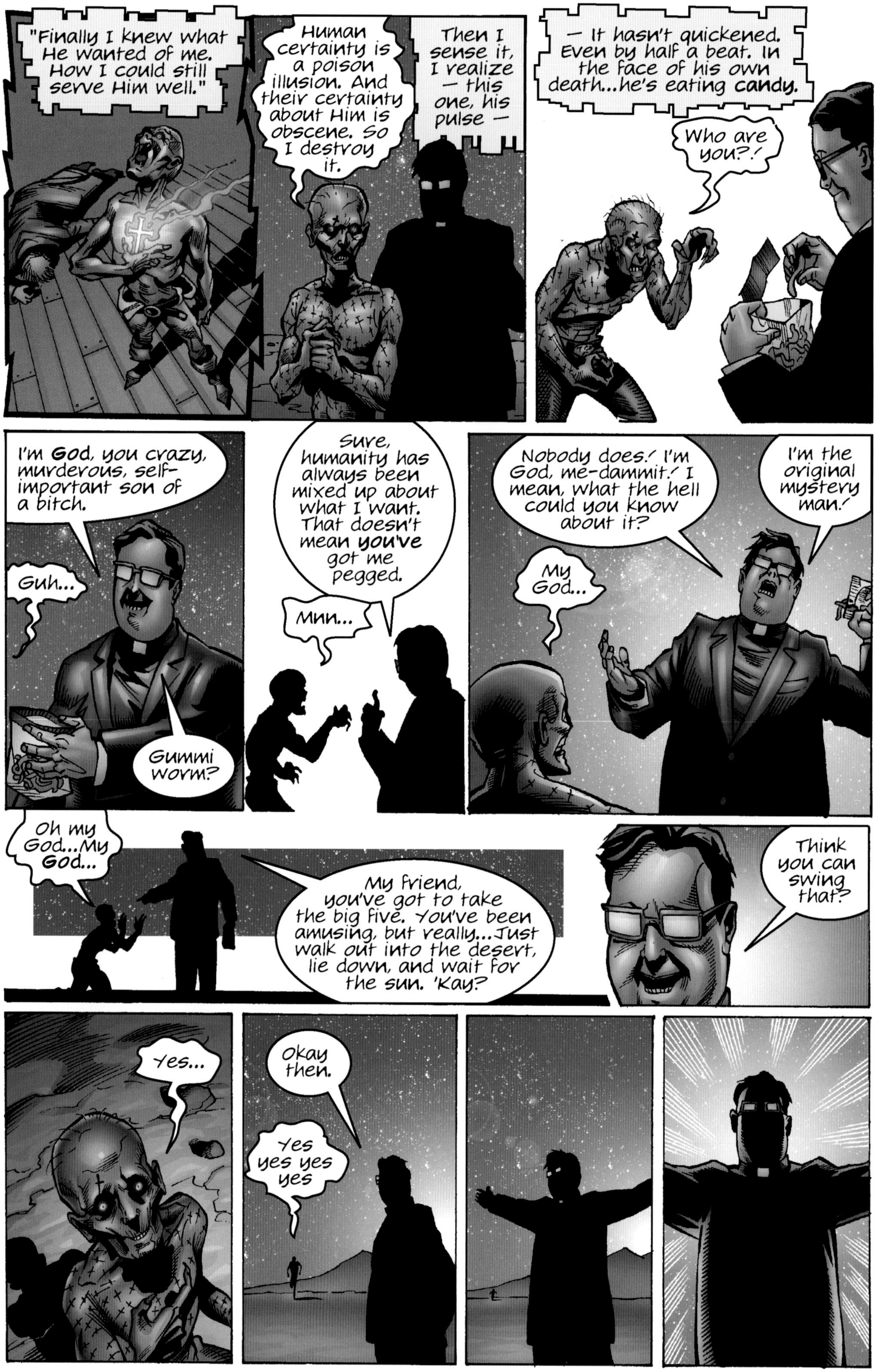

"Finally I knew what He wanted of me. How I could still serve Him well."
Human certainty is a poison illusion. And their certainty about Him is obscene. So I destroy it.
Then I sense it, I realize — this one, his pulse —
— It hasn't quickened. Even by half a beat. In the face of his own death...he's eating candy.
Who are you?!
I'm God, you crazy, murderous, self-important son of a bitch.
Guh...
Gummi worm?
Sure, humanity has always been mixed up about what I want. That doesn't mean you've got me pegged.
Mnn...
Nobody does! I'm God, me-dammit! I mean, what the hell could you know about it?
I'm the original mystery man!
My God...
Oh my God...My God...
My friend, you've got to take the big five. You've been amusing, but really...Just walk out into the desert, lie down, and wait for the sun. 'Kay?
Think you can swing that?
Yes...
Okay then.
Yes yes yes yes

***TICK* COMIC-BOOK CREATOR** and *Firefly/Angel* producer Ben Edlund made his triumphant return to comics in a story of religious zeal. Originally, the cover was meant to have the vampire on a cross, but it had to be toned down so as not to upset anybody.

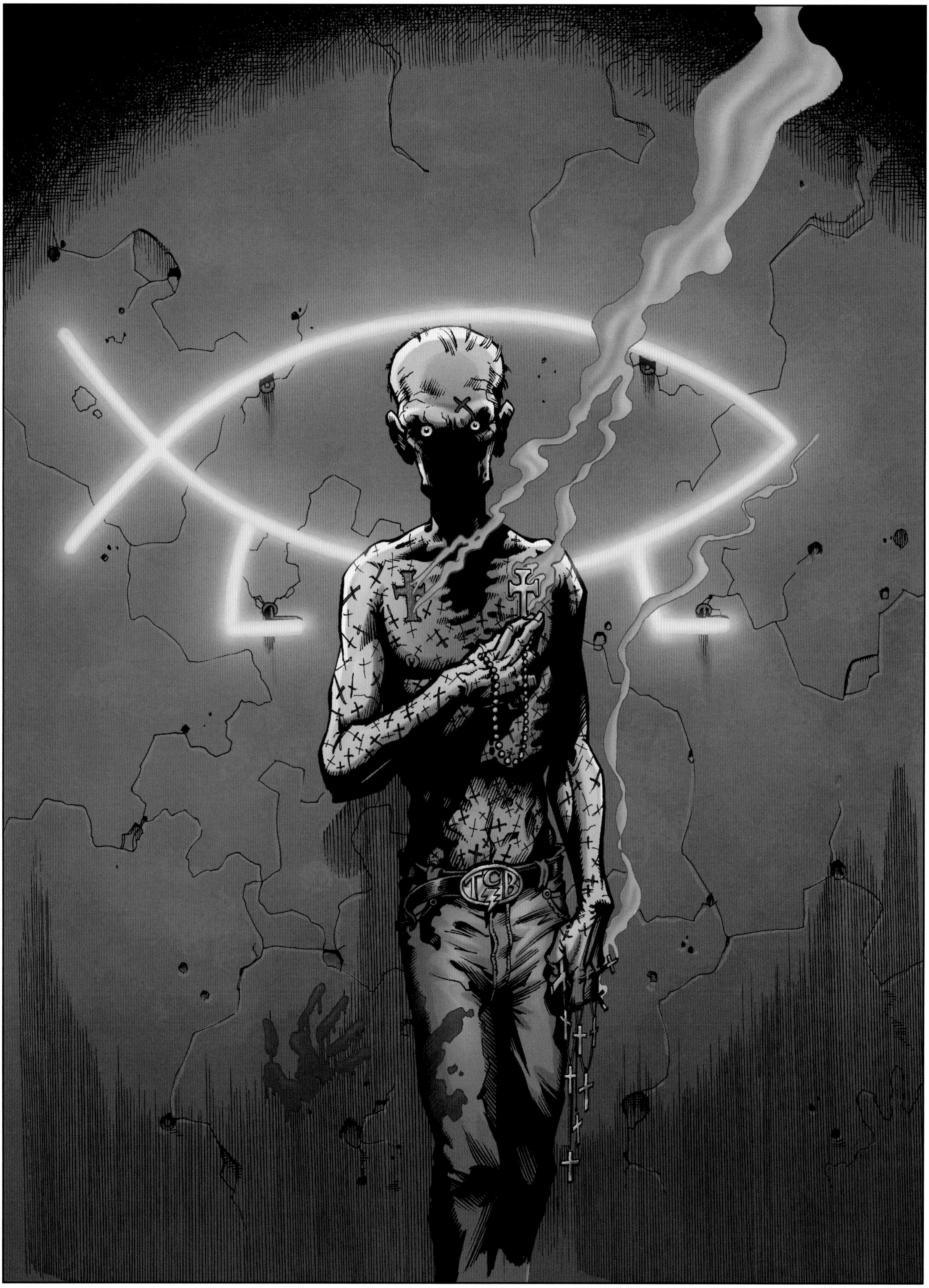

Opposite: Script and pencils by Edlund, inks by Derek Fridolfs, colors by David Nestelle, letters by Annie Parkhouse. Above: Pencils and inks by Edlund, colors by Michelle Madsen. Interiors from "Taking Care of Business," and cover, *Tales of the Vampires* #4, March 2004.

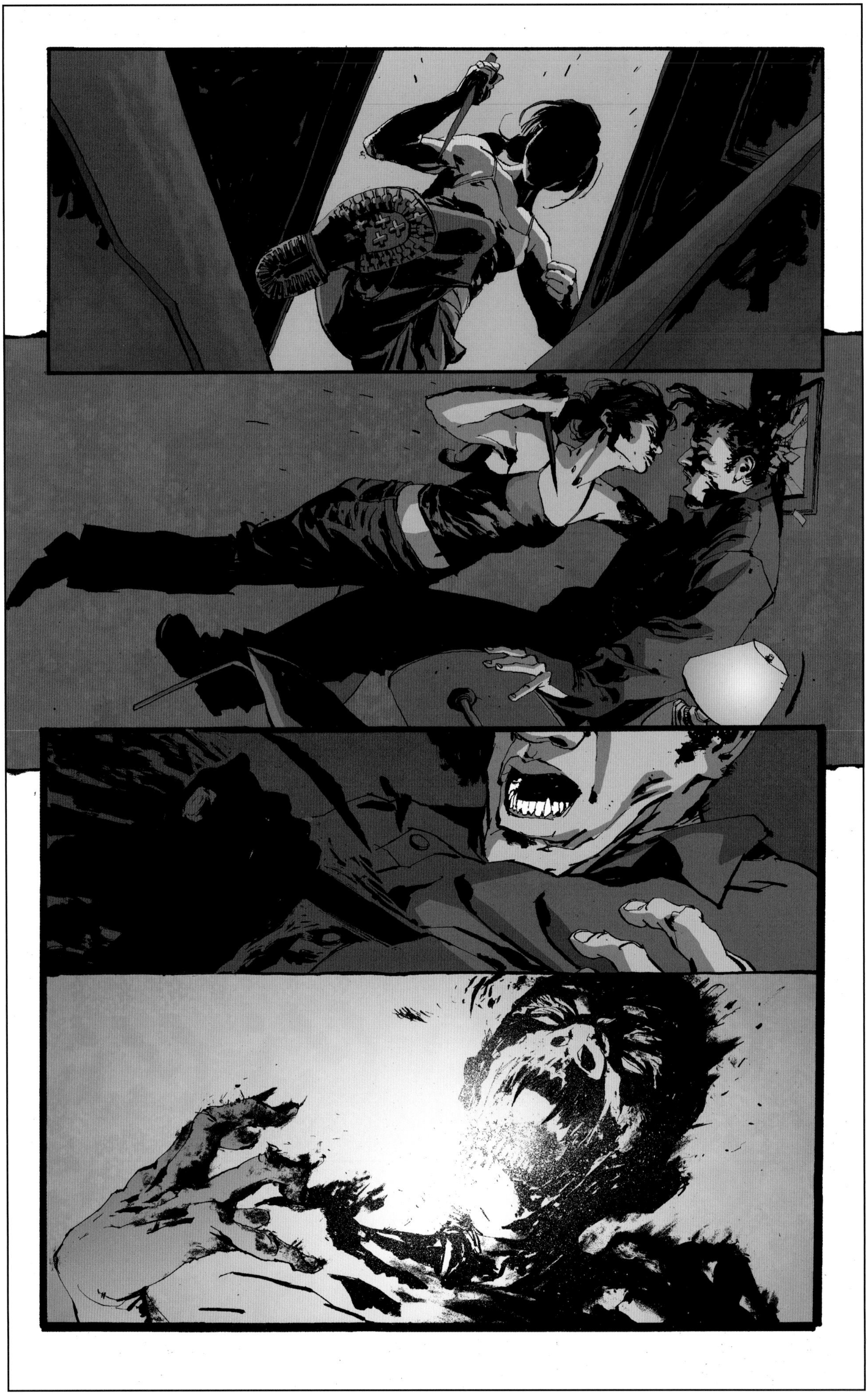

 Script by Jane Espenson, pencils and inks by Jason Shawn Alexander, colors by Madsen. Interiors, "Father," *Tales of the Vampires* #3, February 2004. Opposite: Pencils and inks by Mike Mignola, colors by Dave Stewart. Cover, *Tales of the Vampires* collection, November 2004.

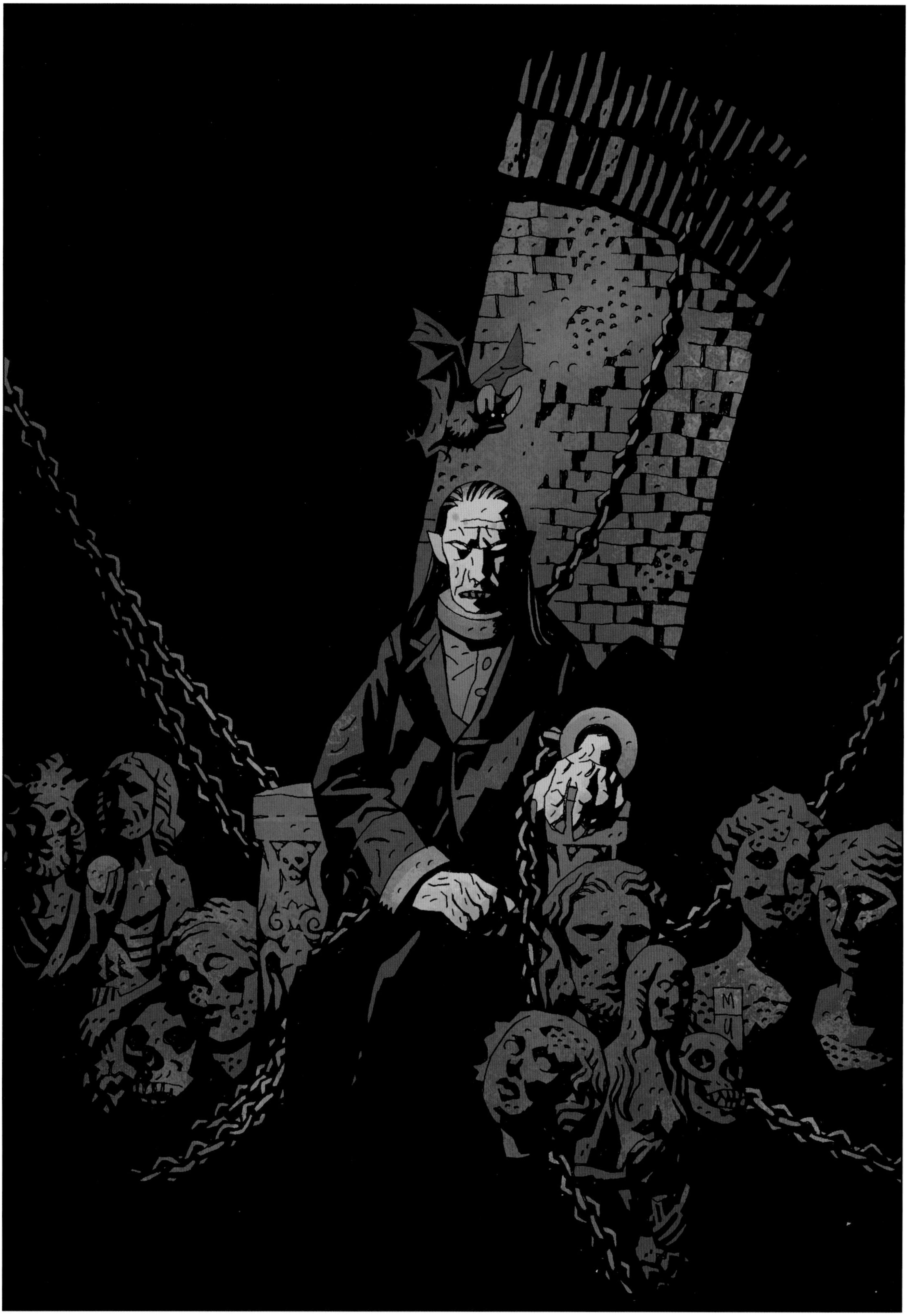

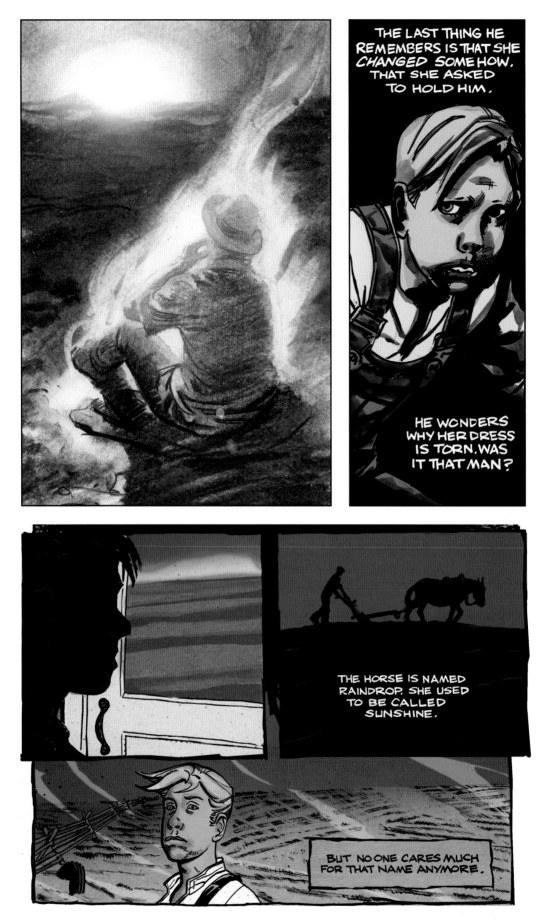

THE LAST THING HE REMEMBERS IS THAT SHE CHANGED SOMEHOW, THAT SHE ASKED TO HOLD HIM.

HE WONDERS WHY HER DRESS IS TORN. WAS IT THAT MAN?

THE HORSE IS NAMED RAINDROP. SHE USED TO BE CALLED SUNSHINE.

BUT NO ONE CARES MUCH FOR THAT NAME ANYMORE.

SEAN PHILLIPS DEPARTED radically from his signature stark, realistic style for his *Tales of the Vampires* story. Each time I've worked with Phillips he's presented a style that I'd never seen before, one that fans would never recognize as his. That kind of chameleon behavior is unusual in this industry, and really exciting to be involved with.

The monthly *Buffy the Vampire Slayer* series had only recently ended when Joss's *Tales of the Vampires* launched, helping the first run of *Buffy* comics to go out on a high note. At the time we talked about relaunching *Buffy* within a year, but other things kept us busy until early 2006, when the script for *Buffy the Vampire Slayer* Season Eight #1 arrived on my desk, and we started talking about artists all over again.

188 Top left: Script by Brett Matthews; pencils, inks, colors, and letters by Sean Phillips. Interiors, "Dames," *Drawing on Your Nightmares*, October 2003. Top right and bottom: Script by Jane Espenson; pencils, inks, colors, and letters by Jeff Parker. Interiors, "Dust Bowl," *Tales of the Vampires* #4, March 2004.

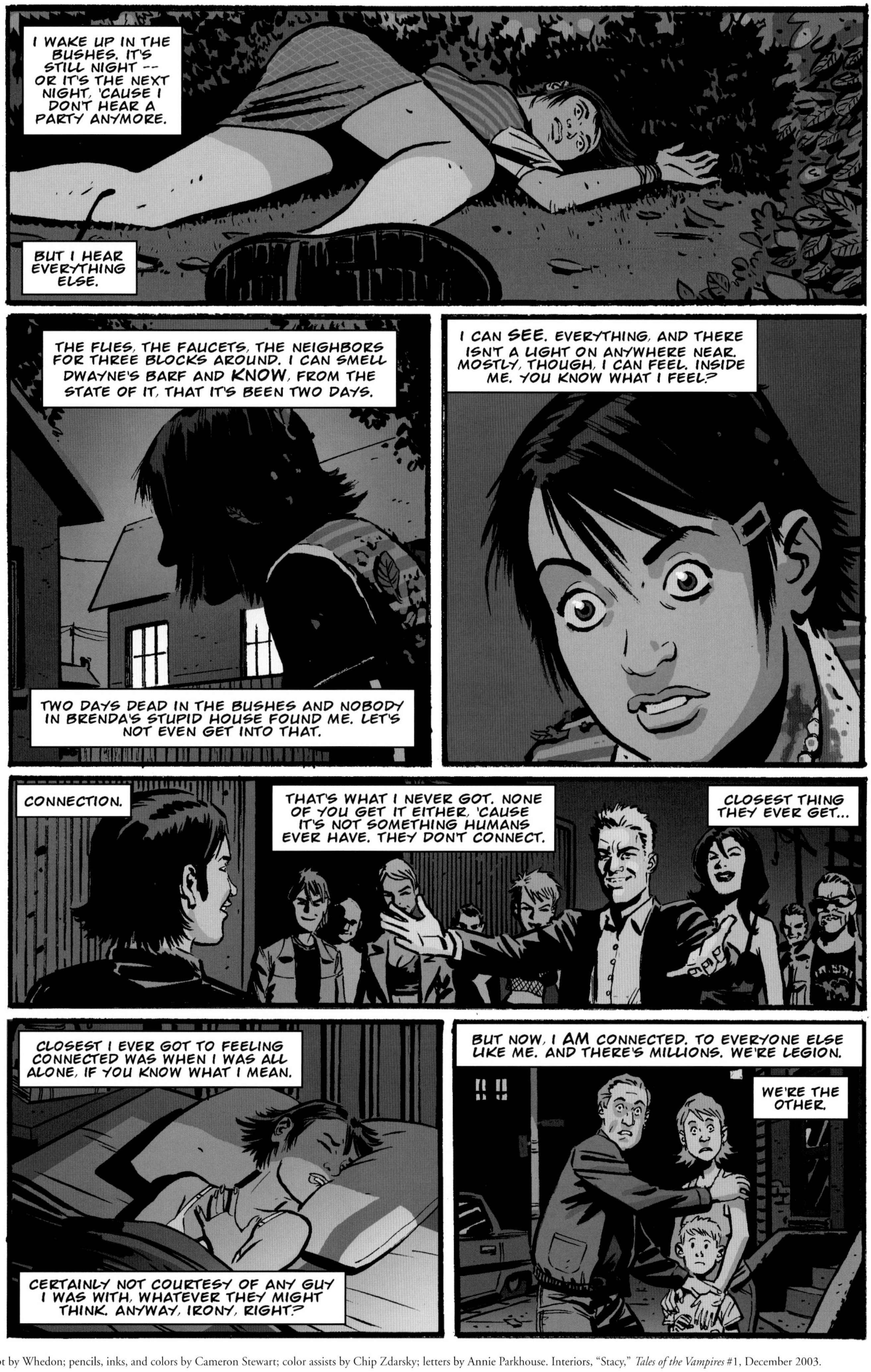

I WAKE UP IN THE BUSHES. IT'S STILL NIGHT -- OR IT'S THE NEXT NIGHT, 'CAUSE I DON'T HEAR A PARTY ANYMORE.
BUT I HEAR EVERYTHING ELSE.
THE FLIES, THE FAUCETS, THE NEIGHBORS FOR THREE BLOCKS AROUND. I CAN SMELL DWAYNE'S BARF AND KNOW, FROM THE STATE OF IT, THAT IT'S BEEN TWO DAYS.
TWO DAYS DEAD IN THE BUSHES AND NOBODY IN BRENDA'S STUPID HOUSE FOUND ME. LET'S NOT EVEN GET INTO THAT.
I CAN SEE. EVERYTHING, AND THERE ISN'T A LIGHT ON ANYWHERE NEAR. MOSTLY, THOUGH, I CAN FEEL. INSIDE ME. YOU KNOW WHAT I FEEL?
CONNECTION.
THAT'S WHAT I NEVER GOT. NONE OF YOU GET IT EITHER, 'CAUSE IT'S NOT SOMETHING HUMANS EVER HAVE. THEY DON'T CONNECT.
CLOSEST THING THEY EVER GET...
CLOSEST I EVER GOT TO FEELING CONNECTED WAS WHEN I WAS ALL ALONE, IF YOU KNOW WHAT I MEAN.
CERTAINLY NOT COURTESY OF ANY GUY I WAS WITH, WHATEVER THEY MIGHT THINK. ANYWAY, IRONY, RIGHT?
BUT NOW, I AM CONNECTED. TO EVERYONE ELSE LIKE ME. AND THERE'S MILLIONS. WE'RE LEGION.
WE'RE THE OTHER.

Script by Whedon; pencils, inks, and colors by Cameron Stewart; color assists by Chip Zdarsky; letters by Annie Parkhouse. Interiors, "Stacy," *Tales of the Vampires* #1, December 2003.

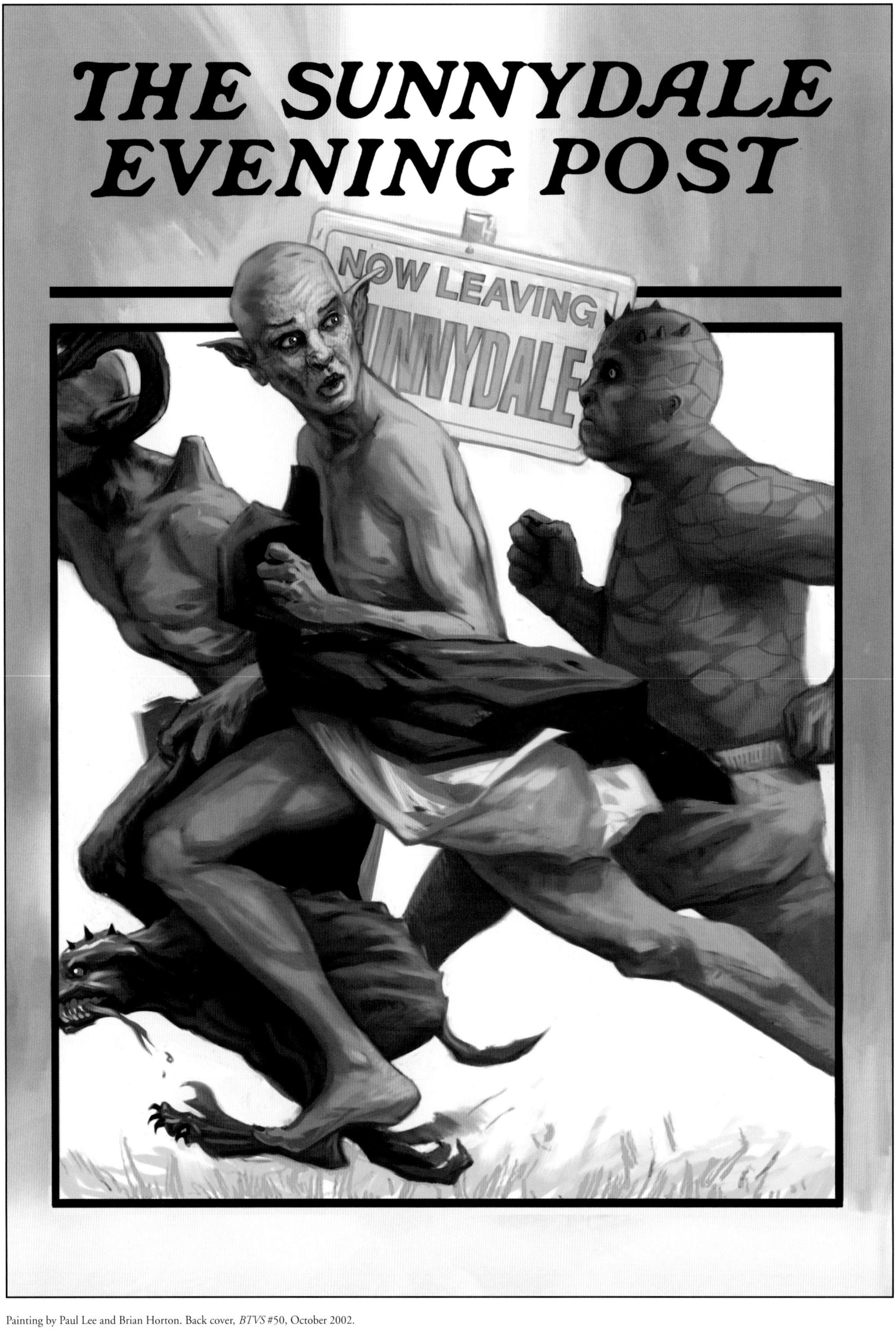
THE SUNNYDALE EVENING POST
NOW LEAVING
SUNNYDALE

 Painting by Paul Lee and Brian Horton. Back cover, *BTVS* #50, October 2002.

Buffy the vampire slayer

WANT MORE OF THE BUFFYVERSE?

BUFFY THE VAMPIRE SLAYER SEASON 8: THE LONG WAY HOME VOL. 1
Joss Whedon, Georges Jeanty, Jo Chen, Andy Owens, Paul Lee, and Dave Stewart
Buffy creator Joss Whedon brings Buffy back to Dark Horse in this official follow-up to Season Seven of the smash-hit TV series!
ISBN-10: 1-59307-822-6
ISBN-13: 978-1-59307-822-5
$15.95

BUFFY OMNIBUS VOL. 1
Joss Whedon, Fabian Nicieza, Paul Lee, Eric Powell, and others
This first massive volume begins at the beginning—*The Origin*, a faithful adaptation of creator Joss Whedon's original screenplay for the film that started it all!
ISBN-10: 1-59307-784-X
ISBN-13: 978-1-59307-784-6
$24.95

BUFFY OMNIBUS VOL. 2
Scott Lobdell, Fabian Nicieza, Jeff Matsuda, Cliff Richards, and others
Follow the newly chosen Slayer from Los Angeles to Sunnydale, through her parents' divorce—with Dawn in tow—as the vampire with a soul, Angel, makes his first appearance, and the not-so-souled Spike and Drusilla cleave a bloody path toward the West Coast.
ISBN-10: 1-59307-826-9
ISBN-13: 978-1-59307-826-3
$24.95

TALES OF THE VAMPIRES
Joss Whedon, Ben Edlund, Tim Sale, Scott Morse, J. Alexander, and others
The creator of *Buffy the Vampire Slayer* reunites with the writers from his hit TV shows for an imaginative and frightening look into the history of vampires in the world of the Slayer.
ISBN-10: 1-56971-749-4
ISBN-13: 978-1-56971-749-3
$15.95

TALES OF THE SLAYERS
Joss Whedon, Amber Benson, Gene Colan, P. Craig Russell, Tim Sale, and others
Buffy is the latest in a long tradition of young women who've been trained to give their lives in the war against vampires. The writers from the television series, including the show's creator, Joss Whedon, present the tales of these girls with the help of comics' greatest artists.
ISBN-10: 1-56971-605-6
ISBN-13: 978-1-56971-605-2
$14.95

CREATURES OF HABIT ILLUSTRATED NOVEL
Tom Fassbender, Jim Pascoe, Paul Lee, and Brian Horton
An old friend of Spike's is in town, and he's getting every teenager in Sunnydale to trip the light fantastic at some very special underground raves. He has a plan that could mean big things for vampires everywhere . . .
ISBN-10: 1-56971-563-7
ISBN-13: 978-1-56971-563-5
$17.95

BUFFY THE VAMPIRE SLAYER: PANEL TO PANEL
Chris Bachalo, J. Scott Campbell, Jeff Matsuda, Mike Mignola, and others
Take a look back at the most dynamic and memorable line art and paintings from the first ten years of the Slayer in comics.
ISBN-10: 1-59307-836-6
ISBN-13: 978-1-59307-836-2
$19.95

ALSO BY JOSS WHEDON . . .

FRAY: FUTURE SLAYER
Joss Whedon, Karl Moline, Andy Owens, Dave Stewart, and Michelle Madsen
Hundreds of years in the future, Manhattan has become a deadly slum, run by mutant crime-lords and disinterested cops. Stuck in the middle is a young girl who thought she had no future, but learns she has a great destiny.
ISBN-10: 1-56971-751-6
ISBN-13: 978-1-56971-751-6
$19.95

SERENITY: THOSE LEFT BEHIND
Joss Whedon, Brett Matthews, Will Conrad, and Laura Martin
Joss Whedon unveils a previously unknown chapter in the lives of his favorite band of space brigands in this comics prequel of the *Serenity* feature film.
ISBN-10: 1-59307-449-2
ISBN-13: 978-1-59307-449-4
$9.95

SERENITY MERCHANDISE

SERENITY ZIPPO LIGHTER
#13-189 $29.99

SERENITY ORNAMENT
#13-420 $19.99

SERENITY IN DISGUISE VARIANT ORNAMENT
#14-686 $24.99

SERENITY PVC SET
#10-664 $17.99

INARA'S SHUTTLE ORNAMENT
#14-977 $29.99
coming Feb. 2008

DARK HORSE COMICS®
darkhorse.com

AVAILABLE AT YOUR LOCAL COMICS SHOP OR BOOKSTORE!
To find a comics shop in your area, call 1-888-266-4226.
For more information or to order direct visit darkhorse.com
or call 1-800-862-0052 Mon.–Fri. 9 A.M. to 5 P.M. Pacific Time
Prices and availability subject to change without notice

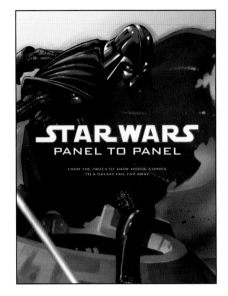
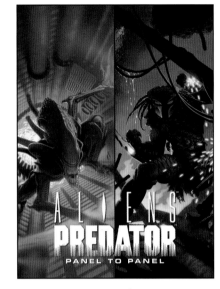
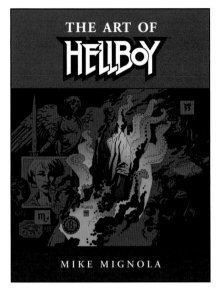
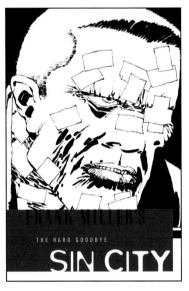

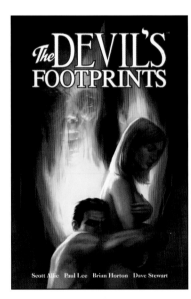